DAUGHTERS OF CORNWALL

1918: The Great War is over, and Clara Carter has boarded a train bound for Cornwall — to meet a ̶ly that would once have been hers. But they ̶ never discover her secret . . .

9: Hannah has always been curious about her ̶ther's mysterious past, but the outbreak of the ̶econd World War casts everything in a new light. As the bombs begin to fall, Hannah and her brothers are determined to do their bit for the war effort — whatever the cost.

2020: Caroline has long been the keeper of her family's secrets. But now, with her own daughter n̶ ̶ing her more than ever, it's time to tell the tr̶ ̶n — to show Natalie that she comes from a long li̶ ̶ of women who have weathered the storms of li̶ ̶, ̶s hardy and proud as the rugged Cornish c̶ ̶ine . . .

DAUGHTERS OF CORNWALL

FERN BRITTON

ISIS

LARGE
PRINT

First published in Great Britain 2020
by
HarperCollins*Publishers* Ltd

First Isis Edition
published 2020
by arrangement with
HarperCollins*Publishers* Ltd

A catalogue record for this book is available
from the British Library.

ISBN 978–1–78541–929–4

Published by
Ulverscroft Limited
Anstey, Leicestershire

Set by Words & Graphics Ltd.
Anstey, Leicestershire
Printed and bound in Great Britain by
T J Books Limited, Padstow, Cornwall

Here's tae us. Wha's like us? Damn few, an' they're a' deid.

A toast adopted by Scottish regiments everywhere, and drunk to the memory of the First Battalion The Scottish Regiment, who in late 1914 prepared peacefully for summer camp, and yet who by 1918 were mostly dead.

In memory of my great-uncle, Second Lieutenant Herbert Edward Hawkins of First/Fourteenth Battalion of the (London Scottish) London Regiment, 1887–1917.

Prologue

Caroline, Callyzion, Cornwall

Present day

It is said that the failings of a family bloodline repeat themselves through the generations until eventually someone, possibly centuries later, breaks the mould. Whether they break that mould with a newly acquired error of personality, or by bringing in a fresh bloodline with its own chaotic genetic make-up, it's hard to tell.

Whatever, I am certain your family will be no different to mine; a long line of women who have toughened themselves on the anvil of life. All with broken marriages, broken hearts and long-held secrets.

The story I am about to tell you is the one I have observed from my birth. Tales I have picked up, as any child does, sitting quietly and forgotten, eavesdropping as the adults reveal their shocking truths.

They dropped their pebbles in the pond and the ripples spread outward through their lives and into my own, where they lap still.

Everything I have, I have worked hard for.

Everything.

I bear no grudge.

I am not a materialistic woman. I am a widow living within my means watching my beautiful daughter take the leap from adolescence to adulthood, carving her own path. She will find a suitable boy, settle down and be a wonderful wife and mother. As I was.

As my mother almost was.

As her mother, Clara, certainly wasn't.

Glamorous, strong and passionate, she lived her life by one rule. "To be a liar, you have to have a very good memory."

And she should know.

I didn't know any of this until very recently, and I must say it has rather disturbed my equilibrium. I like to think of myself as a woman who does not wear her emotions on her sleeve.

Losing my mother was dreadful, of course, as was my husband's illness and death. I was proud of my outward stoicism; my resilience in the spotlight of grief.

That was until I overheard one of the church ladies talking about me behind my back. I heard them in the choir stalls discussing my "lack of emotion", my "cold-bloodedness", and then something I would prefer not to think about, it being so crude and unpleasant. All I will say is that their unkind laughter followed me for days afterwards.

I miss my husband dreadfully. His kindness. His affection. His success. He climbed the ladder of the corporate world and gave me the secure world I craved. Darling Tom.

2

He knew how hard my fatherless upbringing was and how hard I have striven to lead a normal life after the rackety one my mother brought me into.

All that has paled into insignificance now, for I have discovered another family skeleton. My mother was not the only one to have her secrets. To get pregnant out of wedlock.

Everything I thought I knew is a lie.

It arrived on my doorstep just a few days ago. A huge steamer trunk made in the days when people travelled the world by ship rather than hopped on an aircraft. The courier thrust his docket at me to sign. "This has travelled a long way to find you," he said, as if personally affronted. "All the way from Malaysia, via Singapore and Kent, by the looks of things. And it's bloody heavy."

"Are you sure you have the right address?"

"You are Caroline Bolitho?"

"Yes. Well I was, that's my maiden name."

"Then yes this is the right address. I went to the Vicarage just up the road in Callyzion first. But the woman there said the only Bolitho she knew was you and she gave me this address." He handed me a docket.

"Sign and print please, and I hope you don't find a body in there." He laughed until I gave him "The Look", the one my husband and daughter feared.

I signed the piece of paper and opened the door wider for him to carry it into the hall for me.

"Sorry, love. My job is to deliver to the door. That's as far as I'm allowed to go. Cheers. Oh, hang on." He patted the top pocket of his shirt. "Here. You'll need this. It's the key." He handed me a small brown envelope and left me with the mysterious cargo.

By the time I had dragged the trunk into the lounge, I needed a cup of coffee to give me the energy to open the thing. To be honest I was more than a little wary of the contents. What could they be? Why had it been sent to me? Who had sent it to me?

I finished the last of the two digestive biscuits that I had allowed myself and rinsed my coffee cup, putting it on the drainer.

"Come on, Caroline," I told myself. "The time has come."

Back in the lounge, the trunk sat waiting. I circled it, reading the various labels. Most were aged and illegible but there was a name printed along the front edge. I went back to the kitchen and got a duster and an aerosol can of furniture polish.

The trunk was leather and, as I removed the grime, the natural hide began to shine. I made out the letters E.H.B. and an address for a rubber plantation on the island of Penang, Malaysia. I recognised the initials. Ernest Hugh Bolitho, my grandfather. My mother's father. All I knew about him was that he had died in Penang, back in the Seventies, having never returned to his English family.

I kept on polishing until the entire bag emerged, old but gleaming. I had been through so much of late that the idea of opening up the past was both comforting and terrifying. I had kept my family tucked out of sight for years and only Tom knew the circumstances of my birth.

4

I often wonder if keeping my secret to myself actually pushed people away from me.

Tom was my first boyfriend. I couldn't believe it when he spoke to me one Easter Sunday after Church. His parents were High Anglicans and kept the sort of decent, normal home that I had longed for as a child.

The trunk was almost clean now but I kept on polishing until there was nothing more to do.

The time had come to open it.

PART ONE

PART ONE

CHAPTER
ONE

Clara, Kent to Callyzion, Cornwall

December 1918, one month after the
First World War ended in Armistice

I came up from Kent last night.

Just me.

I knew, as soon as I got the letter from Bertie's mother, that I had to go. I packed my bag and willed myself to stay strong. I kissed them both, Philippa and Mikey, and told them I would be back soon; then I left them, shutting the front door behind me, and walked away towards the station. I would not let them see my tears. My withered heart — now rigid against life's blows — would make sure of that. And yet there was still a voice in my lungs screaming at me to turn around, go back, give up this fool's mission. I faltered and almost turned, but the pull of seeing Bertie's home and meeting the family that might have been mine was stronger.

In London I found a boarding house close to Paddington Station. "Just for the one night," I told the unsmiling landlady. In reply she pointed to the poster behind her. No noise after six, no gentlemen callers, breakfast at eight and money up front.

I handed over the payment she required and she showed me to my room. It was at the front of the house with a view of a terrace of white stuccoed houses. Really quite pretty.

I didn't sleep well and was up early, fearful that I would miss my 7.35 a.m. train to Cornwall. Quietly I washed and dressed, creeping over the dingy rag rug which barely covered the splintered boards. Obligingly they did not squeak.

Downstairs, I let myself out into the dark morning. From the pavement, through the bow window, I glimpsed a dining room. Tables laid up for breakfast. I hadn't eaten since leaving Kent yesterday, but I was not hungry.

I walked briskly to Paddington, in the cold morning air, my breath coming in cloudy trails. Paddington Station loomed ahead, lit up in the dark, a welcome glow for morning travellers like me.

Even with the sun not yet up, the station was busy. A steady stream of recently arrived commuters was heading towards the exits and the underground. Smart young working women, older men with bowler hats and velvet-collared coats, and young men in uniform, some on crutches, some with missing arms, and one with dark glasses and a white stick. I swallowed a hard lump that popped unexpectedly into my throat. My eyes darted over each of them. Could Bertie be among them? Maybe these men had seen him? Fought with him? Had news of him? Had watched him as he wrote his long and loving letters to me?

The blind soldier was greeted by an older woman, who touched his arm and said his name.

"Mum?"

I had to turn away; the moment was private and I couldn't watch.

"Want help with your bag, miss?" A porter tapped my shoulder, making me jump.

"No. I'm fine, thank you." I held my bag close to my thigh and set off to find my platform.

This would be the longest train journey I had ever taken. Bertie and I had talked about it many times. The excitement of my meeting his parents and brother and sister.

"We'll take a picnic to the beach. There are sand dunes and rock pools full of little crabs and shrimps. Do you like to swim?"

"I haven't tried," I said.

"I shall teach you," he said, wrapping his arms around me. "It'll be cold. But I shall keep you warm."

I had never known anyone as kind.

He kissed my hair. "My parents will love you."

I was nervous now. I had found my platform and my train was waiting.

I almost turned around to go home, back to Kent and the two people I loved so dearly. A swirl of anxiety, panic, was building in my chest. Would I be found wanting by Bertie's family? Or would they accept me immediately, as one of them? They might like *me*, but would I like *them?*

The train carriages had long corridors along one side and a set of small seated compartments down the other, each compartment housing six seats.

"Excuse me." I stopped by a railway employee holding a whistle and a flag. "Could you point me to Carriage C, compartment two, please?"

The man kept his eyes on the passengers surging around his platform. "Next one down."

"Thank you." I found it easily. A piece of white paper, with C marked on it, was stuck to the open door of the carriage.

Stepping on board I turned left and found my compartment. It was empty. Thank goodness. I was not in the frame of mind for idle chatter with strangers.

I settled myself on the seat next to the window, forward facing, with my travelling bag on the seat beside me. Hoping that by spreading myself out like this I might deter fellow passengers.

I removed my gloves and coat and folded them on top of the bag next to me. I was building a rather nice defence. Once settled, I looked out of the window, watching the farewells. Kisses for the women. Handshakes for the men.

"I'll write to you and let you know how it's all going."

"I'll miss you."

"See you soon."

"I love you."

I wondered what their stories were. So many people with smiles on their faces, hiding God knows what in their minds.

Pushing through them I saw an older man, on his own, quite short, with a tiny bristling moustache. He had a folded newspaper under his arm and was making heavy weather of lugging a suitcase down the concourse. I took an instant dislike to him. He had that look of arrogance and entitlement that so many men carried. He was obviously looking for his carriage and, through the window, he caught my eye. I shrank back in my seat.

He lifted his fist and banged his knuckles on the glass. "Is this Carriage C?" he bellowed.

I looked down at my shoes as if I hadn't heard.

He knocked louder. "Is this Carriage C?" he shouted again, as if I were deaf.

I was forced to reply. "Yes."

"Why didn't you say so?" He shook his head and tutted, then bent to pick up his heavy case.

In seconds he was bumping in through the sliding door of my compartment.

"Ah." He seemed to inhale and exhale all the air in the carriage simultaneously. "I do like an uncrowded carriage." He thumped his case on the floor.

I saw immediately that his mission was to spread himself even wider than I had.

He coughed and huffed, moving his case almost up against my own small bag, effectively hemming me in.

I looked firmly out of the window as all this was going on. At least he couldn't sit next to me, and surely he wouldn't sit in the seat directly opposite me? Without turning my head, I slid my eyes around to check what he was doing. He was dusting his bowler hat with his coat sleeve. I suspected it was done to attract my attention. To trick me into some sort of conversation. I stayed silent.

His hat went on the rack above the seats. His coat went next, removed and carefully folded. And finally, brushing some invisible lint from his jacket, he sat down. Exactly opposite me, just as I had hoped he would not, his knees mere inches from my own.

"Ah." He made himself comfortable and opened his paper. "That's better. Beautiful day for travelling, isn't it?"

I did not reply. I did not wish to encourage any dialogue. I turned my eyes back to the window. What did he mean, it was a beautiful day for travelling? There was the station roof above us so you couldn't tell if the sun was up yet, and on the platform there was still people's breath on the chill air.

"I shall open the window for us," he said. "Can't stand being cooped up." He put his paper down and stood again. I moved my knees to one side. He pulled at the leather window strap and lowered the glass, letting it go with a thunk. He sat down. "That's much better."

The smell of burning coal and soot, shouts of porters loading baggage, not to mention an icy blast of December air, flooded the carriage.

I wondered if I should put my coat back on but that would only provoke more unwelcome words.

I could feel him looking at me. Inspecting me over his half-moon glasses. "You look as if you could do with some fresh air," he said, "if you don't mind me saying."

"I'm perfectly fine, thank you."

"Going all the way, are you?"

"Sorry?"

"Penzance?"

"No." I looked down at my lap. My velvet bag which held my ticket, purse, handkerchief, lipstick and cigarettes were in it. How I wished it had held a book or magazine too.

"I am," he continued. "Going all the way to see my son. He's just come back from France. Alive, thank God. Lost a couple of fingers. A miracle really. Hand grenade exploded on him. He made corporal. Like his grandfather in Crimea. Very proud of him. Do you know Penzance?"

I shook my head and again looked out of the window, praying that he would stop. My prayer went unanswered.

"Terrible thing, this war. The war to end all wars is what they are telling us." He lifted his newspaper and waggled it at me. "So many young men gone. Heroes, the lot of them. Apart from the conchies of course." He sniffed loudly. "Cowards." He shook his head and tutted. "They're all right, Jack. They never had to face the enemy, did they? No. And what's happened? We have lost a generation. All those brave lads. The brightest and the best, all gone."

My fingers tightened around my bag, rubbing the weft of the velvet. I'd heard all of this before. People spouting off about stuff of which they had no experience. Patting my hand. Telling me how proud of Bertie I must be. I had wanted to scream at all of them.

Shout at them, "Of course I am proud of him, you fools."

I felt the unbidden anger raging in me again and I gripped my hands into two bony fists, hoping to gain control over the violence within me.

The man kept going. "We won, though, and that's the important thing."

"Please, don't," I said loudly, surprising myself with the vehemence in my voice.

He stopped smiling and looked at me in astonishment.

"What?" he said. "Don't talk about the war? I was only making conversation," he said. "Being civil. I told my wife, I blame the suffragettes. Young women have forgotten how to make pleasant conversation. All that driving ambulances and thinking they can do a man's job . . . " He stopped abruptly, a thought dawning on him. He nodded slowly, "Oh, I see. You've suffered a loss, haven't you? Someone close? I can always tell. A lot of women have suffered. Many sweethearts left behind. I don't suppose you'll ever marry now. Not with all them young men gone. For ever. I feel sorry for you."

He lit the fuse inside me and my bomb exploded. "How dare you. How dare you presume to talk to me in this way. You know nothing about me."

"All right, all right. Keep your hair on, dear. Grief, that's what it is, love. Turned many a woman difficult, grief."

"Shut up. Just shut up and leave this carriage and close the damn window as you leave." My voice was rising in pitch and volume.

"Crikey," he said, gathering his things, "looks like some poor bloke is better off dead than married to a fishwife like you. You'll never get a bloke like that." He stood up to retrieve his hat and coat. "I shall find a more amiable travel companion, if that's the way you are."

Outside on the platform, the last door was slammed shut, a guard's whistle blew and the train suddenly lurched forward. The man fell back almost into my lap. I pushed him off me and he fell forward onto an edge of his huge suitcase, dropping his paper as the wind was knocked from him. He scrabbled to his feet, rubbing his shoulder.

I picked up his newspaper and threw it at him. "I pity the poor woman who married you."

Shaking his head at me, but keeping his lips firmly closed, he left the compartment.

Left in the peace of my carriage, I closed the window and then searched my little bag for my handkerchief, angrily wiping away hot tears as, with another jolt, the mighty train wheels, powered by coal and steam, began to pull away from the platform.

I cried tears of grief and anger on and off for a further hour or so, appalled that I should do this in a public space but glad that it deterred the few passengers still walking the train's corridor from joining me.

And now, several long hours later, I was finally crossing Brunel's great iron bridge, the Royal Albert, taking me over the river Tamar, from Devon into Cornwall.

CHAPTER
TWO

Clara, Callyzion

December 1918

I leant my head on the cold glass of the train window, drinking in the outside scenery. Bertie had described all this to me time and time again. He had insisted on reciting all the romantic names of the Cornish station stops.

"As soon as you are over the bridge you come to Saltash. The Gateway to Cornwall."

"Why is it called Saltash?" I had asked.

"No idea. Then after Saltash it's St Germans, Menheniot, Liskeard —"

I interrupted him. "I'll never remember all those names. Just tell me where I need to get off?"

"I'm getting to that, Miss Impatience." He inhaled comically and continued. "Saltash, St Germans, Menheniot, Liskeard and then Bodmin. I shall be waiting for you at Bodmin."

"Will you really?" We had been lying in the tiny bed of our Ealing home. "I'm not sure I have had anyone wait for me anywhere before."

"What sort of blighter would I be if I didn't pick up my beloved fiancee after she's travelled all that way to see me?"

"You'd be a very bad blighter indeed." I smiled.

He held me closer, dropping a kiss onto my head. "I can't wait for you to meet my family. Father will adore you. Mother too, or though she may not show it at first, she's always cautious of new people. But Amy and you will be great friends. She's always wanted a sister. Brother Ernest can be a pompous ass but he's not a bad egg."

"It'll be wonderful to feel part of a family again."

"You are the bravest person I have ever met." He squeezed me tightly, his arms encircling me. "My stoic little squirrel."

At this point, I am sorry to say I had already told a few lies to Bertie about my upbringing. Needs must sometimes. "My parents were wonderful," I fibbed, "and I miss them every day, but I feel they would be very happy for me now." Shameless, I know.

"Do you think they'd approve of me?" he asked.

"Oh Bertie," I smiled, "they would adore you."

The train guard was walking the corridors as he did before arriving at every station. "Bodmin Road. Next stop Bodmin Road." I readied myself to disembark.

Standing on the platform, I watched as the train chuffed away down the line and out of sight on its journey towards Penzance. The sun had set and the Cornish winter air blew gently on my skin. I took a scented lungful.

Bertie had told me that it was warm enough down here to grow palm trees. "You're pulling my leg," I had laughed. "No, I'm telling the truth. We have one in our garden. I will show it to you."

I picked up my bag and walked past the signal box painted smartly in black and white, towards the ticket office where a sign painted with the word TAXIS pointed. Even now, the half-expected hope that Bertie would be waiting for me made me breathless with longing. I imagined him running towards me. His long legs carrying him effortlessly. His strong arms collecting me up easily, lifting me from the ground so that my face was above his, the look of love shining between us.

"Excuse me, miss." A man with a peaked hat walked towards me. "Would you be Miss Carter?"

"Yes."

"I thought so. You looked a bit lost on your own." He had a kind face but not too many teeth. "Welcome to Cornwall." He held out his hand and I shook it. He had a good handshake. Dry and strong.

"I'm your taxi to Callyzion. Name's Chewton. At your service. Let me take your case, miss."

"Oh yes. Reverend Bolitho wrote to me to explain. It's very kind of you both."

"No trouble. I'll put your case in the back and you sit up front next to me. You'll be warmer."

Chewton was a fountain of all local knowledge. He gave me a running commentary with potted histories of the family houses as we passed, and pointed out a couple of shops he thought I might be interested in.

"There's the post office and a very nice ladies' wear shop. Won't be as good as your London shops, mind, but you're bound to find something pretty to suit you. Mrs Chewton told me to tell you that."

I felt a pang of alarm. "Do many people know I'm coming?"

"Oh yes. You're the talk of the parish. Mr Herbert was loved by us all. We missed him when he was doing his rubber planting in Malaya. What a thing, eh." Chewton shook his head incredulously. "Malaya. Cor dear. He had a pet monkey, you know."

I felt the familiarity of tears pricking the back of my eyes. "Yes. Bingo?"

"That's right. Mr Herbert told me about all the tricks that monkey played. Running off with Mr Herbert's breakfast, hiding things round the house."

The tears tightened in my throat. "I wish I had met him."

"Ah," Chewton smiled, "you may not have met the monkey but you did meet the man."

"Yes." I swallowed hard. "He was a wonderful man, wasn't he."

"Brave man," Chewton replied. "One of the best."

We said nothing more to each other, sitting with our own memories.

We were out of Bodmin now and the headlights struggled in the shadowed lanes. Great tunnels of trees blocked out any starlight. I could make out small cottages, some with their lamps still lit. And as the car came to a sharp bend in the road, a white owl took off from a gatepost and flapped away, calling as it went.

At last we passed a road sign telling us that Callyzion was just one mile away. Winding our way down a steep lane, then bursting out of the darkness of another tree tunnel, we turned left at a tiny crossroads with a small village green. Upon the muddy, mole-hilled grass, a sign advertised CHRISTMAS JUMBLE SALE, CHURCH HALL, 2.00p.m. SUNDAY

Chewton pointed it out to me. "We'm raising money for our village war memorial. Mr Bertie will be on it."

Three houses down he stopped the car. We were outside a large iron gate.

"Here we are, miss," he said as he pulled on the handbrake. "The vicarage. Let me get the door for you."

He carefully helped me out of the car and then lifted my case from the back seat. I searched in my velvet bag for my purse. "How much do I owe you?"

"Nothing at all, miss. The account has been settled by Miss Amy."

I held out a shilling as a tip. "Please. For your trouble."

He waved it away.

"For the war memorial at least?"

He looked at the coin doubtfully before winning the battle in his mind. "Thank you, miss. Very kind. That'll be for Mr Bertie." He touched the peak of his cap. "Have a nice stay with the vicar. He's a lovely man."

He drove off, waving a cheery hand, and left me standing outside the cold iron of the house's gate. Bertie's home lay beyond. I looked up at it. A big house. The sort I would have drawn as a little girl. A front door in the middle and, on either side, four bay windows, two up and two down.

It sat in the middle of a square garden with a hedge that seemed to go all the way around it and a path leading from the gate to the front door.

There were several neighbouring houses; all had wisps of smoke coming from their chimneys indicating the warmth inside. From the vicarage chimney there was nothing. Bertie had warned me to pack twice the usual amount of warm underwear as his parents did not like heating the house unless completely necessary.

"Maybe when there's ice on the inside of the windows," he'd told me, "but not before."

I hadn't told him that I knew all about freezing homes in bitterly long winters. I didn't speak of my cruel beginnings to anyone. My past life was a closed book. My secret. Instead I had told him that my parents had been farmers in Kent. Hardworking but comfortably off and that I was an only child. That bit was true. The next bit was not. I told him of a tragedy that had struck when a fire in one of our oast houses had taken hold. Both my parents and one of the pickers had died trying to put it out. Fortunately, there was enough money from the sale of their farm, I told him, for me to go to a boarding school for young ladies where I had been taught extremely well by very kind women who, with care and love, had helped me to forge a new life. All a lie.

Standing outside Bertie's home now, I was glad he would never discover the truth. What lay in front of me was a fresh chapter in my new life. A chapter without Bertie.

It was getting cold and I was shivering. I wrapped my coat tighter around me, collected up my case and opened the tall iron gate. Taking a deep breath for courage, I walked the chequered tiled path to the front door.

The navy blue paint was chipped, particularly around the letter box. I imagined the letters of condolence that had been dropped through it since the black-edged telegram had been delivered. The terrible news.

IT IS WITH THE DEEPEST REGRET ... KILLED IN ACTION ... GOD SAVE THE KING.

I hesitated before pulling the bell. Bertie would want me to be brave. "No point mooning about, old girl," I could hear him saying.

The bell rang deep in the house.

Inside, I imagined the two servants Bertie had talked about. Dora, the maid of all work and Cook. They would have heard the bell and been expecting me. Dora would be drying her hands on her apron, pushing the escaped strands of hair under her cap, and scurrying from the kitchen, into the chilly hall and to the front door. I thought how Cook would have told her off more than once that day. "Stop your jittering and jumping. She'll be here soon enough. Finish the ironing, that'll keep your silly brain quiet."

And now here I was. The stranger they had been waiting for. Mr Herbert's intended. Clara Carter. A thin, pale woman in her early twenties with hazel eyes that could be lively if they weren't so sad.

24

How would Dora describe me later, downstairs behind the closed door of the kitchen?

"The poor lamb is broken with grief. I could have hugged her there and then."

Cook would clasp her hands over her bosom in sympathy. "Oh, the poor duck. What was she wearing?"

"Black, of course. I think she had rouge on her cheeks to cheer herself up, and red lipstick too."

"Oh dear," Cook would say, "Mrs Bolitho won't like that. Nor Miss Amy neither. What about her hair?"

"Brown and crimped into a bun. And she's so thin. There's no meat on her."

Cook might shake her head sadly. "Well, she won't get fat in this house. Another mouth to feed on the housekeeping that Miss Amy gives me — it doesn't go far enough as it is. What did you say to her?"

"I says to her, 'Hello, miss.' As polite as I could. 'Welcome to the vicarage. Please come in.' And she says, 'Thank you', in a nice voice, and she looked around the hall while I put her case by the hat and coat stand, and then I says, 'Miss Amy will be along presently.'"

She would lead me into the parlour.

"Did you take her coat?" Cook would ask.

"Oh no. I asked her but she wouldn't. Shivering with cold she was."

Through pursed lips, Cook would say, "Miss Amy needs to get that fire alight and quick. Mr Herbert would be horrified to know his sweetheart is upstairs getting frostbite."

25

Dora would shake her head. "I asked Miss Amy if she wanted it lit after lunch to warm the room up but she said . . ." Perhaps Dora would suck her cheeks in and make herself a little taller to speak in a posh dismissive voice, " 'Whatever for?' "

Cook would sniff. "If she doesn't get a move on, Miss Amy is going to be a shrivelled-up old maid. What a way to greet your own brother's fiancee. And where's Mrs Bolitho?"

"Lying down. It's the stress of it all. Or that's what Miss Amy said. If you ask me, Miss Amy is the one who's giving Mrs B stress."

"Pass me the eggs," Cook would demand, "I shall bake a welcome cake. A big one. It's the least I can do for the poor girl."

And now, Dora came to open the door and all that I imagined became reality. She took my bag, led me to the parlour, and left me alone.

I could not stop shivering. The parlour's bleak fireplace was swept clean. No ashes, no kindling, no box of logs at its side.

I wondered if I should take off my coat and gloves. Would it be impolite to keep them on? My gloves were covered in smuts from the train so I removed them and stuffed them into my pockets. Were there smuts on my face too? A mirror was above the mantelpiece. Speckled and so high you would have to be over six foot before you could inspect yourself. Bertie was so tall he would have been able to see himself in it. I took out my rather tear-dampened handkerchief and rubbed at my face.

If Bertie were here he would do it for me. Bending down to make sure I looked presentable. He used to make a joke out of his height. He was at least a foot taller than me.

When we lay side by side, he would wrap his warmth around me and call me his little squirrel.

"I mustn't cry. I mustn't cry. Be strong." I spoke into the empty room.

I put my hanky back in my bag, and felt for the cigarette case lying within. Silver and slim. Bertie had given it to me the first time he'd come home. Before he had to go back to France. We'd been walking on Ealing Common. He'd taken my hand and led me to a small bench where we sat down. "I have something for you." He'd reached inside his army tunic, pressed the little package into my hand and watched as I opened it.

"Bertie!" I remember turning it over in my hands, tracing the ornate engraving on the precious metal. "It's beautiful." I laughed, "Now I shall have to take up smoking properly."

"That's the idea. Every time you put a cigarette to your mouth," he said, rubbing his thumb over my lips, "think of me." He'd bent his head and kissed me.

"I will think of you all the time," I said, trying not to sound too drippy but failing. "I will dream of you when I sleep."

And now, here I was, standing in his house, in a room he knew so well. My knees went weak and I recognised the impending wall of grief that would floor me at any moment.

I pulled a cigarette from the case and tapped it on the lid, tamping down the loose tobacco strands as he had taught me. "Get a grip, old girl."

I lit it and inhaled deeply, my lipstick staining the unfiltered end. A sense of calm filled my veins.

I closed my eyes and tried to imagine Bertie standing next to me; ready to introduce me to his parents.

His pride in me.

My pride in him.

His mother would be happy and welcoming. "You must be cold! I will get Dora to light the fire and get Cook to send up afternoon tea."

I squeezed my eyelids tight, pushing back the inevitable tears, but my silly brain conjured up an image of Bertie as a small boy: crawling under the chenille cloth of the tea table; winding himself in the heavy, bottle-green velvet curtains; jumping from one stiff sofa to its twin, unable to dent the horsehair cushions.

I could smell him. Macassar hair oil and tobacco smoke.

For a fraction of a moment I heard him say my name. I opened my eyes with fright and hope.

It came again. "Clara?"

He was here? There had been a mistake? He was alive?

I reached a hand up to the marble mantel and gripped it hard, willing myself not to faint.

He called again. "Clara?"

He was just on the other side of the door. I could hear his heels on the tiled floor of the hall.

The door opened and my heart leapt into my throat. Tall, smiling. Bertie was standing before me.

I let go of the mantel and opened my arms, waiting for him to embrace me.

He offered his hand to shake.

"Clara," he said. "At last we meet. Ernest Bolitho. Bertie's brother."

He caught my arm as my knees buckled.

"Oh my goodness. The journey has exhausted you."

"I'm so sorry. May I sit down?" I felt for the nearest chair.

"Not that one," he said sharply, "that's Father's. And . . ." He looked at the cigarette burning its way towards my fingers, "I'm sorry, but Mother does not approve of ladies smoking." He took the cigarette from me and crossed the room to open the large sash window that looked out, as I was to discover the next day in daylight, over the back garden.

I could see the bell tower of the church lit up beyond.

Outside, I knew, lay the palm tree Bertie had told me about and, in the middle of the lawn, an apple tree with a swing. "I love that swing," he'd told me. "Best toy Father ever made for us. When I take you home, you shall sit on it, under the apple blossom, and I shall push you so that your toes reach the sky."

"Bertie was always getting caught out with his smoking." Ernest's voice broke through my memory as he threw the cigarette stub out of the window and turned back to me. "I'll leave the window open. Mother

29

has the nose of a bloodhound. How was your journey? You look tired. You're shivering."

"I'm fine, honestly." My eyes were fixed on the bare dark branches of the apple tree outside. Bertie would never push me on the swing under the blossom after all. To my embarrassment and Ernest's discomfort, I burst into tears.

"Oh dear," Ernest said awkwardly. "Has anyone offered the facilities?" he asked, looking around the room; anywhere but at me. "Maybe you'd like to freshen up?"

"Yes, I would," I managed. "Thank you."

"Our maid isn't too bright, I'm afraid. God knows where Amy got her from but," he coughed, "needs must, I suppose."

He pulled the bell rope by the fire and within seconds Dora entered.

"Yes, sir?"

He gestured towards me whilst issuing orders. "Please show Miss Carter to the facilities and ask Cook to organise some tea."

The maid bobbed. "Yes sir."

I gathered myself and gratefully crossed the room to join her.

I was suddenly aware that I was badly in need of the lavatory, and also to cool my face and neck.

"Oh, and Dora," Ernest barked as we left, "put Miss Carter's luggage in her room. Which one has my sister got ready?"

Dora, her eyes darting from mine to Ernest's, replied quietly, "Mr Herbert's room, sir."

I thought I might faint again, "What?"

Ernest hitched up the knees of his perfectly pressed Oxfords and sat on one of the ugly sofas, oblivious to my distress. "Good. Come back when you're settled."

I followed Dora into the hallway and watched as she collected my small case from the foot of the hat stand and began to climb the stairs.

"I'll show you to your room," she said. "It's a nice room. It overlooks the church."

I took in my surroundings rather than speak. Linoleum, cold and bare in patches, covered the landing floor. Dora stopped at the second room on the left. "Here you are." She opened the door with her free hand and stood aside to allow me to enter.

A single bed with a brown headboard faced the one window. A washstand stood in the corner and a heavy mahogany wardrobe against the wall opposite.

Dora put the case on the bed. "Lavatory is out of the door, turn left. It's at the end of the corridor. Miss Amy's room is just across the landing."

Shakily, I thanked Dora, and waited until she had closed the door behind her.

Here I was, here in Bertie's room. He had told me about it. This bed was where he had slept. Those books, haphazardly lying in the bookcase, were the ones he had read. He had sat at that small table, labouring over homework. Biting the end of his pencil and staring at the church at the end of the garden for inspiration.

I opened one of the wardrobe's double doors and was hit by the powerful smell of mothballs. On the rail were three bare hangers, presumably for my use. I opened the other door and stepped back quickly. Hanging there was Bertie's coat. The one he had worn when I had first met him. I reached out and touched its sleeve then pulled it to my nose. Yes, this was him. This was his scent. "Bertie," I whispered into the scratchy wool. "It's me. I'm here in your room. I'm here."

There was a knock at the door and I dropped the sleeve, shutting the doors quickly.

"Come in," I called.

A woman, very tall and bony, entered. She wore a navy blue dress almost to the floor, high-necked and belted, and stood in the doorway without expression. Her sharp eyes took me in from head to toe. "Clara. Mother and I thought this room would be most suitable for you."

"Oh yes, it's lovely. Thank you. You must be Amy? Bertie talked a lot about you."

"Yes." Her eyes alighted on my case on the bed. "But you haven't unpacked yet."

"I only just got here and I'd like to freshen up before I come down. If that's all right?"

"Tea will be served in the parlour. Father will be home at four thirty." She moved as if to leave, then as an afterthought turned back. "I don't like to keep meals waiting."

CHAPTER
THREE

Clara, Callyzion

December 1918

I brushed my hair, put on my smarter cardigan and touched up my lipstick.

The church bell was striking the hour as I went downstairs and entered the parlour. It wasn't looking much more cheerful than when I'd left, but at least there was a fire, albeit struggling, in the grate. What it lacked in heat, it attempted in cheer.

Ernest was on one sofa, as I had last seen him, and Amy was sitting opposite him, with an elderly woman on the other.

"Here she is." Ernest stood up and smiled. "Mother, this is Clara."

"Come closer, my dear." Her smile was clouded with grief. "My eyes aren't what they were and I want to look at you."

"Mrs Bolitho." I went to her. "Thank you so much for inviting me."

Her grey eyes darted over my simple clothes and figure.

"You have a good, ordinary face," she said to me. "I like that. Bertie liked it too. I know. But, too much lipstick."

I stood my ground. "Bertie liked it."

His mother folded her arms and chuckled. "Bertie always liked spirited people. That's good. He also told us that you have family in Kent?"

"Yes."

"And what do they do?"

"They farmed. Apples and hops mostly. But we had an excellent dairy herd too." My lies poured easily into the room.

"How many acres?"

"Goodness knows. Around two hundred at least."

Ernest interjected. "Jolly good."

"Yes," I gave him my practised, sad smile. "But nothing can substitute for the loss of one's parents when one is so young."

"Goodness. We didn't know," Ernest said apologetically. "How dreadful for you."

Mrs Bolitho seemed to me to perk up at this information. "Oh, my dear. Come and sit down next to me here." She flapped her hand at Amy, "Move up, dear, let Clara sit between us." I squeezed my hips down into the over-sprung seat, feeling the thigh bones of the women either side of me.

Amy tried to pull hers as far from me as possible, while her mother wriggled herself around to see me better. "What on earth happened? How did your parents die?"

I hadn't yet thought through a cogent explanation, so I dipped my head and fumbled in my cardigan pocket for a handkerchief.

"Mother," rebuked Ernest, "Clara will tell us if and when she wants to."

Mrs Bolitho covered her disappointment with a sniff. "Well I am surprised Bertie didn't tell us when he had the chance." A sigh and a short pause before asking, "You did tell Bertie didn't you?"

"Yes, of course. I told him everything."

"I am glad to hear it. And how is London? I believe you work there?"

"Yes. As a secretary at the *London Evening News*."

"How interesting. We don't get that newspaper here, of course. My husband prefers *The Times*."

Before I could respond, Amy spoke across me. "Mama, it's time for your cough medicine."

"I am perfectly fine, thank you." Mrs Bolitho focused on me again. "I want to hear all about how you met our dear Bertie. And Ernest, dear, liven up that fire, would you?"

I watched as Ernest got on his knees by the hearth and reached for a log. Every movement reminded me of Bertie and the first time I saw him.

"Bertie and I met at a bridge club. In Piccadilly."

Mrs Bolitho nodded. "And do you play good bridge?"

"Not as well as Bertie." I remembered him sitting opposite me at the small table, his slender fingers holding his cards. "We won a couple of tournaments together."

"You must be pretty good then." Mrs Bolitho turned to Ernest, who was concentrating on the fire. "Clara plays bridge. Perhaps, one evening, we should play."

"Rather," said Ernest. "Amy? Want to make up a four?"

"I'd rather not." She almost shuddered with the thought of it. "Where is Dora with the tea?" She checked her watch. "She's late. I'll go and chivvy her along." She left the room in a rustle of skirts and left the three of us looking at the fire and trying to think of something to say.

"You must think me very rude," I remembered. "I haven't thanked you for the taxi you sent to the station."

"Amy organised that." Mrs Bolitho waved a hand in the direction of where Amy had disappeared. "She runs the house for me. The last few weeks have weakened my spirits." She coughed lightly. "Was Chewton waiting for you?"

"Yes, he was."

Ernest laughed. "I bet a penny to a pound that he gave you a tour of the fleshpots of Callyzion."

Mrs Bolitho tutted. "No need for that language. Your father wouldn't like it." She picked up the small watch pinned to her bust. "He should be home any minute. I told him to be here at four thirty on the dot."

As she finished her sentence, as if on cue, we heard the sound of a key in the front door and a deep manly voice called, "Halloo. I'm home! Has Miss Carter arrived?"

"We are in the parlour," Ernest called back.

The door opened to reveal an enormous man both of height and girth. Bertie had once described his father as "comfortingly solid", and now, seeing him, I couldn't think of any better words. He was dressed in a black frock coat, black shirt, black trousers and black gaiters. The only colour was the snowy white of his dog collar.

"Aha." He looked at me warmly. "My goodness, how wonderful that you are actually here at last." He took two strides to cross the room, and took my hand and patted it. "You are so welcome here. Even though Bertie didn't have a chance to tell us about you we want to know everything for ourselves. You are certainly as pretty as we imagined." He turned to his wife. "Do you not think so, my dear?" Without waiting for an answer, he looked about the room. "Where is tea?"

It took just a few minutes before Cook's Victoria sponge and tiny meat paste sandwiches arrived, pleasing everyone and giving us all something fresh and safe to talk about.

After tea, Rev. Bolitho withdrew to his study and Mrs Bolitho returned to her bedroom for a rest.

Amy bustled about with Dora, giving instructions for supper and returning the parlour to its pre-tea state.

Ernest and I were left alone. Ernest began the conversation.

"Awfully pleased you came. It seems from what his friend Jimmy said, Bertie was quite swept up by you."

"And I by him." I looked at my lap. "It's so nice to be here, with his family. The people who loved him best."

Ernest cleared his throat. "Yes. We miss him."

A spark jumped from the grate onto the rug. Ernest reached out one long leg, without having to get up, and stamped it out. Both of us sat looking into the flames.

"I miss him very much." One log, its bark now catching a flame, shifted slightly, turning the flame from blue to yellow then orange. "How did your parents find my address?" I asked.

"With difficulty." He smiled wryly. "We didn't know about you or your whereabouts. It was only when we received Bertie's personal effects . . ."

I looked up, fearing what they might have found amongst Bertie's belongings. Not all my letters? Not every private, shaming, loving word we wrote to each other? Please God, no.

Ernest was speaking again. "Among his things were letters from his old friends. One of them, Jimmy?"

My heart flipped anxiously. Jimmy was the friend who had rented us the flat in Ealing. "Yes." My throat was dry. "A good friend of Bertie's. What . . . what did his letter say?"

"Jolly lucky really. He mentioned an address in Ealing."

I clenched my hands, waiting to be shamed. "Oh yes?"

"It was the first we had heard of you. He wrote something along the lines of, 'hope Clara is comfortable in the Ealing flat'."

"Did he say anything else?"

"He asked how Bertie was doing. The usual stuff. Talked about his own marriage. So anyway, as we had an address for you, Father decided we ought to meet you and we could share our . . ." He cleared his throat. "Our happier memories of Bertie."

I relaxed. Bless Jimmy. He had revealed nothing.

"I was so surprised and pleased to get your parents' letter," I said. "It found its way to me eventually. I had to leave Ealing a while ago, you see, and return to Kent — a family matter — but I had left a forwarding address. Just in case."

"Well, I am sorry the whole process took so long. But you are here now."

"Yes. Here I am."

"And can you stay for Christmas?"

I was taken by surprise. I thought I would come for a couple of days, soak my grief in the place that Bertie called home and then return to Kent, to where I was needed the most.

"I don't want to be a bother."

"No bother at all. I happen to know that Mother is very much wanting you to stay until the New Year."

New Year? I couldn't stay for as long as that. Could I? "I'm not sure."

"Do you have plans?" I could see Bertie in his eyes, in his voice.

"Well I . . . I haven't brought anything with me." I couldn't stay. I mustn't. What would Philippa think? How could I miss only my second Christmas with Mikey?

"Amy can lend you anything you need," he said airily. "Say yes and it's settled." He smiled at me. Not Bertie's smile but so similar.

"Well, I . . . I don't have any plans."

He stood up. "Excellent. Now what say we have a game of cards? Rummy?"

And that is how we filled the hinterland between tea and dinner. He told amusing stories about himself, Amy and Bertie growing up. Hide-and-seek in the organ loft, swapping their father's sermon for a shopping list and the Easter they all had chickenpox. Ernest was an easy person to be with then. I began to warm to him.

A dinner of beef broth, followed by tiny lamb cutlets and then apple crumble, filled an hour or so of small talk.

We delicately manoeuvred around the subject of Bertie, not one of us wanting to upset the other, and then Ernest announced that I was staying until the New Year, which occasioned much delight in Bertie's parents.

"And, Amy," Ernest went on, "I've told Clara that you would lend her anything she doesn't have." He grinned.

I looked up and caught her giving him a horrified stare.

"No, no," I said quickly. "I will be fine, honestly."

Mrs Bolitho chipped in. "Amy has plenty of nice things in her wardrobe that she can share. She wears so few of them, it will be nice to see them out and about."

Amy gave her mother a tight smile and said quietly, "Mother, you know it would be impractical for me to wear anything special while I am looking after the house."

I felt her embarrassment. "Honestly," I smiled at her, "I wouldn't dream of borrowing your nice clothes. I might spoil them, and then what would you wear for special occasions?"

Mrs Bolitho leant closer to me and, laughing at her daughter, said, "Amy doesn't like special occasions. I can't remember the last time she went out and had some fun."

Amy paled, her hands tightening their grip on her napkin. "Mother, please."

Mrs Bolitho blithely continued to discomfort her daughter. "But you are young and have your whole life ahead of you, darling."

The napkin was released and Amy stood. "I wonder what Dora has done with the apple crumble?" We watched her leave.

"Don't worry about her," Mrs Bolitho said to me.

Reverend Bolitho peered over the top of his glasses and looked at his wife. "Louisa. Let her be."

When Amy returned, we ate our apple crumble in silence.

And when Dora cleared it away, Amy stood again and — looking anywhere but at me — said, "Mama, come along, you are tired and I don't want your cold getting any worse."

The gentlemen stood as mother and daughter pushed themselves away from the table. As Mrs Bolitho passed me she paused to kiss my cheek. "Goodnight, my dear, and sleep well."

When they had left, I waited a handful of minutes before saying, "If you don't mind, I think I shall retire too. It has been a lovely day, though, and thank you for allowing me to stay."

"Clara, what else could we do? It is what Bertie would want and therefore it is what Louisa and I want," Reverend Bolitho said kindly. "You must be tired." He and Ernest stood as I pushed my chair back.

"Goodnight, Reverend Bolitho."

"Please call me Hugh," he said. "If Bertie were here, I would have liked you to call me Father."

Tears sprang to my eyes and my throat constricted. "My dear," he said kindly, "you will always be part of our family now, whatever the future holds."

"Goodnight, Clara." Ernest smiled. "Breakfast is at seven thirty."

"Thank you. You have all been so kind."

"We'll do something tomorrow," Ernest said. "Maybe a walk after breakfast?"

"I should like that."

"Excellent. Goodnight, old thing."

The same words Bertie would use.

Head down, nerves raw with exhaustion, I climbed the stairs to my room. Bertie's room. I was longing to be on my own.

I closed the door gratefully and, leaning on the back of it, cried lonely tears.

CHAPTER
FOUR

Clara, Callyzion

December 1918

I cried until there were no tears left. Exhausted as I was, I pushed myself to empty my suitcase and get undressed. I hung my one good suit, my office suit, in the wardrobe next to Bertie's old coat, then a newish dress that Bertie had liked, and finally the dress I had been wearing.

My clean underwear and stockings I put in the small drawers by the bed, my shoes neatly by the wardrobe and my nightdress on the pillow. Bertie's pillow. I picked it up and buried my nose in it. It smelt of fresh air and lavender, but not of him.

Quickly taking off my underclothes, I wondered whether I should wash them in the bathroom and hang them to dry on the back of a chair as I did at home. Would that be thought wrong? Should I leave them for Dora to do? Or was that not the done thing, either? After much dithering I decided that I would wash them myself tonight and then ask, discreetly, tomorrow what the system for laundering was.

Slipping on my flannelette nightdress, the one Bertie had given me before he last went to France, I wrapped myself in my dressing gown and grabbed my wash-bag.

A meagre towel had been left on the bed, by Dora I assumed, so I rolled my underwear inside it and tucked it under my arm. Fearing any embarrassing meetings on the landing, I slipped noiselessly down the corridor to the bathroom.

Eventually, my washing hanging to dry overnight on Bertie's old chair, I lifted the eiderdown and sheets of his bed and slipped my feet down towards the end. The sheets were cold and slightly damp. I pulled the blanket and top quilt over me but they gave no tangible warmth.

I had an idea.

Getting out of bed, I went to the wardrobe. Bertie's coat slid easily off its hanger. I laid it on top of the bed and slipped under the sheets once more. That was better. I pulled his coat right under my chin. He had worn this coat when we'd got tickets for a recital at the Wigmore Hall. Was it Beethoven or Bach? I couldn't be certain. But I remembered clearly how we had returned to Ealing and made love to keep warm.

I pulled my right hand from the growing warmth of the sheets and reached for the pockets of the coat. My fingers closed around a piece of almost furry paper. I pulled it out. The ticket to Wigmore Hall. I held it tightly in my grip then kissed it. His fingers had been the last to touch it. I held it a few moments longer then slid it under my pillow.

Blowing out my bedside candle, I could see the black night beyond the window. I had forgotten to pull the curtains and was too weary to get out of bed and close them now. I lay wide-eyed, watching a patch of thin cloud moving across the weak glow of a waning moon.

Could Bertie see me now? Could his spirit be in this room watching me?

If he was lying by me now, he would laugh at the absurdity of the two of us in his narrow bed. His coat keeping us warm. The ticket under our pillow. Everything. He was always laughing. He would hold me gently, passing his blood warmth to me and simply loving me.

I dreamt that night that we were back in our little nest in Ealing. I had been pickling onions in our tiny kitchen. It must have been Christmas because I had Christmas cards on the table and a small tree with red-ribboned bows and a robin on the top. The onions were the ones that Bertie had planted before he went to France the last time and this jar was to be his Christmas present.

I was washing up and looking out at our tiny patch of garden. I had used too much detergent and the bubbles were floating free past my eyes, but when I looked again the bubbles were turning into snow and in the garden white flakes were swirling, and standing in the middle of it all was Bertie. He had his big coat on and the bright green scarf I had knitted for him. He was smiling and waving at me, wanting me to join him. I opened the door and ran to where he had been standing but he wasn't there. A snowman, wearing the green scarf, was in his place. A snowball hit the back of my neck, and as I turned I saw Bertie again. Now he was indoors. I ran back, the snowball dripping down my back, and collected up a handful of snow to throw at him. He was in the lounge sprinkling snow onto our little tree. I went to him and put my arms around him. "The war is over," he told me. "I am home."

We held each other and the bliss and joy and love I felt in that moment was like no other. It was real and ethereal in one. To say it felt like heaven sounds glib, but truly I felt that angels were with us. His tears and mine were created by a greater power I now knew existed. "The war is over. I am home," he said again.

I held him tighter but he was no longer solid. The body beneath his coat was slipping away, like mist. I didn't want to open my eyes to see him gone but I did and saw his coat slip from my arms, empty. He had gone.

I woke up in a terror. He was dead. Bertie was dead.

I had known very little of love before Bertie.

I had been born in Ospringe, Kent. My grandfather had been the closest person to me. He had at least cared about me. Given me some pride in myself. When he died and there was no one else to remember where I came from, I began to change. The one dingy room we shared, in an overcrowded almshouse, was stinking and had a family of rats nesting under his old straw-filled pallet. On the day the gravediggers slid him out of his pauper's coffin, the foot end hinged so that the box could be reused again and again, I stood by his graveside and swore I would have a better life. I went back to that room and dragged his bed, the rats scattering and squealing, out into the field in front and set fire to it. I cleared the entire room. Watching as the flames engulfed my old life. All I had were the clothes I stood in, a small broken piece of mirror that Grandfather had found on the village tip, a pair of old boots, an empty room and my wits. There were two children in the almshouse. One aged three, one five. Their mother was pregnant again and I knew she needed some extra space. I also knew she could pay me a few pennies if I kept her children in my room. Over the next weeks and months I saved as much as I could, waiting for the chance that I felt certain life would throw at me.

I had a plan. I would deliberately cut off my old life before it stained me irrevocably. I knew what it was like to be one step away from the workhouse, my mother dead of consumption, my father a drunken sot, my grandfather keeping us out of the poorhouse, picking hops and apples every Kentish summer before dying a wretched death of lung disease after years of winters toiling in the cement works.

I would erase my poverty and lowness of birth. Rewrite my history.

And, I couldn't have chosen a better time.

On 4 August 1914, Britain declared war on Germany. Men of fighting age were leaving their work — on the land, in the mines, in offices, in factories — and were signing up to enlist. Suddenly employers needed women to man (as it were) the tractors, conveyor belts and desks of British industry.

I had belief in myself. An innate confidence. I could read and write, thanks to my grandfather. My numeracy was nimble enough from keeping score in the cribbage games played with him in the old pub. My clothes had been rags, but I took one of my mother's old skirts and a blouse and, with some nifty stitching and darning, made them presentable enough. I took care of my skin as well as I could, and brushed my brown curls with a scrubbing brush, as my mother had taught me.

Back then, I wasn't sure what I was preparing for, but whatever it was it would require me to be smart, bright and pretty. I was certain of it.

The fifteenth of September 1914 was the day Clara Carter, orphan of Ospringe parish, became Miss Clara Carter, trainee typist at the *London Evening News*, in Fleet Street, London.

The *News*, as it was known, had acquired a reputation for employing women. The shortage of manpower created by the surge of men wanting to enlist to serve in the war meant that women were prepared and wanting to work. What the newspaper knew, and found attractive, was that they didn't have to pay female workers as much as their male counterparts. Board members must have rubbed their hands in glee at the prospect. War meant profit. Newspaper sales were up. Wage bills down.

I only discovered this by chance when taking the half-hour walk from Ospringe to my small cleaning job in Faversham.

Miss Hampton's Haberdashery on the High Street was small but busy, supplying all kinds of fabric from seductive satins that fell down in ripples, to tough tweeds, scratchy but windproof. Miss Hampton was a respectable unmarried woman, probably in her late thirties or early forties. I felt quite sorry for her. A lifetime as a lonely old spinster couldn't be much fun, but then when I saw how happy she was, doting on her customers and deciding for herself what she would have for supper, and when or even if she would have it, I rather envied her.

Each week I arrived just before she opened up for the day, to clean the shop, the storeroom, her kitchen-cum-parlour and her small, feminine bedroom.

That morning, I had found on my journey a copy of the previous day's *Evening News*. I picked it up for no other reason than to practise my reading and use it later for the fire at home.

Miss Hampton spotted it immediately. "Good morning Miss Carter, I didn't know you'd taken to reading the news."

"I found it. I've never really read one before and I thought it might be interesting. About the war and everything."

"Good for you," Miss Hampton said, "You could read it to me over lunch if you like?"

"Thank you. I would like that."

"Excellent. We women need to keep up with what's going on in the world. It's our duty to understand what is being done in our name."

Miss Hampton was a suffragette. She didn't know I knew. Suffragettes in our part of the world kept their beliefs quiet. Most men and many women thought they were mannish troublemakers. So, when I found a brooch in Miss Hampton's dressing-table drawer, a circle of purple, green and white stones, the suffragettes' colours, I knew what she was. I admired her, and if she wanted it to be kept a secret, no one would hear it from me.

Miss Hampton carried on. "As women we must stay strong. Keep the home fires burning. Remind those poor devils who are facing the enemy that there is still an England to return to." She folded the paper and tucked it under the counter. "And we'll start with you getting the shop swept."

I loved my days in the shop with Miss Hampton. For a starter, I stayed clean all day. The bolts of fabric always needed sorting and measuring. The ribbons rolling. The buttons counting.

At first, when customers came into the shop, Miss Hampton expected me to disappear and get on with the work in the rest of her home. But a few months back she had asked me if I would like to take home an offcut of soft grey wool and make it into a garment that I could wear at work. She didn't have to explain that my mother's old skirt and blouse were far from decent. I made a simple dress with a neat neckline, braceletlength sleeves and a neat-fitting bodice and skirt that accentuated my thin frame. I wore it to work every day from then on. As soon as I had finished my cleaning duties, I was allowed to be Miss Hampton's assistant to the customers.

Today, after I had the back room in good order and the bolts of fabric lying neatly on their shelves, it was time for our simple lunch. Miss Hampton locked the door at exactly one p.m. every day and I could hear her doing so as I ran water from the pump at the sink, filled the kettle and lit the hob.

"Now Miss Carter," Miss Hampton arrived in the back room and glanced around to make sure all was shipshape, "did you have breakfast?"

"Not yet, ma'am. My grandfather cooked a mutton stew last night so I wasn't hungry." I lied convincingly but Miss Hampton, although never revealing so, knew very well that there had been no mutton stew and that my grandfather lay now in an unmarked pauper's grave.

"Perhaps you could manage a little bread and ham? I made the bread last night."

"Thank you, ma'am. I would."

"You'll find it all in the larder. We'll eat it at the table here."

"May I get the newspaper?" I asked politely.

Miss Hampton was gathering plates and cutlery. "Please do."

The tea was made, and the food set out quickly and neatly.

I was always thankful for these simple lunches. Not only was it good food, but watching Miss Hampton, the cutlery she used and the delicate way she ate and drank, was a valuable lesson in manners. I also studied the way Miss Hampton spoke and tried my best to imitate her soft voice and accuracy of speech.

Taking her last mouthful of bread and dabbing crumbs from her mouth with a napkin, Miss Hampton placed her knife and fork in the middle of her empty plate and picked up my copy of the *Evening News*. There were many pages of war news, but she hurried through them, muttering "Dear God" and "Unbearable", before stopping at an advertisement showing the latest ladies' fashion styles. "Skirts are getting short." She raised her eyebrows, "In my day you would never show your ankles. I still don't."

"May I see?" I asked.

The advertisement read: "The new workwear for young women". The two models were wearing quite different outfits. One a neat, peplum-waisted jacket with a companion narrow skirt, the other posing in a floaty, floral tea dress. "Ideal office wear for any season," I said. "I like them."

Miss Hampton got up and collected the lunch dishes to take them to the kitchen.

I turned a few more pages of the paper and came to the Situations Vacant column.

THE LONDON EVENING NEWS NEEDS YOU.
Are you a young woman prepared to do essential war work?
Be part of our ground-breaking News Team and
become a typist.
Full training, board and lodging available.
Applications in writing to:
The London Evening News
Fleet Street
London

This was the sign I had been waiting for. The moment I had been preparing for.

A job in London with board and lodging, a skill to learn and a wage to be had.

I jumped up and ran to Miss Hampton who was drying a plate. "Miss Hampton, ma'am, can you help me write a letter?"

I haunted the village post office for days waiting for a reply and then it arrived.

Dear Miss Carter,

Thank you for your letter of 17 August.

We should like to offer you a position on the *London Evening News* as a trainee typist.

We can offer a room in a nearby boarding house where many of our female employees live. The rent is deducted directly from your wage.

Assuming all this is in order, we look forward with pleasure to your suggested arrival on 15 September next.

I remain yours sincerely,
Miss Anita Flint,
Office Manager

Miss Hampton had been almost more excited than me.

"You'll need clothes."

I looked down at my grey wool dress. "What's wrong with this?"

Miss Hampton inclined her head. "Well, shall we be reminded that fine feathers make fine birds? And being so thin you don't take much fabric." She unrolled her tape measure. "Stand still."

Out of shop hours, Miss Hampton and I picked out old remnants of fabric, and between us we sewed two dresses, one work suit and two blouses.

"That should do you if you take care of them. Now what about your footwear?" Miss Hampton asked.

"I'll polish these boots up." I looked at my scuffed and thinsoled shoes. "They'll be fine."

Miss Hampton sighed, "They are worn through. No, no. Let me see what I have in the back."

It turned out that Miss Hampton's shoes were a pretty good fit, although my feet were a little thinner.

"Wear thicker stockings to pack them out a bit." Her eyebrows twitched. "You don't have stockings, do you?"

I was embarrassed. "No. Just these long socks." I hitched up my skirt for her to see.

"Oh dear." She rubbed her chin. "What about personal items of underwear?"

I reddened and shook my head.

Miss Hampton smiled. "Dear me. You are a regular Cinderella, aren't you? You are lucky to have me."

Miss Hampton kitted me out with all that she thought a young woman should need when starting a new job in a new city. Not only that, she also let me use her tin bathtub. The first hot, soapy bath I had ever had.

On the morning of my departure for London, I crept out of my shared room, leaving the two children snoring and a note for their mum — if she could read — and took the walk to Miss Hampton's.

Miss Hampton had my travelling clothes hanging up in her back room, with all my other garments packed into a small case she had bought for me.

"Thank you, ma'am," I said as I stood and looked at myself in her mirror.

"Oh," Miss Hampton coughed, hiding her emotion, "it's been fun. I've enjoyed it."

I spun around in a full circle, checking my appearance from every angle. "I can't believe this is happening."

Miss Hampton pursed her lips and was quiet for a moment. "I believe in you. You have a strength of character that will get you through life's challenges. And if you need any help, you know where I am." Her voice was kind and meaningful. "Now then. You've got everything?"

"Yes."

"Don't forget to clean your nails every day and brush your hair well."

"I won't."

"And clean your teeth. And write. Please. I want to know how you are."

"I'll type you a letter," I told her.

"Ah yes. Very good." Miss Hampton began patting her sides in agitation. "I suppose we should embrace or something."

I laughed as I hugged my mentor, and kissed her on her soft cheek. "I will never forget you, ma'am."

"Likewise." Miss Hampton sniffed.

Miss Hampton watched me as I climbed up on the farm wagon that was ordered and waiting to take me on the first leg of my journey out of Kent.

"Bye Miss Hampton," I waved as the cart began to move.

"Goodbye!" She waved in return.

I never looked back.

"Where're you going then?" asked the young cart driver, flicking his reins.

"London." I smiled. I had done it. I had escaped. "Do you know it?"

"Maybe, one day." He held out an arm and caught a dry stalk of grass from the hedgerow. He put it between his lips, rolling it from side to side for a while.

"Know London, do you?" he asked.

"Of course." I didn't feel as if I were lying. This was the new Miss Clara Carter, after all. I tried another one. "I was born there."

He flicked a look at me, still chewing the piece of grass. Then said, "I'm enlisting. Going to France. My brothers are out there."

I narrowed my eyes, "How old are you?"

"Nearly eighteen."

I laughed. "You're sixteen if you're a day."

"Well, how old are you then?"

"It's very rude to ask a lady's age."

"I wouldn't ask a lady."

"Oi. Cheeky." I folded my arms and sniffed. "I'm eighteen, if you must know."

The barrier was broken.

We continued chatting and joshing each other until he stopped the cart and let me down. "Your next one is over there." He pointed at a smart wagon pulled by two horses. "He's a bit dearer'n me."

I pulled a penny from my pocket and gave it to him.

"I only want a ha'pence," he said.

"Well, if you don't want it?" I said loftily, holding out my hand for the change.

"No. You're all right." He pocketed it.

"Keep it for luck then," I told him. "If you ever get to France, you might need some luck."

He handed me down my bag. "Good luck in London," he said. "I reckon you'll need it more than me."

It was evening by the time I arrived in Southwark. I had slept most of the journey, waking only as the deep mud ruts of the Old Kent Road jiggled the sleep from my head.

The driver took my bag down for me, and I showed him the carefully folded piece of paper I had kept in my pocket. "Do you happen to know where this might be; it's the address of a lodging house just off Fleet Street?"

The man gave me directions to cross the river and ask again. Forty minutes later, I found the building I was looking for. Georgian, tall, thin and well proportioned, with square-paned windows and a black front door, over which was painted the words: "The Fleet Women's Dwelling".

My new home.

CHAPTER
FIVE

Bertie, Penang, Malaya

28 July 1914

Penang is a world away from the boredom of home. I have never missed my life in the Cornish vicarage with my hypochondriac mother and bitter sister. The only one I truly miss is Pa. The most forgiving and unjudgemental man. I am blessed to have him as a parent. I miss my younger brother Ernest too, of course. He and I have been very close but not so much over the last five years. Sibling rivalry got between us, as it does in many families. I am jealous of the way he winds Ma around his little finger, and he is jealous of me because Pa backed this adventure to Malaya all the way.

I can't tell you how thrilling it was to wave Callyzion, my mother and my sister goodbye and board the ship at Tilbury Docks to steam south for the Orient.

I was still only twenty-four and had been lured to Penang by the father of a chum I knew from Cambridge. He owned a rubber plantation there and was having trouble finding someone who would be willing to spend a couple of years, away from family and Blighty, looking after it. As it was, I couldn't wait to get away, so when he offered me a decent wage, a share of the business and my passage paid, how could I refuse?

It took six weeks on the boat from Tilbury.

Six wonderful weeks where I flirted with the young female passengers and played endless bridge, supplementing my meagre income most satisfactorily.

I have been here for two years now and have settled in well. The workers, mostly Malay or Indian, respect me, and in return I look after them well, seeing to their medical and domestic needs, within reason.

I was beginning to think I might never return to England. Everything I needed was here. Sun, sea, a good life and good society with the ex-pat community. But, as my father was fond of saying, "Man plans and God laughs."

God's laughter began one day as I was walking the plantation and checking the taps on the rubber trees. I saw my foreman, Nizam, running through the serried ranks of silver trunks towards me. It was a hot afternoon, and being the monsoon season, the jungle floor was steaming from a recent heavy downpour.

"Slow down, Nizam. It's too hot to run," I shouted to him. In response he waved a buff piece of paper in his hand. "Sahib!" he managed. "Important telegram for you. From England."

Oh God, I thought, what the hell has happened? My mind went straight to my parents. Was father ill? Had mother had another of her funny turns?

Nizam reached me, panting hard. "Sahib, the telegram boy say urgent at once."

He handed me the envelope and then bent double, hands on knees, to catch his breath.

My name, Herbert Bolitho, and my address, Batu Rubber Plantation, were written in a pencilled scrawl.

Nizam, breathing less heavily now, was looking at me, waiting for me to read the message.

I did not oblige him. "Would you run up to the house and get some tiffin ready, Nizam? I'll be there shortly"

I could see the disappointment in his eyes. Excitement of any kind, especially from thousands of miles away, was to be shared, but trust him though I did, gossip spread, which is why I spoke Malay at work and English only with the other English planters. We made sure the staff never learnt our language.

I opened the envelope and pulled out a single sheet of paper. The same grey scrawl wrote:

AUSTRIA*HUNGARY*DECLARE*WAR*ON*
GERMANY*STOP*FATHER

My father's usual brevity Telegrams were paid for by the word. His living in the church paid very little so this extravagance was against his nature. He really must be worried.

I could have run back to the house and despatched my own telegram there and then, but I decided instead to finish the job I was doing; checking the trees for their rubber production and marking those that needed to come out. I had twenty acres of them and ninety estate workers. It was a decent living for them, but the system was beset with corruption and fraud. I tried very hard to be a good "protector", as my position was known.

So why had my father sent me a telegram? Did he expect me to come home? Was England going to be drawn into this war? And if we did, would I do the right thing? Did he want me to enlist? Face the enemy and get killed in a pointless war?

I stood under the canopy of my trees and weighed up my options. The truth was that if I booked a boat home tomorrow, the chances were that the war would be over by the time I got there. Then I'd have to turn around and return to the plantation, to find it abandoned by its workers and overrun with rats and monkeys.

I worked for a further hour or so — the trees were in very good stead — and returned for tiffin. The small feast of tea and cherry cake looked delicious, but I headed for a stiff cocktail instead.

I didn't send a telegram that day. I waited to see if the threat of war was real or if my father had overreacted. I heard nothing further, so a few days later I got up early while it was still cool and strolled into town.

The only place to get reasonably accurate information was in the bar of the splendid Eastern and Oriental Hotel in George Town.

The fans on the shaded veranda wafted the early heat around, giving some respite to those customers who were breakfasting outside.

I lifted my hat to them, "Morning."

"Good morning."

I bounced up the steps into the bar and handed my Panama to one of the several bar boys. "Good morning, sahib," they chanted with toothy grins.

"Good morning, boys. My usual breakfast please." I headed to my preferred table.

I settled to watch the street market below and to view the ships in the harbour. Two warships were docked. One British. I felt a small stirring of unease. Good or bad news?

The arrival of my scrambled eggs and mango juice, with a pot of tea, chased thoughts of the presence of Royal Navy warships from my mind.

"Bolitho, old man." I looked up.

"Duncan. Come and join me." Duncan was protector of a much larger plantation a couple of miles from mine.

His Scottish accent rich and rolling. "Have you had news from home?"

"About the war? Yes. My father sent a telegram."

"I had one last night. My father reckons we'll have to step in, the German government haven't responded to us telling them not to take Belgium or else."

"Oh God."

"Aye, quite so." Duncan pushed his thick spectacles further onto his nose and turned his attention to the waiting bar boy. "I'll have the same as Mr Bolitho but add a large glass of Scottish whisky to the order." The bar boy nodded smartly and despatched himself to the kitchen.

"So," Duncan said in a quieter tone, "what do you think it'll all mean?"

"The war? God knows. It seems all very foolhardy. What happened to diplomacy and peace at all costs?"

"You get a couple of madmen sabre-rattling and the monkey is out of its cage," Duncan replied. He frowned at the tablecloth and then, lifting his eyes, asked me, "Would you go home?"

"You mean enlist?"

"Aye."

I finished the last mouthful of my eggs and pushed myself out from the table, crossing my legs in what I hoped was a casual and relaxed move. "Well now. I'm entirely unsure. Are you?"

"It would be the right thing to do if we were needed." He swept his hand across his large ginger moustache.

I had been afraid he might play the "right thing" card. I lit a cigarette as if I were considering his answer. "Yes, there is that, but for God's sake, the whole ballyhoo will be over by the time we get home. Surely?" I fervently hoped this would be true.

"Will it?" His eyes looked into mine, searching for some reassurance. I looked away and down at the busy market, blowing two smoke rings to puncture the tension surrounding us.

"I don't honestly know," I said. "But look here, wouldn't we be better off staying? Surely if we continue to keep our plantations supplying rubber for boots, tents, mackintoshes . . ." I was ticking them on my fingers, "all those things badly needed in wartime, wouldn't that be better?"

"Mebbe."

I was grateful when the bar boy appeared with Duncan's breakfast. Political debate on an empty stomach is never a good thing. I stubbed out my cigarette, lit another, and asked the boy for two large whiskies.

When they came Duncan and I raised our tumblers. "To us," Duncan intoned.

He ate and I drank in silence. The food was always good here and the tea excellent, but the Scotch was better. I felt it hit my bloodstream without apology.

"Anyway," I gestured with my glass, "how the hell do we know if any of this is true? It may be rumour. The folks at home may be the victims of scaremongering by —"

"By who? The Germans? The Russians? The French?" grunted Duncan. He wiped his moustache and said quietly, "But what if it isn't?"

We sat in tipsy, silent gloom.

I stared out to the harbour. "There seem to be warships in," I said after a while.

"Saw them this morning," Duncan replied. "One British, the other French, I think."

"Is it? Resupplying, I suppose," I said.

"Yes." Duncan drained his glass. "Want another?"

I held out my glass and the bar boy rushed forwards, knowing what we wanted before we asked.

"The thing is," said Duncan, watching the boy run to his errand. "The German Navy is technologically superior to ours and is said to be spreading itself around harbours of importance."

I snorted, "Since when the bloody hell has George Town been a harbour of importance?"

"It's close to Singapore. Too close to Singapore for comfort."

"Well why don't they bugger off to Singapore then?"

Duncan, who could take his drink better than me, said simply: "Take George Town, you can take Singapore."

"No," I said. "They can't just come in here and take over. We are a British Crown Colony."

"Exactly."

A creeping realisation stirred in me. "Bloody hell"

"Indeed."

I sat toying with my drink and thinking.

Duncan was the first to speak. "Which service do you fancy? Army, Navy or the Flying Corps?"

"If it comes to it, I suppose the Army. It's what my father would want. His father fought in Crimea. You?"

"Same. My mother's grandfather was killed in 1814 in America. He's a kind of hero in our family. One we all have to look up to, even though we never knew him. When we were small and had done something wrong, my mother would tell us that the ghost of Grandfather Ewan would haunt us all our days. She said he despised naughty children and loathed cowardice. It has been an enormous weight to live up to."

"Good God."

"Something like that."

We had another large Scotch each and changed the conversation to the general gossip of employees, the price of rubber, and when we'd next have dinner together.

After an hour or so I looked at my watch. "Better get back, I suppose."

"Aye, I'd better go to the telegraph office and send a reply to my father."

We said our goodbyes. Duncan plodded off into town and I strolled down to the harbour to check out the warships.

I was stalling for time. I wanted to stay where I was. I loved the plantation and enjoyed the company of the workers who relied on me. They were almost like family.

It was on the evening of 4 August when my hand was forced. Duncan and I and a couple of friends had spent a convivial evening at the Eastern and Oriental. The squabbles in Europe seemed a long way away. We were buoyed up by cocktails, convinced that our lives would remain uninterrupted. Smoking fine cigars on the veranda under a starry night, any war felt impossible. I was in a hibiscus-scented tropical heaven far, far away from any reality back home.

As I looked down on the street below, I heard, then saw Nizam pelting towards us. "Nizam!" I shouted. "What the hell are you doing out this late? Has something happened on the plantation?" My biggest fear was fire.

Gasping at his exertion, Nizam came to a stop below the hotel balcony. "Telegram for you." He panted. "Urgent."

"Come up here and give it to me, then." And on a whim, I shouted down, "I'll get you a drink, old boy."

A minute later he was standing awkwardly next to me. A bar boy returned with a tray carrying an ice-cold beer. Nizam hesitated. "May I take, sahib?"

"Of course. You need it."

Duncan murmured to me in his deep Scottish brogue, "Servants are not allowed to be served in the hotel, old boy."

"For God's sake." I took the bottle from the tray and handed it to Nizam. "There, now I have served the beer. Blame me."

The bar boy looked at me with fear. "Sahib. I will lose my job."

"I will make sure you don't. Now leave us, and Nizam, drink that bloody beer."

Nizam handed me the envelope and gratefully gulped the drink.

Opening the telegram I read:

ENGLAND*AT*WAR*WITH*GERMANY*
STOP*FATHER.

I handed the envelope to Duncan and the other pals.

We looked at each other, each silently asking ourselves the unbearable question. Should we go home?

I returned to England nine months later. It was not cowardice that prevented me from going home earlier. My mind was made up way before I witnessed the terrible sinking of an Imperial Russian Navy cruiser and a French destroyer in George Town harbour. A German cruiser had masqueraded as a British naval ship and torpedoed them both; the war was on my doorstep all these miles from home.

I booked my passage home in the early May of 1915. Not on an ocean liner but a spice boat, taking her cargo to Tilbury Docks.

Six fraught weeks at sea followed. The crew were constantly on the lookout for German hunter boats and cruisers. Mines were a fresh threat and the captain received daily, sometimes hourly, radio messages with information on where the enemy lay and how to avoid them. To calm our nerves, I taught many of the crew to play bridge. The Chinese who ran the ship's laundry — the dhobi-wallahs — were keen gamblers, and I quickly learnt not to bet more than a few shillings when playing them.

We were due to dock early on a Friday morning and I was up before the sun. My things were mostly packed and, after a quick shave, I bade my farewell to the cramped cabin that had been my home. I went up on deck and waited for the white cliffs of Dover to appear like spectres on the horizon. I surprised myself with the emotion I experienced when they finally materialised from the early gloom. It was not yet seven o'clock in the morning but I was ready to come home.

From Tilbury, I took the train to Victoria Station, which was crowded. I noticed that there were four distinct groups.

Men and women in civvies, going about their day.

Young men, proudly clothed in unsullied uniforms. Smiling. Eager to join their units.

The returning men, wounded, with the mud of France still on their boots, their bandaged heads and arms bloodied, crutches under their armpits, sharing cigarettes, struck dumb by the horror they had left behind.

And finally, women. Wan with waiting. Staring at each and every man in the hope that one of them was theirs.

I left Victoria and walked the short distance to present myself at 59 Buckingham Gate, London. The headquarters of the First Battalion of the London Scottish Regiment. As a proud Scot, Duncan had joined the Argyll and Sutherland Highlanders in Stirling, and I promised to join its equivalent in London.

After giving my name to a recruiting officer, receiving a medical test (sight, height and hearing), I was equipped for active service, and embodied there and then.

I was Private number 4192.

Caroline

Present day

I opened the small discoloured brown envelope and shook out the little key.

The clasps on the trunk were cold to the touch as I turned the key in each of the two locks.

The right one was stiff and took a little time before yielding. The left one turned as if new.

Placing the key on the floor, I put my thumbs on both of the clasps and pushed them down and away. I felt the mechanism of the lock click and then release.

The clasps sprang up and open and with a deep breath I lifted the lid slowly. The smell of camphor and old books rose from within and there, on top of everything was a khaki army jacket.

Bertie, Callyzion, Cornwall

June 1915

Ernest was waiting for me at Bodmin Road station.

"Hello, old chap, or don't you speak English any more?" He playfully punched my arm and took one of my bags, swinging it over his shoulder.

I rubbed my arm. "Still got your superb sense of humour, I see."

"I've got the old jalopy outside. She's a bit of a goer actually." He set off towards the station exit.

"Don't tell me Pa bought you a car?"

"Sadly not. Mum didn't want me going off to join the Army, so I had to find a job."

"A job? Do students work?" I joked.

"I graduated with a First in English actually. Better than you anyway." He sidestepped my attempt to swipe him.

"Congratulations. So where are you working?"

"With old Mr Sands."

"He must be ninety." I thought of him servicing our bicycles when we were boys; he'd seemed old even then. "Is his workshop still going?"

"Rather. His two sons-in-law have spruced the old place up a bit. Doing very well. Sell rather snazzy motors on the forecourt. They have even installed a petrol pump."

"I see, so you're a car salesman, are you?"

"Not yet. The sons-in-law do that. No, I'm in the workshop, servicing lawn mowers. I sometimes get my hands on a car engine. It keeps me out of the house, and Mother happy."

"Excellent."

"And occasionally I am allowed to borrow the odd motor." He stopped and pointed at a tiny red car with a canvas roof. "There she is."

I gave a low whistle. "Smart."

We stashed my bags on the tiny back seat and folded ourselves into the cramped interior.

"Fancy a pint before facing the parents?" he asked as he got the engine running.

"I have been dreaming of one," I answered happily.

"Right then. Off we go."

With a clash of gears and a honk of the horn, we left the station and got out onto the lane towards Newquay and Callyzion. "The Rifle Volunteer do you?" he shouted above the noise.

I answered him with a thumbs up and settled back to watch the landscape of home unfold ahead of us.

In The Rifle Volunteer, Ernest got the first pints in and brought them to the quiet table in the nook by the fire.

"Cheers." We solemnly raised our glasses and drank. Wiping his lips with the back of his hand he said, "Mother can't wait to get you back in her clutches. How are you at winding wool?"

"As bad as I ever was," I laughed. "The thing is, Ernie . . ." I began, but he talked over me.

"While you have been away, Bertie, I have been stuck here. And I don't resent you having the chance of freedom and independence, but while you've been doing that, I have been busy being the dutiful son."

I took another mouthful of my pint. I had a feeling I knew what was coming next and I wasn't wrong.

"The thing is," Ernest continued, "I am twenty-two and it's my turn to get out of Cornwall and see the world."

"I understand that," I said.

"Good. Because it's your turn to be the good son. I'm off to fight in France."

I thought of the war papers in my pocket. "Really? Ah well, that's a bit awkward, because I enlisted this morning."

His face turned from unwelcome surprise to anger. "No. I'm the one going to France. I signed up last week. I have my papers at home."

"I have my papers right here." I tapped my top pocket.

"But I enlisted a week before you."

"Makes no odds. Neither of us can back out now."

"You selfish bastard." He looked at the stained yellow ceiling and sighed. "What are we going to do?"

"We are going to have to tell them." We laughed, I realise now quite cruelly, and said, "They'll still have Amy."

At the top of our lane, Ernest turned the engine off and quietly rolled the absurd little car to the vicarage. It was now very late, and all around us the houses lay in respectable darkness, their owners sleeping soundly.

I had my old house key on my watch chain and opened the door to the hall as Ernest brought my luggage in.

"Sssh." He put his index finger to his lips and promptly kicked the front door closed behind him, making an almighty bang. We stood like naughty boys, shaking with silent, terrified laughter, waiting for our father to come to the top of the stairs and tick us off. But no sound came from upstairs.

"Fancy another beer?" Ernest whispered.

"Prefer a Scotch," I whispered back.

He put my case down by the old hat stand and beckoned me to follow him into Father's study.

I shut the door behind me, very gently, whilst Ernest fumbled in the dark for a match to light the old oil lamp that had been on Father's desk for as long as I could remember. Ernest got it going and turned the wick up. At once the cherished room, with all its memories, lay before me as if I had never left.

Nothing had changed. The worn leather chair by the fire. The rag rug Mother had made one Christmas with the scorch marks of a hundred wood spits dotting it.

The curtains were drawn shut, keeping out the night and the draught that always seeped through the old sash windows.

In this room I had received my (un)fair share of whacks on my palm from my father's ruler. It was also where I had been told, with some relief, that I had a place at Cambridge to read Classics. And, it was where

I had brought my mother to tears, announcing that I was off to Malaya to make my fortune.

I had never expected to see the familiar yards of books on the shelves again, or the inkstand with the fountain pen that Father had received from his parents when he was ordained, and the family photo. All five of us. Mother tiny, Amy very tall and angular, me in my old school uniform and Ernest stiff and unsmiling, wearing short trousers, leaning on Father who was sitting on his chair. His throne.

"My God. Nothing has changed." I settled myself by the fire. Ernest, who'd been searching the bookshelves, finally found a bottle of good malt between *Flora and Fauna of the British Isles* and *The Free Church Year Book*, 1912 edition.

"Get that down you." He chinked my glass. "Welcome home, big brother."

"Cheers." I raised my glass to him then drank.

He settled himself opposite me and we sat, easy in each other's company, neither of us feeling the need to speak.

The Scotch was instantly relaxing and I closed my eyes. I was home.

Quite suddenly my mother burst through the door. "Oh my darling, Bertie!" She was standing before me in her nightdress and shawl, shaking off the restraining hand of my father. "Ernest." She pointed at him. "How could you not have woken us?"

"I didn't know you wanted to be woken." Ernest shrugged.

My father said quietly, "The boys have a lot to talk about, I expect."

I stood up immediately, and put the glass down. "Darling, Mother." I embraced her. "You look wonderful."

She kissed my cheek and held me away from her. "Home for the summer! But you're too thin. All that rice and all those spices. Cook will make you some good English food tomorrow. How about shepherd's pie? We can still get good mutton."

"My favourite! And how is dear Cook?"

My mother pursed her lips. "Just the same. Always complaining. Amy deals with her now although how she manages her, I don't know. Constant complaints about the stairs and her bad knees and her kitchen budget."

My father stopped her flow. "My dear, Bertie doesn't want to hear about all that just now." He had gained a little weight and maybe his beard was a little longer, but my father's comforting bulk made me want to hold him, press my face against him and inhale the soothing smell of him. I resisted the impulse and held out my hand to shake his. He winked at me. "Good to see you, boy. Welcome home." He turned to Ernest with a playful smile, "And put that bottle away now."

Ernie produced the whisky from where he'd stuck it behind his back and handed it to my father's outstretched hand. He checked to see how much we had taken.

"Hmm. Still plenty left. We can share it tomorrow, boys, after dinner."

My mother said peevishly, "I can't wait until tomorrow. I want to hear all Bertie's news now."

"My dear Louisa," my father said. "The boy needs some sleep. There's plenty of time for his news now that he's home for good." He looked at me. "Isn't that right, son?"

I saw Ernest's eyes flick towards mine. I kept my gaze set on my father. "I'm sure we have a lot of news to share. Don't we, Ernest?"

CHAPTER
SIX

Herbert, Callyzion, the calm before the storm

June 1915

"Give Bertie more sausages, Amy," my mother ordered from her seat at the breakfast table. "He needs some proper food."

Amy got up without smiling, took my plate and went to the sideboard where Cook and Dora, our maid, had laid a feast of eggs, bacon, sausage, tomatoes and mushrooms. "How many do you want?" Amy asked with her back to me, her shoulders set. "I know that Cook was wanting the leftovers for tomorrow's casserole."

"Amy!" My mother's response was harsh. "Cook will have to make something else for tomorrow."

Amy returned my plate, now laden with sausages. As she sat down she said, "Oh yes, I had forgotten the fatted calf we have in the larder."

Father gave her a stern look. "Gracelessness does not become you, Amy."

I smiled at my little sister, "That's OK. I'm not here to eat you out of house or home."

She fiddled with the napkin on her lap. "I apologise, Bertie." She added, "It is good to have you back home."

"It's good to be home." I meant it. "How have you been, Amy?"

She glanced at Mother who was buttering some toast. "Just the same," she said.

"Any news on Peter?" I asked as I sliced into a sausage.

She shook her head, eyes down.

"Any idea where his battalion is?"

"No."

"But he writes to you?"

She stood up, "Do excuse me, there's something I have forgotten."

When she'd gone, I looked around the table. "I feel I have said the wrong thing."

My mother became very businesslike. "The truth is, she writes to him twice a week but hasn't had a reply for six weeks. She scours the list of casualties in the papers every day, but there is no news."

"Then he must be OK." I tried to sound cheerful. "It must be awfully hard getting letters into or out of France given the circumstances."

My father wiped his lips and beard with his napkin. "We can only pray." He stood up. "My dear, that was very nice. Thank Cook for me."

"Where are you going?" my mother asked testily.

"I am taking the boys into my study. We have a lot to discuss."

"Then I am coming too." My mother stood up.

My father held up a hand. "No, my dear."

78

"But I want to hear all you have to say. All Bertie's news."

"And you shall, but first we have men's things to discuss." He made for the door and signalled for Ernest and me to come with him.

The curtains had been pulled open and the June sun slanted onto the large desk where Father took his seat.

He motioned at us to take our seats. I took my cigarettes from my pocket and proffered one to Ernest. "Thanks, old man," he muttered, searching his pocket for a match.

"Don't let your mother catch you," Father growled, but his eyes gave us his tacit approval. He leant back in his chair, hands over his stomach, and looked at the ceiling. "I am assuming that both of you are going to France?"

Ernest flashed me a look of terror.

I put my cigarette to my lips and inhaled deeply.

Ernest had gone white.

"Yes, Father. I joined up yesterday."

His gaze remained on the ceiling. "The Army?"

"Yes sir. London Scottish."

"Why?"

"It was the nearest recruiting office to Victoria Station."

"And you joined up on a whim? Or for your country?"

I took a moment to think, stubbing out my cigarette and immediately lighting another. "I saw a German boat, masquerading as a British cruiser. It had put up a false funnel, of all things. It was only when the captain ran up the German flag that we realised what was happening. By then it was too late."

I could still hear, smell and see the thrashing, doomed men, screaming as they burned. "It came into George Town harbour and I watched as it torpedoed a Russian vessel."

"What utter bastards," Ernest fumed.

"May God have mercy on their souls," my father intoned.

I shifted in my chair and tried to make light of it. With a smile I said, "Well, you can imagine that after that I decided the Navy was not for me."

Ernest sniggered but Father did not. I continued, "And I'm not one for heights so the Air Force would be no good." I finished, limply, "So, it had to be the Army."

My father asked simply, "When do you go?"

"Six days. Must turn up, you know, like the proverbial, at Abbotts Langley barracks for training."

"I see." He stroked his beard thoughtfully. "And you, Ernest?"

"I have my teaching position at Oundle, as you know," he said shiftily.

"I do know. But I also know that they are not expecting you until the war is over. That was what you wrote to tell them, wasn't it?"

Ernest's mouth fell open.

"I am not a fool, Ernest," my father continued. "I would have done the same as a young man. Which regiment?"

80

"Duke of Cornwall Light Infantry," Ernest said quietly.

My father continued with the rhythmic stroking of his beard. He watched us. We waited.

Eventually he sat up and placed his hands on his desk. "You are not to tell your mother," he said. "I want her to have the next few days without worry. When you both have to leave, and I suggest you leave at the same time, I will hand her the letters of explanation you will each have written to her. Do you understand?"

"Yes sir," we replied in unison.

"Now, not a word of this to anyone outside this room. For the next few days I expect you to be on your best behaviour and to demonstrate the affection you have for Amy and your mother. If anything should happen," he cleared his throat, "to either of you, in France, they shall have the best of recollections." He reached for his fountain pen and filled it slowly from his ink pot. "Now, my sons, I must ask you to leave to allow me to get on with my business."

When we had closed the door of the study, and were standing in the hall, we heard our father praying for our safety. I know it nearly broke my heart.

Six days later, Ernest and I had done as our father had prescribed.

We had told our mother nothing, and had been the perfect sons. I mowed the lawn and mended the old swing under the apple tree. When all was done, I asked Dora to serve afternoon tea beneath the tree. My mother was persuaded to sit on the swing and I pushed her gently. She was so happy. Her sons at home, her daughter setting the tea table, her husband solid and kind. She sat on the swing giggling like a girl.

Then she said, "Oh, my dearest Bertie. It is so good to have you home. I am blessed to have such loving children." The guilt I felt then nearly floored me.

I felt, as I left my envelope next to Ernest's on the hall table, a terrible coward. My father had prayed with us the night before and given us his and God's blessing.

How on earth was he going to cope with my mother when she discovered how he, and we, had betrayed her? I could have stopped it there and then. Written to the War Office explaining that my parents needed me at home for the duration. But instead, I collected my coat and bag, and with Ernest in front of me, closed the front door and crept away.

We walked in silence to the crossroads where the bus to Bodmin stopped. While we waited there, I made some innocuous remark about the early mist rolling in. "It should burn off by mid-morning."

Ernest looked skywards and sniffed like an old mariner. "Mmmh."

The bus arrived and took us down winding lanes and up steep hills, collecting a straggle of early passengers. From our high seats we could get the odd glimpse of the sea through breaks in the hedge and the mist, before the vapour cloaked them again like a magic trick.

At last we dropped down into the heart of Bodmin town and, as we got off, the driver called out, "Good luck in France."

"Thank you," Ernest and I replied together.

I slammed the door and the driver put the clutch in, ground the bus's gears into first and drove away.

"Nice of him." I smiled at Ernest.

"Very." He picked up his bag. "Well, this is where we say goodbye."

"Just *au revoir*," I said, reaching my arms out to him.

Our hug was awkward, what with our heavy bags banging against each other, but neither of us dismissed the affection and importance of it.

My words were spoken into his neck. "Good luck, Ernie."

"You too, Bertie."

The fog from the moor was gathering around us.

"Right." We let go of each other. "I'd better get to the station." I turned my head away. "Look after yourself."

"You too." Ernie was finding his boots suddenly fascinating. "Let's hope the bally thing isn't over before we get there. Toodle-pip."

"Bye."

I watched him as he went; in just a few paces he had all but vanished in the fog. I could hear him whistling as he headed towards his barracks.

I stayed until I could hear him no longer, then set off on the three-mile walk to Bodmin Road station.

Back in London, the sun was shining. I reported for duty at Buckingham Gate and was given a warrant to attend the Abbotts Langley Camp two days hence. Two days! I could have stayed longer at home, after all. I quickly swept aside the guilt I felt for leaving my mother early and decided that if these were to be my last two days in London, I'd have a damn good time.

I had three guineas in my pocket, pressed on me by my father, with an order to go to the Army and Navy Stores on Victoria Street and kit myself out with extra socks, warm underwear, good boots, and a decent razor. The extravagance and pleasure of spending money buoyed me up no end. I even had some money left, so I went to a pub, ordered myself a pint of London Pride, and thought about how I might spend the evening.

The barmaid was very pretty and overtly flirty. She made it clear that, for payment, she would, as she put it, give me a relaxing hour when her shift finished. I let her down gently and politely and, when I paid my bill, left her a small tip for her kindness. She gave me a sweet smile and told me I would always know where I could find her.

I stepped outside into the warmth of the London evening. The city was full of promise and romance. Lighting a cigarette, I strolled south towards St James's Park.

Buckingham Palace stood ahead of me. The Royal Standard was fluttering limply from its flagpole. I caught a glimpse of chandeliers, twinkling from the upstairs apartments. King George the Fifth was in residence. The same king I had sworn to serve only days ago.

The enormity of it all hit me like a club. I am not a religious man, much to my father's disappointment, but at that moment I closed my eyes and prayed that I would be brave enough.

"All right, sir?" A policeman had approached.

"Yes, yes," I stuttered, "Fine." Had he seen my appalling cowardice?

He tipped his helmet to me. "Have a good evening, sir."

"Thank you." I headed down The Mall. The scent of mown grass coming from Green Park on my left and St James's Park on my right was sweet and reminded me of Cornwall.

I passed St James's Palace and turned left, heading towards Piccadilly.

A memory struck me. Somewhere on Piccadilly there had been a bridge club I'd visit with friends when up from Cambridge. Could it still be there?

It took me about a quarter of an hour but I found it: 26B, The Piccadilly Bridge Club.

The familiar door was opened by a chap who was new; after a brief introduction, he pointed the way up the well-remembered, ornate but peeling staircase.

The quiet voices of players hummed behind the grand double doors of the club room, cheering me up. I was looking forward to a game and hopefully finding chaps who remembered me. I turned the door handle and poked my head around to make sure I was in the right place. It was the same room but it wasn't quite the same atmosphere. This had always been a gentlemen's club, but now I saw there were women sitting at the tables. I did what any chap would do in the circumstance, I walked in and went to the bar.

"Scotch, please."

"Righto, sir."

I leant my back to the bar and surveyed the room.

A man on the opposite wall took a cigar from his mouth and waved at me. "Bolitho!" He navigated the tables briskly and arrived in front of me, wreathed in smiles. "Glad to see you. Glad to see you."

"Good God," I said, shaking his hand. "Jimmy. Long time no see."

"How long has it been?" He beamed.

"Well, I've been in Malaya since early 1912."

"How hot is it?"

I laughed. "Is that all you can ask me after all these years?" It was good to see him. "What are you up to?"

"Oh, the usual. After Cambridge, I did Europe, the tour you know, bloody good timing. I hear the fighting is destroying the place."

"Yes. Terrible. I've been reading about it. Can I get you a drink?"

"Scotch please."

I caught the eye of the barman.

"Anyway," Jimmy continued, "I came back because Father wanted me in the family business, you know the thing."

I did know the thing. For generations his family had made their money from the bank bearing their name.

I paid the barman and handed Jimmy his whisky. "And are you enjoying it? The bank?"

He grinned, "Oh, let's not talk about money, I want you to meet someone." He took my elbow. "I have found the woman of my dreams. And she's a damn fine bridge player."

He guided me to the edge of the room where two women were sitting on their own with a pack of cards lying in the middle of the small square table.

"Marianne, may I present one of my best friends from Cambridge, Mr Herbert Bolitho."

Marianne looked perfect for Jimmy. Clearly of good stock. Wearing a short pearl necklace and a good diamond on the fourth finger of her left hand. "Hello," I said. "I'm very pleased to meet you. Jimmy is a lucky man."

Jimmy and Marianne looked at each other and giggled. "He certainly is," she said.

"And this young lady is . . ." Jimmy faltered, clearly not remembering the name of the other young woman.

She spoke for him. "Clara Carter." Her voice was low and even. Her hand felt cool as I shook it.

My first impression was of a young woman in her early twenties, dressed soberly and unadorned. No jewellery or rouge. Her dark hair in a neat bun at her neck. The edges of her eyes turned slightly down, almost sad, but they also shone with an interest and intelligence rarely seen in the eyes of the wealthy, bored women I had met in Malaya. She smiled. Her teeth were even. "Would you care to join us?" she asked. "We can be partners."

"I'd love to," I said, pulling out the chair opposite her.

Jimmy sat down and nudged Marianne. "He's a damned good player. We'd better keep a keen eye."

"Jimmy! Language."

"Sorry m'dear."

Jimmy ordered some more drinks, and we began to play. And, as we played, the more I admired Clara. Not in a physical way but in the way she comported herself. The more we played, the more in tune we became. I liked the way she played, and the way I understood her eyes as they signalled to me what card she might play next and enquiring if I had something to our advantage. If I had concentrated more on the game and less on her, we might have won, but Jimmy and Marianne were ferociously competitive and bickered constantly.

It was almost a relief to let them win.

The barman signalled last orders and the room began to thin out.

"Goodness." Marianne checked her watch. "Daddy will be so cross with me. I told him I'd be in by eleven and it's now almost eleven thirty." She turned to Clara. "He waits up for me. I expect your parents are the same?"

"Unfortunately, my parents are no longer alive," Clara said, without looking for sympathy. "I am my own keeper."

"God, I'm envious," snorted Marianne. "Can't wait to get married. Jimmy and I will be free to do as we please."

"Steady on old girl." Jimmy put her coat, mink by the look, around her shoulders. "I shall have to take a cold bath when I get home."

Out on the pavement, the air had cooled considerably. Jimmy and Marianne said their goodbyes and left Clara and me standing awkwardly together.

"You play bridge very well," I said.

She smiled. "I am a beginner."

"Really? Well you seem to have picked it up very well"

"Thank you."

"May I walk you home?" I asked.

"It's too far," she said, doing up her thin coat.

"Where?"

She hesitated. "The other end of the Strand."

"Well I can't let you go all that way on your own."

"I'll be fine."

"It's not out of my way, I have nowhere to stay tonight yet." I said it without thinking.

"I see." She gave me a look of pure disappointment. "What do you take me for?" She turned on her heels and walked quickly away, tossing over her shoulder, "Goodnight, Mr Bolitho."

"Miss Carter," I called, picking up my bag and running after her. "Miss Carter. You misunderstand me."

"Oh, I don't think I do. I'll call a policeman if you don't leave me alone."

"I am the son of a vicar," I said plaintively. "I am about to go to France."

"Oh yes?" Her look was withering. "That's what they all say. I wasn't born yesterday."

"Honestly. It's true. I arrived in London today and I have forty-eight hours before I go to my training camp in Abbotts Langley."

She was striding away from me now. "Leave me alone."

"That came out all wrong." I went after her in order to explain. "I came up from Cornwall tonight not expecting to be given two days before I have to leave London. I need to book a bed for the night yet, which is why I have no hotel to go to . . ."

"Well, you're not having mine."

I stopped walking and called after her, "I am so sorry. Please, I meant nothing. I won't bother you any more. It's been a delightful evening."

She stopped. "Are you telling the truth?"

"Yes."

"You really are a vicar's son, who hasn't got a bed, and is going to France?"

"Yes. Honestly."

"Well." She paused, giving me the once-over. "You can walk me to my door and that's it. As it happens there are a couple of hotels near me." She smiled. "I can't have a brave soldier sleeping on a park bench, can I?"

"Thank you."

We began walking and I noticed she was shivering.

"May I offer you my coat?"

"No, thank you," she answered, and then looked at me. "Unless you don't feel the cold?"

"I grew up in Cornwall where the westerlies can freeze your ears off." She laughed at that and I took off my coat and helped her into it. "Better?" I asked.

"Much. Thank you."

CHAPTER
SEVEN

Clara, London

June 1915

By the time we had got to my door, he had told me his life story. His upbringing in Cornwall, his father's church, the summers he and his siblings had spent on their beach, rock pooling, swimming and sailing. He built a picture so beautiful, I felt that I had been with him; eating pasties made by Cook, singing in his father's church choir, fighting with his brother Ernest and then the exotic descriptions of Penang, the plantation, the monsoons, the heat of the day.

"I've never left England," I said. "Coming to London was the furthest I've ever been from Kent."

"You must miss it," he said.

I could have told him the truth there and then, but I didn't. I was not that poor orphan any more. I was a working woman. Independent and unafraid. I told him the story I had been telling my work friends, but this time much embroidered.

"My parents died in an accident on the family farm," I said. "I grew up amongst apple trees and hop fields. I miss them every day. And our horses. My father and I would ride out most mornings. We'd go for miles. Checking fences. Talking to the workers." My imagination was spinning my lies into truth. "From my bedroom window to the horizon, all I could see was our land. We had several hundred acres, you see."

"It sounds like a fairy tale." He smiled. "How often do you get back?"

"Oh, I don't. It was all sold. To my uncle. I have nothing of it left, but my uncle did make sure I had a good education, and that is the greatest gift of all. Isn't it? I have nothing else."

"Your uncle sounds rather mean to me."

I laughed. "To be honest I turned it all down. I wanted my parents to be proud of me. I have always been very independent." That much was true at least. "I am a suffragette. Does that shock you?"

"I don't think so, no."

"Good. You see, I believe, as my mother did, that women are the greatest partner a man can have. Not just in running a home and bringing up a family, but in standing together, sharing our different skills."

I remembered my next words, as the ones I had heard a suffragette say. She had been outside our office, talking to the crowd. "A man without a woman is only half the jigsaw."

I could see I had provoked his thoughts with my exposition.

"And that is what you honestly believe?" he finally said.

"Of course," I said firmly. "Don't you?"

"I am ashamed to say I have never thought about it."

"Well, I suggest you do."

We arrived at my door. "This is me."

He looked up at the building. "Which is your window?"

I ignored the question and held out my hand. "Goodnight, Mr Bolitho, and thank you for the walk and the pleasant conversation."

He took my hand and kissed it. "The pleasure was mine."

I remembered his coat and took it off.

"Here. You'll need this. Goodnight."

At lunchtime the next day, I left the office to walk to a small Italian café on the corner of Fleet Street and Bouverie Street. I went maybe once a month as a treat for myself. It was a beautiful early summer day. The shop windows were filled with colourful displays offering holiday outfits, toys and sandals. All the girls in my office had been chatting for weeks about where they would spend their week-long summer holiday. Brighton, Eastbourne, Norfolk.

I thought it all rather pointless. I had never had a proper summer to get excited about. The best bit for me was going to church with my grandfather and staring at the ladies' hats. If I managed to look innocent enough, some of the ladies and gentlemen would pass me a farthing. Sometimes a penny. I didn't feel sorry for myself. Far from it. I could do a lot with a penny, providing my dad didn't find it and take it to the pub.

So, there I was walking to the café when I heard my name called. I knew immediately it was Herbert, even before I turned around to look at him.

"Hello," he said, running to catch me.

"Are you following me?" I asked.

"Gosh no," he said, patting his travelling bag. "Just left the hotel."

"I thought you said you had two days in London."

"Yes." He grinned. "Well remembered. The hotel is full tonight so I have to find another."

I tilted my head to one side. "Yes. You'd better had."

He had the grace to look embarrassed. "I really will find one."

"Good." I began walking again.

"Where are you going?" He fell into step with me.

"Lunch."

"I could join you?"

I let him wait before I said, "Yes. You could."

Café Maria's windows were full of hams, cheeses and salamis. Its very foreignness excited me. Maria herself was exotically beautiful. Glossy black hair wound into an untidy bun, slender legs in black heeled shoes, and wearing a dress that swung as she moved her hips.

"Signorina Carter," she cried across the noise of customers, her eyes taking in Herbert. "You bring a gentleman friend?" She put her hands on her hips, looking him up and down. "Are you good enough for Signorina Carter? You a good boy? I look after her from men like you."

I enjoyed Herbert's discomfort. "Goodness. No. Nothing like that. Miss Carter and I are acquaintances. We only met last night."

Maria whirled a manicured finger at him. "Last night, eh? That is what I worry for."

I stopped her teasing. "Maria. It's all right. I don't think you need worry."

"OK." She smiled at me and then gave Herbert a knowing look. "Remember, Maria see everything. *Sì?* OK, so where you want to sit? By the window? A nice table for two? Follow me. We have good minestrone today."

I ordered the soup and he the Italian ham with bread.

Maria swept up the menus and invisible crumbs from the table. "Good choices. And what will you have to drink?"

"Coffee, please." I had never drunk coffee until I had come to Maria's. Now I loved it. It made me feel sophisticated.

"*Sì.*" Maria raised her eyebrows towards Herbert. "Signor?"

"Do you have beer?"

"You think I am a peasant? Of course I have beer." She chucked him under the chin. "I get you special glass."

She walked away, her hips swinging, welcoming new customers or shouting *'Ciao'* to departing ones.

I looked at Herbert. "I don't believe in coincidences."

"Sorry?" he asked.

"You finding me this morning. Were you watching for me?"

"Oh." He smiled, and rubbed the end of his nose, a sign — I discovered — that meant he felt uncomfortable. "I checked out of my hotel after breakfast and found myself walking towards your building — quite by chance, you understand."

"Uh-ha." I nodded, not believing a word of it. "Go on."

"And I . . . er, spotted you coming out of your front door and noticed that you were heading for the *Evening News* building."

"Uh-ha," I repeated, so that he was obliged to continue.

"And so, I thought I'd wait for you to come out for lunch. I mean, you had to be hungry at some point in the day."

"You waited four hours?" I was, I admit, flattered.

"Well, I walked up and down a bit, you know, enjoying the sun, but yes, I waited four hours to see you again."

"You're mad."

"Possibly."

"This is the sort of thing you often do, is it?"

Maria brought the food, all plates balanced on her slender forearms. "Here you are. Drinks coming. *Buon appetito*."

In the brief disturbance, Herbert had had some thinking time. He looked at me with a depth of feeling I had never been subject to before. It made me nervous.

"Well?" I asked sharply. "Do you follow women often? And join them for lunch?"

"No. But I did wake up this morning feeling an idiot because last night I told you so much about myself and learnt very little about you. And I'd like to know more."

"What do you want to know?"

"What you do at the newspaper."

And I told him. No lies this time. I (really) was a trainee typist and almost at the end of my probationary period. I had been led to believe that I had good speeds in typing and shorthand and that, there being so many vacancies coming up, what with the war taking all our young men from the office, I was looking at a good steady job in the newsroom. He listened until my lunch hour was nearly over and, as I waved to Maria for the bill, Herbert put his hand on mine and stopped me. "Let me."

"Ah, he is a gentleman, this one," smiled Maria. "Don't let the good ones go, eh?"

Outside, I apologised for Maria's words and thanked him very much for his generosity in paying for my lunch.

"I enjoyed it," he answered. We walked on, my head just reaching his shoulder, towards the *News* building.

As we stood at the entrance, he said, "Thank you for your company, both last night and today. If I have been a nuisance, I apologise."

I began to say something but he stopped me. "Clara, would you allow me to write to you, as a friend? When I am in France?"

I hadn't expected that. "I'm sorry?"

"As a sort of pen friend?"

"Do you have lots of pen friends?" I asked; not that it was any of my business if he had a sweetheart — or sweethearts — to write to, or they to him.

"No. None." He took my hand and held it. "Apart from my family, of course." He smiled at me but did not let go of my hand.

"What would you like me to write about?" I asked.

"Day-to-day life. Ordinary things. I want to hear about your summer and London, and your work and what you had for breakfast and . . . normal life."

"Oh."

He let go of my hand. "You don't have to. Perhaps you have a special someone who wouldn't like you writing to me?"

"I haven't," I said, a little too quickly.

He smiled. "My mother's letters are sweet, but full of the price of yarn and her bronchitis. I'd like something rather more fun."

"Well, yes. I should love to. To be honest, I have no one to write to. At all! I see my friends every day in the office. No need," I said a little too honestly. "But I shall need your address."

He thought for a moment, "Let's exchange addresses tonight."

"Tonight?"

"Over dinner."

"Only if we go Dutch," I said seriously. He had saved me a lot of my wage by paying for my lunch, so I could afford to pay for my own dinner.

He laughed. "Very well."

We arranged to meet half an hour after I had finished work so that I could tidy myself up.

"Goodbye. See you later." He shook my hand.

"Goodbye . . . Herbert." I smiled as I watched him go, his bag bumping his thighs, and as he disappeared amongst the shoppers and office workers, I realised how much I was looking forward to seeing him again later.

Caroline

Present day

The jacket had been folded and packed beautifully, with tissue paper in between each fold and filling out each sleeve. I stood up and held it against me. The wearer must have been very tall because the hem came almost to my knees and the sleeves were at least ten centimetres too long. Was this my grandfather's? It must be, surely. The initials stitched into the collar fitted and so did the connection with Penang. But who would have sent it to me? And why now?

I laid the jacket gently on the sofa, then got back on my knees in front of the trunk. It was deep and full and willing me to search further. So, naturally, I did. Wouldn't you?

CHAPTER
EIGHT

Bertie, Abbotts Langley

July 1915

It had not been my intention to ask her to write to me. Lord knows where the words came from and Lord knows what I was feeling for her at the time. She was completely unlike any woman I had been attracted to before. She wasn't flirtatious and yet I liked her company. She wasn't a chocolate-box beauty but she had an attractiveness that spoke of humour, intelligence and integrity. She was far too slender for my liking, no bosom to speak of, and yet I found myself thinking of how I would like to undress her and touch her and bury myself in her nakedness. It shamed me that I could think of such carnal things whilst barely knowing her.

Anyway, the endless training we endured at Abbotts Langley, which was rather like a scout camp, only less luxurious, kept my mind away from Clara.

It was in the quiet moments that I couldn't get the damn woman out of my head.

I had been too forward with her already, so I decided to wait and see if she would write to me first. I waited four days before I cracked and wrote to her.

Abbotts Langley Camp
July 1915

Dear Miss Carter,

It's your new friend here, Herbert. All my friends call me Bertie so I do hope you feel you can do the same. My brother always called me Sherbert until I set about him in his bedroom. My parents were not impressed, as you can imagine.

Well, how is London? Abbotts Langley is very nice. Lots of countryside for us to practise our route marches on. The weather remains good and my companions are pleasant. We are all in the same boat and learning to come together as a regiment. However, after all the physical training and runs at dawn, etc., the men and I are so hungry we will eat anything. The cook house does good, basic food. There's plenty of it too, so no man goes hungry.

Please don't feel under any pressure to write back immediately.

Kind regards,
Bertie Bolitho

Our letters must have crossed, for the very next morning I had two letters, one from my mother, complaining that Cook insisted on making lumpy porridge and that my sister Amy could not find the right fabric to make a new summer dress, and another from Clara.

Room 6, Victoria Mansions

July 1915

Dear Herbert,

I am sorry it has taken me so long to write to you. The office has been at full throttle gathering the accounts of our returning soldiers from Ypres. It all sounds rather grim. One of our British boys, he came back wounded on the train, told a reporter that he would say nothing other than he had "been at Ypres". I think he would rather not let us know how hard it was. Brave man. However, it seems now the atrocious French weather has halted fighting. May that continue. I hope you don't have to go there, and if you do you really must take warm clothes.

London is cool for summer but my little room in the boarding house is not too bad. Did I tell you about my friend Elsie who lives across the landing from me? She is on the same trainee typist course as me and we didn't pal up until quite late. She's a dear. Tonight, we are sharing a feast of the last two ounces of cheese that I have, with a fresh loaf of bread that Elsie made this morning. She has some mustard to mix with the cheese and I have some eggs and apples so it should do us. The shops are getting very low on food. People have selfishly been stocking up their larders since war was declared and there's little for the rest of us. I shall be hunting out something for the weekend. I'm hoping for sausages. Elsie and I thought a picnic in Hyde Park, to celebrate her birthday, would be fun. I just hope the sun will come out. I have made Elsie a little pin cushion from some fabric remnants I was lucky to find in a haberdasher's on Holborn. It's rather jolly. Green velvet on the outside and red linen on the inside.

I expect you are getting very fit with all the exercise. Is the marching in time very hard?

I hope you have enjoyed reading my nonsense.

In friendship,

Clara Carter

I read it twice, then carefully folded it into my pocket before heading out to the parade ground and that morning's drill practice.

I wrote to her that night.

Abbotts Langley Camp

Mid-July 1915

Dear Clara,

Your nonsense was gratefully received and enjoyed. How was the feast? And Elsie's birthday picnic? Did you find sausages? We have plenty of eggs and sausages here. Shall I post them to you? They may arrive as a sausage omelette but I am sure a resourceful girl like you will do something splendid with it.

Life here is OK. The men I am with are all good chaps. We are all very keen to get going now. Thank God for the Canadians' victory at Ypres. We have been training with gas masks in case there are any more gas attacks so you needn't worry about that!

I will be in touch as soon as I know when we are off.

Your friend,
Bertie

PS (Six hours later) I have just heard that we could be shipping out in the autumn. I might get some leave and would like to catch up with you before I go. If you would like to?

Clara

Of course I wanted to see him before he went to France, but "autumn" was a very loose term. It could be the beginning of September or the end of October. August was already around the corner, and so within four weeks he could be in France, facing every danger I read about each day. I felt sick to think about it. In the office I read every war report that came in on the wire and I saw how censored each one was too.

Our editor was close to the prime minister, as were all editors of the papers at that time. The edict was that nothing should be printed that would alarm or upset the general public. The enemy were suffering, we were winning and morale was high.

I knew that wasn't true. I had read of the blood and mud, the brutal murdering of friend and foe alike. The lack of sleep, warmth and humanity.

How could I tell Bertie that I knew these things? I was as bad as any newspaper editor and wrote him letters full of lies by omission.

Room 6, Victoria Mansions
August 1915

Dear Bertie,

The summer heat has been pretty awful in the office. We have kept the windows open these last few days but several of the girls have felt terribly faint. I almost wish we had the cold of July back. We all have our lunch under the trees on Embankment. Watching the river flow by is almost like being on holiday. I have saved a little money to buy a cotton dress from an inexpensive shop around the corner. It is blue with little white flowers on it. It was a bit big in the waist so I altered it slightly. When the other girls saw my needlework they immediately wanted me to do their alterations. It gives me something to do in the evenings — and earn a little pin money too. I think you'd laugh at me. I sit on the floor, cross-legged like an old cobbler, in as few clothes as possible to stay cool. Goodness knows how you manage to march in your hot uniform! Elsie bought a chicken yesterday from the butcher's! A whole chicken! Such luxury. While I sew tonight she is going to roast it for our supper and then make soup and possibly a pie with the leftovers.

I didn't imagine you'd be sent to France so soon. I was hoping — well, we were all hoping here — that the war would be ending by now. I would like very much to meet up with you if you can. Even if it's only on the platform so that I can wave my hanky at you as the train pulls out.

I will be very proud of my friend the soldier, but I also hope very much that the war will be over quickly and that you won't have to stay away too long.

I bought myself a book the other day. Second-hand in one of the Charing Cross Road second-hand bookshops. It's a volume of poetry. I shall read it tonight but I think it'll be awfully good at lunchtime by the river too. One's brain needs to have beauty poured into it while all these horrid things are happening in the world. I'll let you know how I get on.

Your friend,
Clara

Abbotts Langley
Late August

My dear Clara,

A whole chicken! How wonderful. However did Elsie bag that? Or perhaps I'd better not ask!

Forgive my delay in replying. Your letter was held up in the post but anyway I couldn't have replied sooner as I have been laid low with a bout of food poisoning. Something to do with our egg supplier, the medical officer suspects. Several of us went down with it, so the last few days have been pretty quiet. The MO gave us some ghastly mix of a thing called kaolin and morphine. It completely knocked me out for a number of days but now we are back in training. Yesterday we did a ten-mile march in full kit. The chaps were singing songs which certainly lifted our spirits. Some of the tunes you may know, but I won't sing you any of them as the lyrics are a bit roisterous. All good fun though.

Word has it that we will be off to France at the end of this month, with no leave before then. Rumours, rumours, but we have to be at the ready at a moment's notice. The War Office is keen to get as many of us out there as possible to beat the Hun quickly. I would have liked to have you wave me off! Maybe we can still manage it.

Roll on the autumn.

Your,

Bertie

PS I like the sound of your dress and can picture you very well sewing in the evenings.

PPS Can you send a couple of chicken recipes for the cook house? Ha-ha.

PPS One of my favourite poems is by Gerard Manley Hopkins. My father always recites it. "Glory be to God for dappled things — For skies of couple-colour as a brinded cow; For rose-moles all in stipple upon trout that swim . . .' I can't for the life of me remember more!

Clara

I wept as I read that. Bertie wrote so amusingly and with great sweetness. Was he doing the same as I was doing to him? Omitting his fear? But at least he hadn't shipped to France, yet.

Room 6, Victoria Mansions
September 1915

Dear Bertie,

I have just come back from the music hall in Southwark. I have never been before but Elsie is a great fan. We saw Harry Lauder and Marie Lloyd. Her songs were very funny and everyone was laughing. Then at the end we all sang, "It's a Long Way to Tipperary". Do you know it? It was very uplifting. Marie Lloyd is very pretty and I think a good actress. Elsie was too busy looking at the chaps in khaki around us. One wanted to walk her home, so I chaperoned them. He wasn't too pleased, but I think nor was Elsie.

I am thinking about getting my hairstyle changed to be more like Miss Lloyd's. Do you have an opinion?

France at the end of the month? I have trust in all the training you have done. Lord Kitchener wouldn't allow you to go if you were not ready. But I still pray every night that the war will end tomorrow. And tonight I will pray that I will have the chance to wave you off.

Fish and chips for supper!

Thinking of you,

Clara

Abbotts Langley
September 1915

Dear Clara,

I have never been to a music hall, but I have heard a lot about them from the chaps. I prefer to go to a lunchtime recital, something by Bach. Do you like classical music? Maybe we could go one day after all this is over.

I had a letter from Nizam, my foreman in Penang, a couple of days ago. It is rather out of date as it came on the boat, but it did leave me with a longing for some warmth. How I miss walking the rows of my rubber trees. Just as a dairy herdsman knows his cows by name, I know my trees by number. It seems the war is leaving Penang alone. I can only thank God for that. I may only have been there a couple of years, but I know I will go back, one day. Maybe you will come out to see me? As long as you can stand the heat. But I would love to show you everything. You could stay as long as you like.

Things here are the same. Training day in day out. Very little spare time. Semaphore, knot tying, physical drill, company drill, but at least we are now fully equipped. I have enclosed a photo of some of the chaps and me. Do you like our kilts? I am sorry it's a bit bent. I had it in my coat pocket and some oaf sat on it. Please keep it. It should make a lasting memento of this adventure.

Goodnight,
Bertie

PS As far as I remember your hair is perfect as it is.

Clara

I already knew I wanted to go to Penang to see him. I could think of plenty of women who would put up with the heat just to be with him. Jealousy bit at my heart. Even if she were Princess Mary herself!

I wrote a short note, quickly scrawled, commenting on his photograph.

110

My dear Clara,

I am glad you like the picture. I thought my knees were not knobbly! Perhaps you could send me a picture of you if you have one? I ask because we are now under orders for overseas service and waiting to proceed. Popping up to town will be out of the question so I shan't see you until I get back. It's all a bit top secret. Even we don't know exact timings of embarkation. But as soon as I get there and am able to write, I shall. Don't worry. I'll be fine.

Your letters mean so much to me. Please don't stop writing.

Your

Bertie x

CHAPTER
NINE

Clara, London

October 1915

Bertie is in France.

He left Southampton on 9 October.

What had I been doing when he stepped aboard that ship? Had I been darning my stockings or laughing at Elsie's nonsense? How had the sea crossing been? Had he thought of me? I had felt nothing out of the ordinary that day, yet I had been so sure I would have known, deep down, the moment he was torn from the safety of home.

I only got the news two weeks later.

Western Front, France
October 1915

Dearest Clara,

Well, here I am. I am not allowed to tell you exactly where, but I can tell you it is raining. I expect like the rest of us you'll be glad when the weather improves, for there is no doubt about it, it has been rough lately.

Two days ago the king crossed the Channel. Can you imagine the ballyhoo that created? We were up before dawn and on parade by 06.30, then marched eight and a half miles to our position where we would meet him. When he arrived, he rode his handsome black horse along the line and was heartily cheered by us all. We later heard the same horse had spooked and reared, throwing His Majesty to the ground. No bones broken, but the top brass had him evacuated back home immediately. Lucky him.

Since then we have been in forward reserve, occupying old British trenches. Hardly The Ritz, but it is surprising how resilient we all are. I must say from where I am sitting and writing this to you (a reasonably comfy dugout), I can see the most lovely line of trees dressed in their autumn finery. I am so very sorry that I didn't get to see you before we came out here, but do keep writing your silly letters. I do enjoy them.

My return address is on the envelope. Please send me a photograph, it would cheer me up no end.

With great fondness,

Bertie x

I read that letter twice through. Picturing the line of trees and the French sun falling on Bertie's dear face. Back in its envelope, I held it to my bosom and surprised myself by praying.

113

Oh God, in whom I don't believe, look after my Bertie. Amen.

I had never had my photo taken before, and didn't know how to go about it, but once I had confided in Elsie, I discovered that she was friendly with one of our staff photographers and that he would take one of me.

I did feel a fool as he had me perched on a bench by the river feeding the reluctant ducks. He told me that he usually photographed young society brides. I told him that that was very far from who I was and he said that yes, he could tell that on account of the clothes I was wearing. That did nothing for my confidence. But Elsie was there to help and she made sure I had extra rouge and lipstick.

When I saw the photograph, I must admit I was rather pleased and you couldn't tell that my skirt was too big for me on account of the rationing or that I had no stockings to wear.

I posted it to Bertie with a note explaining how awful the ducks had been.

November 1915

Dear Bertie,

Here is a picture as promised. I am not sure it will cheer you up. I am not smiling, too nervous. The ducks were most unprofessional, nipping at my fingers or shoes and then relieving themselves wherever they pleased. Elsie thought we should kidnap at least two and have them for Sunday dinner!

Good news, I have passed my typing and shorthand tests and have been promoted. I am now working for the subeditors, and I'm in charge of three other young typists. I get to read all the news as it comes in from France and I must say I try to work out exactly where you are. I wonder if you have any dry clothes, enough food to eat, somewhere warm to sleep?

The autumn weather here is very wet and cold. It seems such a long time since I wore my blue summer dress.

This'll make you laugh: last night I went to bed wearing *two cardigans* as well as socks. I couldn't get to sleep because I was so cold and then I thought of you shivering in a trench. I shall knit you some socks and a muffler. Elsie is going to teach me.

I am going to make up a little parcel for you with some chocolate and Bovril. Please tell me what else you would like me to send.

Keep safe and know that I am here thinking of you always,

Clara x

I waited almost three weeks before his next letter.

Western Front, France
December 1915

Dearest Clara,

After twenty-four days in the trenches, we have returned for a week's rest away from the front line.

Your parcel was waiting for me and was received with joy. The picture of you is awfully good. Your hair has grown, I think, and, even though you say you don't smile, I can imagine your smile is brighter than Piccadilly Circus at midnight! I keep you in the breast pocket of my tunic, next to my lighter, so that whenever I have a cigarette, I can see you.

The chocolate I shared with my unit and the coffee I eke out. Just one mug a day. I have your socks on now and you will never know how much I appreciate them. The muffler too is very dashing; the boys say the green matches my eyes — or at least the bags under them, sleep being on ration as well as sugar!

The weather has been a little unkind too. Rain, sleet, cold night fogs that make everything sodden, even under cover. The mud in the trenches is now deep and thick. This morning I accidentally stepped into a very unpleasant patch and almost lost my boots to the suction. Everything is wet and it's impossible to get dry or keep dry. The other night a snap frost froze all the water to ice, turning our sandbags into solid bricks which then tumbled down into the trench. Woke up one of the new young lads, Smiffy, who had gone to sleep sheltering under them. Poor chap has a bruise the size of a hen's egg on his head. How glad we are to be back in reserve ground now. I'm not ashamed to say we are completely exhausted.

Congratulations on your promotion. I am so very proud of you. When I get back I shall take you to The Ritz to celebrate! Let that thought keep you warm.

Fondly,
Bertie xx

Bertie, France

December 1915

The rain hadn't stopped in twenty days. Rain, mud, bullets and death. Clara's letters were so warm and amusing and I thanked God for every moment that she didn't know the truth of this sickening war. I longed to tell her how much I loved her. How much I wanted to be at home and in her arms. But how could I?

Her life must not be dirtied by the truth. I pictured her with Elsie, walking arm in arm, the pair of them chatting and laughing, talking about the theatre and knitting wool and what to have for tea.

The socks and scarf she'd made for me were already muddied and sodden.

Mud. It was everywhere. In my eyes, my nose, my mouth, my ears.

Men were going mad. Screaming in their short fits of sleep. The dying calling for their mothers as they took their final breath.

If hell exists, surely it is here.

Our progress in this war was slow and torturous. Twenty days spent fighting in the rain and the filth and it had got neither us nor the enemy a single step further.

We fight, we carry the dead, we fight, we carry the dead.

I'm so tired I sleep standing some days, and the cold is set in my bones. It snowed overnight and is snowing now. Thick flakes I would have loved as a child, but which now freeze the hair in my nostrils.

The heat of Penang feels so far away. I sometimes hear the tap, tap of the silver tool, cutting into the bark, letting the latex flow. Tap. Tap. Tap. I dream of the heat of the sun on my back, the cool beer . . . and then realise the tap, tap is the sound of bullets. The men lie where they die. We can't keep on top of the dead. But we do all we can for our men. The guns have been quiet for an hour now. The enemy need to sleep too. I will get a mug of tea, write to Clara and try to sleep.

Clara, London

Through the long winter of 1915-16 we wrote to each other many times. I tried to keep upbeat and not let him know how sick I felt as each casualty list came into the newsroom. Christmas came and went. There was no reason to celebrate as far as I was concerned. During that period I heard nothing from Bertie. I was getting very anxious, but I kept my letters up, just in case, until finally, this arrived.

Dearest Clara,

Forgive my lack of letters. You must be furious with me. We have been entrenched for almost two months. Snow and mud, up to our knees. The snow at least brightened the place up a bit, but a few of the men, laying communication wires, got trapped and had to lie in no man's land for two days. We threw some bread rolls over the top to them, knowing they'd be hungry, but the enemy merely shot at them like clay pigeons. Unfortunately, a couple of the men didn't get back.

In the middle of all this I was surprised to be invited for an officer's commission. Believe me, it's not because of any particular heroics, but because we have lost so many of our officers.

A brigadier turned up, looking very smart. No mud on his uniform. God knows what he thought of us. Unshaven and filthy as we are. Anyway, he called seven of us into the officers' dugout and interviewed us "in the field", as it is known. We were each given our orders and signed the agreement to become officers. The upshot is that I am coming home. Leaving France soon to take my place at cadet school. I feel awful leaving my pals here. They have become family to me. But, as an officer, I can hopefully do a lot for them when I return. At least I fully understand what they are up against, having been one of them.

Clara, my dearest wish is to see you again as soon as we can. The thought of you has made my days here bearable.

I'll buy you tea?

Bertie xx

CHAPTER
TEN

Clara, Waterloo

27 July 1916

Bertie finally returned to Waterloo Station on 26 July and I was there to greet him. I was one of maybe a thousand women all in their finest hats and coats, waiting stoically for the train to arrive, and when it did I almost got trampled by the push of so many surging bodies pressing towards the platform. The men coming off the train looked thin and strained but the joy on seeing their loved ones was palpable. Not being very tall I decided to stand on one of the benches near to the platform gate. I can tell you that the fear I had of not seeing him, or of him not seeing me, was great. My stomach was in a twist and my heart hammering as I desperately searched the crowd. I was sure I had missed him and was about to leave until I heard him shout my name and there he was. His loss of weight made him look even taller. His face thin, his nose red from the French sun. I jumped off the bench and ran, slipping through the endless elbows and shoulders around me until he was in front of me.

"You came," he said.

"I thought I'd missed you." I was shaking.

We stared at each other and then he bent and kissed my lips. I, who had never been kissed by a man, kissed him back.

When we broke apart he laced his arms around my back and pushed his face into my neck. I could tell he was crying. I held him and stroked his hair.

"I'm here. It's all right. I'm here."

"I'm sorry," he said, his voice so dear. "I'm so sorry."

"Whatever for?" We stayed as we were, clinging onto each other as if our lives depended on it.

Eventually the crowd thinned around us and a porter asked us to move as another train was due.

I gently took Bertie's hand and, not knowing what else to do, I walked him to the station buffet.

I spotted a table and ordered him to keep it while I joined the longish queue to order tea and teacakes. It was the most suitable thing I could think of.

By the time I got to the table he had blown his nose and looked almost recovered.

I poured the tea and set it in front of him with his teacake.

He put his hand out to mine and I held it tightly. Words were unimportant.

Later we walked to my lodging house. I had often imagined him being in my room. Bending his head to get through my little door. Sitting on my one armchair, his long legs sprawled out in front of him. And now here he was.

"What can I get you?" I asked as I hung his greatcoat on the hook behind the door, next to mine.

He looked so tired I don't think he had the energy to make words.

"How was your journey?" I asked. "You must be hungry?" He smiled at me, creases around his eyes that I didn't remember.

"Thank you for coming," he said.

"I wouldn't not." I went to the kettle and filled it from my one tap then lit the gas on the ring. "I'll make you some tea."

Warming the pot and adding the tea leaves, I chattered inconsequentially, and when it came to adding the sugar to his cup I asked, "With or without?" I turned to him, spoon poised. He was asleep.

I sat and watched him sleep for a long time. Not daring to make a noise to disturb him. I heard Elsie come in from work and knew that she would soon come to check on me. I had told her nothing of Bertie. I cannot tell you why. Or maybe I can. It was to keep him special. My secret. I could not have borne the endless questions about him from the girls in the office. I was not like them. They enjoyed relating every piece of their lives outside the office, and if, as happened several times, one of them had heard that their brother, cousin, or sweetheart had lost their lives serving their country, it seemed to me that all the other girls took the pain as their own, almost enjoying their public outpourings of grief and the attentions it garnered.

I had to get to Elsie before she came knocking.

Opening my door softly, I crept over the landing. Elsie's door flew open before I had time to knock.

"Hello," she said, rather too loudly. I didn't want her to wake Bertie. "I was just going to check that you are feeling better."

I had made up a bad headache that morning in order to have the day off and get to Waterloo.

"A little better, thank you," I lied. "But it has left me very tired. I was just coming to tell you not to come over tonight. I'm going back to bed."

"But you're dressed?" she observed.

"Oh yes. I did try to get up, you know, but really even that wore me out."

"Oh darling." She looked at me so sympathetically. "Have you eaten? Can I bring you a sandwich or soup?"

"I am still feeling rather sick." I leant on the door frame, as though even standing there talking was too much. "I'll be fine tomorrow, I'm sure," I managed, sounding, I hoped, rather wan.

"Understood. But call me if you need anything."

"I shall."

We embraced gently and she watched as I walked the four steps to my door.

"Goodnight," she said.

I gave her a grateful smile and shut my door behind me.

My armchair was empty.

Bertie was now on my bed. Asleep. He had taken off his jacket and was lying in his shirt and trousers, with his braces hanging loosely.

I didn't know what to do. I couldn't very well get into bed with him, so I sat and read for a while until it got dark. I was getting rather tired but I was not going to wake Bertie up. In all honesty, I did not want him to go. I was enjoying watching him. He was in a deep sleep, mumbling occasionally but never waking. I put my book down and began to pad about my room, discreetly getting undressed and washed before hurriedly putting on my nightdress and dressing gown. He was on top of my blankets and pillows so that, even if I had wanted to, I would not have been able to get under them.

I curled myself into my chair, using my coat as a pillow, and slept.

I have no idea how long I slept, but it was still very dark when he woke me. He was shouting. It sounded like "Get down", repeated each time with more urgency. I could see the sheen of sweat on his face. I went to him and touched his arm gently.

"Herbert? Bertie? It's OK. You are safe."

He sat up quickly and looked at me with terror. "Get fucking down!" he shouted.

I stepped back and said coaxingly, "Darling. It's me, Clara. You are safe in London. In my room."

His eyes darted from me to the room to the bed he was lying on.

He ran his hand through his short hair. "Where are we?" he asked.

"In London."

"Not in France?"

"No." I tried to soothe him with my voice and smile.

125

"Oh, thank God." He took a deep breath in and out then lay back on my bed. "I must have fallen asleep."

"Yes."

He held his right arm up to me. "Please sit with me?"

I did so. He was so warm and smelt strongly of exhaustion and sweat. "Is this your bed?" he asked.

"Yes."

"Are we alone?"

"Yes."

He tried to swing his legs from the bed. "I must go."

"Where would you go? It's the middle of the night."

"But it's wrong for me to be here." He looked at my nightclothes. "I am compromising you."

"I am glad." I reached out and stroked his head in the same way I had at the station. "Stay."

He stopped my stroking hand and pulled it to his lips. "I want to stay."

"Good."

"But only if you lie down next to me and we stay here together." He was like a frightened child.

"OK."

I lay down next to him and I had never felt closer to another human being in my life.

In the morning he must have woken first because I heard the gas pop as it took the match's flame.

"Good morning," he said. "Did you sleep well?"

"Very." I saw that my dressing gown had come loose and that he could see the top of my nightgown. I didn't bother to tie it back up.

"Tea?" he asked.

"Yes please."

He brought the tea to the bed and I inched over, making space to lie together.

"I am sorry about yesterday. I haven't slept for a couple of days. I must be a terrible inconvenience to you. Not to say embarrassment."

"What are friends for?"

We sipped our tea in silence.

"It's very quiet up here," he said.

"Yes, we are well above the traffic."

Mundane conversation. Wonderfully normal. No strain between us.

There was a knock on the door.

"Don't worry. It's Elsie," I said. I raised my voice slightly, "Elsie, is that you?"

"Yes, darling. How are you?" She tried the handle but I had locked it last night.

"I still don't feel well."

"Oh dear. Have you been sick?"

"Yes," I lied. "Most of the night. Can you let the office know I won't be in today?"

"Of course, I will," Elsie replied. "Is there anything you would like me to bring home tonight?"

"No thank you, dear. I have everything I need." I looked at Bertie.

"Well, it is Friday," she went on. "You've got the whole weekend to recover. I may not be in until late. George has invited me out for an early supper."

"Who's George?" whispered Bertie.

I put my finger to his lips. "Oh, that sounds nice," I told her. "Have a good time."

"I will. Toodle-oo."

"Bye, darling."

Bertie and I kept quite still and quiet until we heard Elsie's footsteps fade away, down the stairs and out of the building.

"You lie very well," Bertie said. "You would make a very good secret agent. And who is George?"

"He's a Westminster reporter. He mixes with the prime minister and his Cabinet. Gets all the inside information. He's full of himself. Elsie has been playing hard to get."

"Not hard enough by the sounds." He put his tea cup on the floor by the bed and stretched out. "I'm feeling very sleepy again."

"Me too."

"Here. Lie on my arm and I'll keep you warm."

We lay in our innocent embrace and slept until the early afternoon.

"God I'm hungry," Bertie said when he woke up. "What do you fancy for dinner?"

"You mean go out?" I asked worriedly. It was all very well him being in my room, but it was a very different thing to be seen sneaking out of the building in daylight.

"Yes," he said, clearly relaxed about the situation. He rubbed his chin. "I need a shave and a bath first though."

"The only bath is on the next floor and we are only allowed to use it once a week."

He laughed. "Worse than being in the trenches! What do you do?"

"I boil a kettle in the sink and have a wash."

"Right then, that is what we'll do. You first."

I hesitated.

"I promise I won't look."

"It's not that . . ." I was embarrassed.

"Yes, it is."

"Yes. It is."

"You can trust me. And remember, I do have a sister so I know how to behave."

I did trust him but nonetheless I washed very quickly and as covertly as possible. I wished I could have washed my hair too, but a lick of a hot flannel does wonders.

I dried myself and got dressed. "OK. The coast is clear."

He rolled over to face me. "That was quick. You must teach my sister how to do that."

"I've put the kettle on for you. I hope there is enough."

I turned my chair from its position by the window and faced it towards the blank wall.

I settled down and closed my eyes, enjoying the sound of the water splashing in the sink and then the scrape of a razor over his chin. I had never seen a man shave and listening to it was curiously exciting.

"Pass me my kitbag, would you?" he asked.

It was close enough for me to reach still sitting. I grabbed it and held it behind me without turning my head.

"Thank you."

I could hear him rummaging in the bag and shaking out what sounded like clean clothes.

"You may turn around. I am respectable."

He looked to me like the most handsome man in the world. Tanned face. Clean-shaven. White teeth. Hair brushed back and shining. His shirt was crumpled but clean. "How do I look?"

"All right."

"Do I smell a bit better?"

"Yes. What is that?"

"Macassar oil for my hair. You like it?"

I nodded.

"What perfume do you like to wear?" he asked, putting on his tie.

"I have never worn it. Pears soap is the closest I can get."

"One day, I shall buy you a bottle. For your birthday. When is your birthday?"

"March."

"Mine's February. Both spring babies. That must be lucky."

I laughed. "I don't believe in luck."

"Oh, but you must! Even if it doesn't exist, you must believe, in case it does. Do you see what I mean?"

"Sort of."

His tie done, he pulled up his braces and put on his jacket. "Come on. I'm taking you to a place I know."

We went to a small supper club just off Leicester Square. We ate lamb and drank champagne. We danced to the music of a small band. Several people, seeing he was in uniform, came and thanked him for the work he was doing. At first he was polite and thanked them, but I could tell that it began to wear him down.

I interrupted the final interloper by touching Bertie's arm and saying, "I am so sorry but we must go now."

Out on the street, Bertie took my arm. "Thank you."

"I could tell it was annoying you."

"I try not to be rude but if I told them the truth. Of what it was like out there. They wouldn't sleep."

I looked up at him. "You woke up shouting in the night."

He patted his pockets. "Do you have any cigarettes?"

I accepted his change of subject. "No, but we can get some at the kiosk in the station."

It was the first time I had seen him smoke. It wasn't going to be the last.

It seemed natural for him to come home with me and even more natural as we undressed each other and got into bed. "I have never done this before," I whispered, afraid.

He said nothing, but the look of affection he gave me was everything.

When it hurt me I stayed silent. Our eyes locked. Our bodies joined. I fell in love.

CHAPTER
ELEVEN

Bertie, London

31 July 1916

I had found a woman who had got into my bloodstream. Making love to her was quite different to the women I'd met before. She didn't tease, go coy, tempt. Her underwear was not frivolous. Her beauty regime was simple. No pots of powder and paint. Just her red lipstick. I asked her once why she wore it and she answered, "I like it." And because she did, I did. She wore it with uncalculated bravura. It was as much her as was her hair. Shoulder-length, wavy, always secured in a neat bun at the nape of her neck. I would lie in bed and watch her brush it in the morning, winding it through her fingers, pinning it. There was nothing about her that didn't fascinate me. She wanted nothing from me. Not money. Not promises. She just wanted to be with me as I did with her.

She shut from my mind the trenches, the blood and mud, the lost limbs, the screams, the terror, and filled me with the balm of simplicity. When we were together there was nothing else in the world. No France, no war, no Cornwall, no family. Just us, together in her tiny room in a boarding house on Fleet Street. It was what glued me back together. I dared to dream I had a future.

I did not ever want to leave that room or end our nighttime forays to find food in quiet cafés, to dance on tiny dance floors, and then the following morning to watch her dress and go to work while I lay in bed. But all things come to an end.

"Dearest?" I asked from the bed where I lay watching her pull her stockings on.

"Yes?" She smiled at me through her small mirror.

"I have to go to Cornwall. To see my parents."

She fastened her last suspender and turned to look at me. "Of course you must."

"I would rather stay here. You know that?"

"Yes." She sat on the bed and put her hand on mine. "But you'll come back." It wasn't a question.

"I will. The thing is." I rubbed my eyes, not wanting to tell her. "From Cornwall I have to go straight to Lichfield."

"Lichfield. Why?"

"Officer training."

She stood up and reached for her skirt. "Oh. How long will that take?"

"Three or four weeks."

"I see." She did the final button on her skirt then began on her blouse. "And will I see you before you go back to France?"

"I'm not sure."

She tucked her blouse into her skirt and found her jacket. "When will you be going to Cornwall?"

"Tonight."

"Right." She did her jacket up and pulled it down to straighten any creases. "Will you be here when I get back from work?"

"No."

She picked up her hairbrush and threw it at me. "You bastard!"

I leapt out of bed and tried to take her in my arms but she fought back. "Don't touch me. What a fool I have been. I never want to see you again." She pushed past me and ran to the door. "Never!"

She opened the door and almost knocked over a stout and fearful-looking woman who was standing on the landing. Clearly the landlady we had been avoiding. She took in the scene before her. A furious Clara and a naked me.

Hoisting her considerable bosom in front of her, she attacked. "Miss Carter! I am disappointed in you! I shall have to ask you to leave this establishment, at once. You know the rules. *No. Men.* You must pack immediately and be gone, with *your friend* —" she gave me a filthy look — "in the next hour, and before you ask, I will not be refunding the week's rent. I thought I had made myself clear when you took the room. I will not tolerate shouting, drunkenness or immoral behaviour." She finished on a crescendo, *"Do you understand me?"*

Clara slammed the door in her face and burst into tears. I went to her. "I'm so sorry." I pulled her to me and held her to my chest, hoping her angry sobs would subside, stroking her hair and thinking hard.

"I will go today and find us somewhere. I promise."

She shrugged me off. "I have to go to work."

"I know, but I'll pack up our things and find us a place by tonight."

"You have to go to Cornwall."

"I shall telegram my parents and pick you up from work. This is my fault and I shall work something out."

It didn't take me long to pack up. The landlady, arms folded, stood at the bottom of the stairs and watched as I carried my bag and Clara's few belongings out, before banging the front door shut behind me.

It was a warm July day, too warm. The air was heavy with a promising storm. I hailed a taxi and gave the driver the address of my old friend Jimmy's bank.

"Bolitho, old man, what a lovely surprise. What brings you here?"

"I need your help, Jimmy. I am in a bit of a fix."

Jimmy had always been the kindest of men and listened to my story without judgement.

"Well, you are in a pickle," he said. "This calls for a Scotch."

I took it gladly.

"Now then, let me see what I can do."

By lunchtime he had secured a bedsit in Ealing, west London. "Best I can do, old boy."

"I can't thank you enough," I said in all honesty.

His family rented many properties around London and this one was a large three-storey Victorian house, not far from Ealing Broadway, which had been split into six bedsits. Two on each floor.

"It'll be a bit of a commute for Miss Carter, but it's on a good bus route."

He described the flat. One large room, ground floor, shared bathroom and garden. "You're lucky. It's recently been vacated. Might need a lick of paint."

"Jimmy, you have saved us."

"My pleasure." He beamed. "We can't have Miss Carter shamed and homeless." He gave me a questioning glance. "Hope you'll do the right thing by her, old boy. I am doing this for her as much as you, you know."

"She is everything to me and I shall never let her down."

"Good show. Just what I feel for old Marianne. Married life is to be recommended."

We stood up and shook hands. "Thank you again," I said. "You know that if ever there is anything I can do for you . . ."

He prodded my chest. "Just make her happy."

"I will."

The earlier storm had passed, leaving the pavements wet and London grey. I asked the cabby to drop me at the small café across the road from the *Evening News* building. A table in the window was free so I stationed myself there and ordered a cheese sandwich and a pot of tea, settling our belongings under the table. I tried to imagine how Clara was feeling.

When she eventually came out of the office, she looked anxious and tired. I wondered whether that was from a hard day in the office, or was she getting cold feet? In reality we didn't know each other very well and perhaps I had been too bombastic? It was my fault she was homeless and I had jumped in telling her I would find her somewhere to live.

She was waiting for a gap in the traffic and biting her lip.

I scrabbled out from behind the table and ran onto the street. "Clara," I waved. "Over here."

The house in Ealing was red brick, tall and welcoming. The key was under the flower pot as Jimmy had described. The front door opened onto a wide hallway that was dark and smelt of two-day-old cabbage.

To the left there was a staircase and straight ahead of us was a door numbered 1A. Our new home.

I gripped Clara's hand firmly, nodding towards the door. "That's us." I gave her no chance to hesitate.

"Here we go." I warmed my voice with confidence then gave her back her hand, reached for the key in my pocket and fumbled with the lock. Finally, I pushed the door open.

Clara's hands flew to her face and for the second time that day she burst into tears.

The evening sun had banished the rain clouds and the room was bathed in late sunshine. "Is it OK?" I asked nervously.

"It's wonderful." She began to smile through her tears, "Look!" She walked quickly across the room, to the French windows. "A garden!"

She tried the handles. "Do you have another key?"

"I do." I was so happy that she was happy. "Let me try?"

As the doors swung open, the warm afternoon sun fell into the room, bringing with it the scent of roses that lined an uneven, slabbed path to a washing line.

Clara slid her arm around my waist. "It's wonderful."

I watched as she investigated every corner of the small, scruffy patch. "Look, a perfect place to grow vegetables!" She swung into my arms. "What do you like? Potatoes? Broad beans? Spinach? Lettuce?"

I hugged her to me. "Everything. I like everything."

She didn't acknowledge my answer because she had spotted a cracked coal bunker and a dwindled log store. "Do you think we have a fireplace in the flat? No more icy winters?" Her joy was infectious. "And, look at that apple tree!" She pointed to a gnarled tree laden with ripening fruit. "They look good too."

"Well you are the expert," I said.

"Expert?" She looked at me, puzzled.

"Yes. But it's only one tree, not the hundreds you are used to."

"I don't follow," she said, her eyebrows softly knitted.

"I mean it will remind you of home. Kent. In a good way, I hope."

Her face cleared and a faint blush climbed into her cheeks. "Oh yes. My father's farm, you mean."

She turned away from me and I could see her mood had changed.

"Darling, have I upset you?" I asked. "That was very clumsy of me. Bringing up old memories. Forgive me."

138

"No no. It just surprised me that you remembered." She turned back to me and smiled. "Sorry. Just the shock, I suppose."

From an open upstairs window someone was playing "Alexander's Ragtime Band" on a gramophone.

Clara grinned. "Would you care to dance?"

"I'm not too hot at the modern dancing."

"Can you do the cakewalk? I'll teach you."

I was hopeless, but she looked so beautiful dancing around that tiny garden, her long slender legs jigging in time to the music, that I felt I was the happiest man alive. When the music finished we were both breathless, but she grabbed my arm and dragged me back to the house, pointing out a mint bed and a honeysuckle on our way, then, "Come on, we need to explore our little home. I want to find the fireplace, and the kitchen."

The kitchenette was behind a curtain but had a full-sized gas oven, a large sink and a hot-water geyser. Clara was delighted. "I can make you a roast Sunday lunch. And bake cakes. And look, a cold shelf in the larder! No more putting the milk out on a cold windowsill."

She was like a child in a toy shop.

I found the fireplace behind an old, embroidered firescreen. We pulled up the two small but comfortable armchairs and she flopped down, her hands to her chest with joy. "I shall sit here and sew, or read, and toast crumpets." She gave me a smile that melted my heart. "And write my letters to you."

"I shall picture you just as you are. Your hair loose from the dancing, and your eyes so dark and bright."

139

"Stop it," she said, laughing at my teasing.

"And I will come home to you," I said.

She looked at me hesitantly, "Is this *our* home?"

"Do you want it to be?"

"I do."

"Clara," I needed to know something, "will you wait for me? After the war? We have no idea how long that will be, but if —"

"Yes," she said.

"Even though I lost you your room, and this place is so much further from your work?"

"Yes."

"I just want you to feel safe."

"I know."

"And do you?"

"Safer than I have ever felt in my life."

We spent that night putting out our few belongings and moving the bed (larger than we were used to) to a position where we could take full advantage of the garden view.

As the sun set, we lit one of the two gas lamps and lay in bed watching as the bats in the garden came out, catching insects on the wing.

I made love to her gently. Her body, so thin, but still warm and yielding. I never wanted to leave that room. Never.

But, early the next morning, I had to leave her. I had a ticket for the first train out of Paddington for Callyzion and my parents.

I climbed out of bed and washed and dressed while Clara still slept. She was lying peacefully in our muddled sheets, her long hair loose, strands curling on the pillow, and one hand flung above her head.

How could I go?

I took her a cup of tea and roused her. "Darling." I stroked her sleepy cheek. "Clara, would you come to Cornwall with me?"

"Of course I will," she murmured with half-closed eyes.

I checked my watch. "Can you be up and ready to go in half an hour?"

"What do you mean?" She leant on one elbow and pushed her hair from her face.

"We should just make it if we leave soon." I gave her the tea and kissed her nose. "Ma and Pa will be so surprised."

"No. I can't come to Cornwall today." She smiled at me lazily. "You silly thing. I meant I'll come when they know about me. You haven't seen them for months. They will want you to themselves."

"Please?" I pleaded.

"No darling. You must see your family by yourself or they will hate me for taking you from them."

I bent over her and kissed her. "I will talk of nothing but you while I am there."

"Good." She put her arms around my neck and pulled me back to her lips. Desire sprang in me as I freed her breasts from the sheet and her small fingers worked at the buttons of my shirt. "Just once more," she whispered. "And then you can go."

CHAPTER
TWELVE

Clara, London

2 August-October 1916

Bertie went to Cornwall this morning. We have been lovers for only a week, but those days have been an eternity of bliss. My life at last has meaning and purpose. I have someone who has provided me with a roof over my head and a reason to be the person I always wanted to be. I can hold my head high and tell the world I am loved by a man, a brave man, a soldier. When this bloody war is over, we will marry and I shall be the wife of a plantation manager. I shall travel the high seas to the Orient and be his strength. His missing piece of the jigsaw. Together we will build a life and a family and I shall never know loneliness or hardship again. I just had to get through being alone, in our adorable little home, and to wait for the war to be over.

I met Elsie in a Covent Garden teashop later that day. She was agog with my banishment from the boarding house and wanted to know everything.

When I arrived, she was waiting and greeted me warmly.

"Darling, Clara, are you OK?"

"I am."

We quickly ordered our tea and buttered teacakes and I told her my story. I don't know why, but I found myself embroidering the truth, although there was no need.

"The Old Dragon told me about finding you in a compromising situation." Elsie's eyes were wide with questions. "Who was he?"

"My fiance." That was the first fib. Why did I say it? Wishful thinking?

"You dark horse!" Elsie grinned. "Why have you never told me about him?"

"His parents. They are rather well-off. Gentry in Cornwall." Another slight colouring of their circumstances. "They may think I am a gold-digger. After all, I have nothing."

Elsie was affronted on my behalf. "You? The sweetest, gentlest woman I know? And anyway, you come from wealthy landowner stock yourself. Probably of better blood than them."

"Oh, I wouldn't want to talk about my parents and their sad end," I said quietly, pouring us each a cup of tea. "The fire was terrible, but them losing all their money . . ."

She nodded sadly, then frowned. "I thought you said all the money went to your uncle and he gave you your education as your inheritance?"

I put my tea cup down to give me time to think. "Oh yes. Quite so. He was very generous, but my poor parents, what I meant to say was that they lost

143

everything, if you see what I mean." I looked her square in the eye and saw that she believed me. I used to ask myself why I did this — but after a while the lies got easier and I wanted to believe them. I remembered my mother always saying, as she pocketed any coin she found, or pilfered, "Never let your left hand know what your right hand is doing." I saw myself once more as the dirty, straggle-haired, shoeless girl I had been, and still was, deep down: A girl not worthy of decent work, a place to live, a man to love her. I clenched my hands under the table as unwanted tears stung my eyes. If Bertie knew my lies, he would run a mile. I was not worthy of him.

"Clara. Clara!" Elsie was shaking my arm. "Darling. I have upset you. I am so sorry."

She spoke the same words Bertie had the night before when he said the apple tree in our garden would remind me of my "home". I should have told him then and there the truth about who I really was. What a fraud I am. "Be sure your sins will find you out," my mother had warned. I screwed my eyes against the tears that threatened to spill.

Elsie was passing me a handkerchief. "Here, darling. Take this. I have smelling salts in my bag if you need."

I composed myself. "I must apologise. I am fine."

"You poor darling," she cooed. "I am sure love will carry you through all his family nonsense. What is his name?"

"Herbert. Second Lieutenant Herbert Bolitho." He wasn't second lieutenant yet. I was lying again, so I

144

corrected myself. "Well, he soon will be, after officer training."

"An officer! How romantic. Tall, dark and handsome?"

I nodded, wiped my eyes and drank some tea.

"How marvellous!" She clapped her hands. "How did you meet?"

I wanted her to think the best of me and I wanted to make myself the princess in the fairy tale. So, I told her the story, changing the timeline a little. Made it seem that we had known each other for ages, trying to keep our romance a secret until the war came to an end, whenever that may be. Elsie sighed wistfully. "Oh, it all sounds so wonderful and I am so happy for you both. When can I meet him?"

"Not for a while. After Cornwall he has to go straight away to officer training. From there it is expected he will have to go immediately to France. He is very much missed by his men."

"And you," Elsie smiled, taking my hand across the tablecloth.

"Yes. And me."

"Oh, but where are you living?"

I smiled, "He has many good friends, one of them owns a bank." I was trying not to sound as though I were bragging.

"A bank?" Elsie was agog.

I nodded my head, smiling broadly. "Isn't that lucky? And he has properties and was able to rent us a dear little place, with a garden!"

Elsie fairly swooned. "A little place with a garden — oh but how heavenly."

"It is. And I have a real fire I can light on cold nights."

"How romantic. Where is it? Can I come to visit?"

"It's in Ealing, near the common," I finished proudly, then added with regret, "I shall have to ask Bertie if it's OK. I think his friend may not allow it."

Elsie might have had her cunning wiles with men, but she fell easily for my explanation.

"Oh, I quite understand. Being a banker and all. He doesn't want every Tom, Dick and Harry knowing his business, does he?"

I caught the waitress's eye. "This tea is my treat." I took my purse from my bag. "But only if you promise not to breathe a word to anyone about Bertie, or Ealing."

"Mum's the word," she said in earnest.

I had a letter from Bertie a few days later. He had had a mixed time with his parents. His mother wasn't well and Amy, who had heard only in the last week that her sweetheart, Peter, was missing presumed killed in action, had joined the Land Army, working on a farm nearby, and her long hours meant she couldn't do all her mother wanted of her. I felt enormous sympathy for her, especially when Bertie wrote that Amy had also discovered Peter had been writing to another girl in the village. There had been a huge upset, probably what had led to his mother taking to her bed, and Amy had decided to work her grief out on the land.

To add to this cauldron of domestic tension, Ernest, Bertie's younger brother, had arrived in Aden, and was facing all sorts of horrors defending the harbour. Bertie had tried to bring them some cheer by telling them about me, but there had never been the right time to start the conversation.

I had to wait another four weeks before I saw him again, as he had travelled straight from Cornwall to Lichfield for officer training. In those four weeks I made our home in Ealing a sanctuary for him to return to. Each weekend our local church, St Stephen's, held a second-hand sale to raise money for the war effort, and I began to haunt it, gleefully picking up two saucepans, a frying pan, some pretty unmatched plates, a teapot, a pair of bright curtains and lots of balls of wool. I would carry each find home and set about brightening up our room. My greatest find was a bag of scrap material which I fashioned into a patchwork quilt for our lovers' bed.

Elsie kept asking to visit but I did not want her to see our home. It was ours, Bertie's and mine. Private. Not to be shared by another's thoughts or judgements. I told her that our landlord had refused my request.

I felt a little guilty but not enough. Elsie was a wonderful friend, but a friend who didn't belong in our home. It was bad enough that she knew about Bertie, but she had kept her word and told nobody about him.

I loved my work and had had a small pay rise with another promotion to chief sub's secretary, and I loved going home to our special place. Putting the key in the lock of our own door was heaven. I would make myself a tomato sandwich and take that, with a cup of tea, out into the garden, where I would sit in the August evening sun, knitting socks for Bertie and dreaming of him being home soon.

His letters were full of his training and full of longing for me. I held each one to my heart before and after I opened it. I would sleep with them under my pillow. My letters back, I filled with news of the office, my brilliant purchases and my yearning for him.

We both counted down the days to his return. Four weeks. Three weeks. Two weeks. Seven days. Twenty-four hours.

I felt I would die with the excitement and then, at last, he was standing before me. Wearing the kilt of his regiment, tanned and handsome. I could hardly breathe with the nervous excitement that rushed through me.

"Hello," he said and kissed me. I led him into our room and made him a cup of tea. I needed that moment to feel real, to cut him a slice of cake, to pour him some tea. To walk around our little garden hand in hand, to show him the peas I was growing. Finally, I showed him our new patchwork quilt and he was home.

In that seventy-two hours we were never apart. No further than an arm stretch away. He took me to a concert at the Wigmore Hall and later we walked on Ealing Common. He gave me my silver cigarette case and I gave him three more pairs of warm socks, blue this time, that I had knitted. We were building our life together. Our dream. Our married life to come. A life after this bloody war. And we would go to Penang where I would never be found out as the liar I was. Or the poor, destitute girl I used to be.

The weekend flew by but I would recall every second over the years to come. In four more weeks he would be trained and I would be allowed to travel to Lichfield where there was a nice pub in which we could stay. "I will book it for Mr and Mrs Bolitho," he said as he held me for the last goodbye on the platform. "Because, in my heart, you are Clara Bolitho."

Just four more weeks to get up, work, water my peas and knit, and we would be together again. He had managed to wangle a family ticket for me to see him pass out as "Second Lieutenant on Probation". "I have told them my sister is coming," he said. "My sister, of whom I am inordinately fond."

Neither of us spoke of France or the war.

On that morning he left, he made me a boiled egg with toast soldiers. He brought them to me in bed with a cup of tea. I felt queasy as soon as I had finished it all and had to run to the kitchen sink to be sick. He held my hair from my face and rubbed my back. We agreed it must have been a bad egg. The sickness went on for the next three weeks. Always in the morning and sometimes at night. I mentioned it to no one. It was just a bug.

Four weeks later and the bug had cleared up. I was relieved as I hadn't wanted to travel all the way to Lichfield with the embarrassment of having to use the train's public lavatory. He was waiting for me as I stepped off the train and I wept with the joy of feeling his arms around me. I wept as I watched him receive the honour of becoming The London Regiment Cadet Herbert Bolitho, Second Lieutenant on Probation. I wept when we made love and I wept as I folded his clothes and placed them on the end of the bed at the end of each of those three days. Then I wept as he put me on the train back to London. France was getting closer. By now we knew that fewer men came home and the ones who did were not the same men who had gone away. He had been told they could be sent any day now.

I clung to him and he to me, then he whispered, "Clara, will you wait for me?"

The stationmaster was walking the platform, slamming doors as he went. He was getting closer to us as I hurriedly replied, "Yes. Yes, I will wait for you, however long."

The stationmaster was one door away from us. "All aboard," he shouted.

Bertie held my hand as I stepped onto the train and lifted my small bag up for me.

"Shut the door, sir, please." The stationmaster had his whistle ready. "He'll be back, miss, don't you worry."

He blew his shrill whistle, waved his flag and the train began to move. I hung out of the window and waved for as long as I could see my beloved, then wept all the way home.

I heard from him two weeks later. He was in France and his new officer's pay meant that he could send half back to me to cover the rent and save as much as I possibly could, for when he came home.

He couldn't tell me exactly where he was but it sounded grim. His battalion were all exhausted and in need of rest after weeks of brutal fighting. He described his position as being close to a wood, within which enemy snipers hid.

Bertie's battalion had the dangerous job of digging a sevenfoot — deep cable trench across a huge field in plain sight of the enemy. That week they had lost three men, picked off by the snipers like ducks in a shooting gallery.

Bertie had wired back to the command post some three miles away, to explain the danger and the profligate waste of three human lives, but the orders came back the same. "Keep digging."

There was no protection from the constant rain, and they were again working in liquid mud. The trenches, sited at the bottom of a valley, were shallow and needed the communications cables. Every man worked with the enemy shelling them or shooting them, incessantly. Apart from one night, when they had discovered shelter in a bombed-out farmhouse. None of them had slept under shelter since he had arrived. Bertie wrote to me that night before he slept. "I cannot know the limits of human endurance. Many times I have thought we had nothing left to give and every time I am confounded."

As I sat in the comfort of our Ealing home, the fire crackling in the grate, my heart broke for him. He finished his letter with this: "There are no men tougher than these. We each trust each other with our lives. We share everything to make certain no one has less than the other. My socks are a source of much envy and, my

151

darling, I must tell you that three English men are feeling the warmth of them tonight. This war must be over soon. It is not for want of bravery that it has not ended before. Thank God I have you. You are with me, always. Bertie xxxx".

How do you reply to such a letter?

I began, and abandoned, many replies. What I wanted to shout, to scream, was "Come home." But I couldn't ask for that, could I?

Could I tell him all the dreary tittle-tattle of office life and what I had for lunch, when he was living between life and death without a roof over his head? Could I complain that our garden was one big puddle when I was sitting cosily, eating warm soup in the comfort of our little room?

The other thing I couldn't tell him was that I had missed two of my monthlies and that maybe the boiled egg hadn't been bad after all.

I had to believe that he would be home by Christmas.

I fantasised about Christmas Eve. We would be sitting on the floor by our fire. Me wrapping presents. He toasting muffins. We'd have a small tree — I had never had one — twinkling with glass baubles, under which we would place our presents to each other, and as midnight came I would tell him the joyful news that we had a child coming. We would marry on New Year's Day and, after we had exchanged our vows, an old man would enter the church, banging the ancient wooden door at the back of the church open and bringing with him chill air and snowflakes. The guests would turn

152

their heads as his heavy booted steps came down the aisle towards us, waving his hat and shouting, "The war is over. It's over!"

There would be celebrations, not just for us the happy couple, but for the whole world.

Then, we'd get the train to Callyzion and I would meet my new family who would cosset and fuss over me as the pregnancy neared its end.

And we would have a boy, a son, and we would call him Little Bertie.

All good stories would end like that, but neither Herbert nor me nor anyone with a loved one fighting this terrible war could know what ending we would have.

I pulled another piece of paper towards me and lifted my pen.

Ealing
October 1916

My dearest Bertie,

How brave you all are. Please tell the men that I shall bake a decent fruitcake for you all and post it. I have never made one before but I have looked out a recipe. What else can I send you? I hear, from the office, that there is a shortage of razor blades, soap, matches and tobacco. I will send you anything you need. I have finished two pairs of socks this week and I shall post them with this letter.

London is much the same. Everybody is cheering you all on. When all this is over, they are talking about throwing a huge parade to honour you all.

Our little home is safe and I am waiting for you always. I can't tell you how proud I am of you. Something to tell your grandchildren. How Grandpa won the war!

Elsie is well and sends her regards. She has got engaged! Imagine that! A nice enough chap who couldn't join up on account of his polio as a child. Elsie is constantly going on about flowers and what she will wear. She found a lovely pair of shoes in Selfridges but she'll have to save up for years to afford them!

I love you with all my heart, Bertie.

Forever yours,

Clara xxx

CHAPTER
THIRTEEN

Bertie, France

2 November 1916

I am unable to get any rest and have no time to write to Clara. Conditions here are so hellish that the mailbags with our precious letters from home cannot get through. I miss those letters so much. Clara has an ease of writing that makes me feel I am in whatever story she is recounting. I feel the pavement under her feet, the rattle of her bus to work, the sanctuary of our bed. When I get home, I shall marry her. I dare not propose with a letter as I may not be able to fulfil my promise, things being as they are. I almost proposed to her as I held her before putting her on the train from Lichfield back to London. Asking her to wait for me was all I could beg of her.

I am sitting now, bunkered into a hole held up with wooden beams, a roof of tarpaulin and sandbags above my head. As an officer I am allowed this privilege, and even have use of a lower bunk bed. There are three bunks crammed in here and my cell mates are all good men. But tonight, two of the mattresses will remain empty. At 14.45 today, or was it yesterday, we were engaged in hand-to-hand fighting with the enemy. A first for all of us. We charged a line of old gun-pits, hoping to surprise the enemy, but, naturally, they retaliated with heavy machine-gun fire. I killed five of them with my bayonet. I am not proud of it. They were men with families who, in any other time of life, might have been friends. But we are all soldiers and we kill.

When the horror had finished and the adrenaline subsided, I found an unseen place where I could be as sick as any dog.

It had been our first attack against an enemy post rather than a trench line. At daybreak we counted the men we had lost. We had gained nothing. I have never known such terror.

After that we were withdrawn from the front and marched along the muddy road to Amiens. We reached our billets and were given ten days' rest. Rest! There was no rest. We refitted, reorganised and trained.

Within two weeks we were sent to the Belgian border to relieve the men who had been working to strengthen our lines. The enemy welcomed us with a cruel bombardment as the relief was taking place. We had few casualties (thanks to a God whose existence I question), but all the good work done by our predecessors was blown apart. We got stuck in and began to rebuild our defences.

It took us all the winter months to achieve. Compared to the Somme, we were grateful for the relative peace. Of course, we would send the enemy odd bouts of artillery fire at inconvenient times and they would return the compliment, but in lots of ways it felt like a holiday. At least we weren't being shelled.

And we began to get post again.

Near Belgium
4 December 1916

My dearest Clara,

How worried you must have been not to hear from me for so long. But here I am, ripe as ninepence. You cannot get rid of me easily!

Our postal service was halted due to unfortunate circumstances, i.e. mud, more mud, and the possibility that the dear postie might get shot. But it appears that normal service has resumed. First of all, I must ask you for more cake! It kept us going for a week and the men are badgering me to ask you.

Is Elsie married yet? I hope she is happy. It makes me think of how happy we shall be when I get back. I have never told you that I love you, have I? I knew I loved you in that first week when you stowed me away in your little room across the hall from Elsie. I wanted to tell you many times but I felt it would be unfair to you. Supposing you met someone else? I would hate for you to miss out on happiness because you were waiting for me. But I did ask you to wait for me, didn't I? And you said you would and I believe you have. It was very unfair of me. In Lichfield I should just have got on one knee and damned well proposed to you. So, darling, if I were to ask you to marry me now, would you say yes? I would understand if you cannot give me that promise. We shall say no more about it and be friends. But I hope that won't be the case. Please write to let me know as soon as you can with an answer.

Tonight the snow is falling. We keep ourselves warm with drills for everything: battalion, physical, gas, etc., etc. Some nights we play football or have a singsong.

My darling, I still have your picture with me. I am looking at it as I write.

With true love,

Bertie xx

Ealing

7 December 1916

My darling,

Yes yes yes yes, please. You have made me the happiest of women and I will be the best wife a man could have. I love you too. So very much, and I have a special thing to tell you too. I hope it won't change how you feel. You see, I am expecting your child. I think I must be almost four months along now. Which means the baby will arrive in May. A spring birthday. Just like us.

I have told no one and will have to resign my work at Christmas as I don't want the girls to gossip about me. Elsie has already been asking questions as I cannot do up the dress I am wearing for her wedding next week. I have told her that I must be eating too much cake (I will send you one at the weekend).

I will also have to leave our home. I shall go to Kent. My uncle has lost his housekeeper (she's ancient and cannot do all she used to do), so he has asked me to look after the cooking and cleaning for him. I hate to leave our Ealing home but when you get back, we can find somewhere else with the money I have saved.

I know this must all be a terrible shock to you as it was for me, but I am so happy. I pray you will be back in time for the birth. If you don't mind, I shall tell the doctor that we are married. There's nobody but you and there will never be anyone but you, my darling.

What a pretty picture you paint of snow and singsongs. I am glad you are in a safer place.

I am so happy.

At last, when this war is over, you shall have your own little family to come home to.

With my eternal love,

Clara xxx

Bertie, Northern France

14 December 1916

I was to be a father. I held the news like a light in my heart. The weather had taken another turn for the worse, and we were all doing what we could to keep our

159

spirits up. We moved inches and the loss of men was becoming intolerable.

I kept Clara's precious letter with news of our baby in my top pocket; it gave me more strength than a man could put into words. I was acting now only on raw instinct. I could not hear my thoughts, even if I wanted to, which I didn't.

For nigh on fifty hours we had taken the brunt of enemy shelling. In the last one hundred hours I had had no more than six hours' sleep, and that was broken into fifteen-minute splinters if I was lucky. We lost our motorbike messenger less than ten minutes ago. It was he who delivered this miraculous news of a baby. We hadn't seen him for over a week, so when we heard the putter of his engine, a small cheer went up. I watched as he delivered his packets and letters through the trench and when he got to me he said, "Post been rather delayed, sir. Apologies. I hope you're not expecting a Harrods hamper?" This was a joke we shared every time we met. My response was always, "Never mind, Private Thompson, it'll arrive in time for next Christmas."

He handed me my letter, the last in his bag, saluted me and began the long walk of the trench to return to his bike.

I gazed at the envelope and savoured Clara's handwriting. I put my nose to the paper and inhaled, imagining the scent of her hands still upon it.

I opened it and read what she had written. My hands started to shake. A baby? I was to be a father. I looked to where Private Thompson had gone, hoping to shout to him the good news, when the loudest bang yet, far too close for comfort, coming from the far end of the trench, shook the ground beneath us and the mud above us, so that a hail of damp earth, sharp pieces of metal and the blasted remains of Private Thompson rained down upon us.

"Jesus Christ," one of the men shouted, "the bastards have killed Tommo."

One small lad, only seventeen, clutching a parcel from home, threw up, whilst one of his mates picked up his rifle and climbed the ladder shouting, "Prepare to fucking die, you bastards." Before he went over the top and met a hail of bullets.

As the officer in charge, I screamed at the men to gather their senses. This was war, not a bloody pub brawl. We were the British Army and we were to damn well fight as we were trained. Not die from stupidity. And if I saw anybody, *anybody*, doing anything stupid again I would have them shot. *Did they all understand?*

Yessir, came the answer.

The shelling began again.

Wheeeee . . . boom . . . wheeeee . . . boom.

I couldn't take it. My head felt as if it would explode with the pressure of emotion and exhaustion and sheer bloody homesickness. I marched to my dugout, threw myself on my wooden bed and screamed until there was nothing left.

And now I was lying on my bed holding Clara's letter and feeling the light in my heart pierce my darkened thoughts. For strength, I tucked the letter into

161

my top pocket. I was to be a father. I had a reason now to make it through this bloody war.

My brave Clara had left London to return to Kent and the sanctuary of her childhood home, her uncle's farm.

To be alone at such a vulnerable time. My admiration and respect for her grew every second — just as our child was doing. This war could not go on for ever. Each day and every night I held onto the hope that I should be there when our child was born. I would. I knew I would. I felt it.

Christmas was coming and the men and I would make the best of it. Why should I be sad when my heart was full of joy. If Clara could be brave, so could I.

Clara, London

15 December 1916

Today was Elsie's wedding. Just four of us attended and I could barely sit down, my dress was so tight. Elizabeth — Elsie's old friend and the second witness — and I threw rice at the newlyweds as they went to catch their train to Brighton for their three-day honeymoon. Elizabeth and I exchanged the usual pleasantries. How nice it was to meet each other after all this time. How pretty Elsie had looked. And then we said our good byes and I went to the office to hand in my notice. I would work until 19 December.

I was now in our little Ealing home and sorting through what to keep and what to give away. I had to

162

tell Bertie that I was going to stay with my nonexistent uncle or he would be afraid for me and the baby. This way, he won't worry so much. I must keep his spirits up. And when, after the war, he wants to meet my uncle, I shall have to think of a short illness — flu maybe — that will have finished him off; tell Bertie that the farm was heavily mortgaged and the bank repossessed it.

I felt the baby kick. "It's just a teeny little fib to make Daddy happy. That's all. And I haven't lied about going to Kent, have I?"

Dear Miss Hampton,

It's me, Clara Carter. I hope you are well and that the shop is busy. I have had a very exciting few years since I last saw you. I can never forget what you did for me and I still have the clothes we made together.

Life at the *News* has been very exciting and I am now, or will be until this Friday, the chief subeditor's secretary. I couldn't have done any of this if it weren't for your encouragement and help.

I expect you are wondering why I am writing to you now when you haven't heard from me since the day I left Faversham? The truth is, I am in a bit of a fix and I have no one else to turn to . . .

CHAPTER
FOURTEEN

Bertie, Northern France

Christmas Day, 1916

My darling Clara,

Happy Christmas to you and our little one. How is he coming along? Are you very big? Oh, how I would love to put my arms around you both. You will tell him Pa says Happy Christmas, won't you?

And don't be cross when I keep saying he! I just have a feeling . . . I am so glad that you are settled in Faversham. Your uncle's farm does sound very rundown and your bedroom unsuitable for human habitation. But it was good of him to find you lodgings in the town. I can see you doing your daily shopping and cooking for him, then getting back to Miss Hampton's for good female chat.

Please tell Miss Hampton that I will never let you down, and thank her for me for looking after you. I shall be there before either of us know it.

I dreamt about you last night. Standing in the window of a sunlit cottage, our baby in his cot beside you, sleeping soundly, while you arranged lupins — of all things — in a vase. That dream made me so happy and gave me all the more determination to be with you as soon as possible.

We were up early this morning for church parade. Thick snow fell last night but today the sky is clear blue. The broken buildings and burnt trees look rather beautiful clad in white and Gerry, only two hundred yards away, have popped their heads over the trenches to wish us Happy Christmas. Tomorrow we'll be trying to kill them. My father has sent me a pamphlet of seasonal religious verses to keep my spirits up but, and please don't tell him, my faith in God has left me. How can this be God's plan? Yesterday, one of our boys was in his hut with six others and he saw an enemy grenade under his bed. Must've rolled in there during the last attack. He picked it up and saw that the pin was out. He knew he had to get it out of the hut but his hands were shaking so much that he couldn't undo the door latch. He knew the thing was about to go off, so he covered it with his own body and was blown to bits. His five friends survived, although two were badly wounded. The padre said that God and his angels had been with him, but I cannot believe that.

Oh my darling, I am sorry to tell you these awful things, but if I don't tell you, who do I tell? The thought of you keeps me strong, as strong as you.

Just had a thought, maybe you could have lupins in your bridal bouquet?

With my deepest love. Merry Christmas and here's to 1917,
    Your Bertie xxxxxx

Clara, The Haberdashery, Faversham

New Year's Eve, 1916

My letter to Miss Hampton told her the full truth of my condition and my fibs. She wrote by return and welcomed me into her lovely home without a blink. Her beautiful little shop, as I arrived, was twinkling with Christmas trimmings and gewgaws. When I opened the door, the bell still jangled, and the scent of oranges and cinnamon was on the air.

Miss Hampton came from behind her counter, her arms wide. "Clara dear. I am so glad you came." She held my arms to look at me. "You're tired. Come through to the back parlour while I shut the shop for the rest of the day."

She made me sit comfortably and gave me her footstool, lifting my feet onto it and removing my shoes. "Now. A cup of tea? I have made some mince pies if you'd like one?"

I held her hand before she could walk away. "Thank you. Thank you for all this. I don't know why you are being so kind. I owe you so much for helping me."

"You owe me nothing. We are women, and as such have to look after each other when life gets a little awkward."

166

She went to her little kitchen and, as she busied herself with kettle and cups, I looked around this room that I hadn't thought twice about leaving. I was so lucky to be back.

As the afternoon wore on and night began to wrap the village in darkness, Miss Hampton sat and quietly listened to my story. I told her everything. I left nothing out.

"May God forgive me for my lies," I finished.

"He will," she said. "Have you got a picture of this young man of yours?"

When I showed her she nodded. "That's a face that will do you well. Now then. Have you seen a doctor?"

Miss Hampton insisted that I should see the doctor the next morning. "The appointment is for ten o'clock," she told me briskly.

"But what am I to say? What will he think?"

"You will tell him that your husband is away in France and that I, your aunt, on your mother's side, am caring for you until the war is over."

"Really?"

"We women sometimes have to brush over the truth in order to save our men the absolute truth." I knew this all too well. She put her hand in her pocket. "You had better put this on your wedding finger."

She passed me a gold ring. "It was my mother's, so look after it."

"I can't take it." I tried to hand it back.

"You will take it. And you will return it to me as soon as your fiance buys you one of your own. Now put it on."

167

Dr Channing's surgery was in his house and overlooked the front path, in order, I thought, to see who his next patient was.

Miss Hampton looked at me as we approached. "Stand up tall. You have nothing to be ashamed of."

An elderly woman opened the door and ushered us in. "Miss Hampton, how lovely to see you. We see you so rarely here."

"I am blessed with good health." Miss Hampton kissed the woman on both cheeks. "But how are your rheumatics, Mrs Channing?"

"Mustn't complain." She looked at me, "And you are Miss Hampton's niece? I had no idea."

"No," Miss Hampton said quickly. "Dear Clara's mother and I had a silly falling-out years ago, I honestly can't even remember what it was about now, and sadly it is too late to ask her forgiveness. We lost her in the spring. As soon as I heard, I wrote to Clara and here we are."

Mrs Channing looked with suspicion at each of us. "Well, it's a pleasure to welcome you to Faversham." She tapped her chin. "I feel we have met before, Mrs . . . ?"

"Bolitho." I smiled graciously. "Unfortunately for me I have never been to Kent before. I grew up in London."

Miss Hampton noted my easy fib. "Yes, Chelsea. By the river. Do you know it, Mrs Channing?"

"Er, no. I have never been to London."

"You must visit," I said, enjoying myself. "The Royal Academy has many delightful paintings, and after a visit you can just pop across the road to Fortnum and Mason for tea. I do it once a month."

The door to the surgery opened and revealed a tall, handsome man with even white teeth. I thought he might be a patient leaving the room but he introduced himself as Dr Channing.

"My son," said the old lady. "He took over his father's practice when dear Arthur died."

"Thank you, Mother." He stood back to let Miss Hampton and me enter his room. "I shall look after the ladies now."

He closed the door on his mother's pinched face and offered us the two chairs in front of his desk.

I saw him take in my swollen stomach as he took his seat. "How may I help you?"

I blushed and my mouth went dry but Miss Hampton, who had insisted on coming with me, said, "My niece's husband is in France, and until he gets home, she has no one to care for her but me." She looked at me. "Clara, dear, explain your situation to the doctor."

I took a deep breath. "I am expecting a child."

He nodded, and with kindness said, "I did notice." He stood up and walked to his leather examination couch. "Have you had this confirmed by a doctor?" He went to the sink next to the couch and began to wash his hands.

"No."

"And how far along would you say you are? When did you have your last monthly?"

"I'm not sure. August, I think."

169

"Well, let me check you over and we'll see." He indicated for me to get onto the couch. Miss Hampton stationed herself resolutely next to me, and held my hand all the while, as the doctor lifted my skirt.

Dr Channing's cool hands pressed against my skin, feeling all around where the baby lay. He said nothing as he did this and then he reached for a small wooden trumpet, not unlike the earpiece of the phones we had at the *News*.

"Just breathe normally, Mrs Bolitho. I'm going to see if I can hear baby's heartbeat." Dr Channing placed one end on the skin of my stomach and the other to his ear.

Miss Hampton squeezed my hand tighter. "It's all right. Try not to move."

"Is the baby OK?" I whispered.

"Shhhh."

"Sorry."

The trumpet was moved to another part of my tummy, then another and another.

At last the examination was over. Dr Channing went to the sink to wash his hands again, saying nothing.

Miss Hampton broke the silence. "Is the baby all right?"

He picked up a towel and dried his hands. "I am glad to tell you that all is well and you and the baby are in good health."

I smiled and could have cried tears of relief. "Thank you."

"Not at all." He went to his desk and began to write some notes and let me reassemble my clothing.

"And when will the baby arrive, Dr Channing?" asked Miss Hampton.

"I should say May, the early part."

"Oh." My knees buckled at the reality of it all. Dr Channing came straight to me and helped me into a chair. "A little lightheaded? Only to be expected. Let me get you a glass of water." He asked me lots of questions and took many notes before pronouncing that I was perfectly fit and well and that there was nothing to be concerned about.

We left his surgery promising to return if I had any worries.

"Your aunt will keep an eye on you."

Miss Hampton took my arm and said in all innocence, "What else are aunts for?"

My respect for her was growing at an alarming rate, and when we were out of earshot I asked, "What do I call you?"

"From now on I am Aunt Philippa."

Bertie, Western Front, France

January 1917

I was counting the days until May. I needed to be home looking after Clara and my unborn child. The days and nights here ran into each other like tears on a watercolour painting. The colours that once were bright and pretty had run together and turned into the brown of dog muck. The mud, the khaki, the sun, the blood, the food; all shit.

171

We had been moved back to the Western Front. The top brass had told us to prepare for one last big push to win the war. "The enemy are withdrawing," they said. "We can advance and break through their new lines of defence."

Lies. We were nothing but cannon fodder. They had known it and we had known it and we knew that now. Which is why I *had to* get home. Before I became part of the mud and shit. Stamped into this earthy swamp, never to be found.

I was ready to die. Expecting to die but not hoping to die. I had to get back to my child. I could not be a father my child didn't know. My name carved on a village memorial to be glanced at once a year.

The weather had been a bit better. No rain for a few days.

The long routine of trench fighting was over and, so they told us, "Morale was high."

Mine wasn't. I kept that bit of news a secret. As far as my men were concerned, Second Lieutenant Bolitho was a "chap with a smile. Always a comforting word. A brave soldier. The sort of fellow you want by your side."

Let them think that if it made them feel better. Braver.

In reality I spent my waking hours with my brain screaming in terror as unseen tears poured from me. My soul was breaking. I couldn't sleep without the nightmares. I couldn't think for the scream in my head.

I *had to get home*. How had I been spared a bullet in the head? My father and his parishioners must have been sending the right kind of prayers for me.

Take me home.

I wanted chocolate that was clean.

I wanted beer that wasn't watered.

I wanted sherry trifle with raspberries and thick cream.

I wanted . . . I wanted . . . I wanted the screaming in my head to stop and *I wanted Clara*.

I needed to feel her, smell her, taste her.

I needed to stay alive.

Clara, The Haberdashery, Faversham

February 1917

I was worried about Bertie. I hadn't heard from him for almost two weeks. I had read that the government thought the war might be nearly won and that morale amongst the troops was high. I imagined Bertie, keeping his men motivated, getting the fighting done, finding no time to sit and write to me.

I had bought several bars of chocolate. He liked Fry's. I had kissed each bar so that when he bit into it a little bit of me stayed with him. Sounded so silly, but in these awful times, I thought all of us, waiting to hear news that the war was over, would do anything to make the wait bearable.

If he were with me now he would be so proud of our growing baby. I could not fit into any of my old clothes now, but I had made two new loose dresses out of Aunt Philippa's gifts of remnants. She cared for me so well and noticed when I was sad with longing.

I had even started going to church. Every Sunday I prayed urgently to the God I had never believed in to return my Bertie as soon as possible. The vicar told us last Sunday that when we prayed we shouldn't just send the prayers upwards. We should send them sideways and forward and backwards so that the whole congregation could feel our prayers. I must have been very wicked because I only ever prayed up and for Bertie. Nothing and no one else.

Bertie, Agny

March 1917

Clara's parcel of chocolate arrived two days ago. I shared it with the men. One square each. It cheered us all for almost the entire morning.

The enemy appeared to be retreating further, but I didn't trust them. It might have been a plan to draw us into a trap.

We were training hard for God knows what.

Billeted in a ruined village and living in a cellar. We made our recces at night, like blind hedgehogs marching in darkness, falling over jungles of barbed wire, falling into bomb holes, to dig fresh trenches. It felt pointless.

During the day, observer planes flew over, strafing anyone foolish enough to emerge from the cellars for a breath of fresh air or a piss.

Clara, The Haberdashery, Faversham

April 1917

I could hardly move for the baby now. I waddled everywhere.

The doctor was pleased and thought the baby would be here in around four weeks. Since God didn't appear to be listening to me, I sent my prayers now to Bertie's commanding officer. "Let him come home. Please. Our baby is due and I need Second Lieutenant Bertie Bolitho by my side."

I was definitely going to hell for the blasphemy but it was worth it. Maybe I should make a pact with the devil tomorrow.

I had nothing to do but walk the lanes, full of primroses and daffodils now that spring had truly arrived, and rest and wait. I had heartburn and swollen ankles. I had to have Bertie home. I just had to. I couldn't do this on my own.

Bertie, Western Front, France

May 1917

Easter had come and gone with deadly fighting at Vimy Ridge. The Canadians captured it but there had been terrible loss of life. Once again not a single piece of shrapnel nor stray bullet got me. I was beginning to feel invincible. I was meant to survive this and be a loving father and husband.

We were now settled into old dugouts to consolidate. A welcome respite which wouldn't last. Our orders were to be back on the front line in twenty-four hours. This could be the end. The enemy were brave and not afraid to use their weaponry, but they had pushed back so far that we thought they realised we were the better Army.

I would be home soon, never to leave Clara again. I would teach my son how to play football instead of war. Teach him to understand the wonder and fragility of peace and the love and understanding we must give to every human, no matter what nationality or belief.

CHAPTER
FIFTEEN

Clara, Kent

11 May 1917, 8.00 p.m.

I have had an ache in my back all day. I have come to bed and Philippa is making me a hot drink.

"Here you are, my dear." She puts the cocoa by my bed. "Would you like me to rub your back?"

"I would. Thank you." I move onto my left side and immediately feel a great need to go to the lavatory.

She helps me up and takes me to the WC, whereupon, sitting down, a great bloody whoosh of water gushes from me.

"Ah," Philippa responds. "This is exactly what the doctor told me might happen. The waters around your baby have broken, which means that the baby is coming soon."

I begin to cry from fear and call for Bertie.

Bertie, Cavalry Farm, France

11 May 1917, 8.30 p.m.

I am crouched ready with my men to lead a minor operation to capture an advanced enemy trench of about five hundred and fifty yards. We have split into four attacking groups and are ranged equidistant apart in a line facing them. "A" company are far right, "B" company in the centre, "C" company hold back, protecting our line, and I, with "D" company, am on the far left.

The signal is given to move forward and immediately German flares and rockets go up, asking for help from their men.

Clara

8.35 p.m.

Dr Channing is here and I am relieved. He is examining me. "You are doing very well, Mrs Bolitho. Nothing to be concerned about."

He turns to Philippa. "Would you go and get the midwife? I think this baby may be in a hurry to get here."

Philippa gives me a calming nod and disappears.

"What do you mean the baby's in a hurry?" I ask Dr Channing.

He checks his watch and takes my pulse. "You may have your baby in your arms by midnight," he says.

"Oh." I begin to cry again. "I want my husband."

Bertie, Cavalry Farm, France

8.45 p.m.

As the flares go up and light the ground around us, I see how visible we are. Ahead there is a small wall. Partially demolished but it will give us some shelter. I raise my arm for the men to follow me. All of us arrive safely and we huddle closely as enemy gunners put down a heavy barrage which goes over our heads and into our trenches behind. We can hear the enemy ahead shouting. They are certainly surprised.

Clara

9.00 p.m.

The midwife, Mrs Ellery, is here. She has sent Philippa off for towels and hot water. A pain so strong grips my abdomen and I scream.

"There there, Mrs Bolitho," says Mrs Ellery. "Just breathe in and out."

"I want to push," I shout at her.

"No, no, we don't want that at the moment. You are doing very well, dear, just keep breathing."

Bertie

9.15 p.m.

I am looking at my men. I give them their orders.

"When I give the signal, we will sprint to the trench and take it. Clear?"

"Yes sir," they replied as one. I had been listening to the enemy trench ahead and they had grown calmer.

"It sounds as if they were not expecting us to be so close, which is good." I smile to reassure the men who would go anywhere, do anything I order them to do.

I have my gun in my hand, poised to strike. I count in my head five, four, three, two one . . . *Go*."

Clara

9.45 p.m.

"It hurts."

"Hold my hand." Philippa grips me.

Another wave of agonising pain sweeps through me. "Aaaarrrggghhh."

"That's right dear, nice big breaths."

"It's breech." Dr Channing is sweating.

Bertie

9.50 p.m.

We are above the trench and running down its walls, firing as we go. The German soldiers at the bottom of the trench are completely surprised. They have no arms or equipment. Two to the left are running away. In front of us, seven put their hands up in surrender.

180

Clara

10.00 p.m.

"That's a good girl. Keep as still as you can." Mrs Ellery has her hand inside me.

I scream at her, "You are hurting me!"

Bertie

10.12 p.m.

I am looking around for snipers as we take the seven soldiers into our custody.

"Well done, men."

"Thank you, sir."

I hear a rustle to the far left. There are bushes. A blaze of light and the unmistakeable sound of a bullet being released from its chamber. It catches me unawares. I feel a thud in my chest. Another in my leg. I am down in the mud.

Clara

10.35 p.m.

I hear a scream and surprise myself with the noise I can make.

"Push now dear."

"Aarrggh. I am bloody pushing." I am pushing my insides out. The pain is enveloping me to the point that I know there is no returning from it.

"One last push."

I want to sit up and slap Mrs Ellery's pious face and now the pain stops. Something has slithered from me. Dr Channing is picking up a small blue body covered in slime. I am sick.

Bertie

10.36 p.m.

My face is in the mud but I can just about breathe. I can see my men organising themselves into two groups. The larger group to escort our prisoners back to our trenches, and the smaller group, just two of them, to come for me. I can see they think I am dead.

"Lieutenant Bolitho?" one asks.

"Get down. Sniper in the bushes," I whisper.

I'm not sure he has heard me because he repeats what I have just said. "We'd better get down. The sniper must be in those bushes."

"Good men," I whisper.

"Right," says the other, "we'll carry Lieutenant Bolitho back, once we've got the bastard who shot him."

"I can wait," I whispered. "Just do it."

They lie either side of me on their stomachs and turn their guns on the bushes. I can hear them make their guns ready.

"Quick," I urge them.

They fire four rapid shots.

"Got him."

Clara

10.40 p.m.

We have a son. I am staring at him. He is screwing his eyes up and mewing like a kitten. I have done it. The pain is gone. Mrs Ellery is tolerable now.

"Shall I show you how to put him to your breast?"

Gently she guides us, mother and son, and we begin to get the hang of it.

"You're a natural, Mrs Bolitho," smiles Dr Channing, rolling down his sleeves and shrugging on his jacket. "Congratulations."

"Well done." Philippa is smiling down at me. "Cup of tea?"

There is only one thing I want in the whole world right now. My Bertie. I shall write to him first thing.

"Tea would be lovely. Thank you."

Cavalry Farm, France

11 May 1917, 11.00 p.m.

Bertie's rescuers found his body lying in the mud; they lay down either side of him, searching for the sniper who had killed him.

They spoke in whispers. "He's in those bushes there."

"Yeah. I saw it. Let's get the bastard."

They took just four rounds, happy to empty their bullets into the bastard who had killed their officer.

"That's for you, Lieutenant Bolitho."

183

"God bless you, sir."

Second Lieutenant Herbert Bolitho's body was carried back over the expanse of no man's land he had crossed less than two hours before.

Clara

It was Philippa who answered the knock at the door. I was upstairs feeding our little boy.

"Two men," she told me, her voice shaking, "two men in uniform are downstairs. They want to talk to you."

I knew immediately why they were here.

"Very sorry to inform you that . . ."

I screamed.

I saw their mouths moving.

"Killed in action. He was a very brave man, a great soldier. You can be proud of him."

Anger surged through me and I shouted at them, "I have always been proud of him. Did *you* know him? Were *you* there?"

They shuffled a bit and looked uncomfortable. "Unfortunately we didn't get to meet him as we serve in the London office."

"Cowards," I spat again. "Get out. You are not worthy of saying his name."

My baby boy would grow up without a father. I had stories to tell him and a photograph, but that was not much, was it? He was the bastard child of a woman who wasn't even a widow.

184

Philippa tried hard to cheer me with outings and tasty morsels. She began to read books to me in the evening. She helped me find my love for my son when all I wanted to do was die.

And I did love our son. So much. I was on constant alert for danger. I couldn't leave him in the garden in his pram in case a cat sat on him and he suffocated. Or a crow pecked his eyes out. No. I had to be by his side every minute to protect him.

Dr Channing saw me often. "Just keeping an eye on you . . . How are you sleeping? . . You are losing a lot of weight . . . How often do you cry?"

On and on, every week, until I screamed at him to shut up. "Just shut up and leave me with my baby."

He replied calmly. "These feelings can be very overwhelming."

I laughed. "If you really want to know how overwhelming they are, I will tell you. I want to die. I could die today, right now, and have no regrets."

"You would leave your son alone?"

When he said that I burst into uncontrollable tears.

There followed two months in a convalescent home. Once a week Philippa would bring my son to see me.

"I think it is time you gave this little chap a name," she said.

"Is it?"

"Have you thought of any?"

"No."

"Try and think of one for when we come to see you next week."

I knew I didn't want to call him Herbert. There was only one Herbert as far as I was concerned, and no one else in the whole wide world deserved to bear his name.

And then it came to me, almost in a dream. Michael. Michael Carter. A boy with his own name and his own life.

I left the convalescent home feeling that I could, just about, face the world again. Philippa was my strength. A mother to me and Mikey. The summer turned to autumn. Mikey turned from babe in arms to crawling baby. He and I would sit on the grass of Philippa's small garden picking up leaves or examining snails. His pudgy little hands always finding something he'd like to touch and taste. He and I grew stronger together. We were settled, and I was not going to let anything or anybody into my life again.

And that is what I believed, but at the beginning of December the post brought me a letter with a Cornish postmark. I read it several times over the next week and knew what I had to do. I explained it all to Philippa and took her mother's wedding ring off my finger. "Keep this until I get back," I told her.

"Mikey and I will be waiting," she said.

"I will return as soon as I can," I replied. And at that moment that is what I fully expected to do. I had no idea of what would happen next. How my heart would be shredded by yearning and fear. To live in terror of being found out. Of denying all that had been, for the sake of all that was to come. To be a liar.

186

Caroline

Present day

The trunk was inviting me to plunder it. Beneath
the uniform jacket were some shorts and cotton
shirts, spotted with age, which I imagined my
grandfather wore for the tropical heat of Penang. I
lifted those out and beneath them I found some
books. Just cheap paperbacks. A lot of Agatha Christie
and several Dorothy L. Sayers novels. I riffled through
them hoping to find a lost letter or a pressed flower,
but no luck. I turned to each inside page and found
my grandmother's name, Clara Bolitho, neatly
inscribed.

I placed them in two piles on the carpet, and dug
deeper.

A book with a lock I couldn't open. Possibly a diary?
An old Bible and three books of poetry: Yeats,
Masefield and Kipling. I did Yeats for my O levels and
searched the index for any poems I remembered. I saw
another name written inkily on the top right-hand
corner. Herbert Bolitho, 1915.

Herbert? I had never heard of him. A relation clearly,
but of whom? And what had he been doing in Penang
with Grandfather?

In the index I saw the first line of a poem starred in
the same black ink as Herbert's name.

"Lake Isle of Innisfree".

The one I had to learn by heart. I tried to remember
it and spoke aloud:

"I will arise and go now, and go to Innisfree, And a small cabin build there, of clay and wattles made; Nine bean-rows will I have there, a hive for the honey-bee, And live alone in the bee-loud glade."

I was rather pleased with myself. I placed the three books of poems next to the paperbacks and the locked book and picked up the Bible. Not as large as an old family Bible but nonetheless heavy.

I had never been a Bible reader, but I did run my hands over a couple of the papery pages with their dense and tiny print, wondering who the last person had been to do the same. There were no fancy lithograph prints.

I turned back to the first of the inside pages and saw it. A family tree. Going back at least six generations. *My* family tree.

I knew none of the early ones but as I got further down the page I saw the name "Reverend Hugh Bolitho", and next to it "*m*. Louisa Jayson".

My great-great grandfather whose parish was Callyzion.

Underneath them were the names of their children: Herbert, Ernest and Amy.

I knew Ernest was my grandfather, but I had no idea he had siblings. Herbert, the one who liked poetry? Must be. Beside his name was *d. 1917*. Poor man. A casualty of the war. Unmarried and childless.

I was enjoying this now. A little treasure hunt into my past, although I still had no idea why it had come to me and who had sent it.

My grandmother's name, Clara, was beside my grandfather Ernest's, and under them were the names of their children: Edward, Hannah, and David. My mother and her two brothers. My name should be underneath and I was tempted to find a pen and put it there, but before I could, I saw a small edge of paper escaping from the body of the book. Was this the letter that would answer the mystery of why this trunk had come to me? I opened the pages to where the letter had been tucked. There were two letters. One obviously yellowing, addressed to my grandfather in Penang and dated 1948.

PART TWO

CHAPTER
SIXTEEN

Hannah, Trevay, Cornwall

1938

I was hanging out of my mother's bedroom window, drinking in the beautiful Cornish day. The sky above Trevay was bright blue, the seagulls were laughing and playing in the warm breeze, and from where I leant, I could just see the sparkling Atlantic, and a small flotilla of fishing boats, off to their rich hunting grounds, bouncing across the waves. I was Cornish on my father's side and Kentish on my mother's, but I had been born in Penang, Malaysia. A bit of a mongrel, my father told me. "Good," I told him. "Mongrels make the best and most intelligent dogs, so I am happy to be one."

I had finished my morning jobs, and should have been with Mum downstairs, in the shop, but I had been having fun playing with her make-up and taking in the beautiful day.

She called me from downstairs. "Hannah?"

"Yes, Mum?"

"Would you please come down? There are customers who need serving."

"Coming." I quickly wiped her rouge from my cheeks and bounded downstairs.

Mum was standing behind the counter, chatting to two regular customers, Mrs Pengelly and Miss Pritty.

"Is that my rouge?" My mother looked at me, eyebrows raised but not angry.

"Just a little."

"Well, I hope you put it back. You don't need make-up."

"This can never be little Hannah, Mrs Bolitho? asked Mrs Pengelly, a stout woman with a bristly mole on her top lip, who stared at me beadily through her horn-rimmed spectacles. "Look how much she's grown!"

My mother sighed. "Yes indeed."

"She's lovely," said Miss Pritty.

My mother put her hands on her hips and observed me ironically, "Do you think so?"

Miss Pritty reminded me of a fairy-tale princess, preserved like a rose under a glass dome. A faded beauty with greying blonde curls and a delicately crinkled skin.

Mum thought her rather wet.

"Thank you, Miss Pritty," I grinned.

Miss Pritty continued, "I don't know how to cure myself of the desire to come to your shop, Mrs Bolitho. The sight and smell of it all continually thrills me."

The walls were lined with bolts of the finest silks and cottons, all in jewelled colours or bold patterns. Mum's shop, "Clara Bolitho Silks", was her emporium. She imported them from Malaya where I was born.

I had grown up loving everything bright and colourful. To me the Far East was a magical place and I imagined I would miss it.

I had left Penang for England when I was five and, in my blurred memories, I still saw palm trees, still felt the sun on my cheeks, still remembered the perfume of warm air after rain.

My father, Ernest Bolitho MBE, remained in Penang. He owned a rubber plantation and worked for the Malayan Civil Service.

"Buttons," said Miss Pritty. "To match this chiffon." She lovingly ran her fingers over a new roll of soft lilac fabric. "Isn't it pretty?"

"One of my newest favourites," my mother affirmed. "Pure silk."

"How many buttons do you need?" I asked, already looking for something suitable in one of the two glass-fronted, glasstopped counters. Beneath were rows of open wooden drawers, with hundreds of buttons, ribbons, lace and embroidery threads.

Miss Pritty placed her nose close to the glass, looking for the perfect thing.

"The pattern suggests small and round. Six of them," she said. Then she pointed, "Ooh. Those could be just the thing."

My mother took over. "They arrived yesterday from Singapore. Silk-covered and as light as a feather. Perfect for the chiffon."

Mrs Pengelly, who had been ignored throughout this, tutted. "I was here first, Mrs Bolitho."

Mum was unfazed. "Hannah will assist you."

Mum knew I liked Miss Pritty better, but I knew Mum liked to convince customers to spend more than their budget, and Miss Pritty was fair game.

"Mrs Pengelly," I smiled, "how can I help you? We have some very fine gloves."

I worked in Mum's shop every Saturday while my older brother, Edward, played rugby and my younger brother, David, played cricket.

Edward and I had been the first to come to England from Penang. Our father had decided we would be safer in Cornwall due to the political unrest in Malaya. I had been five and Edward nine. Our parents had brought us over on the ship, promising us a glorious holiday with our grandparents in Cornwall. They had not told Edward and me that they were leaving us in Callyzion while they returned to Penang without us. So, when they left, waving goodbye from their taxi, my father calling "See you soon", I had no reason to be concerned. I spent the next week with my face stuck to the front window, expecting them to reappear. I didn't see my mother for seven years. I didn't see my father for many, many more.

Life at my grandparents' home was not what either Edward or I were used to. For a start, our English was not very fluent. Because my father's work was highly confidential, the only time my parents spoke English was to each other, in private. Our parents spoke only

Malay in front of us and the staff to ensure the staff didn't learn any English.

You can imagine the difficulty we had in understanding and being understood when we got to Cornwall. At school in particular. We were singled out as savages for leaving our shoes outside and walking indoors in bare feet, something that was expected of us back home. We were labelled disobedient.

Our favourite time of each day was when Grandfather came home from the church. He was kind to us and always had a toffee in his pocket or time to share his big armchair with the two of us as we chatted in pidgin English or drew communicative pictures together.

Grandmother was kind, too, but suffered from her nerves. I had no idea what that was but it meant we had to be quiet around the house and not disturb her frequent naps.

Dora, the maid, was a sweetheart. Always ready to have a game of draughts with us or play a game of hide and seek. Cook was always telling her off because she spent more time with us than at her chores, but we soon found that Cook was all bark and no bite.

She taught us to bake jam tarts and sponge cakes, buttered eggs and baked potatoes, and when Edward and I told her how much we missed eating curry, she looked out a recipe and made us kedgeree for breakfast.

Aunt Amy was the one person we both avoided. She didn't like children, especially ones like us. We loved to snoop around her bedroom when she was out. Our secret raids into her lair had gone unnoticed for so long that we thought she would never catch us, but one dull and rainy afternoon, just as we were under her bed about to read through a box of envelopes addressed to her and signed by someone called Peter, she came in. Edward, being tall for his age, didn't manage to get one of his feet under the bed quickly enough before she spotted him. Immediately her bony fingers swooped down like an eagle's claw and pulled him out, burning his cheek on the rough carpet.

The scariest thing about Aunt Amy was that she never raised her voice. Quiet menace was her chosen weapon.

"What do you think you are doing under my bed?" she hissed.

"Nothing." Edward got to his feet.

"Don't lie to me, you little savage. What did you find under my bed?"

"I didn't find anything," he continued bravely.

From my viewpoint, still under the bed, I could see her narrow black boots tapping on the rug. "Where is that little sister of yours? If the brat is under the bed right now . . ."

I had no time to move. I saw her bend down and whip up the edges of the candlewick bedspread. Her furious eyes blazed into me. "Come out now, or you will be very sorry indeed." I could see spittle on her lip.

"Yes, Aunt Amy." I crawled out and stood next to Edward, who felt for my hand. I still had one of Aunt Amy's letters in it.

When she saw it, her scalp twitched and I swear I saw flames in her eyes. She advanced towards me and lifted her hand. I squeezed my eyes shut, terrified of the smack that was coming to me. And as it did, I wet myself.

My cheek stung from the slap and my humiliation.

"Give me that letter." She was an inch from my face and had not noticed my disgrace.

I gave her the letter.

My knickers and socks were warm and wet. There was a puddle building on the rug. "I'm so sorry," I whimpered.

"Did you read this?" She held the letter against my face. "Did you read my personal letters?"

"No," Edward said stoutly. "Neither of us did."

She took her eyes from me and stepped towards him. She was poised ready to swipe him too when her black boots gave a little squelch. She stopped and looked down. She was standing in my pee.

Edward took advantage of her rigid horror and took my hand shouting, *"Run!"*

Grandfather gave us a very serious telling-off and we were sent to bed without supper. To upset Aunt Amy was one thing, but to upset Grandfather was much worse. He was the adult we respected and loved. He was everything to us, and to have him say how disappointed he was hurt more than twenty lashes of the school's cane.

We never disappointed him again.

As we grew older our lives became more regimented. As soon as we arrived, Edward had been made to go to church every morning before school, and by the time I was ten, I was joining him. On Sundays we had to go twice. Morning and evening. We also had to write weekly letters to our parents.

As time went on, Grandmother was becoming weaker. Eventually she stopped coming downstairs altogether. She began to express her need to see us confirmed in the church. She insisted that our confirmation classes should be held at her bedside so that she could listen to Grandfather's weekly teaching and join in the prayers for our salvation.

We had never been allowed into her bedroom before this, and I must admit my mind often wandered as I knelt by her bed and managed, through half-closed eyes, to squint around her room.

It wasn't a glamorous room but it was feminine. On her tidy wooden dressing table there was a small crucifix, a silverbacked hairbrush, a hand mirror, and a painted vase always holding a fresh spray of simple flowers. There was also a sepia photograph of my father in army uniform. I longed to get closer to it. To pick it up and stroke the face I missed so much. But the fear of going near anyone's private property had been powerfully instilled in me.

Our confirmation became a huge topic of conversation in the vicarage. Cook and Dora fussed about what we'd wear. Grandmother and Grandfather presented us with our own small prayer book, but Aunt Amy just sniffed. One night, as she came to see we were tucked in bed, she told us that we were not good enough for God. "The devil wants you for his own," she said, before turning the light out and leaving us in darkness.

"Silly bitch," Edward whispered once she'd shut the door.

"Edward." I gasped with shock. "That word is very, very bad."

"If the devil exists, which I don't believe, it's her."

"But Edward, if the devil doesn't exist, then God doesn't either. It's all part of the same story."

Edward lay staring at the ceiling. "I don't believe in God either."

"What? But that is what we must believe to be confirmed." I was scared and tears began to form. "Oh Edward. You might go to hell and I'll never see you again because I will be in heaven." I wiped my eyes on the sheet and placed my hands together. "I am going to pray for you to be saved."

"Don't bother," he grumped, and turned over so that I couldn't see his face.

The Bishop of Gloucester was to officiate and there was to be a good turnout of parish children who were also willing to renew the promises to God that had been made for them at their baptism as babies.

But with a week to go before the big day, Grandmother took a turn for the worse. The doctor said she had had a stroke. I thought that sounded rather lovely. There was a cat next door who loved being stroked and I liked having my hair stroked by Dora, but this stroke had made our grandmother fall into a deep sleep.

Edward and I were sent to bed early that night, and once our lights had gone out and our door closed, I heard Aunt Amy crying on the landing.

"She's never going to wake up, is she?"

My grandfather was with her. "Hush, my dear. Your mother must rest. We must not upset her. If it's God's will she recovers, we shall thank him. If she leaves us she will be with our dear Bertie and we will be thankful."

I lay in the dark and pondered this. "Edward?" I whispered. "Edward."

"What?" He turned over and looked at me over the space of floor between us.

"Have you heard of anyone called Bertie?"

Edward yawned. "No. Go to sleep."

Grandmother died two days later. The news was broken to us the next morning by Grandfather in his study. I didn't know whether to cry or not. I didn't feel the need to cry, so I said nothing but tried to look sad. Grandfather looked very tired but he tried to be cheerful.

"Cook is making you breakfast in the kitchen today as I have things to see to," he said.

The kitchen was fine by us. It was always a treat to sit by the warmth of Cook's range.

"Come on, you two. I'm making pancakes and I have some sausages too."

"Is Grandmother still in the house?" I asked Cook.

"Now now, let's talk of happier things, shall we?"

"What happens to her?" I really did want to know. "Does God take her straight away to heaven?"

Edward tutted. "Her spirit goes to heaven. But her body has to be buried."

"Oh! Is she buried already?"

"Not yet, Hannah." Dora was red-eyed and snuffling. "They have to lay her out and we can pay our respects and then she's buried in a few days."

"Oh." I thought about this for a moment. "What does 'lay out' mean?"

"That's enough of that. Have another sausage."

Aunt Amy came in. She looked very grey and thinner than ever. To my surprise, Cook went and gave her a hug. "My poor Miss Amy. You have done all you can. No mother could have had a better daughter." Edward and I looked at each other in amazement.

Amy burst into tears and Cook rocked her gently saying, "There, there. You've had so much loss."

"I will miss Mama so much," Amy croaked. "I thought my heart was broken after Peter but this," she gulped, "this is unendurable."

"But you will endure it." Cook patted Amy's back softly. "You will be strong, just as your mother was after poor Mr Bertie."

That name again. My ears pricked up. "Who is Mr Bertie?" I asked.

Aunt Amy pushed Cook away and wheeled around in fury. "How long have you been there? Listening in on other people's conversations now, are you?"

Cook moved quickly to shield me. "Hannah and Edward are having their breakfast in here for a change."

"Well, breakfast is over." She stretched a thin arm out and pointed a bony finger at the door. "Go to your grandfather's study and wait until I call you." Aunt Amy was shaking.

Edward stood up immediately. He was always more obedient than me. "Come on, Hannah."

As we walked to the study, Dora was letting four men through the front door. Sombrely dressed, their heads bowed, they passed us in the hall and followed Dora upstairs.

Edward shushed me into the study and closed the door, but I put my ear to it and listened.

"Come away," he said to me.

"I just want to know what's going on," I replied, cross that he should try to boss me about. But I did come away and we both sat. Me in the chair by the empty grate. Edward in Grandfather's chair behind his desk.

We sat like that for a long time until I heard four sets of plodding feet, walking in rhythm, coming down the stairs and heading slowly for the parlour.

"It's those men," I whispered. "I think they've come from Grandmother's room." I put my hand on the door handle. "Shall we go and see what's happening?"

"No." My brother gave me a look of dread. "I think they've put Grandmother in there."

I was puzzled. "Do you mean they have carried her downstairs to sit by the parlour fire? Have they made a mistake and she's got better?"

He rolled his eyes dramatically. "No, you idiot. They have brought her down in her coffin to stay in the parlour until her burial."

"Oh." A dead body in the room next to us was a sobering thought. "Well, at least she'll be warm when the fire's lit."

"Are you a complete fool?" Edward sighed. "They'll keep the room cold or else her body will rot and the flies will come into the house and then probably rats."

I covered my ears with my hands. "Stop it. You are scaring me," I shouted at him.

My grandfather entered looking very sad. "Why are you scaring your sister, Edward?"

"I wasn't, sir."

Grandfather looked from me to Edward and back again. "Hannah, there is nothing to be scared of. Grandmother loved you very much and will never scare you." He held his hand out. "Come. I will show you. She looks as if she is just sleeping. Come and say goodbye."

"Is Edward coming?" I asked. My knees had begun to knock.

"He certainly is." He looked at Edward and held out his other hand, "Aren't you, my boy."

The parlour was where we had Christmas games and birthday parties and warm crackling winter fires, but now it was cold, dark and heavy with the smell of candle wax. As my eyes grew accustomed to the gloom, I could make out a dark wooden box, the length and width of Grandmother, set upon the best table.

Aunt Amy was sitting at one end, whispering a prayer. As we arrived she finished and beckoned Edward and me to join her. I had a sick feeling in my tummy and I wanted to run out of the house and into the fresh clean air of the garden, but Grandfather had his hand on my shoulder.

"Come closer, both of you," said Aunt Amy. "Your grandmother would like you to say goodbye to her. You must thank her for all she's done for you."

I couldn't lift my eyes from the floor. I knew I would see the flies and rats. "Do I have to?" I asked in a tremulous voice.

Edward came to stand next to me. "Let's do it together. Ready?"

I took a deep breath and nodded.

"OK." He steadied himself. "Now."

We gripped each other's hands and peeked inside the box. Grandmother was tinged yellow but looked very much asleep. There were no flies or rats. She wasn't twitching and her eyes were closed, and I could tell she wasn't there any more. She had gone.

Bravely I allowed myself to look along the full length of her. She was wearing a cream lace dress which covered her feet. Her sleeves were buttoned to the wrist and her hands were folded comfortably on her chest where she held the sepia photo of Father in his army uniform.

"Is Father going to be buried with her too?" I asked Grandfather.

"No, child. He is in Penang with your mother. What makes you say that?"

"The photo of him, that Grandmother is holding?"

"Bless you, Hannah. That is not your father, that is your father's brother. Bertie. He was killed in the Great War."

"Our uncle?" asked Edward.

"Where is he buried?" I asked.

"In France, where he died," said Grandfather.

"Why wasn't he buried here, in your churchyard?"

Aunt Amy spoke. "Soldiers who die on the battlefield are buried where they fell. But at least he has a grave. And a headstone." She stood up, her mouth working hard to get her words past her tears. "Peter hasn't. My Peter. Who stepped on a mine, which blew him into tiny millions of pieces that were trodden into the mud by his comrades, who had to forget all about him and carry on killing the enemy. He has no headstone." With a sob, she ran to the door, Grandfather following.

Edward and I were left with Grandmother.

"You asked too many questions," Edward said, then added admiringly, "but they were good ones."

"Why has no one ever told us about Uncle Bertie? Did you know about him?" I asked.

"Nope. All the grown-ups have been keeping it a secret because they didn't want to upset us, I suppose."

"Oh yes." It made sense to my child's mind. "Shall we sing Grandmother a song to make her happy?"

"OK."

And that's how Grandfather found us. Singing "It's a Long Way to Tipperary", which Edward and I agreed seemed the most appropriate.

CHAPTER
SEVENTEEN

Hannah, Callyzion

Spring 1936

Aunt Amy had been suffering from her nerves. I supposed she got it from Grandmother. She didn't live in the vicarage any longer. She had moved to a convent where Cook said the nuns were very kind to her. I had to say the house was a happier place without her.

Grandfather had been very sad and his knees had been hurting; he used a stick to walk now but Edward and I did all we could to look after him. I helped Cook and Dora with the house. Edward was sixteen now and had taken charge of the garden. Last winter he had planted lots of daffodils and now it was spring he had been mowing the grass and fixing Grandfather's old swing. The other day the sun was so warm and the daffodils so pretty that I set up a tea table under the apple tree as a surprise for when Grandfather came home. I even made a Victoria sponge. It drooped a bit in the middle but Cook shook some icing sugar on the top and said it looked pretty good.

Grandfather said he enjoyed it but that the garden was a bit too cold for his knees, so after a cup of tea we all trooped back into his study. We rarely used the parlour any more.

On the morning of my twelfth birthday, a Saturday, so no school, the postman knocked, as he always did, and I ran down the stairs to greet him, as I rarely did.

He wished me a Happy Birthday and handed me a bundle of post. Most of it was for Grandfather but I could see several birthday cards addressed to me and a letter addressed to Edward and me with a Penang stamp.

"Edward," I called up the stairs. "Ed! There's a letter from Mummy and Daddy for us."

We now had separate bedrooms. I was still in our old room, which I liked because it had a view of the apple tree, while Edward had been given the room which looked out over the church.

"Coming," he shouted down.

I bounced into the kitchen which had become the hub of the house. Dora and Cook burst into "Happy Birthday", and Grandfather, sitting in a rocker by the range, joined in.

"Thank you." I kissed them all and handed Grandfather his post. "Mummy and Daddy have written to us." I sat down and waited for Edward before reading it out loud. The whole household of five of us loved to hear news from Penang and the funny jokes that our parents added.

Edward clattered in and sat at the table. "Morning Grandfather, Cook, Dora."

"Good morning, Edward," they chanted.

"Where's the letter from home?" he asked me, reaching to check the envelopes in front of me.

"Uh-uh," I said, pulling them out of his reach. "Not before you wish me a Happy Birthday."

He looked horrified and put his hand over his mouth. "Oh no. Is it today?"

I gave him such a glare. "How could you forget?"

He smiled. "Wait. Hang on. What's this in my pocket?"

He pulled out a small white box tied with a piece of blue ribbon. "Happy Birthday, Hannah."

"It's from all of us. Me, Cook and Edward," Dora grinned.

Cook began laughing so much she threw her apron over her head, which made us all laugh as well. I undid the blue ribbon and opened the box. Inside was a small silver cross on a fine silver chain.

Edward said shyly, "We thought you'd like it now you are confirmed."

"Two years late." I looked at him fondly as I put it around my neck.

"Things like that are never too late," said Grandfather, reaching into the inside pocket of his jacket. "And this is from me."

He opened his hand. "It was your grandmother's."

In his palm lay a dainty gold band clasping a pearl and a small diamond. I held my hands to my chest. "Is it really for me?"

"It is. Try it on," he said.

I slipped it onto the middle finger of my right hand. "Are they real?"

"Oh yes. Does it fit?" Grandfather asked.

I felt the tears in my eyes. "It fits perfectly."

"Good."

Dora, a true romantic, sighed, "Like Cinderella's slipper." Which made me laugh. I got up and hugged Grandfather tight. "Thank you."

"It has been handed down to the first daughter through the generations, and you are next. Keep it safe."

"I will."

Cook wiped her nose on her apron and said, "Who wants some fried bread?"

I forgot about my birthday cards and the letter from Penang until later when Dora brought them to me in the study. "You left these on the table. I found them pushed under your plate."

"I'll keep the letter from Mummy and Daddy until Grandfather gets home."

"That would be nice." Dora smiled. "You know how Cook and I love to hear their news."

My birthday cards were from friends at school and two of the old ladies from the church. I put them all on the bookcase for Grandfather to see later. My parents' letter was the real present. I smoothed the envelope and examined the stamp and even sniffed at it in the hope that Mummy might have left some trace of her perfume on it. I was longing to open it but I had to wait until Grandfather got home at four o'clock. Another five hours to wait.

I spent the day tidying the meagre belongings in my room and admiring my ring. Holding my hand this way and that so that it sparkled as it caught the light. Then I remembered the necklace, my first, and spent at least an hour trying to put my hair up in a bun like Mummy's so that I could better see how it sat and showed off my neck.

By early afternoon I was bored and, after skipping around the garden and playing on the old swing, I went to the kitchen to see Cook.

"Out!" she said, putting her foot in the door to stop me going further. "There's nothing for you to see in here until teatime."

I sniffed the warmth coming from behind her where she blocked my view. "Did you bake me a birthday cake?"

"That's for me to know and you to find out!" she said smartly, and closed the door on me.

I laughed excitedly and jumped up the stairs from the kitchen to the hall, clapping my hands and singing a happy little tune. Edward would be back from Saturday rugby soon and then we'd have my tea party.

I went into the study and read my birthday cards again, then felt the letter from Penang in my pocket. Any minute now, we would all be in the house and I could open it.

Grandfather and Edward finally came home but made me wait even longer as they got themselves washed up and ready. But, at last, I was called to the kitchen where they had all assembled. I walked in with my eyes closed as ordered. I could hear the scrape of chairs being pulled out and starched aprons being smoothed, stifled giggling and whispers.

"When I count to three," Edward said, "you can open them. Ready?"

I nodded furiously.

"OK. One. Two . . . Wait for it . . . three!"

I opened my eyes and saw the kitchen table covered in treats. Triangles of bread and butter, cheese, ham, boiled tongue and, my favourites, tiny sausage rolls. And in the centre a big birthday cake iced with my name and twelve candles aflame on top.

"Happy Birthday to you," they sang to me.

This had happened every year since we had come to live here; each year it filled me with a mixture of happiness and the feeling of being loved, and the hollowness of missing my parents.

"Come on then," said Grandfather. "Blow those candles out before they burn the house down."

I took a deep breath and took them out in one blow to a round of applause.

And then the feast began. Cook's sausage rolls were delicious and I fought Edward for the lion's share.

"I'm hungry," he wailed. "I've played rugby all day. What have you done?"

"I have been waiting. And waiting makes one very hungry indeed," I replied, collecting up another two.

"Leave some room for the cake, young lady," Cook scolded gently.

"Yes," said Dora, "I had to beat and beat that butter and cream to make it extra light. Look at my muscles." She held her arms up, strong-man style, and Edward

213

said, "That's nothing, feel mine." And then we all started to laugh.

It was so much fun that I again forgot about the letter sitting in my pocket. It was Grandfather who reminded me.

Wiping my sticky fingers on my napkin, I carefully opened the envelope.

I cleared my throat, unfolded the pages inside and began to read aloud. It was dated six weeks earlier.

Dear Edward and Hannah,

I hope this letter gets to you before your birthday, Hannah. And we are very sorry not to be with you. Daddy sends you all his love. He is very busy with the rubber trees and also at work.

You'll never believe it but we have had a plague of frogs on the plantation and I have been out with the workers catching them and collecting them in buckets. Some of them are very big and they are so quick, jumping so high and far. We don't know why there are so many or where they have come from, but they seem to have brought the snakes with them. Sadly one of the plantation stray dogs was bitten by one. A very dangerous cobra. You remember me telling you about the little family of monkeys that I have adopted? Well, Mrs Monkey fought the cobra off and almost saved the dog, but it was too late. It wasn't all sad, though, because that dog had had three puppies who were ready to leave her anyway, so now I am training them to live with us. They are so sweet and clever. Two boys and one girl. I have called them Flopsy, Mopsy and Cottontail. Flopsy is black, Mopsy is black with a white blaze and Cottontail (the little girl) is golden. Even Daddy likes them!

How are Grandfather, Cook and Dora? Be sure to send them my love and tell Cook I am missing her good cooking. Are Grandfather's knees feeling any better? Daddy uses Tiger Balm for his aches and pains. It's a kind of ointment that seems to cure everything.

Our house boy, Ngai, does his best and is very good at curries, but the mystery of a good roast and Yorkshire pudding is still unsolved by him. I dug out a recipe for pasties for Daddy's birthday, but Ngai managed to produce something between a scone and a savoury Eccles cake.

How is school for you both? Edward, I am so glad to hear you are doing well in all your subjects. Daddy says that you should be a doctor because your grades for maths and sciences are so high. He is also very proud that you have made the school first XI rugger team.

Hannah, your last report was very promising indeed. Have you managed to stop talking and start concentrating more?

Now, I have some very big news! I am coming home! And not just for a visit. I am coming back to live in Cornwall. Daddy can't come because he has to help with the government here, but — and this is the big surprise — I shall not be travelling alone! I am bringing a special person with me. A small person who is very keen to meet you!

As soon as our travel arrangements are confirmed, I shall telegram Grandfather to let you know the date.

All my love,
Mummy x

"Oh my gosh!" I jumped up and showed the letter to Edward. "She's coming home!" I danced a little jig on the spot while my brother read the letter for himself.

I was full of questions. "Who is she bringing with her? Could it be the puppies? The monkey? All of them? This is the best birthday ever!"

CHAPTER
EIGHTEEN

Hannah, Callyzion

Late summer 1936

Mummy's train was due into Bodmin Road station at teatime. Edward and I loved our rare trips out of Callyzion, and the station was always a favourite destination. Once, we actually got on a train and went to Plymouth, crossing the big iron bridge that Edward was fascinated by. I looked down at the sparkling river far below and the naval boats tethered at anchor and the small yachts sailing along like breezy toys. Grandfather had hired a taxi that had two rows of seats behind the driver, giving us plenty of room for Mummy, her surprise visitor and their luggage.

I had been longing for this day ever since my birthday but, now that it was here, I was filled with anxiety. Would she recognise me? Would I recognise her? Would she still love me as much as she ever did? I dreamt that I had pushed my way through the crowds to find her, and I introduced myself just in case she didn't know it was me. It would save her embarrassment. Then I'd introduce her to Edward and all would be well. Would I be allowed to hug her now that I was twelve? Did parents hug a child over the age of five? I would take her lead. If she wanted to put her arms around me then I would do the same. I talked to Edward about it. I think he had missed Mummy even more than me; after all, he had been nine when she left us to return to Penang with Daddy. He had loved her for four years longer than me.

"Edward?" I had asked that morning in his room.

"What?"

"Do you think you will have to shake hands with Mummy at the station? Now that you are almost grown up? I mean, you are sixteen now."

Sixteen and over six foot tall. He towered over Grandfather now.

"I shall shake her hand, kiss her on the cheek and carry her bag to the taxi," Edward said. It only occurred to me years later that he must have thought hard about his plan.

On the day itself I looked at myself in the long mirror inside his wardrobe door. I had on a red checked summer dress, socks and sandals. My long hair was in neat plaits done by Dora. "Do you think she'll see me?" I asked Edward. "I shall stand in front of her and see if she wants to kiss me."

The platform was shimmering in the afternoon heat. The station looked so pretty. There were flowerbeds edged with railway sleepers, overflowing with pink roses, scarlet geraniums, and saffron marigolds bordered with little tufts of blue and white flowers. I skipped up and down the empty platform, humming to myself and burning off the nervous energy that was building in my stomach.

When I hopped past Edward, he put out a restraining arm. "Stop it."

"Why?"

"You are too noisy for Grandfather."

Grandfather was sitting in the shade on a bench beneath the black and white signal box. He must have been very hot in his trousers, waistcoat and jacket. He had at least taken his hat off and was blotting his brow with his handkerchief.

"Sorry," I said, going to sit next to him.

He winked at me. "I don't know where you get your energy from."

The stationmaster came out of his office holding his flag and whistle.

Grandfather looked at the big station clock above us. "Train should be here any minute. If you listen quietly, you'll hear the tracks singing before it arrives."

This was the magic of trains. Edward came and joined us on the bench and we all listened. I heard it first but Edward said he had. Grandfather didn't hear it until the train appeared around the corner and was coming down the track.

Nothing more was said until the huge engine broke the peace of the afternoon, thundering slowly, hissing and squealing its way to a stop.

As steam and smoke billowed around us, we could hear doors being opened and voices calling. The stationmaster and two porters who had appeared began to help the passengers and their luggage out of the carriages. The platform was now a noisy crowd of people giving orders and identifying bags.

I tugged my grandfather's arm, "Can I go and look for Mummy?"

"We shall stay here." He touched my shoulder. "She will find us."

A sense of shyness hit me. I took Edward's arm and half buried my face in his sleeve. "What are you doing? Get off me." He shook me off.

Grandfather shakily got to his feet. "I think I see her," he said.

Edward and I stood too. I saw he was clenching his jaw. His teeth seemed locked together.

I put my eyes down and squeezed them shut briefly. "Please God, let her like us."

"Hello!" A half-remembered voice was calling to us. I opened my eyes.

"Mummy!" I ran to her and into her open arms.

"You've grown, darling." She hugged me tightly. Over my shoulder she must have seen Edward. Not letting me go she opened her right hand and hauled him into her embrace. "My boy, my boy. How I have missed you both."

I stood like that for a few more seconds until she saw Grandfather.

"Hugh, dear." She stepped towards him and kissed his cheek. "Thank you for coming."

He returned the kiss. "Good to see you back home, Clara."

"Ernest sends his regards. He is so sorry he couldn't get home this time."

"He's busy, I know. The world is a precarious place."
He sighed. "But at least you are home and safe."

Mummy touched his arm with fondness and then
quickly looked behind her. "Oh, my goodness! David,
come and meet your family." A skinny boy with tanned
skin and very dark eyes stepped forward. He looked
very scared. "David, this is your grandfather, and
Hannah is your sister and Edward is your brother. Say
hello."

His bottom lip quivered and tears welled in his eyes
but, to my eternal respect, he held out his tiny hand
and said, "Hello. I'm David."

We each shook hands with him, not knowing what to
say. I was brimming with questions but Edward held
me back with a silent look.

Grandfather called a porter over and Mummy's
luggage was transported out of the station, with
Mummy holding David's hand, Grandfather next to
her and Edward and me bringing up the rear.

In the taxi, Mummy insisted that David sit in
between Edward and me on the back seat so that we
could get to know each other.

I began to chatter nervously. I told him about our
school, and the beach nearby which we didn't go to
very often because we had jobs to do in the house and
church and homework. I told him that Edward was in
his last year at school and was going to be a doctor.
David listened to this with his huge brown eyes but said
nothing.

Edward had been silent all this time. He told me
later that he had been working over in his mind why

Mummy and Daddy hadn't told us about David before. It had shocked him and also, he slowly admitted, made him feel resentful that this small boy had had our mother to himself all these years while we hadn't. However, during the taxi ride he managed to push all of that to one side with one huge mental shove, and show David his one magic trick. He took a penny, and his handkerchief, from his pocket, wrapped the coin in the hanky, blew on it, said some magic words, unwrapped the hanky and the coin had disappeared. I never knew how it was done and was incredibly proud of Edward for doing it. My friends all loved it too, which gave me an increased layer of respect for him.

When he did it for David, I clapped and smiled. David smiled shyly.

When we got home, David was handed to Dora with instructions to look after him while the rest of the family caught up with all our news. I was delighted because now I could have Mummy to myself. To be honest, I didn't like David much. His face was sallow and moody and I didn't like the way he clung to my mother and hid his face in her skirts.

Cook had decided to serve a grand tea in the newly aired parlour.

Mummy stopped in the hall to hang her coat and parasol on the stand. I took her hand and said, "This way, Mummy."

"I know the way, darling." She smiled at me but I saw her falter slightly at the doorway as her eyes swept the room. "Nothing has changed," she said almost to herself.

I was delighted to see that the table was groaning with small sandwiches, bread and butter, scones, a fruitcake and a Victoria sponge. I headed for one of the ancient, uncomfortable sofas. "Mummy, you sit here and I'll sit next to you." Again, I sensed a reluctance in her to join me, but as Edward and Grandfather were settling themselves on the opposite sofa, she had no choice but to take the seat nearest the empty fireplace.

Grandfather opened the conversation. "How was the ship?"

"It was a banana boat actually." She looked down at her hands and laced them. "Much less expensive than the scheduled passages. I played a lot of bridge."

"Did you? Any luck?" replied Grandfather.

Mummy smiled. "Yes, actually. Enough to pay for the little extras."

Grandfather smiled. "Well done. And how about David? How did he find life on board ship?"

She smiled fondly. "He suffered a little from seasickness but the crew were very sweet to him. By the time we got to the Bay of Biscay, he had truly found his sea legs."

I was getting sick of all this attention on David. I tugged Mummy's arm.

"Were Edward and I good sailors when you and Daddy brought us to England?" I asked.

Mummy put her hand on mine. "You were both very good indeed."

"I remember it being rather rough at times," said Edward. "I think I was sick."

Mummy laughed. "A bit, yes, but you got better quickly. And now look at you! As tall as Daddy nearly. How is the rugger going?"

"Not too bad." Edward was very good at rugby but he always liked to play it down whereas I liked to play my achievements up.

Grandfather said, "He's being modest. He's very good. Last weekend he scored two of the winning tries."

Edward beamed shyly. "Team game," he said.

Rugby bored me, I wanted to know more about David, my rival to Mummy's affection. "How old is David?" I asked Mummy.

"Five."

I remembered being five. It was when I'd left Penang and Mummy and Daddy had gone back without me. I felt the first stirrings of jealousy.

"Why didn't you tell us we had a little brother?"

"Well, I —"

Grandfather interrupted. "I think your mother might be hungry. Hannah, why don't you tell Cook we are ready for a nice cup of tea and then we can make a start on her wonderful feast. Eat this up and she won't have to make you any supper before bed, will she."

Unwillingly I left the room.

A sullen David joined us for cake and sandwiches. He still hadn't spoken to me but did look a little happier having spent some time with Dora.

"And has he been a good boy?" Mummy asked her as she pulled David onto her lap.

224

"Yes, Mrs Bolitho. Very good indeed," said Dora. "He liked the old swing. We even had a smile." She directed the last bit to David who buried his face in Mummy's neck.

"Gosh." Mummy turned to the window looking onto the garden with a sad look in her eye. "The swing under the apple tree? Is it still there?"

"It nearly wasn't but I fixed it," Edward told her. "Grandfather made it when Dad was a boy. Did you know that Dad had a brother called Bertie?" Edward added. "His real name was Herbert and he died fighting the First World War."

Mummy stopped stroking David's hair and looked, to me anyway, as if she hadn't really heard what Edward had just said.

Grandfather replied. "Yes, indeed, your mother did know Bertie. They were friends. It is how she met your father."

My eyes widened in excitement. "How lovely. What was he like, Mummy? Did he look like Daddy?"

"Yes," she said slowly. "Very similar. When I first saw Daddy it was in this room, and I thought he was Bertie."

I laughed. "Oh, that's funny. They could have played a trick on you and pretended to be each other! You might have married the wrong one!"

"Yes. I might have."

"Oh my word, look at the time," exclaimed Grandfather. "Would you like to see your room, Clara? Dora has put you in Louisa's old room with a little bed next to it for David."

"That's very kind of you. David is tired." She got up, still carrying David, who was indeed looking very sleepy.

"Can I help you put David to bed?" I asked, jumping up. I was going to make Mummy love me more than David by being the helpful child.

"No, no darling. You stay here. I won't be long."

I sat down and waited. Edward and Grandfather were talking together and barely noticed me, so I got up again and walked around the room, running my hands over the familiar books and ornaments. I had an idea, I would count how many times I could go round the room before Mummy came back, without David.

On my sixth lap, Dora returned. "Mrs Bolitho sends her apologies. The journey was rather tiring and she is having an early night."

"Quite understood," said Grandfather.

I was heartbroken. "Can I go and kiss her goodnight?"

Grandfather saw how close I was to tears and distracted me. "You can have the whole day with her tomorrow. Why don't you and I have a game of Scrabble before you go to bed, eh?" He always knew how to make things better.

I couldn't wait to get down for breakfast the next morning. I cleaned my teeth and, as the weather was so warm, I chose to wear my shorts and a white broderie-anglaise cotton blouse. My legs and feet were bare.

In the kitchen, Cook was spooning kedgeree out of a pan and into a special dish I hadn't seen for a long time.

226

"Shall I lay the table?" I asked her.

"Dora is laying the table in the parlour."

"But we always have breakfast in the kitchen."

"Not today." She passed me a milk jug and sugar bowl. "Take these in to her, would you?"

Dora had made the table look so pretty. The best china and cutlery were laid out with the best napkins.

"That looks lovely, Dora."

"Thank you. Would you like to pick some special flowers for the centre?"

"Yes, please!" I skipped off out into the garden, thrilled to be given such an important job. I walked all around the small flowerbeds, taking my time to decide on what Mummy would like. In the end I picked some yellow-scented roses with lavender and some mint. In the kitchen, Cook helped me choose one of Grandmother's silver vases. It was just right.

Carrying it carefully, I met Grandfather and Edward coming down the stairs. "Is Mummy up yet?" I asked.

"She's on her way." Grandfather shooed me towards the parlour.

As I put the vase on the table I heard her.

"Good morning everyone."

She was wearing a grey dress with a pleated skirt and a white collar. She had a cardigan over her shoulders and wore thick stockings. She looked me up and down. "Aren't you cold in those shorts?"

"Oh no. It's going to be a hot day," I told her.

She pulled her cardigan closer to her. "Maybe my blood has been thinned by the tropics."

David clung to her side. "I'm cold," he said.

I was confused. "But it's summer."

Mummy took David's small hands and rubbed them. "Feels like winter."

"Does it?"

She looked at me kindly. "You don't remember the hot summers of Penang, do you?"

"No," I said, with a jab of resentment. "I suppose I don't."

She turned her gaze to Edward who kissed her cheek. "Morning, Mother."

"Good morning, Edward. Did you sleep well?"

"Yes, thank you."

She looked at the table. "Doesn't all this look lovely!"

"I picked the flowers," I said immediately.

"Did you? They are very nice, darling."

Pleasure, and the smugness that comes from one-upmanship, coursed through me.

The door opened revealing Dora and Cook carrying two large trays of hot food.

"And here comes breakfast," Grandfather looked relieved. "Take a seat everyone."

I made certain that I sat next to Mummy. She made certain that David was on her other side.

"Good morning, Cook," she said as Cook laid the bowl of kedgeree down followed by crispy bacon and grilled tomatoes. "So sorry I missed you yesterday. David and I were rather worn out by the journey down."

"Very good to see you again, Mrs Bolitho. And this is the little one, is it?" Cook gave David a doting look which I didn't appreciate. "He's lovely, isn't he?"

"Say hello to Cook, David," Mummy coaxed.

"Hello Cook," he managed.

"And doesn't he speak good English! Better than these two did." She looked at Edward and me. "It took a while before we all understood each other."

"I only began to teach him a little English, a few months ago. When I knew we would be coming back. Up until then he spoke only Malay," Mummy said this a little too proudly for my liking and went on. "I suppose Edward and Hannah have lost their Malay now."

Grandfather shook out his napkin. "I am quite sure that they'd pick it up again quickly if necessary," he said kindly "Now then, what have we got for breakfast?"

Dora laid down two full toast racks, a plate of butter and a bowl of marmalade. "What would Master David like?" she asked.

"Pineapple please," he replied, which flummoxed her and Cook.

"No darling. We don't have pineapple in England," Mummy said sweetly

David's face dropped. "Mango then."

"Or mango. But look what we have! Bacon, tomatoes, toast."

Cook pointed to her dish of kedgeree, "And I have made something special for you. Your brother and sister's favourite." She lifted the lid like a magician pulling a rabbit out of a hat. "Kedgeree!"

"Can we go home now, Mummy?" David said.

229

As the week went on I got to really dislike David. He was awkward, demanding, and took up most of my mother's time. I tried to make friends with him. I read him stories, pushed him on the swing or played games, but as soon as he grew tired of the story or a game, he would leave me in search of Mummy.

I was not as happy as I thought I would be. I wanted Mummy to spend some time with me, alone.

The adults seemed not to notice. They were in the small boy's thrall.

Edward just shrugged when I tried to tell him how I felt. "Ignore it, Toots." He had got this new nickname for me from going to the pictures and watching American films. "I do."

"Yes, but you can go out with friends and do what you like. I have to stay in, like a child."

"Then stop behaving like one. David's all right really. Just a bit spoilt, perhaps."

"A bit spoilt? How does he deserve to be spoilt when you and I haven't ever been spoilt? We had to get on with things without Mummy running around after us every second." I began to feel the familiar hurt swell in me again. "It's not fair. And why is everything such a secret? Why is he more important than us? Why hasn't Daddy come to see us or even written to us for ever?"

Edward collected up his rugger boots. "I haven't got time for this mewling. You need to grow up."

He left his room and I threw myself onto his bed in a fit of anger, loneliness and tears. I heard him downstairs, yelling a cheery goodbye to everyone then slamming the front door. Not a single person came to look for me.

Eventually my bitter internal storm abated.

I was hungry.

Cook usually had the two hours after lunch and before dinner to herself, leaving the kitchen free for me to find a tasty treat. I came down the stairs quietly, hoping no one would hear me. The study door was closed. I stood and listened for a moment. Mummy and Grandfather were talking quietly. Good. That meant that David would be out with Dora, the only other woman in his life and somebody else I missed from my own.

In the kitchen I found some ham and made myself a sandwich. I put it on a small plate, poured a glass of milk and decided to take it to my room where I could sulk more comfortably.

Passing the study door again, I heard muffled tears and Grandfather saying something soothing. I put my ear firmly to the wood.

"Oh, my dear Clara. Is there no alternative?" Grandfather asked.

"I have tried, Hugh. So hard. But the war and losing Bertie has changed him. I can't stand him shouting at me any more. David is frightened of him and so are the servants. Socially he is as charming as ever and brilliant at work, but I can take the bullying no longer." She blew her nose. "The disappearing for hours — sometimes days — at a time without telling me where he's going or when he'll be back. I hear him at night, in his bedroom, shouting out. If I go to him he almost attacks me until he wakes and then he's embarrassed."

"Poor Ernest."

"Poor David. He has had enough to cope with. You know how hard it was for him when he was born. So early and so little. Then the malaria. I nearly lost him several times. You know I miscarried two babies before him. I thought I'd never have another child. I was so happy, happier than Ernest. He had made sure Edward and Hannah came back to Cornwall to be safe, and now here I was bringing another child into a country that wasn't secure, he said, for children. I would have stayed there but things got worse between us."

"Oh, my dear. You must always know that Cornwall and this house is your home for as long as you want."

"I don't want to say these awful things about Ernest. He's your son and my husband. But . . ." Her voice thickened. "But, he began to get, not violent exactly, but he pushed me a little too hard and . . . hurt me."

"Oh, my dear," Grandfather said slowly. "I am so very sorry."

"It's not your fault," Mummy sniffed. "It was the bloody war."

"You should have come sooner."

"It was hard to get the money for the tickets. That's why we came by banana boat. Thank God I can play bridge. It meant we could at least have one hot meal a day on board."

"That cannot have been easy."

"Well, we are here now, and I can't thank you enough for taking us in."

232

The leather of Grandfather's chair creaked as he changed position. "Edward and Hannah missed you greatly, and I think Hannah is finding it hard to compete with David for your attention."

"She's so grown up, though. Not the little girl I left here all those years ago. I feel she doesn't need me any more, whereas David does."

"She needs you as any daughter needs her mother. I wish you had let me tell them both about their little brother. But I promised you I wouldn't and I didn't."

My heart began thumping hard in my chest. Grandfather had kept David a secret? I tried to still my shallow breathing, determined to hear more.

"If David had died," my mother went on, "I wanted to spare them the grief. I couldn't have done that to them. Better not to know they had ever had a brother than to find out he had died without them ever meeting him."

"I understand. But sometimes a secret is even more of a cross to bear." The silence between them hung heavily for a moment. "So, what are your plans now, Clara? Do you intend going back to Penang soon?"

"No, Hugh, I don't. I have left Ernest."

I stood stock-still, all this truth making me feel sick with anger. Would I never see my father again? How could all these adults that I had loved and trusted keep all these secrets?

"I see. How do you envisage your future here with three children?"

"I am not going to be a financial burden to you. It may be wrong of me, but I have been hiding a little

233

money from Ernest over the years, perhaps already thinking of life without him. I've been wondering about opening a small shop, and I would like to buy a little car."

"Well, well," my grandfather said, "you are a doer. I think a drink might be in order. A small sherry, perhaps?"

"No thank you. But thank you for listening. I feel a lot better. I am so sorry to burden you with all this. I have kept it all in for so long." I heard the rustle of her dress as she stood up. "Do you think Cook would mind if I made myself some tea?"

I ran, with the uneaten sandwich and undrunk milk, back to the kitchen.

I sat at the table, my breath coming too fast, just as Mummy came in. She started when she saw me.

"Hello Mummy," I smiled brightly. "I just made myself a ham sandwich. Would you like a cup of tea?"

Hannah, Trevay

1938

My mother did as she said she would do. With a loan from my grandfather, and much searching for a suitable property, she leased a shop in Trevay and bought an old Austin 7 car. She drove very badly, either so slowly that people honked to get past her, or so quickly (sometimes on the wrong side of the road) that other drivers flung their motors onto pavements to avoid her. "I am a very good driver," she'd exclaim if any of us dared take a sharp intake of breath, the last before we surely died. "I have never had an accident!"

To which Edward would reply quietly, "No, but we've seen plenty behind us."

Mum's shop had been a wool shop before she took it on. The stock of wool left by the previous keeper stayed with us to keep the custom coming, but gradually, as she imported more of the Eastern silks, the customers remained with her and changed their tastes. Over time her shop became, in Cornwall anyway, rather famous. You couldn't get better anywhere else in the county. Including Truro.

Trevay was a small fishing village some ten miles up the coast from Callyzion. The harbour front was built with rugged fishermen's cottages and a pub, The Golden Hind. Beyond the harbour wall lay the open sea. Along the harbour wall was a jumble of fishing boats, large and small, and on its granite walls the men would land their catches and mend their nets. The Cornish accent here was broader than in Callyzion. It was hard to tune my ear to it, getting only one word in three or four, but as time went on my own accent grew the same. My mother was always correcting me. "Darling, please don't use the Cornish vernacular. If it's a rough day say it's a rough day, not your other nonsense."

She was right, I had begun to say "'Tis helluva hooley" instead, because it was such fun. "Yes Mum."

"And when things are right, say so. Just using the word 'ideal' will not do."

Her shop was in the back street, behind the harbour cottages, in the middle of a short run of shops. There was a butcher, greengrocer, hairdresser, tobacconist-cum-newsagent, a baker who sold out of pasties every day by ten in the morning, and us. We were between the hairdresser and the greengrocer. All these buildings were built by the Victorians and so were well organised within. We had a dry cellar below the shop, a room behind the shop with a kitchen curtained off, and the next floor housed the four of us in two bedrooms — I shared with Mum — and two further letting rooms above that housing two lodgers. One was Mr Tomlinson, the St Peter's Church verger. The other was Miss Penrose, a young woman who taught at the junior school.

Sometime in the mid-1850s the railway company built a branch line into the village, capitalising on the popularity of seaside holidays to quaint destinations. With the train came a hotel. An enormous edifice commanding a high point above the harbour. Mum loved to go there. They held a weekly bridge night and she was soon a much admired and respected player.

I was 14 and still at school. I could legally leave now but Grandfather had insisted I stayed until I was sixteen in order to take my General School Certificate.

Edward had been accepted at medical school in Bristol, and David, now seven, had developed into a much more easy-going boy. Miss Penrose, who taught him, said he was one of the brightest in the school. He was interested in all kinds of engineering, questioning every construction he saw and occasionally tinkering with the Austin. He was also very funny. I had managed to bury my initial jealousy and come to enjoy his company. He was still quiet at times but no longer afraid of us.

Of Dad we heard very little. His letters were succinct. He was well. Rubber prices were good. He worried about Mr Hitler, and he was glad Edward had got his place at Bristol.

I didn't tell anyone what I had heard that afternoon in Callyzion. The things I had overheard about my father I put away, not wanting to hurt either of my siblings. If David remembered any of what he had seen or heard in Penang, he kept it to himself, and I never asked.

Mum was happy. Dad was doing well. We were OK.

I wouldn't, couldn't, ask for more.

Mum was doing so well that she took on a half-share in a teashop newly opened on the harbour front. The inevitable had happened and Mr Tomlinson and Miss Penrose had conducted a love affair under our noses and got married. The new Mrs Tomlinson gave up her work at the school and became Mum's partner in the business. Our two letting rooms became their bedroom and sitting room. Mum insisted that she make the bride's dress and organised the flowers for the church. I couldn't understand why she wanted to be so involved, but I overheard a conversation between Mrs Emery, the hairdresser next door, and a customer that seemed to have something to do with it. It was a warm day and Mrs Emery had the shop door open to let the breeze in and the heat from the hairdryers out. Due to the noise in the salon she had to talk loudly to be heard. "I hear the teacher next door has to get married. How could Mrs Bolitho not know what was going on under her own roof? Never did like her much. Very pleased with herself, she is. What I'd like to know is, where is *her* husband? Hmm?"

She couldn't see me from where she was talking, so I made my presence known by stepping into her eyeline and giving her a filthy look through her window. It shut her up but I would never forgive her for speaking about my mother like that. And what did she mean about Miss Penrose having to get married? She was in love with Mr Tomlinson and that was enough, wasn't it?

Mum got rather overcome by the marriage service and shed a few tears. Poor Miss Penrose's parents couldn't come for some reason, so I suppose Mum felt as though she was standing in for them. She cried very rarely, and then only when she thought I didn't know. Perhaps she missed Dad more than she let on.

In November of 1938, Mrs Tomlinson gave us some happy news. She was going to have a baby in the spring. I was thrilled and hoped it would be a little girl. "I can babysit for you," I told her, and she said yes that would be lovely but that she was going to keep the baby in a pram in the teashop so that all the ladies in Trevay could cuddle it while she was working.

Christmas was very busy in the shop and Mum let me decorate the windows with little snowmen I made out of bits of wool. There was a competition for the Best-Dressed Festive Window, and Mum went all out with her display of silks. She even made me an elf suit to wear behind the counter and a Mother Christmas outfit for herself. Mrs Tomlinson baked mince pies for us to give out to customers, and Mum had a small bottle of sherry to offer them too. "It'll open their purses a little wider," she laughed, giving me a nudge. I loved it when she treated me like one of her grown-up friends, and she was right, purses were opening, very nicely.

Grandfather came to spend Christmas Day with us. He had retired by then and, apart from helping at midnight mass the night before, had no other commitments to the parish. Edward took the old Austin to bring him over while Mum and I made lunch and David laid the table. He and I had collected a Christmas tree the week before and garlanded it with paperchains and cut-out icicles. Mum had made our fairy years ago by dressing one of my old baby dolls in a dress of white silk shot through with silver thread, and pipe cleaners bent into wings. It had always been my business to place her on top of the tree, with the top branch of pine needles scratching her little pink legs, but this year David wanted to do it. I was about to argue with him when Mum gave me one of her looks, and I was forced to capitulate.

"Good girl," she muttered. "Fancy a sherry?"

"Really?" I had never been asked before.

"You will be fifteen in a few months' time and it is Christmas." She brought out the almost empty bottle that she'd offered the customers over the previous week and held it to the light. "Just enough for two of us."

I poured it carefully and evenly into two small glasses with green bases.

"Here's to us." She raised her glass to me and I raised mine to her. "Happy Christmas."

The sweet warmth filled my mouth and slid into my stomach. I laughed. "It's heating me from the inside."

"Warming your collywobbles," she laughed back, then checked her wristwatch. "You'd better get the bread sauce on before your brother gets back with Hugh."

"Here we are," called Edward, opening the back door a few minutes later.

"Merry Christmas," said Grandfather from behind, pulling the rain and cold in with him. "Edward drove very well"

"I am glad to hear it. Give me your coat." Mum took his wet coat and kissed him. "Happy Christmas, Hugh." Then set about giving her orders. "David, put Grandfather's coat on a chair to dry, would you? Hannah, put the kettle on. Edward, could you reach up and open the latch window, it's getting so steamy in here. It's from the pudding boiling."

Eventually we were all settled and our lunches in front of us.

"For what we about to receive, may the Lord make us truly thankful," intoned Grandfather.

"Amen," we replied, and tucked in.

The conversation around the table was jolly and fun. David was itching to get to the small pile of presents under the tree; there was a large box-shaped parcel labelled to him from Grandfather, but Mum had decreed we weren't to touch them until teatime.

"Please, can I open it now?" he wheedled.

"No darling, I have told you. You have your stocking gifts to play with."

It was true. David had woken us all too early and insisted we went downstairs to see if Father Christmas had been.

"Come on then." Mum had got out of bed and wrapped herself in her warm dressing gown and slippers. "We may as well get the fire lit for the day."

Edward, who could sleep all day if allowed, got up and got the fire going, while I put the kettle on and made us all a morning brew.

The stockings hung bulging and invitingly from the mantel.

We sat in a tight group on the rag rug in front of the fire and rapidly pulled open our gifts.

Mum had given me a small bottle of Devon Violets cologne. I swiftly unknotted the purple ribbon around the bottle's neck and carefully pulled the cork stopper out. I put it to my nose and inhaled deeply. Soft and alluring, the light scent made me feel like a grown woman.

"Don't spill it," she said.

"My first bottle of real scent." I hugged her, my knees digging into the knots of the rug. "I love it. Thanks Mum."

Drinking our tea, we got busy opening our small gifts. I had made shortbread biscuits for Mum, knitted fingerless gloves for Edward and, for David, I had found a tiny model of Mum's car. He immediately began running its little wheels all over the floor, making the noise of Mum's infamous clashes of gears as he went.

Mum was not amused. "It's the clutch, not me," she exclaimed as Edward and I laughed till we cried.

Now, sitting around the table with my small family, Grandfather tinkled his water glass with his pudding spoon. "I'd like to make a toast. May 1939 be a year of peace for us all."

"Peace for us all," said Mum as we drank.

"And," continued Grandfather, "for Ernest who cannot be here but to whom we send our loving thoughts."

"To Dad," Edward replied.

"To Daddy," I echoed.

Mum got up and went to the clock on the mantel. She pulled a letter from behind it. "I have a message from him."

"Has he sent me a present?" David asked.

My heart flipped. We hadn't heard from Daddy for a long time. I had written him two letters since the summer, telling him about school, and Mum's shop, and about how we all would like him to come to Cornwall and stay. Be a family. He hadn't replied, yet. He had remembered David's birthday, but not mine. Had I done something bad? Is that why he had left me in England when I was so little? I wanted to have him home so that I could talk about him in the same way my friends talked about their fathers. The fun they had. The closeness. A daughter and father relationship I

242

could see was different to mother and daughter. A father can lift you on his shoulders and hold you on his knee. He is the first man a girl can love and the one her husband will forever be compared with. Mum's father died in a fire with her mother. Did she compare Daddy to him? I don't think my parents could have properly loved each other, but I think she needed him to look after her. Or maybe she was too independent and capable? Magazines are always saying that men want a nice wife who will look after them. Mum looked after us very well, but perhaps she didn't look after Daddy? Perhaps I would be the same when I married; after all, I only had Mum as my role model and she could do anything without a husband. Was Mum the same as her mum? I was on the brink of being a woman and I was beginning to see the world through a woman's eyes.

Mum had opened Daddy's letter and began reading aloud.

Hello my dear old things and Happy Christmas to you all,

I am so sorry not to be with you for another Christmas and to share your Christmas turkey. As I write, the monsoon rain is falling heavily and the heat and humidity is rising. I am imagining you in the cold. Is Jack Frost biting your toes? It's a long time since I felt him.

On Christmas Day I will be thinking of you and hoping that you are all together eating well and singing Christmas carols. I am thankful that you are all safe in Cornwall. I shall go to our local

Protestant church and pray for you before our "English" Christmas lunch at Government House.

I am afraid I shall be staying out here for longer than any of us expected. I cannot tell you exactly why, due to confidentiality, but the government in London has asked all British territories to stand fast during what might be a spot of bother in Europe and elsewhere.

I enclose some photographs of the little monkeys that come to share my breakfast each day, a snake charmer, some of the temples that Clara will remember, and Cottontail's grand-puppies, which are all growing up quickly, just as you all are.

God bless you all,
Ernest/Daddy

Mum stopped reading and exchanged an unreadable look with Grandfather, before saying, "Daddy also enclosed ten shillings for you all to spend on a present from him. Isn't that kind?"

This jolted a memory in David. "Can I open my presents now?"

Mummy refolded the letter and put it back in its envelope. "When Edward and Hannah have washed up."

David looked at us solemnly. "Hurry up, please."

Edward and I dutifully stood and started to clear the table. We left Mum and Grandfather to sit by the fire while we went to the curtained-off kitchen.

"Toots," said Edward quickly, checking that the adults couldn't hear us.

"Yes?" I whispered.

"If we were to go to war with Germany . . ."

"Oh, not this again." I rolled my eyes. "We won't go to war. Not after the last one. Who would want to?"

"Me."

"What?"

"My friends and I have been talking about it. If we have to, we would go."

"Mum wouldn't let you."

"She couldn't stop me."

"But you are going to medical school and will be a doctor."

"I can do it afterwards."

"I don't think so." I was getting upset. "We need doctors."

"And we need pilots."

"But you are going to medical school," I hissed.

"No, I'm not." He ran a plate under the cold tap, rinsing off the suds. "I've written asking for a postponement. A lot of students are doing the same."

I silently dried up the last of the dishes and folded the tea towel before hanging it on the oven's rail. "When are you going to tell Mum and Grandfather?"

He gave me a steady look.

I shook my head. "Not tonight. No. You can't spoil their Christmas."

"I thought later, before I took Grandfather home."

"Absolutely not. Promise me." I sounded pleading, even to myself.

He sighed and rubbed his eyes. "Well when?"

"After the New Year. When all this —" I waved my hand towards the room beyond the curtain — "this happiness is over. Promise me."

"OK. I promise."

"Thank you."

CHAPTER
NINETEEN

Hannah, Trevay

January 1939

The weather had become increasingly wet and gloomy, and then a cold snap over the southwest brought with it deep snow over the moors. With no way of getting over Bodmin Moor, Cornwall was cut off.

We didn't expect that Mum's shop would be overly busy during the first part of the year, people having spent their comfort money over Christmas, but we didn't expect it to be dead. The whole of Cornwall, not just Trevay, was in a financial hole. Farmers couldn't get their beasts to market and the rest of England couldn't get their goods to us.

The Trevay fishing fleet was out every day. We depended on them and they on us. Whatever time of day they returned, we were waiting on the harbourside. But, before the weather got better, it got worse. The thermometers were below freezing and the inner harbour had frozen over. The fleet were stranded offshore for almost three days.

It's a funny thing that in times of near disaster one can only remember the warmth of community spirit. Mum opened up the café from 8.00 a.m. until 7.00 p.m., asking Trevayers (as we began to call ourselves) to bring with them whatever they had to share so that as a village we could sit as one, in warmth, and not feel hungry or lonely. She brought everyone together. Families buried feuds, friends forgave each other for past slights, children made new friends and even one or two love stories bloomed.

When at last the harbour ice melted, we welcomed the crews home with warm fires and hot food.

We even made a story in the local newspaper, the *Trevay Times*.

"Mrs Clara Bolitho Welcomes the Hungry and the Lonely" read the headline. I was terrifically proud of it and bought two copies. One to put in my scrapbook and the other to carry in my small purse in case I came across anyone who hadn't already read it.

During all this disruption, Edward hadn't had a chance to break his news about postponing medical school. That was until breakfast one February morning, when the postman dropped two letters through the door.

Mum was buttering toast in the kitchen. "I'll get it," I called to her. Two letters were on the mat. One for Edward with the crest of the Bristol medical school on it, and one addressed to Mum. Out of curiosity I turned the envelope over to see if it yielded any clues. In black ink and in a clear hand it read, "Michael Hampton, Faversham, Kent".

Edward and David came chasing down the stairs having some sort of game, and I held up Edward's letter. "For you," I said, raising my eyebrows.

He snatched it from me and hurriedly put it in his trouser pocket. "None of your beeswax," he said and sat down at the table.

"Hannah," Mum called to me. "Take the tea tray to the table for me, would you?"

"Yes Mum." I put her letter in my cardigan pocket and did as I was asked.

"Tappy eggs and soldiers," Mum said, putting a bowl of boiled eggs and a full toast rack in the middle of the table.

David grabbed one and let it go quickly. "It's hot."

Mum tutted and helped him put it into his egg cup and then take the top off.

"Can I have butter in mine?" he asked.

"No," said Mum firmly.

I remembered the letter in my cardigan.

"This came for you." I handed it to her.

She reached for her glasses and read the front. She paled and bit her lip

"Do you recognise the handwriting?" I asked.

She turned the envelope over, as I had, and read the back. A shadow crossed her features. One I couldn't decipher. A sadness perhaps? Shock? She got up and threw it into the fire without opening it.

We three all looked at her. "Why did you burn your letter?" asked David.

"It's from someone I used to know," she said, sitting down and picking up her tea cup.

"Who?" I said.

"It's a grown-ups's thing."

"Oh. Was it somebody who was horrible to you?" I persevered.

"Quite the opposite." I opened my mouth to question her further but she got up briskly and said, "Look at the time. You'll be late for school. Edward will walk you on his way to the butcher's. Is that OK with you, Edward?"

The three of us trudged up our street and turned left up the hill to school. "You don't need to walk me to school any more," David complained.

"I'm going to the butcher's for Mum, aren't I?" Edward enjoyed his position as Mum's second in command and used it to shut us up at moments when we wanted to know what was going on.

"Mum wasn't happy about that letter, was she?" I said. My mind had been burning with all sorts of explanations and had landed on the most obvious one I could think of. "I think it was a love letter," I said. "From an old admirer."

"Pooh," said David.

"What do you think, Edward?" I asked.

"It's for Mum to know and us to respect." His self-importance inflating wildly. "Right. Off you go and have a good day."

As I ran into the playground with David beside me, he said, "I hate it when Edward gets all big for his boots."

He said it so seriously I couldn't help but burst out laughing. "Me too!" I said, and we laughed all the way to the assembly hall.

When we got home, I could sense something had changed. "Mum?" I looked in the kitchen and then the shop, but I saw that she had turned the sign to closed. Something was not right. Business had begun to pick up again and, even if she couldn't tend to customers herself, she always had Edward to call on. He was surprisingly good at selling things to the women who shopped there. Mum always said it was because he was so tall, handsome and charming. "Your charm will either get you a long way or into terrible trouble," she would tease him.

I backed out of the shop and went upstairs. "Mum? Edward?"

I heard a movement in the bedroom that Mum and I shared. I opened the door slowly. The curtains were drawn shut and it was clear that Mum had been lying down because she was now sitting on the edge of her bed, with her back to me, looking for her shoes, whilst running a hand through her loosened hair.

"Mum? What is it? Are you not feeling well?"

"Is that you, darling? How was school?" She still wouldn't look at me and I sensed she had been crying.

"Yes. I wrote an essay about Oliver Cromwell."

"Oh, good girl." She reached for the hanky she almost always had up her sleeve and wiped her nose.

"Why are you in the dark? Do you have a headache? Can I get you an aspirin?"

"No thank you." Over her shoulder, she glanced at me with a small smile. "I'm fine."

I went to sit next to her. "Did that letter upset you this morning? The one you burnt?"

My hands were in my lap and she took one of them and patted it. "A little."

"Was it from a Gentleman? From the olden days before you met Daddy?"

She smiled sadly. "Where do you get these ideas from?"

"Was it?" I persisted.

She took her hand from mine and used it to take my chin while she looked deep into my eyes. "Darling, life is a long road full of potholes. Some you can walk around and others you fall straight into and get hurt."

"So the letter was from a pothole?"

She laughed. "Something like that."

"Will you tell me one day?"

"That's enough for now." She smoothed her blouse and stood up. "Were you looking for me?"

I remembered. "Oh yes. Where's Edward?" I asked. She sniffed and wiped again. "I don't know. Have you looked in his bedroom?"

Suddenly I didn't want to find Edward. If he had told Mum about not going to medical school, on top of the other letter that had upset her, I absolutely didn't want to find him.

"I'll make you a cup of tea if you like."

"Yes please. That would be lovely."

In the kitchen I found the breakfast things unwashed and no apparent sign of a luncheon snack having been made. That wasn't like Mum. Or Edward, to be fair. He was a pretty good housekeeper. Being Mum's "man of the house".

David wandered in. "Can I have a biscuit? Oh yuck, smelly old eggs."

I busied myself around him. "Mum has a headache." I pointed at the biscuit tin. "You may have two biscuits and a glass of milk while you do your homework. I'll clear up a bit and then, if Mum still doesn't feel right, I'll make us cheese on toast for supper. How does that sound?"

"Nice. Where is Edward?"

"I'm not sure but he'll be home soon."

"I need his help with my fractions."

"I can help if he can't. Now off you go and do what you can."

I ran a bowl of water for the washing up, my brain spinning again. I was scared.

I had never seen Mum like this before. I had seen her angry, frustrated and tired but not so obviously upset. If Edward's letter had added to her sadness, I would kill him. Mum was both mother and father to us. What would we do if anything happened to her?

Suddenly I understood something vast. Why had I not seen it before? Mum was the centre of our lives. She had no husband, no partner to take the helm in stormy times. No shoulder to rest her head on. She was alone.

Daddy *had* to come home. I would write to him, without anyone knowing, and make him come back. Especially if an old admirer was sending her letters. Mum needed him. How could he not look after us? If I explained how things were here, I was sure he'd come back.

I washed up and got the kitchen straight while the kettle boiled, and then took Mum's tea up to her.

"Here you are," I said, putting it on her dressing table.

"Thank you, darling." She had moved from the bed to the small stool and was brushing her hair in the mirror.

"The kitchen is all tidy and David is doing his homework."

"Thank you, darling," she said, looking at me through the mirror. "What would I do without you and Edward?"

Her eyes looked so sad. "What would we do without you is the better question," I answered, and began to straighten her pillows and blanket. As I did so I felt the sharp corners of an envelope, caught in the bedding. I pulled it out. It was Edward's letter from this morning.

Mum's eyes saw the anger in my face as she watched me in the mirror.

"You might as well read it," she said.

The gist of it was the medical school could no longer hold a place for him and, if and when he wished to, he would have to reapply, with no guarantee he would be accepted second time around. It ended by wishing him luck in the RAF.

Anger, born from Edward's utter selfishness, swelled in me. How bloody dare he show this to Mum before telling me?

"I am so sorry, Mum," I said.

"What for? He's a grown man and he wants to do the things he wants to do."

254

"But you need him here. We all do."

"Yes. But does he need us? The truth is that women hold the family together. Men know that."

"Is that why Daddy stays in Penang?"

"Partly."

"Don't you want him home?" I was anxious to know the answer.

"I had better find something for supper," she replied.

"Mum." I stopped her. "If I wrote to him and asked him to come home, you wouldn't have to work so hard. He could give you the money for food and school clothes and the bills, and we could be a family."

She looked at me with more love than she had ever shown me.

"Darling Hannah." She rested one hand on my shoulder while the other tenderly stroked my hair. "You are growing into a wonderful woman and you have your whole life ahead of you. My life with Daddy was fun, but after a while I missed you and Edward more than I wanted to be with Daddy. And he didn't mind because he loves Penang. He loves all of you very much and maybe, one day, he'll come back to walk you down the aisle on your wedding day. How does that sound?"

I knew she was trying to make everything sound normal but I didn't believe it.

"If he did, that would be lovely. But Mum, I don't want you to be doing all this on your own. Maybe, one day, you'll meet another nice man, a companion, who will take you out on treats?"

She smiled and almost laughed. "That's a sweet thought, but I am happy as I am with my three lovely children, thank you. What I really want is for you all to be happy."

"Even if you are unhappy? Even if Edward will go into the RAF and not be a doctor?"

She sighed. "Yes. Even if. Because, my darling, if you have a daughter, you will love her as much as I love my daughter and as much as my mum loved hers. Men are wrong in thinking we are the weaker sex. It is they who are weaker. Granny, me and you. We are the strong ones."

Hannah, Trevay

3 September 1939

Nine months later we declared war on Germany and our — my — quiet life came to a jolting stop. It felt as though a terrible darkness had fallen over us. Two days before, Mr Hitler had invaded Poland. He had already invaded Czechoslovakia and Austria, but our prime minister, Mr Neville Chamberlain, who for years had tried to appease and prevent another war, decided enough was enough. We were at war. The four of us sat in our back room and listened to the news on the radio. Mum grew very stiff and still, her hands trembling as she reached for a cigarette. David found it rather exciting, I think, and began to jump up and down, firing his small toy gun. Edward stood almost to attention, swivelling his glance to Mum first and then to me. I shook my head at him, sending a message of silence. Mum didn't need to hear his plans to fight.

"You can turn the radio off now please, Hannah," Mum said.

I was nearest to the set so only had to shift an inch or two to reach the knob.

David's noise was becoming unbearable. "Shut up," I snapped. "And put that bloody gun down." He looked at me in shock, his bottom lip quivering. "For God's sake." I stood up. "Who wants a cup of tea?"

Mum got on with her daily life in the shop, still smiling and chatting to the customers, who were always eager to hear about Edward's progress. But in her bed in our shared room, I knew she didn't sleep.

Within a month Edward had joined up and was on a boat to Canada for pilot training. He was nineteen.

Of course we all thought the war would start immediately. A Home Guard troop was created from older fishermen who had fought in the First World War, and younger boys who were too young to enlist as yet. They met at the St Peter's Church hall and began training with nothing but pitchforks or an occasional homemade wooden rifle. When they marched around the harbour or took shifts in scanning the horizon for Hitler's invasion, the town either sniggered or applauded them, or both. David started a platoon of his own in the school playground, ordering his chums to march in precision and salute him at the end of each session. Mum encouraged him, knowing he was only eight and, for the foreseeable future, would remain safe.

I was fifteen and itching to do my bit. I knew I had to wait until I was seventeen, and began to almost hope the war would not end before I got a chance. My father had been in the Army so I began to research how I could join too, though I never told Mum.

Every night, Mum and I listened to the wireless news, constantly expecting to hear that German soldiers had landed along the south coast and would soon be at our front doors. But oddly, all was quiet. People began to call it a Phoney War. To believe that Mr Hitler would never be able to reach us.

Edward stayed in Canada for Christmas and New Year, and was not expected back until the spring. He was doing well, he wrote, and hoping to be made a bomber pilot.

I was in the last term at school and about to take my General School Certificate when things changed. In May 1940, Mr Chamberlain stepped down as prime minister and Mr Winston Churchill took over. Mum was pleased. "Come the hour, come the man," she said, drinking the cup of tea she always made to have while listening to the news.

I began to dread the nightly broadcasts and the man who read them.

"Good evening, this is the news from the BBC. France has fallen to the German Army. The Battle for France has ended in defeat for the British and their Allies."

"Oh dear God, no," Mum breathed, and reached for her cigarettes. I watched her and saw the trembling of her hands and the deep lines around her mouth.

I was scared. "Mum, the Germans won't come to England, will they?"

Her quick smile hid her own fears, "Of course not, darling. We have the Home Guard and Mr Churchill and very brave soldiers."

"But they might not be able to stop them."

"I think they will. We shall all have to fight back. Very hard."

Over the next few days we heard about the rescue of hundreds of thousands of British and Allied forces in France who had been beaten back to a little town called Dunkirk by the German Army. Thousands of boats, large and small, captained by ordinary people, sailed the Channel to rescue them. It was a miracle, and at church on Sunday we all gave thanks.

But now Mr Churchill called on the RAF.

He told us, via the wireless, that although the German Air Force had more pilots than us we still had more planes, including the fast and deadly Spitfires and Hurricanes that would take on the terrifying task of battling for Britain. There was no doubt that German forces were just a few miles over the Channel. If the Channel had been fields instead of deep water, they could have walked the twenty-odd miles over to us and that would have been that. I began to imagine what I would do if they parachuted into Trevay. How would I fight them? I began checking that all our windows and doors were secured day and night, and slept with David's cricket bat under my bed. I even asked Mum if she thought it would be sensible for David to move into our room and not be on his own in his.

"No, darling." She patted my hand. "That's very good of you, and I do appreciate all your extra security measures around the house, but the house is feeling like a prison, and believe me Hitler is not interested in coming to Cornwall."

"Why not?" I asked anxiously.

"Because we will never give in, just as Mr Churchill told us."

In the end, Mr Hitler didn't invade us because our fighter planes made it so difficult for him. Instead he launched a terrible bombing blitz.

Caroline

Present day

It is my mother's birthday. I always mark the day, and Christmas and Easter too, by visiting her grave. I usually go early so that I can park on the verge by the churchyard gates without trouble, and also so that I don't run into the boy who mows the grass.

Or any other visitor.

I prefer to talk to my mother in private.

Today was quite warm so I took my lightweight coat. I had first seen it in the large department store where I take my daughter, Natalie, for lunch when she's down from London, but I hadn't been sure about its colour.

She had persuaded me to buy it. "Mummy, it's lovely on you. And that mint green is really flattering."

I had looked at myself in the long mirror and turned from side to side, hands in pockets then fiddling with the collar.

"How is it from the back?" I'd asked.

"Not pulling anywhere and your waist looks really tiny."

That had pleased me. "Right, I'll have it. As long as I can change it if it looks different at home." The strip lights above me had glowed powder-puff pink. "These lights are either too flattering or not flattering enough. I can't tell."

I had looked at Natalie's shabby reflection in the mirror behind me and tried not to sound judgemental. "Can I treat you to a new coat?"

She'd smiled. "I am perfectly OK with this hoodie, thank you."

"But your denims have holes in the knees. That's got to be draughty? How about a new pair of slacks?"

"Mother, this isn't 1952. These are vintage designer jeans with rips that cost me a lot more than your coat will cost you."

I had said nothing, preferring to look pointedly at her feet.

"And these boots," she'd said, "will ensure my feet aren't deformed by ill-fitting shoes, which is why your generation have bunions and mine doesn't."

I had folded my new coat over my arm and sniffed, "Well, at least we knew how to look feminine."

She had thrown her hands up. "Mother. There are at least a hundred different genders out there now! Feminine men, masculine women, asexual, bisexual, lesbian —"

I had stopped her. "Shh. Keep your voice down. You are in Truro now, not North London."

Oh God. I had been wondering for some time that she might declare she had a girlfriend.

I had divulged my worries to my friend Annie, one of the church flower ladies, as we washed vases under the outdoor tap in the churchyard. She was a woman whose common sense I then appreciated.

"Caroline, it's a phase, that's all." She had put her hand on my shoulder, comfortingly, "But you could have a lot of fun buying two wedding dresses. One for Natalie and one for her wife." I almost dropped the vase I was holding.

Anyway, today was my new coat's first outing, and I must say it was very comfortable to wear in the car. I could reverse the car without any restriction at all.

On the seat next to me I had a spring bouquet for Mother. All blooms picked from my own garden. When Tom, Natalie's father, was ill, he made me promise to look after his lawn and flowerbeds after he'd gone, and I have. This year the tulips are magnificent. Ramrod straight. I have the usual gay red and orange in the back garden, encircling the grass, but last October, in the front just outside the porch, I planted two huge tubs of pale pink and black tulips. The postman has been most admiring of them.

Today I picked only the reds and oranges from the back garden and mixed them with forget-me-nots and three white hyacinths.

They are almost over and browning a little at the edges, but the perfume is still good and Mother would understand.

Her headstone I had made from Cornish Delabole slate. Not a great big showy thing, but small and effective. It had her name "Hannah Bolitho" and her dates carved into it.

Below I'd had inscribed: *Loving mother and grandmother. Much missed.*

Simple and suitable and, after the cost of the slate, all that was needed.

Mother had been a complicated woman. Mainly, I think, because her own mother, the sainted Granny Clara, had been so "bohemian" herself.

I thought back to my surprise delivery. The Trunk. It was revealing some very interesting answers to the many questions I had pondered growing up. The letter I had found inside the Bible, and a diary lying among the knick-knacks were most illuminating. Well, at least the first half was, I hadn't finished it yet.

The letter was from Granny Clara to my Grandfather Ernest and it was about my mother and me.

Trevay, 1948

Dear Ernie,

Thank you for your last letter and generous cheque. It was very kind of you and will help Edward and Shirley pay off their last bills for the wedding. It was a very happy day and Shirley is very good for Edward. He adores her.

It was good to hear all your news too. Please send Nizam and his family my very best wishes. I can't believe he's fifty! How many years has he been with you now? Almost thirty years I suppose. He's a better house keeper to you than I ever could have been. I am so glad that we can look back now without pain.

Unfortunately my health is not very good at the moment. Probably just bronchitis. The family cluck around me as if I am a dying duck, which I am not. My doctor is extremely kind and keeping a good eye on me. Thank goodness I was fit for the wedding. Hannah looked so lovely as the bridesmaid. So lovely, that she attracted the attention of one of Edward's RAF boys. They saw each other a few times and then he did the disappearing act. He rather broke her heart, but he did leave a gift behind. You are a grandfather. I realise this may be a shock to you but you have a beautiful granddaughter called Caroline. She is the baby in the enclosed photo, sitting on Hannah's knee. Hannah has taken it all in her stride as has the whole family and none of us can remember a time when Caroline was not here.

I think Hannah would like to hear from you. Be kind.

Yours affectionately,

Clara. x

I knew that I had been born out of wedlock. My mother had never kept that from me. But I had always hoped she would tell me who my father was. Now, I don't think I shall ever know.

So Granny Clara had been supportive to her pregnant, unmarried daughter. And to be fair I did grow up in a very loving home. But I had always yearned to have two parents, a neat bungalow overlooking the harbour and a father to whom I would be Daddy's Girl.

I longed to be at boarding school and have wonderful adventures like the girls in the Enid Blyton *Malory Towers* books. The children at my school said horrible things about my mother — and especially about the absence of my father so that in the end I made up all sorts of stories about him. He was a spy and an actor in Hollywood. He drove sports cars and took me to Paris for my birthday. The trouble was I wasn't very good at remembering my stories, so the lies were always discovered and children who might have been friends drifted away from me.

In the end I said he was dead.

Killed on a space mission.

That shut them up.

My grandmother, who died when I was a baby, drummed into my mother that, "To be a good liar, you have to have a good memory." She must have had a *very* good memory, because the diary I found in the trunk was hers and very revealing it was! No wonder she kept it locked! When she left for England and brought Uncle David home with her, she must have left the thing behind. How her heart must have raced when she discovered it wasn't in her bags. Luckily for her, I think no one even thought twice about opening it, and packed it up never to be looked at until now.

And what a hypocrite!

She didn't have three children. She had four. Her first born was a boy called Michael, or Mikey as she wrote, the son of Herbert Bolitho who was killed in action in the Great War and who was the older brother of my grandfather Ernest. Now that must have been a huge secret to keep.

I have never lied to my daughter Natalie. And she has never lied to me. Apart from the time Tom and I had our last weekend away together, while he could, and we left her looking after the house.

"No boys. No booze. No drugs." Those were the last words we said to her as we drove off.

You can imagine what happened.

It was the neighbours who told us. I have never been so embarrassed. We grounded her for a month. Since then, good as gold.

I hope she might still be a virgin. She's only twenty-two and I am sure she would have told me if anything had happened.

Tom and I were very lucky. She could have gone off the rails at uni, but she found a lovely girl, Lucy, in her first year in halls and they stuck together as housemates until they graduated. They share a flat in Camden Town now with Lucy's boyfriend, Ryan.

If I were Lucy's mother, I'd be worried sick. I have spoken to Ryan on the telephone when I ring Natalie and he always sounds as if he is laughing at some private joke.

I am sure Natalie is saving herself for Mr Right.

As I tidied Mother's grave, I told her all this news. Including the revelation of Granny Clara's illegitimate son. I wanted her to know that her own weaknesses, inherited from her mother it seemed, were not inherited by her daughter and granddaughter. I wanted her to know this and be proud of us. I placed the flowers under her name and stood up to brush the grass from my knees.

"See you at Christmas if not before," I said, and blew her a kiss as I always did.

PART THREE

CHAPTER
TWENTY

Hannah, Trevay

1940

Our nightly news bulletin listening was now a litany of how much damage was being wreaked on our great cities. The number of dead, orphaned, widowed and homeless was heartbreaking and Mum and I could only thank God that we were so far away from the horrors of yet another world war.

Edward's training was almost at an end and he was due home after the summer. His letters were full of the fun and excitement he was having with his fellow students and the great news that he had been accepted to fly heavy bombers.

Mum removed her spectacles and put his letter down. "He'll be flying over Germany."

"Good." I was very gung-ho in those days. "We need to give them some of their own medicine. David will be so excited."

Mum reached out a hand to my knee and held it tight. "No. Don't tell David. Better not. We don't want to frighten him."

"But he'll be so proud of his big brother," I told her.

She let go of my knee and reached for her cigarettes. "And if he's shot down? Killed? Taken prisoner? What then?"

"Mum, he'll be fine. It's Edward. He'll be all right."

She inhaled deeply and blew a plume of smoke towards the ceiling. "It's a deadly game, darling. We shoot *them* down, they shoot *us* down."

"That's what I want to do. As soon as I am seventeen I am going to join up and shoot down the enemy planes."

"Do you think you can protect Edward?"

"And his friends, yes."

"Well, we'll see. You won't be seventeen for a while yet."

"Ten months. That's all. Then I can join the Auxiliary Territorial Service."

"The ATS?" She rubbed her head with the hand holding her cigarette. The smoke wreathed around her hair. "Why on earth do women feel the need to be killers?"

"I don't want to kill anyone. I just want to shoot their planes down. They'll parachute out and be taken prisoner."

"Ha." She sucked harder on her cigarette and coughed as she stood up. "Cup of tea before bed?"

I watched her stub out the cigarette. "Mum, I'm serious."

She headed to the kitchen. "Let's cross that bridge when we get to it."

272

By the time Edward was due to return later in 1941, rationing was in full swing. Food, fuel and fabrics were now all at a premium.

It was impossible for Mum to get any shipments of silk for the shop as the sea lanes were vulnerable to attack from the bombs, torpedoes, mines, or all three. But business was still good. Mum was a resourceful woman. She got out her old sewing machine and offered remodelling of outdated garments. She was extremely good at it. Taking in, letting out, adding extra panels to maternity dresses. She made customers' clothing coupons go much further than they had expected.

"I shall not be beaten," she would say. "Women could run the world, given half a chance."

Mum hadn't used the old Austin since Edward had gone, but now she had David and me washing and polishing it and topping it up with the last of the petrol in the gallon tin she had been saving.

David was ten now and as tall as Mum, but not quite as tall as me. "I can drive us to the station to collect Edward if you like," he suggested nonchalantly. "I know how to."

"That's as may be, but you are too young and I shall drive."

"But you haven't driven for ages. You will have forgotten."

"No, I have not forgotten and you are not driving."

I listened to this with amusement. The truth was that he probably could drive better than Mum — who couldn't? When the old car was mothballed in the boat sheds at the top of the town, David and I had breathed a sigh of relief. Not just for our own safety, for the safety of the whole of Cornwall.

"Actually, there is something you can do, David." Mum smiled beguilingly, "You can check the oil and make sure the bloody thing still starts."

With Mum driving too fast down the winding lanes to Bodmin station, I distracted myself from thoughts of certain death by looking at Cardinham Woods across the valley. The leaves in the soft autumn sunshine were gleaming amber and scarlet. If I was to die today, at least it would be surrounded by the beauty of it all.

David was the first to shout, "Look out, Mum."

I switched my gaze to the view coming at us through the windscreen. We were entering a dark tunnel of trees where the leaves lay thick and damp on the road which was dropping away before us and bending sharply to the left.

"Don't shout like that, David," Mum said, turning her head to the back seat to look at him. "You must never distract the driver —"

We hit the hedge on the opposite side of the road, which lifted the back wheels off the ground, then slewed over the wet leaves onto the other side of the road where we finally came to a stop.

"Don't you ever do that again," Mum shouted at David. "Never distract the driver! Look what you have made me do!"

"Are you both OK?" I asked, rubbing my knees which had hit the metal under the windscreen and were throbbing. "David?"

274

He had slid off the back seat and was stuck in the space between it and my front seat. "Yeah. Fine."

"Mum? How about you?"

"I need a cigarette."

She fumbled for them and the matches.

"Mum, get out of the car first," David said quickly. "There may be petrol spilt in here."

"Oh, for goodness' sake." But she did get out and sat down on the roots of a tree that were growing thickly through a stone wall.

I got out and joined her. "Mum. Are you sure you're OK? You look a bit pale and your hands are shaky."

She lifted her head and stared up into the tree branches. "Sorry. I didn't mean to scare you."

A few minutes later a car approached us and slowed down.

"Everybody OK?" said the male driver.

"Yes, thank you." Mum smiled lightly. "Just a small skid on the leaves."

"Treacherous in this weather. Can I give you a hand to push you back onto the road?"

"That would be kind. David, help the gentleman please."

The Austin had a bit of a dent on its front bumper and one of the headlights was broken but not much else.

As we drove away, waving our thanks to our rescuer, David checked his watch. "Train due in ten minutes, Mum."

"We would have had time to wait with a cup of tea if you hadn't made me skid." She sniffed.

275

When Edward stepped off the train, all three of us screamed his name. David jumped up and down waving and Mum fluttered her handkerchief, packed especially for the purpose.

My eyes drank in his familiar features. His eyes were so blue in his tanned face, his uniform lent him a dashing air and he had grown a moustache. This was the longest we had ever been parted and I suddenly felt how much I had missed him.

"What's that under your nose?" asked David, pointing at the new moustache. "Newsprint?"

Edward cuffed him, "Jealous. Hi Mum."

"Darling." Mum took him in her open arms. "You look so handsome."

Over Mum's shoulder he smiled at me. "Hey Toots. Did you miss me?"

Mum handed Edward the car keys. "You drive, darling, if you're not too tired?"

David and I shared a wide-eyed glance.

"OK." Edward tipped the front seat up and threw his new kitbag onto the back seat. "Room enough for you two?" he asked.

"What about your suitcase?" David asked.

"You can have that on your lap, Shortie," Edward laughed. He helped Mum into her seat and, once we were all settled, he set off at breakneck speed, throttle on the floor and jamming the brakes on hard on every corner.

Edward laughed. "I've been away too long. These lanes are so narrow compared to Canadian roads."

"I suppose you drive on the right in Canada, do you?" Mum tried to sound calm. "Only we are still on the left here, darling."

"I know." With one hand on the wheel and the other draped across Mum's seat, he leant the car to the left. "Light me a cigarette, would you?"

"Are you allowed to smoke now?" asked David, leaning over Edward's shoulder.

"Sure. It keeps my brain clear. A pilot must stay focused."

"Mind that cyclist," shrieked Mum as he veered to the right again.

"Never distract the driver," David and I chorused, and fell about laughing.

At last we were back in Trevay.

"Welcome home, darling." Mum pulled Edward through the back door. "Cup of tea?"

"Do you have any coffee?" he asked, dropping his kitbag and suitcase on the floor.

"We haven't seen coffee for a long time." Mum filled the kettle and lit the gas. "Not that I mind. I prefer tea."

"In Canada you can still get everything," Edward told her, walking into our back room and sitting in an armchair. "Hey, Shortie, pass me my bag, would you?"

"Stop calling me Shortie," grumbled David, doing as he was asked.

Mum brought the tea tray in and sat at the table. "Hannah, I forgot the biscuits. The tin is on the side."

"In Canada they call biscuits cookies," Edward said, rummaging in his bag. "I have presents for you."

"Cookies?" asked David hopefully.

"No. But I do have an . . ." He pulled his hand from his bag, "An orange!"

"Oh," said David, disappointed.

"An orange! I haven't seen one of those for . . . well, I can't remember," Mum said.

"I have four of them. One each. Got to have them for our eyesight." Edward handed us our oranges. "And I have for you, Mum, something special."

Her eyes were suddenly lit with a joy I hadn't seen since Edward went away. "Oh?"

"Now close your eyes and put out your hands."

She obliged, laughing.

Edward put a slim paper bag in her hands. "You can look now."

Mum looked at the bag with anticipation. "What have you done, you silly boy?"

"Open it."

She lifted the edge of the bag and peeked in, wanting to keep the mystery alive just a little bit longer. "Oh." Her mouth dropped open in awe as she pulled out the packet. "Stockings! I can't believe it." She put one hand to her mouth, suppressing tears. "Stockings!"

"They're silk," smiled Edward. "Do you like them?"

She clutched the packet to her bosom. "I love them."

I was curious. "Did you go to a ladies' shop to ask for them, Edward?"

"How embarrassing," sniggered David, for whom ladies' underwear was still wildly amusing.

"Yes, I did. Nothing embarrassing about it. I am used to the ladies in Mum's shop, aren't I?" He turned

278

to Mum who was still hugging her present. "How's business?"

We sat and swapped news and drank our tea and ate sausage and mash with onion gravy (Edward's favourite) until it felt as though we were as one again.

Edward began to tell us stories of his training.

"So, there I was with my friend, Clarky, flying our two-seater trainer plane, just a little single-engine kite, when we heard a terrible noise coming from the front. Clarky looked underneath and pulled at a few things and the noise stopped. 'I don't what I've done but it's fixed it,' he said, and I said, 'You certainly have, the propeller has fallen off.'"

David was lying on the floor, his hands under his chin, rapt. "What did you do?"

"The old training kicked in. We had been taught how to glide our aircraft to a safe landing because in battle we may well have to do that if we've been damaged."

"But where did you land?" I asked.

"In a field. As soon as we got out a farmer and his son came running to us. They had the propeller. When it fell they knew what must have happened and picked it up then watched where we landed."

"Did you fix it?"

"Sure. We were up and out of there before anyone knew anything."

"Wow," breathed David. "You are so brave."

"All in a day's work," Edward laughed.

"David," said Mum. "Time for bed. Off you go."

"Oh." His shoulders slumped and his mouth turned down. "Can't I stay up a bit longer?"

"No."

Edward caught his hand as he walked past him to the stairs. "How about I come up to say goodnight when you're ready?"

David perked up immediately. "Yes please. Can you tell me more stories?"

"Bed!" Mum said sternly.

When David had finally been tucked up, Edward came down and Mum offered him a beer while I made our nightly tea and she turned on the wireless for the news.

"The Imperial Japanese Navy Air Service have launched a surprise attack on Pearl Harbor, Honolulu, Hawaii. The White House is expected to announce its formal entry into the war tomorrow.

"At home, the City of Plymouth, in Devon, has been bombed heavily. The Devonport Naval Dockyard has taken the worst of the attack but there are many civilian casualties in the city. There are warnings across Devon and Cornwall that there could be more raids in the days to come."

Edward leant forward, elbows on knees, and listened intently to the report and the advice given on how to stay safe.

Mum waited, smoking quietly, for the bulletin to finish, and for Edward to give her the news she was dreading.

"I'm being posted to Scampton, Lincolnshire. Bomber Command need all the air power they can get," he told us.

"When?" asked Mum.

"I'm waiting for orders. Couple of days perhaps."

"Two days!" I couldn't believe it. "But you've only just got home and we haven't seen you for so long."

"It's my job, Toots."

"And you'll be on bombing raids over Germany," Mum said. It was not a question.

"Yes. Anywhere we can help." He reached for one of his Canadian cigarettes. "Want one?" he asked Mum.

"Thank you." He put two between his lips and lit them both, then passed one to her.

"They could shoot you down?" I said.

"They could, but I won't let them."

I felt tears prick the back of my throat. "I don't want you to go."

"Hannah. Time for bed," said Mum.

"But Mum, you need him here." Even to myself I sounded like a whining child.

"Bed," she said.

I did as I was told, but not before I had flung myself around Edward's neck. "I hate this war."

"Toots, listen to me. We are going to beat them. I promise." Moving my fringe from my forehead he kissed me. "And I am going to tell Grandfather that when I see him tomorrow. Want to come with me?"

"Can I, Mum?"

She rolled her cigarette between her thumb and middle finger, thinking.

"No. You have school. You can see Grandfather any time, but Edward must see him before he goes."

"Because he might get shot down?" I was angry. "Or maybe Grandfather might die? That's what you mean, isn't it?"

Mum pulled on her cigarette deeply, then took her time expelling the plume of smoke. "No, darling. It's because you have to go to school."

CHAPTER
TWENTY-ONE

Hannah, Trevay

1941

Edward was doing very well at RAF Scampton. He was now a sergeant pilot and his squadron was waiting to take delivery of a fleet of the new Lancaster bombers. He said they would win the war.

We had Grandfather living with us now. The arthritis in his knees — all that praying on cold church floors, Mum said — had got very bad. Cook and Dora were still in Callyzion, though, looking after each other, which was nice. Mum and I made Edward and David's old room comfortable for Grandfather. He spent a lot of time in bed nowadays, but could still manage the stairs when he wanted to.

David was nearly eleven years old now and had made one of the top rooms his bedroom. The walls were covered with maps and clippings of our advances and losses. I told him Mr Churchill would want him at the War Office soon, and he shied a comic at my head for my trouble.

The remaining upstairs room was Mum's workroom. She had a large cutting-cum-sewing table and three dressmakers' dummies of varying sizes. When the shop was shut she often went up there to work, though I still took tea up for Mum and me to carry on our tradition of listening to the nightly BBC news hour together.

Over the last few weeks we had begun to notice that Grandfather was getting very forgetful and a little bit confused. The other night he thought David was Daddy and we had to explain that Daddy was still in Penang. I'm not sure he understood even then.

Daddy's letters had become fewer. Maybe one every couple of months. As I explained to Mum, it wasn't his fault. The ships had more important things to do than carry a letter all the way to Trevay. But we always wrote a weekly letter to him. We hadn't heard from him for almost three months.

"Here is the news from the BBC.

"Singapore has fallen. It is thought that more than fifty thousand Australian and Indian troops and government officials throughout the Malay Peninsula have been captured. Mr Churchill has called it the worst capitulation in British military history, but has said that it is 'one of those moments when the British race and nation can show their quality and their genius.'"

Mum tried every avenue to find out whether Daddy was safe and where he was, but we had no news.

But then the war got even closer to home.

Truro was bombed. They bombed the hospital.

A second bomb exploded in mid-air and travelled almost a quarter of a mile, damaging one hundred houses. Fourteen people were killed.

The next day, just after lunch, Bodmin was bombed by two enemy aircraft; the German pilots turned back to see their devastating damage and strafe the ordinary people trying to help the injured.

Later that day, there was a similar raid on The Lizard. Rosevear Farm and four houses were hit. One farmhand was injured and his cattle were killed. Luckily an RAF Spitfire was in pursuit and shot the bomber down, watching as he crashed into the sea.

Mum said when we heard the news, "It's all so terrible. A mother's son, maybe a husband and a father." I knew she was thinking about Daddy and Edward, but all I could think about was standing behind a great big ack-ack gun and shooting the enemy down before they could wreak more damage on us.

We had an RAF station about six miles away at St Eval. It was closer to Callyzion than us but it soon came in for a pasting. The work being done at St Eval was pretty hush-hush, but rumour had it that it flew reconnaissance missions to photograph what the enemy were up to and that they also hunted for submarines.

The worst attack on the airfield was in July. The runway was the target. Without that, our boys couldn't get in the air. After the raid, the planes turned for home, passing over Callyzion and emptying their bomb bays onto anything that looked like a sitting duck. Cook and Dora would have known nothing about it. Killed outright, in their beds. I knew what I had to do.

I joined the ATS. I was just eighteen.

I was ready to leave home but not to leave Mum. She was outwardly very supportive but I knew she did not want me to go.

David was growing up and his interests outside home were pulling his attention. Mainly the engines of the fishing boats and a fascination for anything that needed grease.

Grandfather was now bedridden and a tremendous burden on Mum. Not that she ever said so. She always had a cigarette dangling from her lips ticked mouth and some silly story to make us laugh.

But when I left for my basic training she behaved as if I was just popping into Truro for the day.

"Bye darling." She kissed me. "See you soon. I shan't wait to wave you off. Grandfather will be wanting his lunch." She left me, on the harbour with my kitbag and a gang of other new recruits, with a brief wave. I climbed onto the coach and watched her walk away, expecting her to turn and wave again, but she didn't.

My fellow raw recruits on the coach were a good bunch. Most of us knew each other by sight and one or two I had been at school with. The chatter and laughter started the moment we turned up the hill and out of Trevay. The driver was an older man with a bald head and wispy ginger strands combed from ear to ear.

"How long before we get to Salisbury?" a girl called Shirley shouted to him. "Only I might need to powder my nose soon."

"It's a good six hours," the man grumbled. "Should have gone when you could."

"I did," she laughed, "but I'm only small. Me mum's tea runs through me quick."

He scowled at her then turned his attention back to the road.

"What's your name, Mr Driver?" Shirley tried again. "My name's Shirley."

"I'm Mr Thomas to you," he said without looking at her.

"Oh, that's nice. I knew a Mr Thomas once. Perhaps you know him?" Shirley asked politely.

"Mebbe. What's his first name?"

"John. Mr John Thomas." Shirley shrieked with laughter and so did the girls around her. I had to ask someone what the joke was, and when she told me I found it shocking but very funny.

As the journey went on and the daylight started to fade, so the conversation became quieter. I must have nodded off at some point because Betty, sitting next to me, woke me. "Look. Stonehenge!"

"Where?"

"It's a bit dark to see but look, there, can you see the shadows in the moonlight?"

That was my first glimpse of the stones but not my last. Salisbury Plain was to become very familiar to me.

We arrived, at a very late hour, at our camp, stiff and hungry and needing the lavatory. A male officer greeted us with little warmth and gave us directions to our Nissen hut and instructions to freshen up. The entire camp was in blackout and it took a little while to adjust our eyesight to find the neat paths leading to our accommodation: a large shed. Thirty beds were set in two lines with a coke stove at the far end. I picked a bed halfway down on the right-hand side, near enough to get some heat from the stove but far enough to allow the girls who might really feel the cold to have the benefit.

Shirley was at the far end of the hut, looking for the bathroom. "Where's the lavvy? I'm not joking. I shall wet my drawers in a minute."

The officer had followed us and pointed back the way we came.

"The ablutions are twenty yards out to the right, Miss . . .?" I saw the sarcasm in his eye.

Shirley went towards him, holding out her hand, "I'm Shirley. Pleased to meet you. What's your name?"

He bared his teeth. "I am Company Sergeant Major Stewart," he barked. "And I am your worst nightmare. From now on you will address me as Company Sergeant Major, or sir. Do you understand?"

All of us stood a little straighter.

"Yes, sir, Company Major Sergeant, sir," Shirley said.

CSM Stewart quelled the giggles in the room with one, long, death stare. "Dinner is waiting for you all in the cook house. I suggest you get some food inside you and get some beauty sleep. I shall be waking you up at 5.00 a.m. You are in the Army now. You have forty-five minutes before lights out."

The wash house was a bleak and basic hut with a row of basins down the middle and WC cubicles and showers arranged around the outer walls. Once we'd done what we needed, we found our way to the cook house, where the cook had ready cottage pie and apple crumble. CSM Stewart stood surveying us from a corner, which dampened any chat we might have had about him or the food.

We ate up and cleared the tables before thanking the cook, saying goodnight to the CSM and heading for our thin beds.

We got through six weeks of intensive training, all at the double. We were assessed for fitness, hearing, eyesight and nerves. If we were to be gunners on the anti-aircraft heavy ack-ack guns, we had to prove we had nerves of steel.

Health-wise, we were well looked after. I didn't like the inoculation jabs that we seemed to get every few weeks, or indeed the FFI every Friday. It stood for Free From Infection. We had to present ourselves to a female nurse, naked, for a full and intimate examination. I found it very embarrassing and couldn't think why it was deemed necessary, until one of the girls, who had been enjoying the company of a soldier in the Tank Regiment, was treated for pubic crabs.

Once the shock of that was over, we all wondered how the hell she had time to get pubic crabs, given that every waking hour was spent marching, doing PT, cleaning our hut, polishing our shoes, church parades, manning fire equipment during raids, and then more marching for good measure. It was utterly exhausting and I loved it.

Mum couldn't come up to watch me pass out, but Edward got leave to see his little sister become a gunner in the British Army.

Once the parade was over we fell out and went to find our friends and family.

"Did I look OK?" I asked him. "Were we marching in time?"

"You looked very smart and the marching was pretty good. Better than mine was at this stage."

"Really? Oh, thank you. And thank you for coming in uniform. I have been dying to show you off."

"Come on, Toots." He took my arm. "I'm hungry. Take me to the nearest pub and I'll treat you to lunch."

Shirley caught up with us looking ravishing in her uniform. "Hello. You must be Hannah's brother? Edward? I'm Shirley. I have heard so much about you." She took his other arm and walked with us. "You're flying Lancasters, I hear."

I could tell from the way Edward had turned all his interest towards Shirley that we were not going to have our lunch alone.

I had a week's leave to go home and breathe the fresh sea air of Trevay. I had not had much time to miss it all but, as the coach lumbered down the hill and pulled up on the harbour, I drank in every feature of the town. St Peter's spire, the flock of seagulls arguing on the harbour wall and the rich smell of tar and diesel.

I jumped down the coach steps and said goodbye to the girls as we all hitched up our kitbags and walked proudly towards our homes in our uniforms.

"Hi Mum. I'm home!" I called as I opened the back door.

"Hannah!" David ran from the back room and almost knocked me over with a strong hug that left me breathless.

"Mind my jacket," I laughed as I pushed him off. "You've grown a helluva lot."

"Of course I have. It's what happens." He ducked as I tried to swipe him, then shouted, "Mum. Hannah's home and she's hitting me already."

I saw the curtain between our back room and the shop swing back and Mum stood there grinning at me. "Welcome home, darling."

"Oh Mum." Tears started filling my eyes. "I have missed you."

I took Grandfather's lunch up to him. "He doesn't eat much," Mum explained, handing me a tray with a saucer of the tiniest amount of fish, potato and peas on it. "He'll be so pleased to see you in uniform. Here, take this spoon. You'll have to feed him. Just very small amounts. He doesn't swallow as well as he did. He likes a little drop of water too." Mum put everything that Grandfather and I might need on a tray. "He might not remember you at first, but that doesn't matter; he will just be so pleased to see you."

I went up the stairs and into his room. He was lying in bed awkwardly, slipping down on the pillows.

"Hello, Grandfather," I said, putting the tray down. "Shall I make you more comfortable?"

His faded eyes turned to look at me, his voice creaky from lack of use and with a bubble of phlegm. "Hello Louisa. Where have you been?"

I smiled down at him and said brightly, "It's me. Hannah."

"Hannah? Who is Hannah?"

"I am your granddaughter."

"Are you?"

"Yes. Shall I help you sit up a bit?" He was almost weightless as I pulled him up straighter and re-plumped his pillows.

"What's it like in France?" he asked, fixing me with his gaze. "Have you seen Bertie?"

I hesitated before answering, thinking of what might be the right thing to say.

"France is in a bit of a mess actually." I picked up the saucer of his supper and sat by his bed. "You have something to eat and then I will tell you all the news."

He took a tiny amount and took his time chewing and swallowing. "Water." He reached out his arm, the skin dry and the veins blue through it. I held the glass to his lips and helped him take a couple of sips.

"How is Bertie?" he asked.

"Last I heard he was fine." I smiled to keep up the pretence. My uncle Bertie had been dead for twenty years but to Grandfather he was clearly very much alive. I fed him a piece of fish. He swallowed and asked for water again.

"I feel so sorry for Clara, you see." He put his cool hand on my arm. "He loves her so much. When do you think he'll come home?"

Poor Grandfather. It was awful to see him so muddled. One son killed in the Great War, the other thousands of miles away in brutal captivity. There was no point in upsetting him with the truth. I remembered how kind and strong he was for Edward and me when we first arrived in England. Now I must be kind and strong for him. I smiled. "She married your son Ernest."

He frowned and his jaw began to work from side to side, trying to express something he couldn't remember.

"Ernest? No no. It was Bertie who married Clara and then Ernest went to Penang."

"That's right, Ernest went to Penang," I said truthfully. "With Clara. Uncle Bertie, he," I thought for a moment, "he's in France. But I was born in Penang with my brothers Edward and David."

"Were you, by Jove? Did you meet my boys?"

"Only Ernest. He is my father."

"What is your name then?"

"Hannah. Hannah Bolitho. The same name as you."

"Good God." He tapped the side of his head with his crooked fingers. "Who are you married to?"

"No one, yet. I am your granddaughter."

"Really? But you're in the Army? I like your uniform."

"Thank you."

"Very smart. My boys, Bertie and Ernest, are in the Army." He looked at my uniform again. "Are you in the Army too?"

"Yes."

"Good girl." He patted my hand again. "Good girl. Ask Louisa to come to bed now."

"How about one more spoon?" I concentrated on getting one pea and a little corner of potato on the edge of the spoon, but by the time I had it balanced he was asleep.

As my week's leave went on, I could see how much Mum was enduring. Running the shop, caring for Grandfather and dealing with the adolescent David couldn't be easy. I took over Grandfather duties and made sure Mum got her feet up when the shop was closed for lunch, but it wasn't a solution.

"Mum, maybe you could get some help in the shop? Or maybe a daily woman to help with Grandfather and the house?"

"And how do you think I can afford that?"

"Edward and I can send you money."

"I can look after myself. It's very kind of you Hannah, darling, but we will be just fine. David's getting better around the house. He wants to go to university when the war is over, to do his blessed engineering, and if the war isn't over he wants to join the Navy."

"To be an engineer?"

"What else?" She lit a cigarette and coughed.

"Mum, Grandfather was talking about Daddy's brother again this morning."

"Oh yes." Mum turned her eyes to the window and our nextdoor neighbour, who was hanging laundry on a thin line draped from one drainpipe to another. "Silly woman, that one. It's going to rain this afternoon."

"How well did you know Bertie, Mum?"

She flicked her ash into the small pot she kept for the purpose. "Oh darling, it's all so long ago." She sighed. "He was a very nice person. I wouldn't have met your father if it hadn't been for Bertie."

"Where did you meet him?"

"In those days people bumped into each other all over the place." She checked her small wristwatch. "Right, I had better get the shop open for the afternoon. I'll have a cup of tea if you're making one."

Before I had to return to Salisbury, I helped Mum with all the time-consuming jobs she couldn't do with the shop and Grandfather to look after. I did some spring cleaning and cleared out cupboards that hadn't seen the light of day since the war started. The linen cupboard at the top of the stairs gave up its treasures unwillingly, but I found enough good white linen sheets and fine lace tablecloths (all from the vicarage in Trevay) for Mum to make several wedding dresses for her customers. She was so pleased.

"Darling. I had forgotten all about these. These are Granny Louisa's. She made the lace, you know. She had very nimble fingers. She tried to teach me during my first Christmas with her but I was useless. You have the blood of some very fine women in your fingers, you know."

David would have helped me to sweep the cellar if it hadn't been for his great fear of spiders, but he made up for it by handing over the toys he had grown out of long ago which the Women's Voluntary Services were most grateful to receive.

I tried to air Grandfather's room, but he didn't like the window being open or the noise of me brushing the carpet so in the end I gave up and sat and read to him as he dozed. He seemed to enjoy crime fiction and in particular the Lord Peter Wimsey novels by Dorothy L. Sayers, though I am not sure how well he followed the plots. I could see he was getting weaker and his chest wasn't good. The last two or three nights I was still at home, his coughing kept Mum and me awake, but she refused to let me go to him. "I know how he likes things. I shall go."

On my last morning I called the family doctor to him.

"Thank you for coming, Dr Cunningham."

"You look well, Hannah." He wiped his feet carefully on the back doormat. "Army life suits you."

I led him up the stairs and he strode into Grandfather's bedroom, leaving me to hang back at the door.

"Good morning, Reverend Bolitho. I hear you have a bit of a cough. That must be tiring. Let me have a look at you."

I watched as he opened his doctor's bag and took out his stethoscope and thermometer.

"Right. Let's pop this under your tongue while I take a listen to your lungs."

Grandfather was looking very pale and did as he was asked. "How old is he now, Hannah?"

"Nearly eighty-five."

"He's done very well." He wrapped his stethoscope up and put it back in his bag, then removed the

296

thermometer and examined it. "He's running a temperature."

"What's wrong with him? How can we help him?" I asked anxiously. "Is it serious? Only my leave ends today and I have to go back to Salisbury tonight. If needed, I could try and get some compassionate leave."

I looked at Grandfather, so vulnerable and lost-looking.

Dr Cunningham knew what I was thinking. "He is eightyfour and we can expect things to start to wear out. However, his heart is strong so I think he's going to be all right for a while yet. He has a chest infection and we don't want that turning to pneumonia, so I shall prescribe medication. He's to take it three times a day. It should perk him up and I shall come again tomorrow to check on him." He closed his bag and added, "Fresh air is best. Open his window and make sure he has plenty of liquids."

Grandfather stirred and lifted his delicate eyelids. "Don't let her open the window."

The time came for me to leave. "The coach will be waiting on the harbour, Mum."

"Would you mind if I didn't walk down with you, only I worry about Hugh on his own."

"You didn't wave me off the first time."

She put her hands on the tops of my arms. "Because I couldn't bear to see you go. Because I worry about you, and Edward, all the time. Because I love you and I miss you. That's why." She lifted one hand to brush a tear from my cheek. "That's why."

I hugged her, crying onto her shoulder. "I love you so much, Mum. I will be all right. And so will Edward. But I do worry about you. And when this war is over, Edward and I will come back and look after you. I promise."

Caroline, Truro

Present day

I decided to drive to Trevay today. The diary in the trunk had been filling my mind with old memories of our home and the shop. It was a short drive from my home in Callyzion and the weather looked promising. I needed to find Granny Clara's grave. I had some things I needed to say to her.

The graveyard in Trevay was much less municipal than the one where Mum lay, close to my home. Instead of the beautiful, almost mathematical rows of headstones and footpaths at Mum's, St Peter's churchyard in Trevay was more natural. Ancient, mossy stones leant at alarming angles, the script on the stone weathered to nothing. A few war graves, all the same, spotlessly clean with roses planted at their feet, stood as upright as the soldiers who lay beneath them once had, and the churchyard was not so big that I needed a map to find Granny Clara's grave. I spent a pleasant quarter of an hour looking for her and reading the inscriptions of others, letting them know I was there and thinking of them.

298

Granny's, when I found her, was to the left of the church and close to a clipped yew tree. I stopped and read the inscription.

*In Loving Memory
of Clara Bolitho.
A True Daughter of Cornwall.
We shall miss you always,
Michael, Edward,
Hannah and David.*

I read it again. A daughter of Cornwall? That's a laugh. She had been born in Kent, according to the trunk diary.

And then I realised. Her *four* children were named. My mother and uncles knew about their half-brother?

A handy bench was a yard or two away, so I made myself comfortable and began telling Granny Clara that I had found her out.

"Hello. It's Caroline. I have been reading about you. Recently a huge trunk was delivered to me, and inside it was your diary. I expect you are a bit shocked that I, your granddaughter, a *real* Daughter of Cornwall, am telling you this."

I stopped and put my face to the sky, feeling the light warmth of the sun. I could hear skylarks in the fields behind and the scent of new gorse hung on the breeze.

"So you were orphaned and shot off to London, leaving your old life behind you, to seek your fortune. Some would say that was brave; others might say you were a chancer."

I stopped. I knew I was angry with her and wanted to tell her how angry I was, but maybe she had no choice but to do what she'd done. Perhaps I hadn't taken her circumstances into consideration?

I cleared my throat and spoke to her again.

"I know all about Michael. Your first child. The one you left for another woman to bring up while you found yourself another man and skipped off to Malaya. You completely removed him from your life. Do you know what that must have done to him? He must have spent the rest of his life looking for you. I know how that feels. I would love to find my father but no one gave me any clues at all. Did they?"

I heard my voice growing louder. I was hurling these words at her gravestone and the emotion inside me exploded.

"Neither you nor Mum would tell me who *mine* was!"

And there it was. The reason I had been angry all my life. Why I had insisted on marrying an ordinary, kind man. Both of us being pure on our wedding night. Teaching Natalie to do the same.

I tried to control my sobs and tears but the dam had broken.

"And I am so angry that you and Mum allowed yourselves to let go and enjoy passion and love and danger and excitement. I know it cost you a lot, too, but I would have loved a bit of that. Being as good as I have been allows me to sleep at night, but it is *so* boring."

Hannah, Salisbury

1943–1945

After months of training and endless practice, I joined a battery of women capable of picking off anything that flew in the sky above us. I started as a spotter, able to identify any aircraft flying, moving on to working with plotting instruments and range-finders, which allowed the Predictor to calculate the correct angle for the gunners to fire and bring the aircraft down. I was passed as able to do all these jobs and at nineteen years old I became a sergeant. The work demanded steady nerves under gunfire; at the end of several hours we were mentally and physically exhausted, our ears numb from the noise and our voices hoarse from shouting orders. I preferred not to think about the pilots that were killed in these operations, and we were always relieved to see parachutes deployed. Those men would be taken prisoner, losing their freedom not their lives.

Edward was flying more sorties than were good for him. He had passed the mark where the odds were favourable for him. Now, every time he flew, the odds of his being shot down were getting shorter. It was only a matter of time before he could cop it and he nearly did. He had been on a bombing raid over Essen when his Lancaster was hit by anti-aircraft fire. One engine was hit and began to burn but, using his skills and the remaining engine, he managed to fly his entire crew home over the Channel at a height of only four hundred feet. He had been a sergeant pilot then but

301

was promoted to pilot officer before being awarded a Distinguished Flying Cross by the king. The invitation to Buckingham Palace for his investiture had places for only three guests. He had wanted to take Mum, David and Shirley! But with sisterly persuasion he took me instead. I still had the photo of us all outside the palace.

Afterwards, Mum and David caught the train home to get back to Grandfather, while Edward and I hit the town. In the first pub I had a lemonade, which lasted me all night as I didn't like alcohol, and Edward had a large whisky. Then another and another, but he didn't seem a bit drunk. In the next pub it was the same, but this time we met a party of other RAF pilots who also drank whisky after whisky and yet appeared unaffected.

I asked one of them how they stayed so sober and he told me, "I drink a bottle of Scotch a day when I'm not flying. We all do. It's the only way to get through the job."

When I finally got Edward out of the pub and off to the lodgings that Mum had booked, I took his arm. "Are you OK?"

"Sure, Toots. I'm fine."

"But you have had an awful lot to drink."

"Have I? Doesn't feel like nearly enough."

I looked at him and he looked away, pinching the top of his nose with his thumb and forefinger.

"Are you OK?" I asked again.

I heard his in-breath catching raw in his throat. He still wouldn't look at me. "Sure, Toots. I'm fine."

We stopped walking and I turned to face him. "Talk to me."

302

I saw his face change from despair to fury in a split second. "For God's sake! I'm absolutely fine. Absolutely. It's the others who aren't. My friends. The enemy. God knows they are *not* fine. Blown to bits or drowned in the Channel." His voice was choked now. "But I am absolutely *fine*." He rubbed at his eyes with the sleeves of his greatcoat.

We sat on a bench in the dark and I held him as he cried.

After about twenty minutes, when he had recovered himself, we got up and walked to our digs. We didn't need to say anything.

That night I didn't want him sleeping alone, so I stayed in his room and watched while he slept, and in the morning we got up, had breakfast, and never spoke about that night again.

He and I got on with the work we were trained to do and lived our lives as fully as we could. What would be the point of not doing so?

I began to drink a little and accept offers of dinner out with men who made me laugh. One of them I fell rather heavily for. I gave him my virginity, and for several weeks I was a walking advertisement for young love. Until he became ill and had to have his tonsils out.

I was waiting on the ward to surprise him when he came back from theatre and noticed a very pregnant, pretty woman waiting for someone too. We smiled at each other and would have struck up a conversation together if a nurse hadn't bustled in. "Your husband is on his way soon. Tonsils at his age can be very difficult."

The woman laughed. "Men never grow up. We have two small sons at home and he's just as helpless as them."

I slipped out of the ward and down the corridor, their laughter following me, making my foolishness feel all the greater.

When the girls in my hut found out, they were sympathetic and judgemental in equal measure. Unable to bear their pity, I joined in with their coarse talk of romance and began dating again, burying my pain in men who would take me out to dinner and away for weekends.

Grandfather died in March 1945. Mum's letter told Edward and me that it had all been very peaceful. She had been on her way to bed and made her usual visit to him to make sure he was comfortable. He had taken her hand, kissed it, and thanked her for being such a good daughter to him. It was a rare moment of lucidity, and one of the few times he had called her Clara rather than Louisa. The next morning she took him his tea and settled the cup on his bedside table before opening the curtains and telling him it looked like a fine day for Trevay, and when he didn't answer she knew he had gone.

Edward and I went home for the funeral, a twenty-four-hour pass, and to be honest I was glad that Mum had one less person to think about at home.

In April she wrote to us again. The War Office had given her news that our father was alive but still a prisoner in Changi Jail, Singapore. The Red Cross had been allowed into the prison to check on civilian detainees and had found him emaciated, and showing signs of having been tortured (we later discovered he had had his toenails removed), but he was at least surviving. I hadn't seen him for more than fifteen years and had no idea if any of my letters had got through to him, but the news he was alive made me even more impatient to finish this war. Every enemy bomber we shot down I dedicated to Dad, may God forgive me.

I was twenty-one at the end of April. All twenty-first birthdays in my hut were celebrated in the same way. The birthday girl would be taken to the pub, plied with alcohol, taken back to the hut, stripped of her clothes and left naked in the dark, locked out of the hut. I fought hard but the alcohol had made me dizzy and my efforts to resist were futile. I banged on the door, shouting to be let in, while they all laughed inside.

"You." A male voice in the dark spoke.

Covering my nakedness as best I could, I turned to face our commanding officer, who had with him two colonels I had never seen before.

"Yes sir?" I managed, noting that the girls behind the locked door had gone very quiet.

"Name?" asked the CO.

"Sergeant Bolitho, sir."

"Why are you out of uniform?"

I heard a snigger through a crack in the door. "It's my birthday, sir."

"I see. In normal circumstances I would expect you to salute me and my guests, but I can see that would hardly be appropriate."

"No, sir. Thank you, sir."

"Right, well. I don't expect to see this happen again."

"No, sir."

I could hear the bolts being drawn behind me. The door opened and several hands steered me backwards into the shelter.

The CO ushered his guests ahead of him before saying, "Sergeant Bolitho?"

"Yes, sir?"

"Happy Birthday."

On 7 May, I was in our Nissen hut trying to get some sleep, having been out on duty overnight, when the familiar voice of the prime minister, coming through the camp's Tannoy system, jolted me awake.

"*Yesterday morning . . . the German High Command . . . signed the act of unconditional surrender . . . Hostilities will officially end at one minute after midnight tonight, Tuesday 8 May . . . The ceasefire began yesterday . . . The German war, Mr Speaker, is therefore at an end . . .*"

"It's over," I whispered. "This bloody war is *over!*" I jumped out of bed. "Girls, get up. We've won!"

The ensuing commotion drowned out the next part of Mr Churchill's speech until he got to "long live the cause of freedom! God save the king!" Then, all around me, inside and outside our hut, I heard the growing swell of cheers and running feet. Someone was singing

"God Save the King" and other voices were joining in. All thoughts of exhaustion and sleep left us and we ran out into the crowd. The entire camp was electrified with joy and relief. We were ordinary people again.

I put a call through to RAF Scampton to make sure Edward was safe. "I'm OK, Toots. When you're in London, send my love to the king, won't you."

By happenstance, seven of us from my battery had been given a twenty-four-hour pass for 8 May. We had planned to get the bus down to Winchester to get our hair done for a concert party, but we ditched that and caught the early train to London.

It was standing room only on the train. Anyone in uniform stood, freeing the seats for the young women with children, older women with their friends, young boys, old men, and even dogs. Everyone was going to London to witness the momentous day.

Getting out at Waterloo, we surged through the throng and walked over Westminster Bridge and into Parliament Square.

Some of our gang had never been to London before and were goggle-eyed at seeing Big Ben and the Houses of Parliament. "Blimey," said Jane, one of the best spotters, "to think Mr Churchill lives there. Big, innit."

"It sure is!" A young American sailor with a group of pals surrounded us. "And you ladies sure look swell."

"Hey, I like a woman in uniform," said another, cosying up to one of our posher girls called Fiona.

She flicked his hand away from her waist. "No thank you."

"Aw, come on. The war is over. Time to have a little fun."

"We are having our own fun, thank you very much," Fiona said. "Come along girls, we don't want to miss Mass."

The sailors knew when they were being brushed off and, whistling and winking, they attached themselves to a group of WAAFs instead.

Fiona was walking in the opposite direction and we all followed her. "What did you mean about Mass?" I asked her.

"Just an excuse. They wouldn't want to be stuck with nuns, would they?" She chuckled. "Anyway, if I am going to be chatted up by an American, I want him to be handsome, sober and a general at least. And also, while we are here, I think we should pop into Westminster Abbey before we do the things we'll regret and have a word of thanks with the Almighty. Mummy knows the archbishop very well. Mummy and Daddy were married in the Crypt. Come on."

"Are we allowed to go in? asked Ena, a new girl to our battery and from Manchester.

Fiona tutted, "God's doors are open to all. Follow me."

The shouting, joyful rabble of voices were left behind and dimmed as we entered the quiet gloom of the ancient church. The height of the roof and its vaulted ceiling made me feel tiny and insignificant.

"Bloody hell," Jane said under her breath.

Advancing towards the grave of the Unknown Warrior, we stopped and took our caps off in respect.

Fiona bowed her head smartly, put her cap back on and saluted. After a moment's hesitation, we all followed suit.

Several people in civilian clothes smiled at us. An elderly man spoke. "Thank you."

None of us knew quite what to say. I felt clumsy and humbled. Jane grinned and replied, "Our pleasure, sir."

Then more people appeared wanting to give us their thanks and shake our hands, telling us how brave we were. Not one of us knew how to respond, feeling neither brave nor boastful.

Eventually we made our way down the nave and past the quire, where we found a pew to share. The peace seeped into me. I knelt, thinking of Grandfather and the services he had presided over in his own simple church in Callyzion. Closing my eyes I tried a very unsatisfactory prayer of thanks. The words were clumsy and my thoughts too busy to make any sense, so I stayed where I was, kneeling, until my knees got cold and I could sense the girls wanting to rejoin the outside world of mass celebrations.

As we left the abbey, a cordon of police officers and mounted cavalry were holding the crowd back and clearing a path in the road.

"What's going on?" I asked a woman with a baby in her arms.

"The king and queen are coming, I think," she told me.

"Really?" The girls and I were very excited and pushed our way to a better vantage point. Suddenly a huge cheer went up and an open horse-drawn carriage went past with the king and queen and the two princesses riding in it.

"Bloody hell!" screamed Jane. "Me mam will never believe me!"

As the royal procession moved around Parliament Square and up The Mall, the police cordon and mounted soldiers formed a barrier ahead of us and moved us slowly towards The Mall and Buckingham Palace. Shoulder to shoulder, the crowd moved and swayed like the sea running up a beach. As soon as the message got through that the royal family were safely back home, the cordon broke, allowing us to rush towards the palace gates and jam our faces against the iron railings. The famous balcony was hung with red velvet and gold braid.

"Terrific view from the balcony," Fiona said to me quietly.

"Don't you mean of the balcony?" I answered.

"Princess Elizabeth and I were at school together. At a party once, she took me up to show me the view."

"You're kidding."

"No. Why do you think she joined the ATS?"

"Because of you?" I couldn't believe what she was saying.

"Well, I may have mentioned to her that it was jolly good fun. But don't tell the others, will you?"

I shook my head. "Are you telling the truth?" I said sceptically.

"I'm afraid so, oh look . . ." A huge cheer went up behind us. "There they are!" She raised her hand and waved wildly.

310

"Will they see you?" I shouted.

"I shouldn't think so . . . oh look . . . there's Lilibet and Margaret Rose too. Hooray!" she yelled.

I didn't know if she was telling me the truth or not, but I decided to believe her as it would make a wonderful story for Mum. As I watched and waved my hat and cheered, Mr Churchill himself appeared on the balcony and stood between the king and queen. A huge wave of noise came up from the crowd, which must almost have knocked him off his feet, and yet he remained dignified and unassuming. The emotion of the moment affected almost everybody witnessing the event. Fiona put her arm through mine with tears rolling down her face. "Almost six bloody years and it's over!"

"I don't think it's properly sunk in." I looked around to find the rest of the girls but they must have been swept up in the crowd. "Can you see Jane and the other girls?" I shouted to Fiona.

She stood on tiptoes, a little bit taller than me. "No. They'll be fine though. Don't worry."

We stood as we were, cheering and waving until the balcony was empty and the curtained doors closed.

"I think we need a drink," Fiona said, putting her cap back on. "I want to find my handsome Yankee general."

Together we embraced the moment, ending up in Soho where the music and customers were flowing out of the bars onto the pavements, infecting us with joy. I had never been so drunk or so euphoric. We weren't going to die tomorrow after all. Years later we heard that Princess Elizabeth and Princess Margaret had been out on the town in disguise. If they had half as good a time as we had, I am glad.

Fiona found an American flyer who was charming and handsome and could jitterbug like a pro. I found a British lieutenant who recited reams of Rupert Brooke until I kissed him just to shut him up. The four of us sang and laughed as we made our way down to the Thames Embankment and watched as dawn broke over Waterloo Bridge.

On that night, for the first time, I felt I properly existed. No longer a daughter or sister or soldier, but a free and independent woman with my life ahead of me. My own rules. No boundaries drawn by others. I could do as I pleased. Be true to myself. I was equal to any man and would live my life in nobody's shadow.

CHAPTER
TWENTY-TWO

Hannah, Trevay

1945_1948

At last I could return to Trevay. I couldn't wait to see Mum and David and take a walk on the harbour beach. The fishing village had escaped the worst of the bombing, although St Peter's Church spire had been damaged by machine-gun fire from a burning enemy plane as it flew over and into the sea. The pilot had been rescued by a gang of fishermen and given a couple of pints in the pub before being taken prisoner of war.

My first few days at home, I moved from bed to sofa to bed again, with the occasional meal or bath. I was so happy to be home and Mum spoiled me rotten, filling me in on all the gossip.

One evening, about a week after I got home, I decided to take a walk on the beach. It had been a beautiful June day and the beach still had a couple of families playing cricket and maybe five or six people swimming in the millpond sea.

I was walking along the beach, following the estuary out to sea, when I saw something almost totally

313

submerged but showing red in the sunset. I stopped and, shading my eyes, used the same powers of concentration and focus as I had when I was on ack-ack. It wasn't quite clear enough to see until a small wave made it bob up just enough above the surface for me to be sure. It was a mine, and a big one. These floating mines had been thrown off warships since early in the war. They were, in essence, floating bombs. Large metal globes, filled with explosives and covered in spikes which, when hit by a boat would blow it to smithereens. I looked up the estuary to see if any of the Trevay fishing fleet was coming in on the evening tide. There were three boats, still about a quarter of a mile out.

I shouted to one of the swimmers who was closest to the beach, "Mine! There's a mine." And pointed to where it was travelling gently towards the harbour. "Tell everyone to get out of the water," I yelled.

Then I ran to the family playing cricket, explaining that if one of them could run to the harbourmaster and let him know, I would signal to the three fishing boats to keep clear as they came in. A few people had heard what was going on and had begun to gather on the harbour wall or come down to the beach.

"Get the children away!" I ordered in my best Sergeant Bolitho voice, and then instructed any adult with a spare piece of clothing to take it off and wave it, warning the little fleet coming in. The mine had lifted into the middle of the estuary, running quickly on the tide and pushing ever closer to the harbour wall.

As soon as the fishing boats were in shouting distance, we all yelled and screamed and waved our jumpers, pointing at the mine's position. The sun was dipping faster and we were losing daylight. The mine was getting less and less visible as the golden-red rays glinted off the surface.

Then, at last, I heard the engine of the harbourmaster's boat getting closer.

I kept my eyes on the mine and signalled clearly to where it was. The harbourmaster got as close as he could to it, killing his engine, and then, with a boat hook, began gently to push the bomb to the beach. Seeing what was happening, the fishing boats, like sheepdogs, manoeuvred themselves into a horseshoe shape. I got everyone on the beach to move back onto the harbour wall some two hundred yards away, while the little boats shepherded the mine onto the sand and waited for the bomb squad to come and disarm it.

When I got back home and told David, he was furious I hadn't come to fetch him. Mum was just cross that her supper had been spoilt. That's what war did to us.

Singapore was liberated in August 1945 and soon we had news of Dad. The first was a letter via the Red Cross, telling us that he had been hospitalised and was receiving treatment for starvation and malaria, and then we got a letter from him, in his own hand.

Dear All,

I am home in Penang. Thank God. Not feeling too bad. I received all your letters and apologise for not being able to reply — there wasn't too much in the way of good stationery to be had. It was all rather bloody, actually.

How are you? Cornwall sitting pretty in the sunshine? I shall be thinking of you eating pasties on the beach while I get the plantation back on its feet.

I had really hoped that Father might have enjoyed coming over and seeing it before it was too late. Thank you, Clara, for caring for him and for looking after the children.

Edward, I am very proud of your endeavours as a pilot. Congratulations on the DFM. Assuming you have shelved any ideas of medical school, you must, in my absence, become the head of the family and stay in Trevay to help your mother with the business.

Hannah, if you don't already have a legion of young Lochinvars sighing over you, I am certain it won't be long until you are married with a family of your own.

And, David, if you still remember your old papa, I expect you to present yourself in due course to my old alma mater, for your degree. Dublin is a grand city and Trinity an excellent college. I am sure I can put in a good word for you.

As soon as things here are back on track and I am back to my old self, in around three to five years, I will come to the UK for a long-overdue visit.

With all the best,
Pip pip,
Ernest

Edward, who had read the letter aloud to us, folded the notepaper and we sat in stunned silence.

Mum reached for her ever-present packet of cigarettes and lit one, allowing a curl of smoke to leave her mouth and head to the ceiling before saying, "He's OK then."

"He's not coming home?" David asked.

"The plantation," Mum said. "He has to make sure that it's OK."

"But what about us?" David was confused. "Why doesn't he make sure *we* are OK?"

Edward slipped the letter back into its envelope. "He'll come when he can. Won't he, Mum?"

Mum lit another cigarette from the butt of her dying one. "Of course he will. But he has a lot to see to in Penang and we are all OK, which is the main thing. Hannah?" She turned to me. "Would you look after the shop today? I have rather a headache."

The shop was quiet when Edward brought me a cup of tea and we settled on the two short stools Mum kept behind the counter for lulls such as this.

"At least Dad's all right," he said. "That's something to be grateful for."

I wrapped my hands around my cup and blew gently to cool the tea down. "We haven't seen him for sixteen years. I thought he was dead. He hasn't a clue how that feels."

"He has had it pretty bad, Toots."

"And we haven't? How dare he tell you to 'shelve' your plans for medical school, to get me married off, to encourage David to go to Dublin. No wonder Mum left him."

The words were out of my mouth before I could stop them.

"It was the war parted us," Edward said, not understanding what I was saying.

The letter had sparked a flash of anger in me which was slowly growing.

"It wasn't the war. It was him. Long before the war, Mum was unhappy with Dad. When we were still in Penang."

Edward watched my face, trying to understand me.

"Why did she go back then? After she left us with Grandfather?"

"It was more than that. Dad was . . . well, he was angry, maybe the first war did that to him, and David was frightened of him and . . . I think he hit Mum."

He looked at me in disbelief. "Really? She told you this, did she?"

"No, not exactly," I hesitated.

"You're making it up." He drained his tea cup.

"I'm not."

"So how do you know?"

"It was in the vicarage, when Mum first came back with David. I listened in at the door of Grandfather's study and heard her telling him. She was crying. She said she had left him for good. We would never go back to Penang."

"Listening at keyholes?" He looked at me with disgust. "So why didn't you tell me?"

"I don't know. It just felt too awful and I didn't want to think about it. And . . ." I hesitated.

"Well, come on? What?"

"The reason she didn't tell us about David was because he had been very ill as a baby and she was worried he might die, so she thought it was better for us not to know we had a brother in case he did die and we never got to see him." I could feel the tears constricting my throat. "And she must have been so scared and unhappy, and she was missing us and . . ." Thinking of how lonely Mum must have been, remembering how lonely Edward and I had been, my voice began to crack. "It must have been horrible for her because I know how horrible it was for us."

Edward's eyes searched mine. "Is this a lie? Tell me now."

"I'm not lying. Dad and Mum aren't going to live together again and that's the real reason he's not coming home. Please, never tell Mum or David I told you?"

The announcement of Edward's engagement to Shirley, a month later, came as a surprise to all of us. Mum and I thought things had cooled between them over the last year or so, but now that Shirley was back in Cornwall, and she lived about four miles away in a pretty hamlet called Pendruggan, things had obviously warmed up.

The news was announced during a Sunday lunch that Shirley had been invited to. Mum was a bit shocked but naturally congratulated them. David thought it all very soppy and found an excuse to go upstairs. Shirley was giddy with joy and clinging to Edward's arm like an irritating clump of ivy. I was furious that he hadn't told me and said so while he and I washed up, leaving Shirley and Mum chatting around the dining table.

"Nice of you to tell me," I whispered sarcastically, handing him a soapy plate to dry.

"I didn't realise I had to have your permission," he replied with quiet anger.

"Oh, come off it." I picked up the greasy pork roasting tin and began to scrub at it. "Why now? Have you got her in the family way?"

"Nice one, Toots. Firmly below the belt. And no, I haven't. Is it beyond your foetid thoughts that we might actually be in love?"

"Oh please!" I snorted. "Love?"

I took my hands out of the sink and faced him. "How about all those other girls you have dangling on a string? How did Shirley suddenly come out on top? You've barely mentioned her since we've been home. Shirley is a good friend of mine. She doesn't deserve to end up with a mess like you."

He threw down his tea towel and rolled his eyes, lifting his hands above his head. "Well, I am very sorry if I am slightly messed up after flying bombers over Germany and killing God knows how many people while trying to protect my flight crew, my family and my country."

"Oh, shut up," I spat. "You know what I'm talking about. The only thing you are in love with is a bottle of Scotch."

"Can't a man have a drink now and then?"

"It's more than that though, isn't it? I have seen the bottles under your bed."

"Snooping on me now, are you?" His face grew redder and he lunged at me.

"Don't you hit me!" I buried my face in my arms.

"*Stop it!*" Mum had pulled the curtain that separated the kitchen from the sitting room. I saw Shirley sitting, looking horrified, behind her.

"Edward," Mum's voice was now controlled and low. "Apologise to Shirley."

He straightened his spine. "I am so sorry, Shirley. My sister and I were just having a little argument over nothing. You know how it is."

Shirley's eyes rested on mine. "Are you OK, Hannah?"

I had picked up the discarded tea towel and was drying my hands. "Yes, yes, all fine, we can be terrors when we get going. Nothing to worry about. Sorry to have worried you." I laughed, trying to make light of the obvious tension and anger between Edward and me. "On today of all days! I'll make a pot of tea, shall I?"

Shirley reached for her coat which was draped over Mum's armchair. "Not for me. I told my mum I'd not be late and the bus is due in about ten minutes." She kissed Mum's cheek. "Thank you so much for a lovely lunch, Mrs Bolitho."

"I'll walk you to the harbour stop," Edward tried.

She squeezed past him, reaching the back door, without touching him. "No. You're all right. See you in the week." She flicked her eyes quickly to Edward and left.

"What was that all about?" demanded Mum.

Edward pointed at me. "Ask her."

Mum turned her face to me. "Well?"

I couldn't lie, so I took a deep breath and explained how worried I was about Edward's drinking and his sudden betrothal to Shirley, adding: "Mum, you must have seen the bottles under his bed?"

"Edward is a grown man, Hannah. He can do as he pleases."

"But Mum," I began pleading, "he's drinking so much. Too much. You know how often he goes to the pub. You know how he buries himself in his room after supper."

She looked at Edward. "Shall we go and look under your bed?"

"No," he said, trying to block her way to the stairs. "Hannah's making trouble because she's jealous that I'm getting married."

"No, I am not!" I said.

Edward was standing in front of us now, his arms on either side of the walls to the stairs. "She's made it all up."

I had dealt with enough drunken and bolshie men in my barracks not to be scared of him. "You are being an

322

idiot, Edward. We are doing this for your own good." I got his arm and twisted it behind his back.

"Let me past." Mum's voice was low and unignorable.

Edward relented.

She pulled out four empty whisky bottles and a half-full one. Taking them out in turn, she held them up and counted them.

Faced with the evidence, she didn't need to ask Edward to explain. He had broken down and lay on his floor sobbing.

He was still there when Dr Cunningham arrived and went to examine poor Edward.

We waited anxiously until he came down, alone, and explained what he thought was going on.

"Edward is experiencing what used to be called 'battle fatigue' but what we are now calling 'war neurosis'. I have seen rather too many young men, and some women, who are suffering the same thing. You can't expect to pull an ordinary person out of their lives and turn them into successful servicemen, with all the grisly experiences that job entails, without damaging their minds."

Mum reached to grab my hand and I held it tightly. "Will he recover?" she asked.

"It will take time. You may have noticed some changed behaviour before today's episode. Mood swings. Anger. A need to be alone. Perhaps drinking too much."

Mum nodded. "Yes. All of that. I had hoped it was a phase." She took her hand from mine and fiddled for her hanky up her sleeve. "What can we do to help him?"

"I suggest a little break away. There is a very good place for ex-servicemen to convalesce in Exeter. I can see if they have room for him."

"How long will he be away for?" I asked.

"Hard to say at this point, but a few weeks certainly."

Mum blotted her eyes. "He's getting married."

The doctor smiled. "Good. Something for you all to look forward to." He stood up, "I will be in touch as soon as I hear about a place for him." He shook Mum's hand. "He will get better. It just takes a little time."

CHAPTER
TWENTY-THREE

Hannah, Trevay

1947

Edward came back to us after sixteen weeks of treatment but it took almost twice that before the Edward of old resurfaced. He struggled between bouts of anger or withdrawal and tears.

During this time, Shirley devoted herself to him. She worked four days a week in our local bank, as a teller, but every other waking hour was given over to him.

She became part of us; family, in a way that is rare with outsiders. Together we poured love and security into him until his mood swings grew less evident and stormy, to the point where he decided he could face making a date for his wedding: 16 June 1947.

Mum immediately started making plans for the wedding dress. Shirley and Shirley's mother had no say in it.

"I have been saving some cream satin for Hannah's wedding dress," Mum announced, "but it will do for you, Shirley."

I choked on the celebratory tea I was drinking. "What about me?"

"What about you?" Mum said airily.

Shirley was mortified, "I can't have Hannah's satin."

Mum looked at us both, sizing us up. "Well, you are both very skinny, I might have enough to make your dress, Shirley, and a bridesmaid's dress for Hannah. Then Hannah," she looked over her tea cup at me, "you can use it at your own wedding when the time comes."

"Second-hand Rose? Charming," I said. "And anyway, Shirley might not want me to be her bridesmaid."

Mum smiled at her daughter-in-law-to-be. "Of course you want Hannah as your bridesmaid. You are best friends."

"Oh yes," Shirley had to say. "I was going to ask you, Hannah."

"Were you? Really?" I asked with raised eyebrows. "Mum is very good at making people do what she wants. Aren't you, Mother dear?"

"I don't know what you mean." Mum was all innocence.

Shirley laughed. "I wouldn't let your mother steamroller me even if she wanted to."

So began many nights cutting, tacking, and shooing the groom from the parlour, as the dresses began to take shape. They were very similar except for the necklines. Mine was square-cut and Shirley's sweetheart.

She also had a veil, of course, simple and hip-length, caught on the crown of her head in a tiny sparkle of a tiara.

"Where's this from, Mum? It's very pretty," I said as I took it from its musty tissue nest lying within a small and battered cardboard box.

"I can't remember," she said through a mouthful of pins.

"Was it yours?" I placed it on my head. "Does it suit me?"

"I have said I can't remember."

"What did you wear when you got married to Dad? I have never seen a photograph."

Mum ignored me. "Right, Shirley, hop onto that stool and I will pin your hem. Don't want you tripping over it on your way up the aisle."

I tried again. "Why are there no photographs of your wedding?"

"It was just after the war," she said, irritated. "We didn't have money to throw around." She knelt down and began pinning Shirley's hem.

"Did you have a proper wedding dress?" I persisted.

"Oh, for God's sake," she said crossly, not looking at me. "I have told you it was a long time ago."

"Sorry, Mum. I am just interested. That's all."

She sat back on her heels and studied the hem. I thought the subject was closed until she said, "I got married in an ordinary two-piece suit. Nothing fancy. The tiara was given to me by a friend of mine from Kent, where I was born. I told her I was marrying your father and she sent it to me. She didn't know that I didn't have a wedding dress to wear with it."

"How kind of her." I put it carefully back in its box. "What was her name?"

Mum rarely spoke about her life in Kent. All we knew was that her parents had died in a fire and she had gone to work in London when she was only eighteen.

"Philippa Hampton. A very kind woman. She looked after me when I was on my own." Mum's expression softened at the memory, then tightened again as she said briskly, "She was the person who taught me how to sew."

A bell rang in my head. I thought of the letter that Mum hadn't opened all those years ago. The one she had thrown on the fire. I'm sure the name on the back of the letter was Hampton. "Tell me about her?" I asked innocently.

"She had a lovely shop. A bit like ours but smaller and I used to work for her."

"You never told us this?"

"No well, it's all a long time ago but she was very kind to me when I was . . . very young. We lost touch."

"That's sad. She sounds lovely."

"She was. But . . ." Mum returned her attention to Shirley's hem, "neither of you will be in that church if I don't get these dresses done. Now pass me the tape measure."

The wedding day dawned warm and cloudless.

"Morning." I pushed Edward's bedroom door open with my bottom as I was carrying a mug of tea in each hand. "Wakey wakey. Rise and shine."

"What time is it?" he grumbled with his eyes still closed.

"A quarter to eight. Time for you to have your last cup of tea with your sister in your last hours as a single man."

He pulled himself up and ran his hands through his Brylcreemed hair. "Thank you."

I passed him his tea. "Shove over."

He made some space for me and we sat together, quietly drinking.

"Are you nervous?" I asked.

"No."

"Good."

"She's all right, isn't she? Shirley? You and Mum like her, don't you?"

"I'm glad you asked me that." I turned my serious face to him. "Mum and I have been waiting to tell you how awful she is and what a mistake you are making."

"Very funny, Toots."

I used my elbow to dig him in the ribs. "We love her, you idiot. She's great. Remember she was my friend first and I do have excellent taste."

"This tea is good." He swallowed another mouthful and grinned. "Oh my God, I am getting married today."

"Mr and Mrs Bolitho. Who'd have thought?"

"I wish Dad were here."

"I think Mum is happy he's not. Can you imagine the ballyhoo of him turning up out of the blue."

"I suppose you're right."

I bent to his cheek and kissed him. "I am always right." I got off the bed. "If you've finished your tea, I'll take the cup downstairs. I'm next in the bathroom after Mum, then you, then David."

"OK." He passed me his empty cup.

"One more thing," I said as I went to the door.

"What?"

"Could you please try to look handsome today?"

I closed the door just in time to miss the pillow he threw at me.

Mum, David, Edward and I had decided to walk to the church. Outside the shop, the bright sun lent Trevay the look of a fancy postcard.

"Take a photograph of us all, would you David?" Mum had become photo-mad after we had given her a Box Brownie camera for Christmas. "I want the shop in the background. Daddy would like to see it."

"The shop? What about me? The groom?" Edward teased.

"What about me the bridesmaid?" I preened.

Mum pulled us into her desired position. "Who'll be looking at you two when I am in the photo?"

David took a couple of pictures as directed, then we swapped and I took some of us with a palm tree in the background. "Dad is not the only one with palm trees."

Edward checked his watch. "We'd better get going."

Mum began to fuss around him, checking he had shaved properly and brushing the shoulders of his uniform jacket. "You'll do. Now, David, let me see your hands. The best man must have clean nails."

David held his hands out dutifully. "I did scrub them."

330

"Good boy. Now, Hannah. Turn around slowly so that I can check that your dress is hanging straight. Is it pulling anywhere?"

"No, Mum. It feels lovely."

"Good. Now then, how do I look?"

She was wearing her navy two-piece suit with a felt hat that she had steamed and to which she'd added a silk peony.

"You look lovely, Mum."

Edward held his arm out for her. "Come on, Mum, and no crying in the church please."

"As if," she sniffed.

The three of them left me at the church door to take up their positions within, while I waited for Shirley.

The guests, as they arrived, looked happy and pleased to be there, and commented on my dress and the weather. I noticed a trio of young men, all wearing their RAF uniforms.

"You must be the Scampton gang." I held out my hand to them.

"We certainly are," answered the tallest, most handsome one with a broad smile. "And you are his sister? Hannah?" he said, his eyes so blue I had to look away for a moment.

"Yes."

"Sergeant Hannah Bolitho of the ATS?"

"Well, yes," I blushed.

"I am very pleased to meet you. I'm Greg, this is Dougie and Ian."

"Nice to meet you too," I managed.

"We'd better go in and check on Ed," Greg said. "Don't want him to get cold feet, do we? Catch up with you later?"

"Lovely." I watched as they headed for the old church door and vanished into the gloom within.

Shirley's mum arrived next with a couple of her sisters, looking flustered. "I had a sherry to calm my nerves but all it's done is made me feel hot. Do I look hot, Hannah? Do I need some more powder on my nose?"

"You look lovely." I kissed her and then got tangled up with the aunts who had also been on the sherry and also wanted to kiss me. I managed to peel them off before saying, "You'd better go in. Shirley will be here in a minute." And sent them off like gaggling geese.

"The vicar emerged. Any latecomers?" he asked.

"I don't think so." I turned and peered down the short lane that led to the church. "Can't see anyone."

"Your brother is looking a little nervous." The vicar smiled. "But your mother is handing around toffees."

I laughed. "That sounds like Mum." I heard the crunch of tyres behind me. "Here comes the bride!"

A small, open-topped, blue car, its chrome gleaming, purred up to us. Shirley was waving from the back seat, her veil blowing and tiara sparkling. "I hope I am not too early!"

"It's best not to look too eager," laughed the vicar.

The driver left his seat and opened the back door to let Shirley and her father out.

"You look beautiful," I said to her.

"So do you." She grinned. "Oh God, I feel a bit sick."

"You'll be fine." I showed her the little satin bag Mum had made for me. "I've got a hanky and smelling salts in here if you need them."

"Oh thank you. Is my lipstick OK? Any on my teeth?"

"Show me? No."

"Come on, you two." Her dad was anxious to get on. "Time and tide and all that."

I stood next to Mum during the service, trying, surreptitiously, to spot RAF Greg. He was two pews back from us and it was hard to look at him without cricking my neck, so instead I thrilled to his pitch-perfect singing voice during "Love Divine, All Loves Excelling".

The service went — apart from David playing the fool and pretending he'd lost the ring — without a hitch.

Following bride and groom back up the aisle to the sunshine waiting for us, I managed a sly glance at Greg. He was looking straight at me, smiling. I almost tripped over the back of Shirley's dress in excitement.

While we were in the sunshine having the group photographs taken, I searched for my brother. He was standing behind a gravestone, smoking and chatting with a group of people.

"Edward?" I said out of the corner of my mouth as we grinned to the camera, "ask your Scampton gang to join us. It would be a great picture to send to Dad."

333

Edward fell for it and called the boys over. The photographer organised us into a small group of bride and groom, me and the three RAF boys. Greg was placed next to me and I swear his hand grazed my bottom as he straightened the back of his jacket. I was in love.

The reception was waiting for us in the back room of The Golden Hind pub and the walk down from the church to the harbour was a pleasant one. I found myself strolling alone with a group ahead of me and one behind. The sea below us was at high tide, gloriously lit by the blue skies above. Fronds of pink tamarisk waved gently beyond slate walls and the coconut scent of gorse was on the air. The soft caress of my satin dress on my skin pleased me and I began to imagine my own wedding day, walking this lane with Greg beside me, confetti on his shoulders and his strong arm around my waist. So far away was I in my daydream that it took me a few moments before I registered that someone behind was calling my name.

"Hannah! Hannah!"

I stopped and turned. Hurrying down to me were Mr and Mrs Tomlinson, the couple who had been our lodgers and were now married, holding the hands of a little girl who I assumed was their daughter.

"Hello!" I grinned. "I didn't see you at the church."

"We were a bit late," panted Mrs Tomlinson. "Sophie, say hello to Hannah." The child looked at me with screwed-up eyes and buried herself in her mother's skirts. "She's shy but once she knows you there will be no stopping her," Mrs Tomlinson laughed.

We began to walk together down the hill. "I'm so glad you could come," I said. "How is your new parish, Mr Tomlinson?"

We shared our news all the way to the harbour and The Golden Hind until they spotted Mum and abandoned me.

Greg had gone off with his friends after the photos and must be at the bar by now. Should I go and look for him? Or would that look too desperate? I decided that the noisy throng in the pub could carry on perfectly well without me for a bit, so I wandered to the harbour.

I leant against the warm stone of the harbour wall and tipped my face to the sun. Thoughts of Greg subsided as I stood with closed eyes listening to the separate noises around me. The laughter from The Golden Hind melted into the laughing sound of the gulls above me. The softness of the waves, slapping the wall under me, joined the song of the fishing boats' rigging. I opened my eyes and took a deep breath of the air laden with tar and sea salt. I might have been born on the other side of the world, but the blood of my father flowing in my veins was the blood of a Cornishwoman.

"Excuse me."

I jumped, startled by the unexpected interruption. A man, not much older than Edward, was standing beside me. He had a kind face. One that was familiar somehow. I liked it. I smiled at him. "Can I help you?"

"I hope so. I am looking for someone."

"I know most people around here."

He smiled shyly. "I can see by your dress that you may have been at the wedding today."

"Yes. Chief bridesmaid." I laughed. "My brother was married today. Do you know him?" I wondered if that was how I knew this man's face.

"No, no. I'm actually looking for a friend of my foster mother's. Clara Bolitho?"

"She's my mother."

"Oh well. Goodness." He ran his hand through his hair anxiously. "My name is Michael Carter. Your mother knew my foster mother in Kent. Miss Philippa Hampton?"

"Good heavens." I was astounded. "Mum talked about her for the first time only a few weeks ago. They were very good friends, I believe."

"I believe so. Yes." There was the beginning of a relieved smile.

He began to bite his lip. "Urn. Well yes, but . . . she'll be busy celebrating your brother's marriage won't she? I'll wait a bit. Don't want to give her a shock." He laughed nervously. "I will wait until later."

"Not at all. You can join us for the wedding breakfast. I know Mum would want you to share in our big family celebration. I'll tell her you are here."

"Oh no, no. It's going to be a bit of a surprise to see me, I think. I don't want to intrude on a family occasion. I could maybe see her tomorrow?"

Over his shoulder I spied Edward's dashing RAF chum outside the pub with a beer in his hand. "If you're sure?"

"Absolutely."

"OK. If you change your mind you know where we are."

I put him out of my mind as I left him and sauntered casually over to the pub, knowing that Greg could not miss seeing me.

"Hey." He smiled.

"Hi."

"Nice wedding. Can I get you a drink?"

"Thank you. A lemonade please."

From that moment on I knew we were going to be a couple. Inside the pub he guided me with a hand around my waist and kept me beside him, attentive, always including me, no matter who he was talking to or what the subject was.

When the call came for dinner, he said, "Can I sit next to you?"

"I don't know. Shirley spent ages making the seating plan."

"I can fix that." He steered me towards the top table then whispered something in Edward's ear. Edward spoke to Shirley and Shirley spoke to a waitress and the waitress, when she saw Greg, nodded and an extra place was squeezed in next to mine.

"Well, this is nice," he said, helping me into my chair before sitting down himself. "Now tell me who is who."

I pointed out the more interesting people and then caught Mum, sitting on the opposite side of Edward, giving me a very old-fashioned look. "And that is my mother, Clara."

"She looks amazing."

"She is."

"She's worried about you."

"Of course she is. She doesn't know who you are."

"Introduce me."

"Now?"

"Now. Before our dinner is served."

"OK."

We left our seats and went to her.

"Mum, may I introduce Greg Winter. He's a friend of Edward's."

My mother, not getting up, looked him up and down and gave him her hand. "How do you do."

"I am very pleased to meet you. Edward and I flew together in the same squadron. He is a fine man."

Mum never could trust charm. "Yes, he is. And what are you doing now the war is over?"

"I am a photographer."

Mum was not impressed. "What sort of pictures do you take?"

"My interest is fashion. I have had a couple of things published in the women's magazines."

"Fashion?" My mother looked surprised and impressed. "I am in the fashion business too."

"Are you? How fascinating. I look forward to hearing all about it. Perhaps we could find a quiet corner after we've eaten?"

"I look forward to it."

When we got back to our seats, Greg whispered, "She hates me."

"Oh stop it," I said. "I think she liked you."

"I hope so, because she's going to be seeing a lot of me." He felt for my hand under the table. "If that's OK with you?"

The food was good and the speeches funny; even David, nervous as he was, got many laughs and a round of applause for his best man's speech. And all the time, Greg stayed close to me. When the small swing band began to play, he took my hand and led me to the floor. He danced well and soon I was following him as if we had been dance partners all our lives. Mum watched me all the while.

At midnight the bride and groom made their farewells and left the pub in a shower of rice and drunken ribaldry for our home. The guests and the band took their cue and began to collect their things ready to leave. Saying goodnight to them, I went back to our table to collect my small bag and the shoes I had abandoned before dancing. Sitting on her own was Mrs Tomlinson.

"Hello. Have you had a good time?" I asked her. "Where is Sophie?"

"Harold is putting her to bed. We have a room upstairs." She pointed vaguely at the ceiling and I could see she had had a few too many glasses.

"Oh that's nice." I wanted to get away because Greg was waiting for me outside. "Well, goodnight," I said.

"I have to tell you something." She gripped my hand and pulled me down next to her. "I was remembering my own wedding. What a wonderful day. Your mother was an angel. Without her I don't know what we would have done. You are so lucky to have her as your mum. I love her like a mum. An angel she is. An angel."

She really had had too much to drink. "Ha-ha. Not always an angel but we do love her."

"She's wonderful. A wonderful, wonderful, woman," she slurred.

"Wonderful," I smiled, looking at the door anxiously, hoping that Greg would still be waiting for me.

"I am going to tell you something now. When Harold and I were lodging with you, we fell in love."

"Yes, you did. I know." I was hoping if I let her say what she wanted to say, I would get away quicker.

"We had to get married, you know, because Sophie was on the way and my family cut me off but your mother . . . your mother understood. She was so kind. No one ever guessed."

"Really?" I was amazed. "Goodness. I had no idea." I glanced at the empty doorway again. "I would love to talk more but I'm sure Mr Tomlinson will be wondering where you are and I am rather tired. It's been a very exciting day, hasn't it?"

"You are such a lucky girl."

Thankfully Mr Tomlinson appeared at that moment. "Darling, time for bed. I think you've had a bit too much sherry."

I watched as he gently got her to her feet. "Come on, old thing." He looked at me. "Goodnight Hannah. Splendid day. Splendid."

I watched as he steered her to the stairs and then hurried out into the night air.

340

Greg was waiting for me, enjoying a cigarette in the moonlight. "Would you like one?" he asked. I shook my head. "Shall we walk a little? It's a beautiful night."

Trevay had never felt so romantic. The soft air and starry skies seduced me and gave me the confidence to lean my head on Greg's shoulder without fear.

"That feels nice." He kissed the top of my head. "Edward tells me you were both born in Malaya."

"Yes. We arrived in Cornwall when Edward was ten and I was five. I barely remember Penang. Cornwall is home to me now. Where are you from?"

"Just outside Birmingham. The Black Country. My father was a miner. If it hadn't been for the war, I would be down the pit by now."

"Your parents must be very proud of you. Flying Lancasters."

"It's braver to work down the mines, believe me."

"Do you have brothers or sisters?"

"No. Only child. Apple of my parents' eyes. Spoilt rotten."

"Do you see them often?"

"No."

"Why not?"

"You might hate me."

"I could never hate you. Go on."

We stopped and he tilted his head to the stars with a huge sigh. "Honestly? I want more than they can give. I want to make my name. Be somebody. Live a better life than they have lived."

"You can do that and still love them. Be part of them."

"I know. And they will always love me. But, I don't want them to be part of the world I am beginning to inhabit." He found his cigarettes and lit one. "Does that make me sound very selfish?"

I was too intoxicated by his presence to disagree. "Of course I understand."

He kissed me. Not the determined kiss of a man who wanted sex because he's scared he'll die tomorrow, like the men I had known before. No, this was the kiss of a man who wanted me. Just me.

When we broke apart he smiled at me shyly. "You are the most lovely woman I have ever met."

"Am I?"

"Oh yes."

"Goodness."

He smiled and kissed me again. "Right, I had better get you home or I will have confirmed all your mother's suspicions about me."

We made our way back to my home, stopping constantly to kiss under the shadows of the ships tied up on the quay and the creaking signs swinging above the shops.

I heard Edward shouting even before we turned the corner into our lane.

His voice was loud and aggressive. "Get out. I don't know who you are or who you think you are, but you are upsetting my mother."

We turned the corner and I could see Edward standing in front of the door to the shop and the man, Michael Carter, who had spoken to me down at the harbour hours before, standing with dignity before him.

"Edward, I just want to speak to her," he said. "Please."

"Don't call me by my name. You don't know me and my mother does not know you."

Michael took a step closer to Edward. "I just want to see her. To talk. I am not here to hurt her."

Edward squared up to him. "Just fuck off."

Michael raised his hands in peace. "Please. It's about her friend, my foster mother. She died and she wanted me to find her. Please."

Even though this man, Michael, was the same height, if not a bit taller than Edward, he couldn't match Edward's strength. Grabbing him by his collar, Edward almost lifted Michael off his feet as he threw him off the pavement and onto the road. "I told you to fuck off. I am warning you, if I ever see you hanging around here again, I swear to God, you won't be going anywhere without a wheelchair. Do you understand?" Edward loomed over Michael who had fallen onto the road.

"Yes, I do. But if your mother ever wants to contact me, tell her I am still in Faversham. The same address," Michael said, wiping blood from his hand as he got to his feet.

"Just bugger off." Edward gave him one more glare then walked into our shop and slammed the door. The sound of the bolts being rammed into their clasps echoed around us.

I stood in shock. I had never seen Edward like that.

Greg went to Michael. "Are you OK?"

"I've been better." Michael was pale with shock. "I knew my coming here would be a shock, but I hoped

343

that it would turn out better. I just wanted her to see me. To know," he said.

He ran his hand through his disorganised hair and checked the wound on his hand.

"Is it OK?" I asked.

He gave me a smile of recognition. "Hannah. Hello again. Yes it's just a graze."

"You need to sit down for a moment," Greg said and helped me to the kerb. He sat down and I joined him, putting my arm around his slumped shoulders. "Can I take your message to Mum?"

Michael looked up at the windows above Mum's shop. "It'll keep." His smile was sad. "I just wanted her to see me and to know me. That's all. I am not here to make trouble."

"But why do you want to see her?"

Greg took a handkerchief from his pocket. "You'd better wrap that round your hand."

Michael was surprised to see that the blood from his hand was now dripping onto his trousers.

"That's not a graze." Greg pointed at a broken piece of glass. "You must have fallen on that."

"I'll tie it for you." I took his hand. The cut was small but deep. "There. You'll need to clean it. Where are you staying?"

"Over the hill and faraway." He got to his feet with a hollow laugh.

"We could get you a taxi?"

"No. No. I am fine. You are a kind person, Hannah. But if you knew my true circumstance, I fear you might treat me as your brother has."

"I can promise you I wouldn't," I told him earnestly. "I want to help you."

"You are very kind." He shook Greg's hand and then mine. "I am so pleased to have met you, Hannah. And I apologise for creating such a scene."

"Are you staying in Trevay tonight?" I asked, not wanting him to leave like this. "Perhaps we could meet up tomorrow and we could talk?"

"Maybe." His smile to me was suddenly kind and almost affectionate. "One day perhaps." With a deep breath, he stood tall and gave me a short bow from the neck. "Goodnight. And thank you. I shall not forget your kindness." He nodded to Greg and walked away.

Greg and I watched as he rounded the corner, listening to his footsteps slowly diminish in the quiet dark.

I turned to our door crossly. "I am going to have words with Edward."

Greg held my arm and pulled me back to him. "Edward is enjoying his wedding night and you are not going to spoil that."

"I suppose not," I sighed. "Fancy a cup of tea?"

"No." He put his arms around me. "But I do fancy you."

"Oh Greg."

"Come on. Let's find somewhere we can be alone."

We spent the rest of the night huddled in the bus shelter by the fish market. We talked about everything. He told me about wanting to travel the world with his camera, to be a photojournalist. During the war he had managed to take images from his cockpit of the damage his bombs had done over Germany. He told me how he'd had to close his mind to the people beneath him. The dead, the homeless, the widowed and orphaned. The War Office discovered what he was doing and asked him to continue for their intelligence work.

"It wasn't easy," he told me. "Once you've dropped your payload, you want to get up and out of there as soon as possible. Not be worrying about focus and composition. But when I could get a shot, I did. But what I found is that there are so many stories in the world that can be told in pictures. Have you seen the *National Geographic Magazine?*"

I shook my head.

"You should. Stories about people and places you would never have thought of. Wild, dangerous, colourful places."

"Like Penang?"

"Yes!" His eyes lit up. "I could take you to Penang and you can show me your father's house. His plantation. Look at how his workers live."

"I would love that. We took some pictures of Edward and Shirley today. All dressed up. And of Mum and David and me too. He hasn't had any recent photos for ages. He'll hardly recognise David. He's grown so much."

He smiled. "You see. You get it. Our lives. Their lives and what we can learn from each other."

"It all sounds incredible. I should like to watch you work."

"I will take pictures of you." He looked deeply into my eyes and, as described in any romantic fiction I had read, I melted.

As the eastern sky began to gather streaks of light, the red and green navigational lights of Trevay's fleet of fishing boats pricked the inky sea as they sailed back into harbour.

We walked to the harbour wall and down to the small beach, where we watched them and skimmed stones.

"Stay right where you are," he said to me as I was about to throw a smooth piece of slate.

"Why?"

"With the dawn light behind you, you are the most beautiful girl I have ever seen."

I laughed. "What about all those fashion models you work with?"

"They have superficial beauty but inside there is nothing. They can't match you."

"Oh," I said.

"Yes. Oh," he replied.

We held each other and he kissed me again and then whispered into my neck, "This must be the best day of my life."

"Mine too," I breathed. "What time is it, Greg?"

He checked his watch. "Ten to five."

"Ten to five? Oh gosh. Mum will be mad."

He took my hand and together we ran.

Greg saw me safely into the kitchen and then, with one last kiss, he left me for his guesthouse. I crept upstairs and found Mum sleeping soundly. Not snoring exactly, but breathing through her mouth, puffing out her lips in a small purring sound. I pulled off my bridesmaid's dress and hung it up carefully. In the dressing-table mirror I saw a different me to the one of yesterday. Softer, happier, feminine. Things I hadn't had time for during the war years. I slipped off my underwear, pulled on my nightie and got into bed. My head was full of Greg and my lips were almost bruised by all his kisses. I thought I wouldn't sleep but I did, solidly and dreamlessly, until Shirley woke me a couple of hours later.

"Hannah? Are you awake?"

"No," I said without opening my eyes. "Is Mum awake?"

"Yes, she's downstairs already." She giggled and, lifting up my bedclothes, slid in next to me. "Wasn't yesterday divine?" she breathed. "I can't believe we are now sisters. Edward is the most wonderful man and I am so happy. Last night in bed was pretty good too." She giggled.

"Eugh." I pulled the sheets around me. "I don't want to know."

"And what about you and Gorgeous Greg? Tell me everything."

I opened one eye and smiled. "I can't possibly tell you everything."

She opened her eyes wide. "Oh my goodness! Hannah Bolitho! You didn't!"

"No, I did not. But I might. What time is it?"

"A quarter to eight."

I groaned. "I didn't get in until five. Can I go back to sleep, please?"

"OK." She wriggled down next to me.

"Are you staying?" I opened one eye, "Or going back to your bed of marital passion?"

"I'll stay."

"Well be quiet."

"OK." She was silent for approximately ten seconds. "Something really weird happened last night."

"What?"

"A man came looking for your mum, only she took one look at him and told Edward to see him off."

Suddenly I didn't feel so tired. "Yes. I saw Edward throw him out. I spoke to him. He seemed very nice."

Shirley gave a shiver.

"He must have followed us home from the reception, because he was hanging around outside when we got back. We used the back door as we always do, and kept it open because it was such a lovely warm evening. Your mum and I went into the parlour with David, who by the way had had too much shandy, while Edward put the kettle on. Your mum and I were laughing at David, who was telling us his silly jokes, when we heard a man's voice at the kitchen door, asking if this was Clara Bolitho's house. Well, your mum and I hushed David and listened. We heard the man say his name was Michael something and that his foster mother had known your mum when she was in Kent. Your mum got up ever so quickly to go and see him. I followed her and when she saw the man, she slammed the door in his face. She looked as if she'd seen a ghost. She was so pale I got her a brandy.

"Anyway, the next thing we know is there's a hammering on the shop door and she told Edward to see him off. That he wasn't to hang around here. Well, we heard Edward open the door and tell the man what for. Your mum was very upset. Edward poured her another brandy until she'd calmed down and then she went to bed saying she had a headache."

"So, who was he then? Michael?" I asked. "Did Mum say?"

"No. She said nothing."

"It's funny but I met him yesterday after the wedding. We spoke and he seemed really sweet."

"Well, I think Edward is right. He thinks he might be one of them who has funny thoughts," Shirley said. "You know. Imaginary friends and stuff. I mean, look at some of the people Edward was in hospital with when he was ill. Perhaps he has the same thing Edward had."

"Oh yes. That might explain it." I remember I had thought Michael looked familiar. "He must have been in the same hospital with Edward. He must have heard Edward talking about Mum or something and made a weird connection with her in his brain. Poor man."

"Edward said he'd never seen him before."

"Well, he was on that much medication, he probably wouldn't remember."

"I hadn't thought of that," Shirley said. "That'll be it. Well done, Hannah. Mystery solved."

CHAPTER
TWENTY-FOUR

Hannah, Trevay

1947

Edward and Shirley slotted into married life easily. They took over the two top rooms, Mum moved her workshop back downstairs, and Shirley kept her job at the bank while Edward took on shifts at the pub as well as in the shop.

All I wanted to do was to see Greg again. I didn't hear from him at all over the next six days.

"You're about as useful as a wet lettuce, moping around all the time. Waiting for the postman," Mum chastised me. "Find something useful to do. The bakers are looking for girls."

The bakers were on the quay and famous for their pasties and bread. It wasn't the same as working on ack-ack but it was a job (and paid a bit better than Mum did). It was extraordinary that women who had worked at men's jobs during the war were now subjugated to office work or shop work, while the men took up where they had left off.

I took the job because it was easy and my working hours meant I would have plenty of weekends free to see Greg.

His first letter arrived exactly a week after the wedding.

Dearest beautiful Hannah,

Forgive me for not writing straight away but I have been on a couple of jobs for knitting patterns. The pay was dreadful but will at least allow me to buy you a decent dinner this weekend. Can you come up to town? I would pay the train fare if I could but that would mean no pudding with your dinner. Say you'll come? I can't live another week without you.

Let me know by return of post.

Your Greg x

I told Mum that Greg had booked me into a local hotel, where his parents would stay when they came to town to visit, and he would sleep in his small flat.

She narrowed her eyes and lit a cigarette before giving me a very vague birds-and-bees talk. "Men get very excited and women have to be careful," she said, not filling in any of the gaps between what I knew already. "Women who get pregnant before marriage have only themselves to blame. Your father would disown you if you got into trouble. And imagine what Edward and David would think. It would bring shame on us all."

"Yes Mum," I said primly. "Greg is very respectful and I am not silly."

"I hope so," she said.

I couldn't wait to get on the train or for the journey to end. At Paddington I looked around expecting to see Greg, who had told me he'd be there to meet me, but I couldn't see him so I waited in the station café. He turned up almost an hour late, full of apologies.

"Darling little Hannah, I am so sorry. The bloody designer I am working with is such a prima donna. He actually flounced out after I said that I thought the model didn't look good in the gown he had designed. He started crying, and that set off Francine, who may be delightful to look at but —"

"Francine? Wallis?" My eyes widened.

"Yes, anyway, she started crying, her make-up was ruined and —"

I interrupted again. "She's on the cover of almost every magazine."

"Yes, darling, but believe me, she looks like a screwed-up sock when she's been crying, so then the make-up artist took ages to . . ."

I began to laugh. "But she's the Face of the Year."

He stopped and looked at me. Really looked at me. "Darling Hannah, what am I doing, prattling on about idiotic, neurotic, arty pansies, when I should be hailing a cab and getting you back to my humble abode so that I can kiss you?"

We hurried to the taxi rank. "Ealing please, cabbie. Denbigh Road," he told the driver with an easy charm.

"Righto sir."

In the back of the cab, with Greg holding my hand, I felt born again. This was my future. I had heard girls talking about finding the "one", and how you knew straight away when "It" was "It". And now I discovered for myself that they had been right. I had found my "one".

"Just here on the left, cabbie."

We had pulled up outside a large, red-brick, three-storey house, identical to the others in the street.

"Two shillings and sixpence, please."

Greg patted his pockets. "Oh God, I've left my wallet at the studios. Darling . . ." He pulled his mouth down in an apology. "Could you possibly?"

"Yes, of course." I found the change and gave the cabbie a tip on top.

"Thanks, miss." He smiled then said, loudly enough for Greg to hear, "Make sure he pays you back. Tata."

Greg tutted. "What sort of chap does he think I am? Thank you, darling, I won't forget I owe you."

His flat was at the top of the house. Just one room but large and airy with a view over the street.

"Just temporary," he told me, kneeling to put a match to the gas fire. "It gets a bit chilly up here but the fabulous natural light makes it worthwhile. Even if there is a hell of a draught coming through it."

I thought it the most romantic room I had ever seen. Through the skylight window the sky was cornflower blue. I pictured us lying on the rug by the fire, in each other's arms, and counting the stars as they appeared in the heavens.

The gas fire popped. "Shit. Bloody meter. Hannah, have you got a couple of bob?"

I had and happily handed them over.

"Sorry, darling. I wanted this to be so perfect for you."

"It's rather romantic." I smiled, "Lovers in a garret and all that."

"Lovers?" He raised an eyebrow comically. "You are not thinking of seducing me, are you?"

"Furthest thing from my mind."

He took a step closer to me and said in a low voice. "Mine too."

I took a step towards him so that our faces were almost touching. "Well, that's all right then, isn't it?"

I had never known a man kiss so beautifully. Some were overeager. Tongues like rogue invaders. Teeth clashing. But Greg's lips were gentle on mine, moving with ease and no hurry. I honestly could have stood there being kissed all night. Such is woman's frailty.

When we broke away, Greg busied himself with making us cheese on toast and pouring two large gins from an almost empty bottle.

I knew there was no boarding house down the road, as I had told Mum, and as the gin took hold, I was more than willing to shed my clothes and be made love to on the rug in front of Greg's gas fire. There were no stars above, just the pattering of rain on the glass above us. He didn't ask me if it was my first time and I didn't tell him it wasn't, but I was grateful that he had a packet of French letters to hand.

"Hannah, did you hear anything I just said?" Mum was carrying a basket of laundry out of the back door. "Or are you going to sit there and file your nails all day?"

I put the nail file down. "Sorry, Mum." Greg had told me how beautiful my hands were. He said they were hands that could paint the Madonna or play the violin.

"Sorry," I said again. "Do you need some help?"

She sighed. "Dear God, you're about as useful as a wet dream."

I bit my lip, to stop myself laughing at Mum's unusual crudity.

"Mum!"

"Well, honestly. Since you got back from London, I can't get any sense out of you." She lifted the laundry basket further up her hip to wedge it better. "Get the pegs and help me hang this lot."

It was warm out. The heat was bouncing off the tiny square of brick yard we called a garden. Mum had recently planted a small trellis of sweet peas climbing the wall between us and our neighbour, and a crop of early potatoes were sprouting in an old zinc bath, by the gate.

"These should dry well," she said as we strung the sheets and David's school shirts on the line.

"I'll iron them tonight if you like, Mum." I gave her my most winning smile. She was right, I hadn't pulled my weight since seeing Greg. "I'll cook supper too. What have we got?"

356

She knew I was trying to appease her and gave me a tiny smile as she delved into the front pocket of her floral overall for a cigarette.

"Sausage, mash and beans. And while you're in such a helpful mood, bring me out a cuppa, would you?"

"Of course, Mum. You sit down in the sun and I'll bring it out."

In the kitchen, I took two cups from the hooks hanging under the crockery shelf and waited for the kettle to boil. The smoke from Mum's cigarette drifted through the open kitchen window. I liked it. It was her. I couldn't remember a time when she didn't have a cigarette in her hand or hanging perilously from the corner of her mouth as she pinned a hem or shelled peas, squinting against the smoke.

I made the tea and took it out. She was sitting on the old bentwood chair we kept outside for the warm weather. "There you are."

She threw the stub of her cigarette on the brick floor and took the tea I passed her. She looked tired. "Thank you, darling."

I settled myself on the warm bricks. "You do too much, Mum."

She sipped her scalding tea, coughed and reached for another cigarette. "I'll have plenty of time to rest when I'm in the churchyard."

"Your mum's cough is sounding worse," Shirley said, walking down from church the following Sunday.

"She's always had that cough," Edward answered. "It's just Mum."

357

Shirley turned to me. "Don't you think it's worse, Hannah?"

I thought for a second. "No. Just the same as always." But she had got me thinking. I did hear Mum in the night coughing more than usual, and I had found one of her hankies with a bit of blood on it. "Nose bleed," she had told me.

David left school that summer. He had done well in his School Certificate and had been taken on by the small garage workshop up at the Trevay sheds as an apprentice.

"I thought you were going to Trinity? Dad's old college," Edward said, tamping down his pipe, a new affectation.

David shrugged. "We haven't heard from Dad for ages. Why should I bother when old man Reggie —"

"Mr Davies to you, David," Mum reprimanded.

"Yes, Mum." He began again. "When Mr *Davies*," he emphasised sarcastically, "says he'll have me fully qualified as a mechanic by the time I'm eighteen."

"I could have done with you fixing up my old kite during the war," Edward said, lighting his pipe.

"Could you? Could I still do that?" David asked eagerly.

"Of course, although knowing you, you'd be busy inventing new aircraft with all the gadgets."

Mum laughed as she inhaled deeply on her cigarette. "Oh darling, don't give the poor boy ideas . . ." She broke off, feeling for the hanky up her sleeve, and coughed violently, the noise coming from deep in her chest, until she retched.

358

"Has something gone down the wrong way, Clara?" asked Shirley, getting up ready to hit her mother-in-law on the back.

Mum held a hand up to stop her while holding her handkerchief to her face. She shook her head, struggling to inhale.

"I'll get some water," I said, running to the kitchen.

When I came back, Mum was wheezing badly and Edward, Shirley and David were standing over her looking shocked. I followed their eyes and saw the red clot on the handkerchief in her hand.

Edward took control instantly and got Mum to lie on her side on the floor, instructing Shirley to fetch a cushion and a blanket. "Hannah, get Dr Cunningham," he ordered.

"I'm coming with you," shivered David, and together we ran out of the house.

"Is she going to die?" David said, trying not to cry.

"Darling, of course not," I said, trying to sound as if I believed the words myself. "Come on, I'll race you to the doctor."

The rest of the afternoon went too fast and yet in slow motion.

Dr Cunningham examined her and called for the ambulance. "Just a precaution. Might as well give her a night's rest in hospital and check her out."

Shirley and Edward went with her while David and I ate toast and played Ludo while listening to the radio.

We were still up when Edward and Shirley came home.

David jumped up. "What did the hospital say?"

Edward looked at me. "Toots, put the kettle on, would you?" He looked dead on his feet. "Actually, have we any whisky?"

I found the bottle and poured him a little and, after some hesitation, I put a splash into Shirley's tea too.

"So, tell us. What's wrong with her?"

Edward sat back in Mum's armchair and rubbed his eyes. "They will do some tests over the next few days. Keep her in hospital to rest. It could be that coughing so hard has burst a blood vessel, or it could be just a bit of asthma, or, worst case, it could be TB, but they don't think that's likely."

"Thank goodness." I immediately felt relieved.

Edward drained his glass. "Toots, you are going to have to take some time off from the bakers. They'll understand."

"Hang on." I wasn't going to be taken advantage of. "I like my job, and the money I bring into this house is as good as yours."

"Shirley can't leave the bank and I do enough as it is, working late in the pub and in Mum's shop. It makes sense for you to stay at home and look after the shop and the house."

"I suppose," I answered gracelessly. When was I going to see Greg again if I was tied to the stove and shop?

Edward had moved on. "David, you'll help Hannah. It's all hands to the pump."

"Why me?" David whined. "I work too, you know."

Edward lost his rag. "My God, I am glad Mum isn't here to listen to your selfishness."

Shirley, sitting next to him, placed her hand on his arm. "Teddy, we are all tired and upset. There's no point getting angry."

I picked at a nail while David muttered, "I'm sorry."

"Me too," I said. "I'll tell work tomorrow. I don't want Mum worrying."

"Here's to teamwork," Shirley said, raising her cup.

"Teamwork!" I smiled weakly, but down in my shallow, selfish mind, all I could think of was how I could use Mum's absence as a cover to see Greg.

I couldn't phone Greg because he didn't have a phone in his flat, and if he wasn't at home, he was on a photoshoot somewhere. But I did have his address and I wrote to him that night. My heart wanted to gush about how much I missed him and longed to see him again. My mind decided to affect sophisticated nonchalance.

Dear Greg,

Cornwall is gorgeous at the moment. All I want to do is swim and sunbathe. I am thinking of getting a new swimming costume. Perhaps a little daring? What would you think of a pretty red one with a halterneck and sweetheart neckline? Yes, I saw the picture you took of the bathing belles of Bournemouth in yesterday's newspaper. Do you think one of their costumes would suit me?

You might want to come down to Trevay and I could model for you. I am joking! But it might be fun!

Unfortunately I cannot get to London to see you for a while. My mother is a little unwell and needs rest. She is in the local hospital, very well cared for, but I have to "man the shop".

Actually, it can be amusing. Mum's customers are rather old-fashioned. They are disappointed when they see me behind the counter because they adore Edward. He helps Mum out sometimes and is a whizz at selling anything to them.

Why don't you pop down soon? Edward would love to see you.

Very affectionately,

Hannah

I read it through several times. Would it sound too corny? Did I sound too desperate? Would he accept my oblique invitation?

In the end I stuck a stamp onto the envelope and marched to the postbox where I pushed it straight in and let go before I could stop myself. Done. What was the worst that could happen?

I fretted all that afternoon and evening, imagining scenes where I waited for the postman to empty the box, begging him to give me the letter back. "Can't do that, miss. Against the rules. This is the *Royal* Mail and I am entrusted to make sure it doesn't fall into the hands of criminals."

"But I'm not a criminal!" I would wring my hands in earnest, fear and panic making me want to cry.

"How do I know that? Eh? There could be money or a cheque in the envelope! Now run along, miss, or I will have to call a police officer to take you to the cells."

362

I was ashamed to have sent Greg such a clearly provocative letter. What would Edward or Mum think of me?

Mum! I hadn't thought about her at all. I resolved to go to see her first thing in the morning. Not only was I a harlot, I was a heartless daughter.

Mum looked much better when I arrived. She was sitting up, drinking tea and chatting to a very old woman in the next bed.

"Hi, Mum."

"Darling, I was just telling Mrs Lane here about the shop. How is it going? Did Miss Southern get the lace I ordered for her? I put it aside."

"Yes, Mum, and she liked it very much."

"Oh good; I told her the lilac would be prettier than the blue. Better on her sallow skin. Poor dear." She turned to Mrs Lane and raised her voice. "It's such a godsend to have a daughter like Hannah. She was in the ATS, you know. On the guns. Became a sergeant."

Mrs Lane looked at me and grinned. Her teeth, I noted, were in the glass beside her. "Oh yes." She nodded, extending the "S" to almost a whistle.

"She's rather deaf," my mother whispered to me. "Poor old thing. I chat to keep her busy but I'm not sure how much she takes in." She turned back to Mrs Lane. "This is Hannah. The one I was telling you about. She'll bring me in some wool and my crochet hooks and I will make you a bed jacket. Remember?"

"Oh yes," Mrs Lane whistled again, grinning and flaunting her bare gums. "On Wednesday."

"That's right." My mother nodded as though she were talking to a toddler, then lowered her voice again, "Poor soul. She's not all there. She's obsessed with Wednesday. God knows what happens on Wednesdays."

A young nurse, pushing a medicine trolley, stopped at Mrs Lane's bed. She smiled at Mum.

"Mrs Lane first, then your turn, Mrs B." I stood out of her way as she swished the curtains around herself and her patient.

I pulled a chair up and took Mum's hand. "How are you?"

"Fed up with being in here."

"The rest will do you good. How's your cough?"

"It seems a bit better. They keep coming round poking me and saying I have to give up smoking, then they give me tablets as big as horse pills which," she lowered her voice, "have blocked me up completely. Can you get me some syrup of figs?"

"The nurse will give you some if you ask."

"It's embarrassing enough without the whole ward knowing."

"Oh Mum. We are missing you."

"I hope so."

"We are, and everything at home is fine. Shirley and I do the cooking and ironing between us."

"And the shop?"

"Ticking over. The consignment from Singapore came in yesterday. Some really lovely brocade."

"Good."

"And you? Has the doctor said anything yet? About when you can come home?"

"They don't tell you anything in here."

The curtains beside us swished open again, revealing Mrs Lane with her hair brushed and pillows plumped, sleeping quietly.

"Good morning, Mrs Bolitho. Your turn. How did you sleep?" The young nurse's uniform rustled with pleasing authority.

"Very badly," complained Mum. "It's too noisy and too hot to get any sleep in here."

"Then why," the nurse smiled, taking a pen from her pocket, "did the night staff record that on their hourly checks you were asleep?"

"I may have dozed."

"Oh, I see! I'll let them know that if you're snoring you're just dozing. Is that right?"

I laughed. "Pay no attention to my mother. She's a story-spinner."

"I have noticed." She laughed. "Now then, Mrs Bolitho, the doctor will be coming around soon so I have to get you spick and span for him."

I stood up. "While you do that, I'll go and get us a cup of tea. Oh, and do you have any syrup of figs? Mum needs some." I winked at them both and set off to find the tea trolley.

CHAPTER
TWENTY-FIVE

Hannah, Trevay

1947

The doctor said that Mum's chest was clearing well. It wasn't asthma or TB, and as long as she stayed off the smokes she'd be fine; however, he was going to test some new medication on her and so she was to be kept in for the next week for monitoring.

Walking out of the hospital I felt a lot happier. Edward was looking after the shop so I decided to walk down to the butcher's and get us some nice steaks for supper. A celebratory extravagance. Mum was fine. The sea was sparkling and I was in love. I felt loved too, which meant that I had a spring in my step, a swing in my hips and time to smile and chat to people as I passed. The café on the quay had its tables outside, so I stopped and ordered a pot of tea for one and a toasted teacake; I hadn't had breakfast so what the hell? It was my money.

The war seemed a very long way away now and the life I had been resigned to losing, in those dark days, now spooled ahead of me. The men I had given myself to were nothing. We had to believe we were alive to stay alive. Comfort found where comfort was. And now I had Greg. A man who truly loved me. A man I truly loved and the man for now and for ever.

I shared the last crumbs of my teacake with a young seagull that had joined me, drained the lukewarm drops of tea from the little brown pot, left my payment on the saucer and walked home as if on air.

"Hi Toots." Edward looked up and smiled as I walked through the shop door from the street. "How's Mum?"

I filled him in with all the good news. "Shop been busy?" I finished.

"Dead." He stretched his shoulders where he sat behind the counter. "Oh, this came for you."

He found an envelope that was hidden under a ball of egg-yellow wool.

"Why do we even stock that?" I asked. "It's horrible."

"Mrs Peters is knitting a cot blanket for her expected grandchild."

"Poor little sod."

I took the envelope he passed to me. My heart skipped a beat as I recognised Greg's handwriting.

Edward was moving towards the curtained entrance to our sitting room out back. "I'm going to grab forty winks before I start tonight's pub shift."

I wanted to read my letter before he left me to look after the shop. "I've bought steaks for supper. I'll cook you one before you go to the pub, but let me put them in the pantry first to stay cool, and I need to powder my nose."

Reluctantly he turned back. "Steak. Pushing the boat out, are we? I'll have some of that."

"Yes, well, it's to celebrate Mum's all-clear from anything nasty."

I hurriedly put the steaks away then slunk off to the lavatory, the only room with a lock, where I could read Greg's letter in peace.

Darling Hannah,

I like the idea of you in one of those bathing costumes. I would have it off you in a matter of moments, or maybe not. Maybe I'd let you tease me a bit first.

Actually, I suggested Cornwall as a location for a shoot in *Woman's Own*. The art director loves the idea. So, how are you fixed for next Thursday? Fancy being my Girl Friday? Then, when the shoot is over, I will stay down for the weekend. How does that sound? Know any romantic little B and Bs?

I'll call you when I arrive.

G xx

I read the letter twice more, thrilling to every word he'd written. With a bit of luck, Mum wouldn't be back home until Monday or Tuesday.

I took great care cooking the steaks, and served them up with fried onions and potatoes the way I knew would please Edward.

"Very nice, Hannah," he said, mopping the plate clean with a piece of bread.

"Delicious," added Shirley.

"I'll have your spuds if you don't want them," said David to Shirley.

"Go on then." She pushed them onto his plate with her knife. "I'll do the washing up."

"No. Let me." I stood up and collected Edward's plate. "You've been working all day."

She smiled gratefully. "If you're sure?"

"Absolutely."

"I might go for a bath and an early night." She stretched her arms over her head. "You don't mind, do you, Teddy?"

"I'll try not to wake you when I come in from the pub." He got up and kissed the top of her head, fondly, then reached for his coat hanging on the back of his chair. "See you later."

When he'd gone I said, "I'll make you a cuppa if you want one, Shirl. I'll bring it up to you when I've finished down here."

"Would you?"

"Of course. Now, up you go. And, David?"

"You want me to dry up for you," he said sullenly.

"No. I was thinking you might like to listen to that comedy on the wireless that you like."

He was amazed. "Mum doesn't like me listening late."

"Yes, well, Mum's not here, is she."

"Blimey, thanks, sis."

I washed and dried the dishes and tidied the kitchen, then took Shirley's tea up to her. She was still in the bath so I sat on the edge while she drank it.

"Such good news about your mum," she said.

"Isn't it? She was looking so much better this morning." I yawned theatrically. "The worry has been awful."

Shirley lay back in the water. "You must be exhausted, Hann. You've been so good looking after us and the shop."

"I am a bit tired." I rolled my head from shoulder to shoulder.

"I'll look after everything this weekend," she said sweetly. "You put your feet up."

"I couldn't let you do that," I whispered, rubbing my neck.

"Have you got a headache?" she asked sympathetically.

"A bit."

She sat up quickly, slopping the bath water over the rim and over my skirt. "Careful," I shrieked.

"But, I've had a great idea! Pass me the towel, would you."

I handed it to her and she stepped onto the thin bath mat, wrapping the towel around her. "You need a break."

"Ha!" I said, as if it were an impossible idea.

"No really!" She was looking very pleased with herself. "Get hold of Greg and tell him to come down for the weekend!"

I laughed the notion off. "Don't be ridiculous!"

"I am absolutely serious." She finished drying herself and sprinkled a handful of talcum powder under her arms. "Could you pass me my nightie? It's on the back of the door."

"Where would he stay?" I said, shrugging my shoulders.

She pulled her nightdress over her head and reached for her toothbrush, smiling and pointing it at me. "Why don't you say that you have been invited to stay with an old ATS friend further down the coast!"

"But who?" Again I made it sound impossible.

"Ermm, Faye?"

"I haven't spoken to her in months."

"And you don't have to. Listen," her voice became low and conspiratorial, "I'll tell Teddy that you have been invited to spend a couple of nights with Faye. I'll say that you really need a break before your mum comes home."

"And . . .?"

"And what you will actually be doing is having a nice little Mr and Mrs Smith time in a cosy hotel with Greg!"

I put my hand to my mouth as if in shock. "I couldn't!"

"You can if you want to. I won't spill the beans. Careless talk costs lives, remember?"

I laughed as if astonished. "Shirley! You naughty woman!"

She smirked, "Nothing that Edward and I didn't do before we married."

"I don't wish to know!"

"Oh, come on. I know you had your moments too. We thought we'd be killed at any minute. Remember? Life is for living, sister."

I properly laughed. "Oh Shirley. You are so wonderful."

Getting into bed that night, I felt only a slight guilt at having manipulated Shirley so easily.

Greg phoned two days later. He was coming down on the train the next day, while Francine Wallis would be driven down by her husband, Maurice.

"He's a terrible little man, but very rich," Greg told me. "I can't stand him and he doesn't trust Francine to be away from him for a night, let alone two nights. Poor little cow. By the way, darling, are you any good with a make-up brush? The usual bloody girl has got herself up the duff and had to get herself sorted."

"Sorted?"

"Yes, you know . . . 'See the doctor'; some quack, I expect, but at least she'll be back at work next week."

"Oh no. How awful." I thought of the girls who had been in a similar bind during the war. We had heard later that one girl had actually died.

"Well, they shouldn't be so damn stupid, should they?" He sounded so matter of fact. "What do these girls expect if they don't look after themselves?"

I was surprised that he should think that way. "I suppose." I thought of my own narrow escapes. Some of the men I had known refused to use French letters and it was almost impossible for women to get hold of them, unless they were married and had an understanding doctor. I couldn't imagine going to our

Dr Cunningham to ask him. He'd known us all for too many years.

"That reminds me . . ." Greg lowered his voice seductively. "I had better do some shopping myself if I have got you all to myself this weekend."

I blushed. Not with embarrassment. With passion. "Yes, you'd better had."

"That's my girl. Right. Meet me off the train at lunchtime and try to look like a make-up girl. OK?"

"OK." But he had already rung off.

I told Shirley about the updated plan.

"Lucky you." She grinned.

"Can you explain it to Edward for me?" I pleaded.

"Of course. Let me just get this word perfect. Greg's coming down a couple of days early for a photo shoot and you are going to earn some pin money as the make-up girl. Yes?"

"Yes."

"And then, on Friday night Greg is getting the train back to London while you get the train to Penzance to see Faye for a couple of days."

"Yes."

"But actually you and Greg will be on a train together for a dirty weekend?" She curtseyed as I applauded her.

The story sounded so plausible that even Mum believed it, and was actually pleased that I would be getting a little break before she came home.

"You deserve it, darling, after all you have been doing for the family while I'm stuck in here."

Guilt nibbled at my ribs that afternoon and in bed that night I was fidgety. My conscience nagged at me until I gave up on sleep and went downstairs for a very early cup of tea. I took it outside and sat on Mum's old chair, watching the dawn break over the back of the house. We had a nest of sparrows under the eaves on top of a drainpipe, and I listened as the babies woke and began squawking. I watched as their parents flew out and off in search of tasty morsels for their breakfast. I remembered we had some Rich Tea biscuits left in the tin and I went to collect a couple to break into crumbs. When Mum was home, she was always the first one up and she had told how she could feed the birds from her hand.

Settling myself back in the garden chair, I threw a few crumbs a little way from me and watched as the two birds landed on the wall separating us from our neighbours. They cocked their heads from side to side, beadily checking me out. I kept quite still, and after a few minutes they came down, tucked in and flew up to the nest to quieten the children's chatter. Gradually with each journey they got closer and closer until one hopped onto my open palm and snatched a crumb. I imagined sitting like that in the garden of the house Greg and I would live in. A cottage, hunkered down in its own pretty garden, the sea sparkling beyond the gate. I would take fresh lemonade and warm homemade bread outside for Greg and we would sit in the sun teaching our children, a son first and then a daughter, about the wildlife around us. Greg would build dens for them and I would introduce them to the

374

birds. I rubbed the last of the Rich Tea crumbs from my hands and counted the chimes of the church clock. Six of them.

The sun was climbing and the sky was the palest blue. Greg would be pleased. His photographs should look wonderful.

Back in the kitchen I laid the breakfast table.

Edward was down first.

"You're up early," he said as he did up his tie. "What time does Greg get in?"

"Midday." I went to the stove. "Egg on toast do you?"

"Lovely." He went to the mirror over the mantel and checked his collar. "You're keen on Greg, aren't you, Toots?"

I kept my back to him. "He's all right."

"Listen." He turned to face me. "I know it's none of my business, but watch yourself."

"Whatever do you mean?" I checked the toast under the grill and cracked four eggs into the frying pan.

Edward sat down. "I don't want you getting hurt, Toots. Greg is fun and all that but I'm not sure I want him fooling around with my sister."

I reached for the fish slice and turned the eggs. "You make me sound like an inexperienced teenager. He's not fooling around with me. I like him and enjoy his company."

"I am just saying he has a reputation as a love them and leave them merchant."

I laughed. "Oh for heaven's sake. I am a grown woman who knows how to live her life. I know exactly what kind of man Greg is."

"Do you? To be honest, I don't like him much. I used to but, well he's not exactly the man he pretends to be."

I was furious. "I will be the judge of that."

Edward held his hands up in peace. "All right, all right. I'm just glad he is not hanging around for the weekend, that's all. Mum wouldn't like it." He reached behind him to turn the wireless on.

"Mum wouldn't like what?" Shirley appeared dressed and freshly made-up.

I took the toast from under the grill and handed her a knife. "Butter those, would you? Eggs are nearly ready. Edward was saying that if Greg was going to stay this weekend, Mum wouldn't like it."

Shirley gave me a covert look under her mascaraed lashes. "Why ever not? He seems a trustworthy chap." She smiled at Edward, who was listening to the news. "Hannah," she went on, loud and clear for Edward's benefit, "what time is your train to Penzance on Saturday?"

"Oh, it's just after the one Greg's catching back to London," I said innocently.

"Oh yes," she said, giving me a big wink while Edward started to eat his eggs. "I expect you and Greg can share a taxi to the station. He can help you with your bag."

"That makes sense," I said. "Don't you think, Edward?"

He looked up, "What? Sorry, miles away. Any tea on the go?"

I spent the morning making beds and straightening the house to salve my guilt for the wicked weekend I was about to embark on.

I collected a few things together and put them in my small suitcase and tucked it under the bed ready for Saturday morning.

I washed my hair and shaved my legs; now all I had to do was put a little make-up on, red lipstick and powder, and get dressed. If I was going to be Francine Wallis's make-up girl, I had to look the part. I had bought a pair of denim trousers ages ago, just for knocking about in, but then had seen Marilyn Monroe wearing a pair in a magazine photo, looking sensational. Apparently, they were called jeans; I wondered if that was after Norma Jean. Anyway, I put them on with Mum's old pink gingham work shirt and belted them tightly at the waist. Checking myself in the mirror, I rolled the sleeves up and undid another button. Pretty good. Then I dug around in my wardrobe for my old pair of canvas beach shoes and rolled up the hems of the trousers. I looked even better.

All I had to do was put together a convincing set of cosmetics (powder, rouge, eyeliner and mascara), a brush and some hair lacquer, and I immediately felt like a professional cosmetician.

I arrived at the station with half an hour to spare, found a bench and turned my face to the sun. If I still had any qualms about what I was doing, they cleared like mist in the heat as soon as the London train squealed and hissed its way into the station. I saw Greg step off the train and onto the platform. He was so handsome my heart skipped. His hair had grown a little and was pushed up by the sunglasses he wore on his head. He was wearing loose cream trousers, a white shirt and a navy pullover around his neck. I watched as he stepped down with his camera bag and small duffel bag and put them on the platform. I began to jog towards him and was about to call his name when an elegant, female hand stretched down from the train door and I heard a woman's voice saying, "Darling, G. Help me down, would you?"

A slender silk-stockinged leg appeared next, followed by the model-slim body of Francine Wallis. Greg reached up and effortlessly lifted her down. Their eyes never left each other.

"Hello," I said, walking right up to them. I held my hand out to Francine. "Good afternoon, Mrs Wallis. I am Hannah, your make-up artist for the next two days."

Greg jumped and almost tripped over his bags.

"Hannah." He gave me a small peck on the cheek. "Thank you for helping out."

I gave him a wide smile. "Dearest G. You call and I come running. You know me!" I pointed to the two suitcases waiting at the train door. "You had better bring Mrs Wallis's bags out before the train goes off with them."

Irritably, he did as he was told.

Francine looked me up and down and proffered a limp hand. I shook it heartily, hoping to at least dislocate her shoulder.

Greg, breathing heavily after lifting the enormous cases down, had hidden his eyes with his sunglasses now and said tersely, "Dear Hannah. It really is sweet of you to meet us."

I ignored him. "I had no idea you were travelling by train, Mrs Wallis. Greg told me you would be motoring down with your Mr Wallis?"

"Did he?" she answered with narrowed eyes. "Unfortunately my husband is kept in London with business."

"What a shame." I smiled, then slid my arm around Greg's waist and kissed his lips. "You always have so much on your mind. Don't you, darling?"

He laughed loudly. I could tell he was nervous.

"So, where are you staying, Mrs Wallis?" I signalled to a porter to collect the bags. "I will get the taxi to drop you off."

"Where are we staying, Greg?" she purred.

"Oh damn. Didn't Maurice book you into somewhere?"

"How should I know?" Her peevish tone pleased me very much. If she was my competition, I would give her a run for her money.

"Well, there are always rooms above the pub," I told her. "It's very homely. I'm sure they could fit you in and they do an excellent breakfast."

She shuddered. "I haven't had breakfast in seven years."

Following the porter, we left the station and he whistled up one of the waiting taxis. "Where to, sir?"

Greg was nonplussed, "Er . . . Hannah, anything other than the pub?"

I grinned flirtily, "Well, there is that little guesthouse you stayed in when you visited us last time."

Francine pulled her painted lips into an unattractive pout. "I thought you said you didn't know this place, Greg."

"Ah," I said impishly, "to be honest, he didn't get to see much of the town on that visit. We were having too much fun, weren't we darling?" I nudged him in the ribs.

He gave me a filthy look. "If you say so."

I laughed, then turned to the porter who had loaded the baggage. "Can you think of a suitable place for our guest to stay?"

He lifted the front of his cap and scratched his forehead. "Well there's always The Railway Hotel. It's expensive, mind."

Francine perked up. "It sounds perfect."

I shook my head. "Sadly, they are fully booked. I checked yesterday. But I'm sure the pub will find something for you." Opening the back door of the cab, I ushered Francine and Greg in, then, jumping into the front seat, I said to the driver, "The Golden Hind, please."

CHAPTER
TWENTY-SIX

Hannah, Trevay

August 1947

The pub did have a room for Francine. Rather small with two sets of steep and narrow stairs to get to it, but it was pretty enough. Curtains that matched the counterpane of the single bed. A dressing table with a small mirror only slightly cracked. And a convenient bathroom and lavatory just across the hall, shared with a travelling salesman in the room opposite.

"And look!" I said. "You are lucky enough to have a view of the sea."

Francine gave me a look that told me she knew I was a moron. No surprise there, but she was mollified by the obeisance of the landlord's wife, Olive, who turned out to be her greatest fan.

Olive rustled up a large Bloody Mary and a handful of celery sticks, as ordered, and offered to iron all the modelling outfits, pouring from one of the large suitcases, required for the shoot that afternoon.

I took the decision to snaffle Greg while all this was happening. Pulling his arm, I said loudly, "Come along

Greg, I must show you the location before the tide comes in."

I led him to the harbour, then turned left down to the small beach that bordered the estuary and the sea. He remained silent and brooding all the way.

On the sandy beach I stopped and waved my arm to the view. "The tide is at its lowest now, which is the best time to start. Just look at the colour of the sand against the sky. It's perfect, don't you think?"

I couldn't read his eyes as he was wearing his sunglasses again. After an uncomfortable silence he spoke. "What was all that about?"

"What do you mean?" I said breezily.

"You think I am sleeping with her, don't you?"

"Do I?" I turned back to the view. "It really is a glorious setting. I shall give Francine half an hour to eat her celery and then I will pop back and do her make-up. You can set up while I do that. I'll ask Olive to bring the clothes down. We can put them up on that rock there. It should be dry. I will hold a towel up to save any modesty Francine may have."

"Hannah, stop it," he said, at last looking at me.

"Stop what?" I answered.

"I am not sleeping with her. She is an important, famous model and, as her chosen photographer, I have to keep her happy."

My façade dropped. "I saw the way you looked at her as you lifted her from the train."

"It's what I do," he answered with an exhausted sigh. "To get any model to trust you, they have to think you are flirting with them. It's my job."

"Pathetic," I sniffed.

"Yes, it is, and the way you are behaving is pathetic too."

"And what way is that?"

He took his glasses off and looked at me properly. "Jealously. Darling. Please don't spoil our few days together. I can't wait to be alone with you." He caressed the top of my arm. "You are the one light in my life. Do you think I wanted to spend all those hours on the train, listening to her bitching, her need to be the centre of all attention?"

I drew a line in the sand with the toe of my canvas shoes. "You looked as if you were enjoying it."

He took a step closer to me and wrapped his arms around my shoulders, pulling my head to his chest. "Darling, there is no need for you to worry about her. She's a clotheshorse with a small brain. God, I was furious when she told me Maurice wasn't coming down. They had some sort of argument and he wouldn't even drive her to Paddington. I had to pick her up from their house, while trying to pretend I couldn't hear Maurice screaming insults at her from upstairs. She was crying, he was screaming; it was all most unedifying."

I lifted my head from his chest. "Is this the truth?"

"Yes." His smile melted my heart. "And, by the way, you look so goddamned sexy in that outfit."

"Do I?" I almost purred.

"Uh-ha. You make Francine, with her perfectly groomed face and tailored *haute couture*, look dull, dull, dull. You, on the other hand," he held me away

383

from him, passion flaring in his eyes, "you are a real pin-up."

"Stop it." I laughed.

He took me in his arms again and kissed me, his hands roaming over my waist, hips and bottom. "I could make love to you right now. Right here."

His words gave me shivers. "Maybe tonight?" I said.

"Shall we? A blanket, a bottle of wine?"

"Yes, please."

"Consider it done."

I left him to decide on where and how he wanted to set up the pictures and went to get Francine ready. As I got in view of The Golden Hind I saw a large, blue, open-topped car thunder to a stop outside. A small man with a deep tan and a thick white moustache leapt out and headed for the pub entrance, as a group of interested bystanders gathered to admire the gleaming machine.

By the time I got inside, the man was thumping the polished bar and shouting at Graham the barman, "Where is my wife? I know she's in here somewhere." He saw a door and rushed to it. "If she's with that bloody snapper, I'll bloody kill him."

"Sir," shrieked Graham, "I don't know who you are looking for, but that is the door to the kitchen."

The man, who I now assumed was Maurice Wallis, rounded on him. "Which damn room is she in?" His eyes were bulging as he squared up to the barman. "I'll knock your bloody block off if you don't tell me right *now*."

"The door to the upstairs rooms is that one." Graham pointed shakily.

Maurice growled throatily, "It better had be."

"Excuse me." I stepped up to get between Maurice and the door. "I may be able to help you. Are you looking for Mrs Francine Wallis?"

He stopped. "Who the hell are you?"

"I am her make-up artist for the shoot she is working on this afternoon. I am about to get her ready. Would you like to follow me?"

As we mounted the stairs he began shouting: "Francine? If you are here with that pansy, I am warning you, I will kill the pair of you."

Above us I could hear a door open. "Maurice?"

"Francine? Is that you?"

Francine began to have hysterics. "Darling. You've come. I have been put in this ghastly place under false pretences. I am expected to *sleep* in this hovel. It's awful. I want to go home."

By now Maurice had pushed past me and was taking the stairs two at a time. "If that floppy piece of shit put you in this fleapit, I swear to God I will kill him."

As he got to the final step, Olive appeared from Francine's room, an expression of pure vengeance on her face. "What did you call my pub?"

"I said it's a bloody *fleapit*." He was now nose to nose with Olive, who gave him a good clump on the chin.

"I don't know who the hell you think you are," she said, "but no one speaks to me or my guests like that."

"He's my husband, you stupid woman," Francine screamed.

Olive whipped around to face her. "Oh, you've changed your tune. Stupid woman, am I? After I've got you your stupid celery and ironed your clothes. Get out, the pair of you, and take your lardy-bleddy-dah London ways with you. My husband and I, and our pub, are worth dozens of you."

"How dare you speak to me like that?" Francine drew herself up like a cobra about to strike. "My husband and I have enough money to buy your filthy pub and this village a dozen times over if we wanted to."

"You just go ahead and try," Olive said, sticking out her upturned palm. "But first, you owe me two pounds for the room, six sticks of celery and a bleddy Bloody Mary."

"I'll pay you twice that to get out of here," Francine said rashly. "Maurice, pay the peasant."

Olive laughed. "Oh dear. Insulting behaviour costs. It's forty quid now."

Francine stamped her foot. "Maurice, pay her and take me home."

Patting his pockets, he looked at Olive. "Would you take a cheque?"

"No problem." Olive smiled. "It's sixty quid for a cheque. But be quick about it, or it'll be eighty any minute."

As soon as I could, I went back to Greg. He had rolled up his cream trousers to just above his ankles and loosened a few more buttons of his shirt. His camera was in his one hand as the other was shielding his eyes, looking at the sun.

"Greg!" I called to him as I ran. "Greg!"

He turned to me. "There you are. We've got about two hours of good light." He looked beyond me. "Where's Francine?"

"On her way home." I must admit I couldn't keep the pleasure out of my voice.

Greg's face dropped. "What the hell are you talking about?"

I told him what had happened.

"And you didn't think to stop her?" he asked angrily.

"Well, no. It was all very quick and then they were gone."

"Where are the clothes?"

"For the shoot?"

"Of course, for the *damned* shoot."

He was getting angrier every second, and I was afraid how he would react when I told him. "She took them with her."

"She took them with her? *For God's sake.*" He picked up his tripod and threw it to the sand. "*What the hell am I going to tell the magazine?*"

"The truth?" I ventured quietly.

"Nobody wants the effing *truth!* They want the goods! Jesus Christ." He sat down on the sand, cradling his camera in his lap. "I know she's difficult, but this takes the bloody biscuit."

I went and sat down next to him, putting my arm around his hunched shoulders. "I am so sorry. It's all

387

my fault. I should have booked her into The Railway Hotel."

He fumbled for my hand. "You couldn't help that it was full."

"It wasn't full."

He looked at me and said slowly, "It wasn't full?"

I shook my head sheepishly. "No."

He snatched his hand from mine. "You *stupid* cow."

"I'm sorry," I mumbled.

"Sorry?" he spat as he stood up. "A fat load of good that is. You have single-handedly lost me a good commission job and you say you're sorry?"

"Yes."

"Why don't you just piss off and leave me alone?" He began to walk away to the water's edge.

I sat where I was, confused and hurt by his nastiness. What had I done? I remembered Edward's warning. Is this what he meant? *He's not exactly the man he pretends to be.*

I watched Greg go. He was heading to the open sea. I watched him until he was a small figure against the horizon and the setting sun. The sand beneath my bottom was getting cold so I stood up and saw how far the tide had come in since Greg had left me and I had been feeling so sorry for myself. If he didn't turn around and come back in the next half an hour, he would be cut off, in one of the many rocky bays that the incoming tide made it impossible to escape from or reach.

I swiftly collected up his tripod and camera bag and placed them on the rocks I knew would remain dry, and began running in the direction he had headed for.

He wasn't more than three hundred yards away. Standing knee-deep in breaking waves, soaked from head to foot and furious to see me. "I almost drowned," he shouted. "And I dropped my camera and the bloody sea has taken it."

I was more concerned about getting him safe. "The tide is running in quickly." I reached him and grabbed his arm. "Hold onto me and don't let go."

He pulled me off him. "I'm going to find my camera." As he turned away, a huge bulk of water rose up and dumped itself over us. I lost my sense of which way was up as I was tumbled underwater and scraped sharp sand and slate. My lungs were bursting as I managed to break the surface and gulp fresh air. I looked around but couldn't see Greg. I would have to go under again to find him. The sand and seaweed billowing around me made keeping my eyes open impossible. I was a strong swimmer and pushed myself in what I hoped were ever increasing circles, my arms and hands stretched out, feeling for anything human. I could feel my heart racing with panic. Nothing. I could feel nothing but strings of weed. I surfaced again, took another deep breath and continued my search. I knew it was my last chance. The tide in the estuary had a reputation for taking people under. My only option was to get out and get help. I calculated that the lifeboat was about a seven-minute run away and again swam to the surface and dragged myself out against the suction of the water. I had to bend over, holding my knees to catch my breath before I ran.

After half a minute I stood up, ready to sprint to the harbour, when I saw him. His head and shoulders were lying on the sand. The rest of his body was being nudged in by the incoming waves.

"Greg!" I reached him and dropped to my knees. "*Greg!*" I put my hand to his neck to check his pulse. "Greg? It's Hannah. Can you hear me?" I thought I felt a faint pulse, so I stood over him, grabbed him under his shoulders and pulled him up the sand. I laid him on his side and immediately a gush of water poured from his mouth, making him splutter.

"Greg." I shook him. "Breathe. Deep breaths. Come on."

I saw his chest begin to swell and he opened his eyes. "Thank God," he whispered. "Thank you."

Typical man, he wouldn't let me take him to be checked out by the doctor, so I took him home. Both of us dripping wet. As we fell through the kitchen door, Shirley, who was at the sink, gave a cry of fright.

"Oh, my goodness. What's happened to you two?" She pulled a kitchen chair out and offered it to me, but I pushed Greg down onto it. "You look half drowned, the pair of you! Let me put the kettle on."

"You don't have any brandy, do you?" He shivered appealingly. "Hannah just saved my life." If I knew then what I know now, I might not have.

CHAPTER
TWENTY-SEVEN

Hannah, Trevay

1947

Shirley ran a hot bath and I insisted that Greg was the first one in it. He needed it more than me. Later I got into his water, topping it up with a boiled kettle.

Shirley heated some soup for us.

Greg was wrapped in Edward's dressing gown, and I was dressed in my warmest pyjamas: we sat by the newly lit fire and told our story.

"You were bloody lucky," Edward told us. "Anything could have happened."

"I would have been all right," David said, lounging on the rug in front of us. "I'm too strong a swimmer to let the sea beat me."

Shirley stepped over him to her seat, "That's silly talk. The sea is no respecter of anyone."

"Thankfully the tide washed Greg up." I shivered at the thought of what might have happened. "I am not sure that even the lifeboat could have saved him if it weren't for that."

Greg said, clearly irritated, "You're all making a mountain out of a molehill. I was fine. But I must admit, I was relieved when I saw Hannah was OK."

I remembered his anger at losing his camera and his almost lifeless body lying in the surf, and closed my eyes to block out the picture in my mind.

"You said Hannah saved your life," Shirley pointed out.

"Figure of speech, old girl." He turned to Edward. "Any more brandy?"

"I can't wait to tell Mum," David said.

Shirley prodded him with her foot, "Oh no you don't. You know what the doctor told us. Your mum needs peace and quiet when she gets home."

"Which reminds me," Edward said, "all being well she'll be home on Tuesday afternoon."

"I will have everything ready for her." I realised how much I had missed her. "I'll get the bakers to make her a welcome home cake."

We chatted about Mum's homecoming and the jobs we needed to do beforehand. Edward would do a stocktake in the shop. Shirley got out her notebook and pencil and began to make a shopping list, and David promised to clean his room.

I noticed Greg yawning. Shirley caught him too. "Greg, you are tired. Your clothes are still a bit damp, but when you get back to your room, you can ask if they'll air them for you."

"That's so kind." He smiled sheepishly, "The trouble is, in all the excitement of Francine and her room at the pub, I forgot to book one for myself." He stood up, wincing as he straightened his back. "But don't worry about me. I'm sure I can find somewhere. If you could just tell me where my clothes are?"

Edward got up too. "You can probably have the room Francine had at the pub. I'll walk down with you. I might even buy you a pint."

"Er," Shirley interrupted, "neither of you are going anywhere. Greg can sleep on the sofa down here. It's the least we can do."

"Absolutely," I joined in. "Edward! Greg is your best friend. Of course he can stay here."

Greg shook his head. "I couldn't take any more of your hospitality."

"Of course you can!" Shirley gave me a sly wink. "Any friend of Teddy's is a friend of ours. Isn't that right?"

Blankets and a pillow were found and the sofa made up invitingly.

I checked the time, "It's getting late. David bed, now."

Shirley took Edward's arm, "And it's time for us as well, Teddy."

"And you, Toots," Edward said to me. "You've had a long day. Come on."

There wasn't much I could do. "I'll just get a glass of water."

"Would you bring one up for me too?" I could tell David was spinning the time out. "Yes, yes. I'll be up in a minute."

Greg was settling himself on the sofa and saying nothing.

"Toots," Edward said. "You go up. I'll bring the water."

I knew what he was doing and why he was doing it. "Goodnight, Greg," I said. "I hope you sleep well."

His eyes were closed already. "I will. Night, night."

In bed I cursed my big brother. He had humiliated me and what had I done? Obeyed.

I thought of Greg downstairs. Was he asleep already? Did he have no thoughts of creeping up the stairs to find me? To be fair, that would be very dangerous as he had never been upstairs before and wouldn't know which door I was behind.

Could I wait for another half an hour until Edward, Shirley and David would probably be asleep, then creep down to Greg's sofa and seduce him? Supposing he was asleep and screamed when I woke him? It was a risk. But a risk worth taking?

I waited until I was sure I could hear Edward's snores above me. The house was certainly very quiet. I waited for another five minutes and then inched my way out of bed, across the floor, through the door and downstairs. By the light of the lamp in the lane beyond our back door, I could just make out Greg's sleeping form. I kept still again. Ready to lie if anyone found me. "I was just getting another glass of water," I would say.

I stood stock-still in the silence and counted another minute in my head. Everyone was definitely asleep.

"Greg?" I whispered. "Greg? Are you awake?"

He moved under the blanket. "I have been waiting for you," he whispered back. "Come here."

I slipped under the blanket and his lips felt for my mouth. The passion rose quickly in me as his fingers stroked my breasts, slipping inside my pyjamas.

"I have been thinking about this," he whispered. "Thinking about you. Ever since you promised me on the beach this morning." He moved so that his weight was almost on top of me. "Hannah, I can't get enough of you."

"Darling, Greg." I trailed my fingers down his spine, his nakedness exciting me further.

"Oh shit!" He moved suddenly and began to grip his thigh. "Cramp."

He fell off the sofa and tried to flex his leg. "Grip my toes, would you?"

I did as he asked and after a few seconds he relaxed. "Sorry about that." I could see his teeth as he smiled in the dark. "Maybe this sofa is a bit too small. Is there anywhere else we could go?"

"Not upstairs. Sorry."

"What about the shop?" He began to nibble my neck.

"OK."

In the darkness, the shop enveloped us with the erotic scents of Far Eastern silks, and the sensual, drowning silence of rich fabrics.

He took my hand as he walked me into the middle of the shop floor. "Where is best?"

"I'm not sure. I've never done this before."

"Good." He held my face and kissed me deeply. "I want to be the first one. Cushions. Are there any in here?"

"Yes. On the stools behind the counter."

"Ahh. The counter."

"You mean . . .?"

"Yes, I do mean. Wouldn't that be naughty? What would all your customers think if they knew?"

He found three soft cushions and laid them on the glass counter top. "Hello." He was looking behind me and my heart skipped a beat as I imagined Edward seeing us like this.

"What?"

"A nice big mirror."

It was our old cheval mirror that Mum used during fittings. He picked it up and carried it to the side of the counter. "Now we can watch ourselves."

He lifted me onto the counter and laid me down gently. "See how beautiful you are?"

In the dark I could see my eyes, wide with desire. "I want you," I breathed.

"And I want you," he said.

We finally parted, him to the sofa, me to my room, very late. My childhood bedside clock told me it was after four. Under my cold sheets I felt changed. Loved. My body worshipped. Greg had made love to me in a way no other man had. Selflessly. Passionately. I knew that he loved me and I loved him and that we were meant for each other. There was a future full of happiness and love ahead of us.

Shirley woke me with a cup of tea at 8.30.

"Morning sleepyhead." She kissed the top of my head. "Sleep well?"

"Very well, thank you." I stretched my arms above my head.

"Is Greg up yet?"

"He's gone. Had to get the early train. He left a note." She pulled a crumpled piece of paper from her pocket. "Here you are."

Hannah. Thanks for everything. Greg x

CHAPTER
TWENTY-EIGHT

Hannah, Trevay

December 1947

In the days after Greg disappeared, I tried every means I could to contact him. I even went to London and waited outside his flat for him to come home. I watched from early morning to late afternoon, until a young woman, pushing a pram, walked up to the front door, fumbled for her key and let herself in. When I rang the doorbell asking for Greg, she told me that she and her husband were the new tenants, and no, there was no forwarding address for anyone called Greg.

A month later, I read in a magazine: *The young and upcoming talented society photographer, Greg Snow, is engaged to the Model of the Moment, Francine Wallis. Mrs Wallis is divorcing her husband of three years and tells us that she has never been happier.*

The photo showed them with their arms around each other, leaning against a balcony covered in an exotic flowering climber with a sparkling sea behind them.

That was the first time I threw up.

Two months after that, I knew I was pregnant.

How could I tell Mum? Edward? Shirley? David? The whole of Trevay?

In the end I didn't have to. Mum heard me one morning.

As I rinsed my mouth over the bathroom basin, I felt her standing behind me.

"Darling?" she said softly. "Are you OK?"

I briskly wiped my mouth on the hand towel. "Fine, Mum. Bit of a tummy bug. What are you doing out of bed, anyway? You know you need to rest. Doctor's orders."

"I am fine. But you? You don't have a bug, do you? It's morning sickness."

"Mum. What a thing to say!" I tried to brush past her and get downstairs. She blocked my way. "Mum, please. You go back to bed and I will bring you up a cup of tea. What would you like for breakfast? Toast and marmalade?"

She stayed where she was. "You can't fool me. How far gone are you?"

"Honestly, Mum, you've got the wrong end of the stick."

"No. I haven't. Have you seen a doctor? Tell me the truth."

The weeks of anxiety and anger had exhausted me. The room began to spin and I sat on the edge of the bath. "No. I haven't seen a doctor." I sounded weak and silly.

"Why didn't you tell me?"

I put my head in my hands. "Oh Mum, you don't know how many times I nearly did. I wanted to tell you but . . ."

She sat down next to me. "Who else knows? Does the father know?"

I shook my head. "Nobody knows."

"My poor girl." She put her arm around my shoulders. "You and I will go to the doctor together." I laid my head on the comfort of her bosom, my tears wetting her nightdress.

"Have you thought about what you might do?" she asked gently.

"I don't know." Tears slid down my face.

She hugged me a little tighter. "Listen to me. I think it's too late to stop it now and anyway, you don't have to. The baby has all of us. A ready-made family. You are not the first or the last woman to find herself alone and pregnant, and, here's a secret that is true, you don't need a husband to raise a family. Every baby is a blessing."

"You're not angry with me then?"

"Why would I be?"

"Because, I've let you down."

She raised my chin and looked straight into my eyes. "Listen to me. You will always be my baby, but tonight we are two women sharing this together. I see you, Hannah, for the woman you are, and I love you."

I clung to her as she rocked me gently. "Oh Mum. I am so sorry. I have tried to get rid of it. I ran a hot bath and sat in it drinking gin. During the war, the girls I was with always said that was the best way, but nothing happened, and I'm not brave enough to find a woman to do . . . you know . . . the knitting needles . . . Oh Mum, I am so sorry. Will you tell Dad?"

She put her hand under my chin and raised my face to see hers. "We don't need to tell Dad just yet. What is he going to do? You are going to have this baby and keep it." Her eyes sought mine, "You do want to keep the baby?"

"Would you mind? What would you tell people?"

"We will tell people, without shame or regret, that we are proud of you. This baby is a chance for us all to do the right thing."

"But it's not the right thing. I will be an unmarried mother. Sullied. A slut. An idiot."

She smiled. "Or you could be a great mum to a much-wanted child."

"Aren't you ashamed of me?" I asked.

"Not as much as you would be ashamed of me." She reached for a towel and wiped my eyes, "Now, I think we need that cuppa."

Before telling the rest of the family, Mum took me to the doctor's to be examined. A new doctor had joined the surgery, a woman, Dr Sally Finch.

"When was the date of your last period, Hannah?" she asked kindly.

I told her and she counted the weeks on her desk calendar. "I make that about fifteen weeks. No spotting or bleeding?"

"No."

"Good. Now, if you would just lie down on the bench, I'll have a feel for baby and see if I can find its heartbeat."

As I lay down, I saw that Mum was wiping her eyes. "Are you all right, Mum?"

"You remind me of me when I was expecting for the first time."

Dr Sally looked up. "And was your first baby quite big, Mrs Bolitho?" she asked.

I smiled. "Edward is well over six foot and a rugby player. I don't expect he was tiny."

I looked over at Mum and saw something — some memory, perhaps — flit across her eyes. "Edward was big. All my babies were big. Why?"

"Because this little one," Dr Sally put her hand on my bump, "feels a good size. Like daughter, like mother." She picked up a small wooden ear trumpet and pressed it to my abdomen. "Aha. Yes. There's a good heartbeat there. Hannah, your baby is doing very well."

I was dreading Edward's reaction and asked Mum to tell him, Shirley and David, while I stayed upstairs.

It was Shirley who came to find me first.

"Why didn't you tell me?" she asked.

"I really wanted to, but I was scared."

"Of me?" Shirley sat on the bed where I lay. "You must have felt so alone."

"Ashamed really."

"Is it Greg's?"

"Shh." I looked anxiously towards my open bedroom door. "Please don't tell anyone. Edward would kill him."

"I could kill him. Does he know?"

"No. I couldn't find him and now I don't want to."

"He'll never be happy with that skinny bitch."

I reached for her hand. "I don't want him to know."

"He's a fool."

"So am I."

"No, you are not! He should have used protection."

"I am as much to blame for that."

"And he gets off scot-free. While you . . ."

Her anger on my behalf was kind but I didn't need it. "While I have a loving family to bring this baby into."

Tears formed in her eyes. "Yes, you do."

"Is Edward very angry?"

"He'll come round."

"What about David?"

"He's excited about being an uncle."

"Bless him."

"Bless us all, Hannah. Bless us all."

It was over Christmas that Mum's cough came back. She had gone back to smoking and refused to go back to the doctor.

"I am not bothering Dr Cunningham over his Christmas holiday," she said. "He'll have enough on his plate. I'll see how I go."

I felt guilty because my bump was growing well but Mum was wrapping me in cotton wool. The midwife had told me to put my feet up when I could. Mum took that as an order and virtually had me under house arrest.

I wasn't even allowed to help make the Christmas cake. "It's not good for your blood pressure," she kept telling me.

"But, Mum, the baby isn't due until the end of May early June. I am not even half way."

"Never mind that." She coughed. "You take the rest while you can."

Poor David, he ended up with a lot of my jobs to do.

"I am so sorry," I told him one afternoon as I had my feet up by the fire and he was carrying in a basket of logs.

"Just as long as I have a very big, very expensive Christmas present, I don't mind. And Mum says I am in charge of the Christmas tree this year, which I have never been allowed to do before."

"Just don't hang toy cars and tractors all over it," I joked.

"That's not a bad idea. Thanks, sis."

"Don't make me laugh." I hung onto my tummy. "You'll start the baby."

"Hot water! Towels!" David teased, making me laugh even more.

Mum came through from the shop, "What's all the hilarity about?"

"Just David," I said, hitching myself up to make a space for Mum. "Come and sit down next to me. David, pop the kettle on, would you?"

He groaned theatrically, "Why me?"

"And bring some cake," I added.

Mum sat down and pulled her handkerchief from her sleeve. "What a day."

"Busy?" I asked.

She nodded and began to cough. It sounded different. Chesty with a long rattle. Each time she managed to catch a breath, the cough that came after was harder and took longer to recover from.

I sat up and rubbed her back, trying to soothe her lungs. "Mum. You really must see the doc. This is getting worse."

She shook her head, unable to speak. She looked almost grey.

"Mum, come on. Try to take a deep, slow breath."

She tried but another cough, different again, brought up a clot of blood the size of a two-bob piece.

"*Mum!* David, call Dr Cunningham."

It felt as though I was just getting to know my mum, and I was terrified of what might come.

CHAPTER
TWENTY-NINE

Hannah, Trevay

December 1947

"I am not spending Christmas in hospital," Mum told Dr Cunningham.

"Clara," he said, winding up his stethoscope and putting it in his bag, "you have no choice. You have a very bad chest infection. Possibly pneumonia."

"I can go in after Christmas."

"No, you can't. The hospital has a bed waiting for you and you are going today."

"But I am fine."

Dr Cunningham looked over his glasses at her sternly. "I am your doctor and what I say, you do. Understand? Your family are quite capable of looking after themselves and Christmas in hospital is quite fun. The nurses have decorated the wards and you'll get a stocking at the end of your bed."

He picked up his bag. "Edward will drive you and I will be there to meet you."

I showed him out and thanked him for coming so quickly. "So you think it's pneumonia?" I asked quietly, mindful that Mum's ears were as sharp as a bat's.

"I hope it is." He placed his hand on mine. "But she is a smoker and that can cause all sorts of problems."

The first tendril of fear twisted through me. "Meaning?"

"Let's not get ahead of ourselves. We'll know more once the hospital run their tests." He looked down at my rounded stomach. "And how are you doing?"

"I am fine."

"Very good. It can't be easy for you." He put his hat on, "Right, I'd best be off. And don't worry, I will look after your mum and you look after yourself."

Looking back, that Christmas was one of the happiest we'd ever had. Shirley took over the shop, the cooking, the presentbuying, and supervised David's festive decorations. Only once did she display any irritability, and that was when David had helped himself to her cotton wool to use as snowballs glued to the shop windows.

Edward drove us every day to the hospital and helped to translate some of the more complicated medical terms used by the medics.

Mum was looking so much better as well. She had been put on a medicine that eased her chest considerably but also caused some weight gain. The irony was, she looked fitter than ever.

On Christmas Day, Shirley insisted that we parcel up the cooked turkey and trimmings and take them in to eat together around Mum's bed. It was so silly but such fun. The nurses handed out crackers to everyone on the ward and we all sang carols with our paper hats on.

On New Year's Eve we even smuggled a bottle of sherry in, singing "Auld Lang Syne" at midnight.

Two days later the doctor called us into his hospital consulting room. "Your mother is doing well, but we have found several small tumours in her lungs."

"Cancer," Edward said.

"I don't want you to think that this is all bad news." The doctor opened Mum's file. "We think that a course of radiotherapy could kill the tumours without need for operating."

Shirley took my hand. "That sounds good."

"There are many options open to us, but I would strongly recommend we try the radiotherapy as soon as possible," the doctor continued.

Edward was thinking. "How about you operate to remove them and then do the radiotherapy to kill off anything you missed?"

"That is a good question, Mr Bolitho, but your mother is not a young woman and the operation is highly invasive. It could take a lot out of her."

I said immediately, "Please try the radiotherapy first then. Mum seems so well at the moment."

The doctor gave me an encouraging smile. "Yes, and that is what holds her in good stead. Radiotherapy is not a walk in the park, though. There will be pain and it will take a lot of energy from her, but it is what we think is best."

Edward nodded slowly. "OK. When can you start?"

Mum was out of hospital in three weeks. The doctors were very pleased with her progress and allowed her home on the promise that she would rest and not work in the shop.

Edward went to collect her with David while Shirley and I waited at home. It was a joyful homecoming and wonderful to see her sitting in her favourite chair again. "It's lovely to be home again," she sighed, settling in. "I saw snowdrops in the lanes. Spring is on its way."

We settled into a nice routine. Shirley had given up her job at the bank and had taken over the shop. I helped her occasionally, and eventually I didn't have those flashes of memory whenever I looked at the shop counter and the cheval mirror. I had consigned that to a part of my brain that I never wanted to visit again. If I did think about it, the feelings of guilt and shame were unbearable. I was so angry with Greg. How can a man just walk away and not even think about the devastation he may have left behind? I remembered his description of flying over Germany on bombing raids. "Once you drop your payload you want to get out of there as soon as possible." The crudeness of his remark hadn't struck me then but my God it almost killed me now. What would I tell my unborn child about its father? Should I make up a love affair? Have him killed in a terrible accident? Or tell the truth. Just asking myself those questions unsettled me so much that I had to shut that entire chapter down. I had been a fool. I had had my heart broken, and so what? I was just another foolish woman who had mistaken lust for love. Thank God I had my forgiving family.

Mum was getting stronger all the time. An X-ray check-up showed that the tumours had shrunk enough to take her off the danger list. I am not a churchgoer normally, but I did slip into the empty church that morning and give a prayer of thanks.

Mum was unstoppable. "I want to plant some wallflowers and get some sweet peas in," she told Edward.

"When?" he asked her.

"Well now, of course. Come on."

And she insisted on doing two afternoons a week in the shop plus all day Saturday. "My customers are my friends," she told Shirley. "I need to get back to normal."

At night when my back ached she would rub it with almond oil. "I had a friend, years ago now, who did this for me," she said. "Only another couple of weeks to go. Are you excited?"

"And scared," I said.

"That's only normal." She carried on rubbing me. "Would you like me to stay with you when you have it?"

I had wanted to ask her but wondered if it would be somehow inappropriate. "Would you?"

"Try stopping me."

The contractions started on a Friday afternoon. I lay down on my bed without telling anyone, to make sure that this was the real thing. I must have fallen asleep because a sudden, strong contraction woke me. When it passed, I got up and went down to find Mum. She and

Shirley were in the shop, chatting to a couple of customers and drinking tea.

"Mum?" I said. "I think the baby's coming."

The reaction was extraordinary.

Mum told Shirley, "Run and fetch the midwife."

One of the customers fainted and the other ran about clucking like a hen and being absolutely useless.

Mum shouted, "Pull yourself together, you silly woman, and when she wakes up —" she pointed to the body on the floor — "put the closed sign up and shut the door behind you."

Another contraction stopped me in my tracks as Mum tried to get me to the lounge.

"That's the way. Breathe deeply and, when it has passed, we'll get you upstairs."

Her voice was calm and gave me courage.

Upstairs, she undressed me and got me into bed, and then I heard the solid, dependable footsteps of the midwife.

Caroline Clara Bolitho was born just after midnight on 2nd of June 1947 with a tuft of dark hair and a cross little face. "She looks exactly as you did when you were born," Mum said, and I was glad there was no sign of her father. She had all the love she needed right here, three generations of Bolitho women. The daughter of us all.

CHAPTER
THIRTY

Hannah, Trevay

Autumn 1947

Caroline was universally adored and it was agreed by all who met her that she was the prettiest baby ever seen. Taking her out in her pram, I would get stopped constantly by people wanting to look at her. Only one woman, out with her daughter, said as she walked away, "She's lucky that baby wasn't born with a mark of Satan, being a bastard and all." I wanted to turn back and confront her, but I chose not to feed the unkindness. I couldn't be more proud of my beautiful girl.

It was a glorious autumn and Trevay was bathed in warm sunshine for day after day. The fishing fleet was bringing in good catches and the holiday-makers had flown like the swallows back to where they belonged My life had never been so happy and fulfilled. My mother was well, my baby was good, and I had all the joy I could have hoped for.

Coming back from one of my pram promenades, I turned the corner that led to our back door and I saw

Mum hanging out some of Caroline's clothes. She didn't hear me coming and I could see she had a cigarette in her mouth.

"Mum," I said, making her jump and guiltily throw down the cigarette before stubbing it out with her shoe.

"What did the doctor tell you?" I asked.

"It's just the one."

"You can't have just the one. You will have bought a packet."

"Hello, Caroline." She looked into the pram.

"Don't change the subject. You promised us all that you would stop smoking."

"And I did."

"But you've started again?"

"Just the odd one." She coughed.

"You're coughing."

"It's just a dry throat."

But she picked up little Caroline and swung her up in the air, both the washing fluttering on the line and the laughter of my little girl catching on the sharp Cornish breeze.

She coughed again and my previous euphoria flipped to dread.

Dr Cunningham looked over the results of the new X-ray. All of us were there. All of us hoping not to hear the news we knew he would give us.

"I am sorry to say that the X-ray shows tumours in your throat, lungs and bladder."

Mum, her hands serenely folded, said, "More radiation then."

Dr Cunningham couldn't have looked sadder. "No, Clara. I am very sorry but there is nothing we can do other than to make you comfortable if and when you suffer any pain."

Edward broke down. He dropped his head on his chest and sobbed. "No. That can't be right. It can't be."

Shirley looked at Dr Cunningham angrily. "But he said! Last time. That hospital doctor said there were plenty of options. That she could be operated on. The cancer taken out."

Dr Cunningham shook his head. "I am very sorry."

Mum asked, "How long have I got? Will I see the summer?"

"I hope so," he said.

We left the surgery in shock, David as white as a sheet. I put my arm around him but he shrugged me off angrily. "I have to go to work."

"No, you don't," I said. "They'll understand."

"I want to go." He began to run.

Mum said, "Let him go."

Caroline was four months old when Mum began to spend more time in bed each day.

It was oddly comforting for me to have her to myself. Her and Caroline.

In daylight hours, when everyone was working, I would care for the two of them, fitting the repetitive jobs around them, but at night, well, that was our special time. We had a routine.

After supper I would take Caroline up for her bath. Sometimes Mum came in, depending on how she was

414

feeling, to sit and share the pleasure of seeing Caroline's smiling face as the water lapped her little body. When she was ready, I would lift Caroline onto Mum's lap, where she had a warm towel waiting, to pat her dry and get her into her nappy and nightclothes.

Caroline's tiny cot now sat between our two beds in the bedroom we had always shared.

With the light down low and the curtains drawn against the lengthening nights, I would sit and nurse my daughter while Mum lay in her bed and watched us.

"You are a good mother. You read Caroline so well."

"Thanks, Mum."

"You are a better mother than I was."

"Rubbish. You had three of us, thousands of miles from your family and friends and living in the jungle."

She laughed. "It wasn't so bad. I had your amah to help. A sweet woman who took care of all of you and me included. I learnt a lot about kindness and patience from her. She even cooked for us if I asked. Your father loved her curry."

I was glad she had brought my father into the conversation as there was something I had been thinking about but hadn't known how to broach.

"Mum, would you like me to let Daddy know you are not well?"

She sighed, letting her shoulders drop heavily into her pillows. "What could he do so far away and, honestly, would he care?"

"We are still his family. You are his wife."

"I would rather let sleeping dogs lie," she said.

Caroline had stopped suckling, her tummy full; sated. I lifted her onto my shoulder and rubbed her back to encourage any brewing burp.

"You could have found happiness with someone else."

"I didn't need to. I had you and the boys. I was happy." She was watching Caroline. "I am happy."

"Did you love Daddy?"

"He was kind and made me laugh. That was enough."

"But that's sad. To not have found your true love."

She waved the thought away. "It's all so long ago."

She began to cough, but as I made to get up and help her she held up her hand. "Don't disturb the baby. I'm fine."

"I think she's ready to go down now anyway." I lifted Caroline into her cot and tucked her little blankets around her, then went to lift Mum up her bed a little so that she could cough more freely.

"There. Better now?" I took away her sodden handkerchief and replaced it with a clean one. "Let's get you settled again."

"You are a good daughter." She smiled up at me. "I do love you."

"And I love you."

"What time is it?"

"Time for bed for both of us. Would you like me to read to you?"

"Not tonight, darling. I'm a bit weary."

I kissed her goodnight and by the time I had put my pyjamas on and returned from the bathroom, she was sound asleep.

The next morning, before he went to work, I asked Edward about writing to Penang.

"To tell Dad that Mum isn't well," I added.

"Does he deserve to know? He hasn't exactly been a loving parent or devoted husband."

"I think he deserves to know."

"Have you talked to Mum about this?"

"Yes, briefly, last night. She didn't seem to care."

"A letter may take too long to get to him." Edward spooned the last of his porridge down. "I suppose we could send a short telegram."

"I think it's the right thing to do." I was relieved. "Thank you."

"What shall we put?"

"Something to the point. Dear Dad, Mum seriously ill. Will you come to UK? Edward, David and Hannah."

"OK. I'll drop into the post office and get it sent today."

Dad responded a week later with a return telegram.

DEAR*OLD*THINGS*STOP*NO*PLANS*TO*
RETURN*TO*UK*STOP*SENDING*BEST*
REGARDS* TO*CLARA*STOP

Edward had opened it and, having read it, threw it down on the table. "Utter bastard," he said and stormed out into the garden.

I read it and was shocked by the cruel callousness of his words. I tore it up and burnt it in the grate before David could see it. I was glad that we had never told Mum that we had contacted Dad.

Mum was having more good days than bad now. Dear Dr Cunningham popped in every day to check on her and was slowly increasing her pain medication.

That night she didn't join me for Caroline's bath, but when I got back to our room, Mum was propped up against her extra pillows, awake and waiting for us.

"There you are," she said. "Can Nana have a cuddle, please?" Caroline settled into the crook of Mum's arm and gazed into her grandmother's eyes. "Now then Caroline," Mum began, "I am sorry that I won't see you grow up, but I shall be watching you and looking after you. Your mummy is my little girl, so I want you to be a good girl for her. Do you understand?" Caroline blew a small bubble in reply. "I will take that as a yes."

"Mum." My voice was choked with unshed tears. "I can't bear hearing you talk like that. You might get better."

She looked at me rather sternly. "We both know that is not true. We all have to die when our time comes."

I took her free hand. "I am so sorry, Mum."

"Whatever for? Not for having Caroline?"

"For letting you down. For getting pregnant. For being a single mother. For so many things."

Her fingers felt for mine. "Ssh. I told you before, you need no man to make a child happy and secure. I learnt that a long time ago and it was hard. But you will always be Caroline's mother.

"Some mothers have to walk away, and their hearts never mend. But you will never walk away, I will make certain you never have to."

Caroline began to fret. "She's hungry." Mum smiled, "She had better go to her mummy."

Later, when Caroline was fed and settled, I noticed that Mum wasn't sleeping as comfortably as she had been. She was fitful and mumbling words I couldn't make out. I hoped it was just the extra morphine.

The next morning she was her normal self, so when Dr Cunningham came I didn't bother to mention it to him. In fact he was very pleased with her.

"Clara, I don't know how you do it. Your heart is strong, your chest sounds a lot clearer and I can swear the apples in your cheeks are glowing."

"Flattery will get you everywhere, John." She laughed.

"You keep going like this and we'll have you skating by Christmas. See you tomorrow."

On one of our pram walks, Caroline and I caught a cold which meant we had to move out of our room for a few days. With Mum's chest being so vulnerable we couldn't risk her getting it too.

I had to move out of our room for a week so that Mum didn't come down with it too. David played a blinder by agreeing to let Caroline and me have his room, but he drew the line at sleeping in my bed next to Mum. He offered instead to sleep on the sofa, which we all appreciated, and to read to Mum in the evenings while Caroline and I remained in quarantine.

What we didn't know then was that David was about to play a very important part in Mum's life.

Clara, Trevay

October 1947

I have been thinking so much of the past. I have so much time to think these days. Today I asked David, without telling anyone in the house, to fetch me some writing paper. I had to write to Ernest and tell him about Caroline or else how would he know he had a granddaughter? I hoped he would take the news better from me. After all, how could Hannah tell him there was no father?

David posted it for me, again in secrecy. He is such a lovely young man. Ernest has missed out on so much. My fault. I had taken the children from Penang and brought them back to Cornwall. He could have followed us, but I am glad he didn't. He was not Bertie and Bertie was the only man I ever wanted.

Once the letter was posted I felt a lot better, but my thoughts kept whirring and kept me awake.

Michael, my dear boy Michael, was with me all the time now. In my dreams and in my waking. How could I have denied him when he came here to find me? It was wicked of me to set brother against brother, making Edward turf out his own sibling. I was deeply troubled and I knew I needed to make amends. I had been a wicked woman and I had to atone for my sins before it was too late. I needed someone to help me, but it couldn't be Hannah, she had so much to do, and it couldn't be Edward because I am a coward. It couldn't be a priest because I had no faith. So that left dear David. He was the one child who had been with me always. I nearly lost him to malaria all those years ago, but he had grown into a strong and clever man. I knew it was hard for him being the youngest. Edward and Hannah did reign over him rather, but when they'd been busy fighting for king and country, he had been here, with me, keeping me sane while I worried so much about the other two.

Yes, I thought, out of them all he would understand how important this last mission was to us. He would be here in a minute to read to me.

He was knocking at the door now. "Come in, darling."

"Hey Mum. How are you doing?"

"I am looking forward to another chapter of our book." I reached out and touched his sleeve.

We were reading Agatha Christie's *Sparkling Cyanide*. David loved murder mystery stories as much as I did. I had had a whole shelf full of Christie and Dorothy L. Sayers that I had had to leave behind in Penang. Perhaps they were still there.

"You fell asleep in the middle of a chapter last night," David replied.

"Did I? That's because your reading is so soothing. And actually, David, before we start, I wonder if I could ask you a small favour?"

"Of course, Mum."

"Good boy."

I want to write another letter. Another one no one can know about. But my hands get so tired, would you write it for me?"

"Now?"

"Why not. The writing paper is still on my dressing table and there's an envelope too."

Hannah, Trevay

November 1947

The colds that Caroline and I had went to chest infections and so we couldn't move back into Mum's room for a good couple of weeks. Mum couldn't wait to see Caroline and I couldn't wait to see mum. She was looking a little more frail but otherwise very cheerful. I noticed a sparkle in her eyes.

"You must be so tired," she said to me. "You haven't had much sleep while you've both been ill. I could hear you both coughing at night."

It was true, I can't have had more than three hours' unbroken sleep a night.

"Oh dear. We tried not to wake you. We are absolutely fine now, I hear that you and David have been having fun."

"Oh yes. We have become bedside companions and amateur sleuths. It's been lovely spending time with him."

"It's been good for you both."

She began to cough. I could tell it caused her pain. I took Caroline up into my arms and ran to the door shouting, "Edward, Shirley? Are you there? Could you bring Mum's medicine up?"

We had been given permission to administer Mum's medicine as and when we felt she needed it, and she needed it now.

Shirley ran in. "Here. I only gave her some an hour ago."

"What should the gap between doses be?"

"Doc said four-hourly."

"I just need to sit up a bit, that's all," Mum said wheezily.

"Let's sit her up."

We got either side of her and lifted her to a more comfortable position. She was definitely lighter and frailer than she had ever been. Shirley took the soiled handkerchief from Mum's hand and swapped it for a clean one, while I rubbed Mum's back, taking care not to bruise the skin over the sharp bones of her spine.

"Deep breaths, Mum," I said, willing my voice to sound calmer than I felt.

Shirley caught my eye over Mum's head and mouthed: "She's not been right since last night."

"What happened?" I mouthed back.

"She was very sick. I would have told you but you were sleeping and I didn't like to wake you."

Mum's coughing spell was passing. "Is that a bit better?" I asked her.

She managed to smile and give a thumbs up before lying back on the stack of pillows we had constructed for her.

423

"I will make us all a cup of tea. Won't be a moment." Shirley left us on our own.

"I hear you were sick last night. What was that about?"

"I don't know." She was still wheezy after the coughing.

"Are you in pain?"

"My back aches."

"I'll bring you a hot-water bottle in a minute."

By the time Shirley came back with the tea, Mum had fallen asleep again, and for the rest of the day she dozed.

Dr Cunningham popped in and took a look at her without waking her.

"Her chest doesn't sound good but her heart is still strong and she doesn't have a temperature," he told me.

"That's good. But she's getting worse, isn't she?"

"She has a will to live. It is our fate not to know the day or the hour."

"We won't leave her on her own."

"It's very hard for you all, but at the end you will be glad you were there for her." He picked up his bag. "Get some sleep yourself and I will see you tomorrow"

Over the next two days, Mum began to sleep more and more. When she was awake she was quite chatty, always asking if there had been any post, but we couldn't get her to eat anything. David was eager to finish off the book they were reading and, even though she dropped off before he had finished, she enjoyed hearing his voice.

On the third day she slept for most of the day, her tiny body barely visible under the blankets. Her hands and feet got cold easily and Shirley and I found some mittens and bed socks to warm her up. We were preparing for the end without admitting it.

She woke briefly at teatime and asked for a cup of tea, but she barely managed a drop before falling asleep again.

All of us decided we needed to be in the room with her, and Shirley, bless her, brought us a tray laden with sandwiches to keep us going.

The daylight began to fade and I turned on the small bedside lamp that gave the room a soft glow Together we chatted about our day until David decided he should read the last chapter of *Sparkling Cyanide*. We were all absorbed in the story when we heard a loud knock on the back door.

We looked at each other. "Who the hell is that at this time of night?" Edward asked.

"I'll go," said David quickly.

"Tell them to clear off, whoever it is," Shirley called after him.

Mum stirred and opened her eyes. "Has he come?" she asked.

"It's all right, Mum." Edward leant towards her.

"Someone at the door. David's gone."

The sparkle I had seen in her eyes a few days ago came back. "Who is it? Has he come?"

We heard two sets of footsteps climbing the stairs and David's voice, "She will be so happy to see you."

I flashed a questioning look at Edward. "Is it the doctor?"

The door opened to reveal David with a tall handsome man whom I recognised. Again I looked at Edward who stood up ready to throw him out. He was only stopped by Mum's clear voice. "Mikey, you came." She held her thin arms out to him. "Edward you can sit down. This is Michael. Your older brother."

None of us could speak.

"Let me hold you," she said to him.

He bent over her and she wrapped her arms around his shoulders. "Can you forgive me? I turned my back on you when you came last time."

"There is nothing to forgive. I didn't give you time to think. I should have warned you."

"I was scared. I had told no living soul about you other than Philippa. How could you want to see me when I had left you behind and refused to answer any letters that dear Philippa would send me."

Michael kissed her forehead. David passed him a chair. "I couldn't believe it when your letter arrived. It was like a miracle. Thank you for asking me to come." He took her hands and stroked them.

"What letter?" asked Edward. "Mum, how did you get out to post it?"

"Oh I posted it. In fact I wrote it," grinned David. "Mum asked me to and it was our secret."

"What the hell is happening here?" Edward was nonplussed. "Mum this person could be anybody."

"No Edward." Mum smiled, "This is Michael, my son. Your brother."

"Why the hell have you never told us about him before?" Edward was getting upset. "How did Dad never mention him?"

"Ernest was not his father," Mum said calmly.

Edward got to his feet again. "You had an affair?"

Shirley took Edward's arm and pulled him back. "Teddy sit down and listen."

"I had a love affair, yes, but before I ever met your father. I met a wonderful man who I loved very much. Michael is his son. He was a soldier fighting in France but on the night that Michael was born, Bertie was shot and killed instantly."

"Bertie?" I asked, gradually pulling things together. "Dad's brother?"

"Yes." I saw a tear roll from Mum's eye as she looked at Michael. "Did Philippa tell you?"

"Yes. And she told me about you marrying and going to Penang."

"Was she very cross with me for running away?"

"She explained everything to me in a way I understood. She said you would never have given me to her if there was any other way, but there wasn't."

Mum nodded, her eyes drooping. "I loved her very much. She was a mother to us both in the end."

Michael held Mum's hands as his tears fell on to her fingers.

"Oh Mum." Compassion and understanding welled in me. "That's why you supported me when I was expecting Caroline?"

"Yes, but I would have supported you and Caroline no matter what." She took a long, exhausted breath. "I have been waiting for this day for so long I had begun to think it would never come."

She looked at each of us with the bliss of pure love.

"Edward, David, Hannah, Michael, come closer I want to hold all my children in my hands for the first and last time in my life. Each one of you has given me reason to carry on, and now we have little Caroline too. Hannah, promise me that you tell her about my mistakes and yours. Not that she isn't allowed to find her own way, but to understand that life is not simple."

"I will, Mum."

"Good. Now I am very tired and I need to sleep. Mikey, I want you to stay here tonight. I want to wake up in the morning knowing that all my babies are with me under one roof."

Caroline

Present day

Granny died two days later, having had her greatest wish granted.

I learnt this from the second letter in the envelope. It was from Michael's daughter, Kate. The Trunk had been posted to her from Penang by the granddaughter of my grandfather's housekeeper, a man called Nizam. I know this is very complicated but aren't all family trees?

Nizam had remained loyal and faithful to Grandfather Ernest, Granny Clara and poor dead Uncle Bertie who had been his first boss.

Nizam outlived them all but when he died, his daughter found that he had kept the Bolitho possessions safe in the trunk. His granddaughter, Adik, had somehow divined Kate's address in Kent and sent it on to me, after tracking down the Bolitho name to Callyzion.

I must say I thought her father, my Uncle Michael I suppose I should call him, was treated pretty poorly. At least he got to meet his mother at the end.

Uncle Edward apparently remained rather grumpy because he had always thought he was number one son, not number two. Still, Auntie Shirley always mollified him, and when she had the twins he couldn't have been a more devoted father.

Uncle David became the senior engineer for a racing car team and married a woman who could change a tyre in a pit stop faster than he could. They live in Monaco now.

My mother stayed in Trevay until her death. She became a pillar of the community and ran Granny's shop for another twenty years. She never told me who my father was. "The Bolitho bastard", I was once called at school. As soon as I knew what that meant, I vowed to keep myself pure until my wedding night. A vow I am proud to say I kept and one that I have impressed on my own daughter, Natalie.

I wish I had met Uncle Michael. We had a lot in common. He never met his father and I never met mine. We had both lived in a family where secrets beat at the very core of who we are, or who we think we are. You may be harbouring your own secret. If so, ask yourself this. Is it your secret alone? Or is it someone else's secret that you are not telling them? Something that, if they did know, would turn their world upside down, make them reassess everything they thought they knew. The missing piece to their jigsaw.

The arrival of that trunk has given me answers to a pain I had buried so deep I didn't know it was there. I am proud to be my mum's daughter, but I so wish I had met my father. Or do I? Was Mum protecting me from someone who would not have been a force for good? A man of low morals? Not the hero I have always longed for? Having one loving parent is perhaps enough?

My phone rings and I pick up to hear my daughter's voice.

"Darling, I have just been thinking about you," I tell her. "How are you?"

"I'm fine, Mum. Actually, really well and happy."

"That's nice."

"It is and I hope you will think so too."

"Tell me."

"I'm pregnant!"

I freeze. "What?"

"Mum, I know it's not what you would have wanted for me, but I am really happy and excited and you will love Ade, my boyfriend. It's all been a bit of an accident but we are happy and I want you to be too."

I smile, wanting to laugh, "You're not gay?"

"Mum! What are you talking about?"

"I mean it wouldn't matter if you were gay of course but . . . oh darling, I am going to be a granny?"

430

"I think you'll make a wonderful granny, Mum."

"Do you? Oh darling, all babies bring joy and . . . actually, Joy is rather a good name, what do you think? When can I see you? And can I meet Ade? What does he do? We must arrange the wedding. Spring I think . . .?"

Just another daughter and another mum.

The daughters of the daughters of Cornwall.

Hopefully as wild as the land in which they are born . . .

Acknowledgements

With thanks to the *Guardian* archives and BBC History websites.

I am indebted to the archives of the London Scottish Regiment, Cornwall's Regimental Museum, and all those who served. This being a novel, I have played fast and loose with the timeline of war, for which I hope I will be excused.

Also thank you to Anthony Adolph, a fine genealogist who discovered so much about my great-uncle Bertie.